I0819037

The
CUPID
Dilemma

ALSO BY APRIL ASHER

A Simple Twist of Fate

SUPERNATURAL SINGLES

Not the Witch You Wed

Not Your Ex's Hexes

Not Your Crush's Cauldron

Written as April Hunt

STEELE OPS

Deadly Obsession

Lethal Redemption

Fatal Deception

ALPHA SECURITY

Heated Pursuit

Holding Fire

Hard Justice

Hot Target

The Cupid Dilemma

A Novel

APRIL ASHER

ST. MARTIN'S GRIFFIN
NEW YORK

This is a work of fiction. All of the names, characters, organizations, places, and events portrayed in this work are either products of the author's imagination or used fictitiously.

First published in the United States by St. Martin's Griffin, an imprint of St. Martin's Publishing Group

EU Representative: Macmillan Publishers Ireland Ltd, 1st Floor, The Liffey Trust Centre, 117–126 Sheriff Street Upper, Dublin 1, D01 YC43

www.stmartins.com

Opening chapter art: Arrow © DGIM studio/Shutterstock

Designed by Meryl Sussman Levavi

The Library of Congress Cataloging-in-Publication Data is available upon request.

ISBN 978-1-250-35788-5 (trade paperback)
ISBN 978-1-250-35789-2 (ebook)

First Edition: 2026

10 9 8 7 6 5 4 3 2 1

To Cheyenne and Scarlet and their lovely team of booksellers who kept me in continuous supply of confetti cupcakes, caffeine, and creative air

The
CUPID
Dilemma

1

WHERE WAS A PORTAL TO THE UNDERWORLD WHEN A DEMIGODDESS NEEDED ONE?

Addie

Perspiration suctioned Adalyn Whitlock's once-stylish cocktail dress to her ample curves, and the longer that the horror show played out in front of her, the more sweat that slid down her cleavage.

So. Much. Sweat. Her body spray was seriously being put to the test as a massive cloud of déjà vu hung heavy over her head. This could not be happening again, and yet the screeching alarm assaulting her eardrums told her otherwise.

"Addie!" A familiar voice shouted mutedly. "Addie! Adalyn Whitlock! Snap out of it before I smack you back to reality!"

The panicked tone of Addie's cousin briefly turned her focus from the nearby inferno and toward the surrounding chaos.

People scurried in all directions, like cockroaches evading a light beam, as they fled for safety. Thick trails of sludgy sugar coated the no-longer immaculate ballroom floor, remnants of the once-lavish dessert table knocked over by a wedding guest during the first mad rush for the exits.

Freaking pillar candles.

She'd warned the bride that the tall—albeit gorgeous—gothic candles she'd wanted adorning the reception hall to give her skin a "romantic glow" weren't a good idea. Alcohol, open flames, and a bridal party insistent that they could win a professional dance competition didn't mix.

Ask her how she knew.

But what the bride wanted, the bride got, and now the eight-tier wedding cake with marshmallow frosting and chocolate raspberry ganache filling looked more like an oversized campfire s'more than a confectionary statement piece.

A soon-to-be fully engulfed s'more if the flames got any larger.

Bailey, her cousin—and one-third co-owner of Happily Ever Forever—popped into existence in front of her, their mouth moving with sounds resembling the muffled utterings of the New York City subway.

"Addie!" Bails sandwiched her face between their colorfully ring-bedazzled fingers and dragged her gaze away from the chaos and toward their face. "Pull it together, girl! Don't lose it on me now! What the fuck are we supposed to do?"

Everything and everyone around Addie slowly stumbled back into focus—colors, sounds. The fire alarm blared, piercing her eardrums.

Addie drop-kicked her mental cobwebs. "Get the fire blanket from my emergency bag."

Bailey blinked behind their stylish black-framed glasses. "You stashed a fire blanket in the emergency bag?"

"After the last time? Absolutely. Are you really questioning my preparedness right now?" Addie quipped.

"Hope you packed some good luck in with the damn blanket," Bailey muttered and dashed out of the ballroom to the staff lounge where they'd stashed their gear during this morning's setup.

Addie rolled her neck and kicked off her heels. She could do this. She'd practically lived through the fire academy when she binge-watched that drama a few months ago, never mind that the real thing would probably send her into cardiac arrest on the first day.

Cardio was not her forte.

Addie ran an assessing gaze over the cake table and cursed. Despite the only nature walk experienced by the young socialite bride was the short foot trek from Central Park to a Park Avenue dress boutique, she'd insisted on a *Midsummer Night's*–themed cake complete with nature's foliage.

A lot of foliage.

Take away the kindling, lessen the flames.

With an actionable plan semiformed, and armed with a handful of water goblets, Addie slowly approached the growing inferno, more sweat rolling between her boobs with every step. Within a foot of her target, her bare left foot slipped on a melted sugar puddle and immediately threw off her balance.

She envisioned ass-planting into the gooey sludge as two strong arms banded around her waist, miraculously keeping her upright as she struggled to find both her feet and her balance.

"Exit is the opposite way, gorgeous." The deep, sultry voice sent a tingle down her spine—or that could've been from their close proximity to the fire. "Let's get you out of here, yeah? The professionals with fire-retardant suits should be here soon."

"I can handle it. There's no need for all of that."

As if purposefully challenging her words, something sparked on the cake and the damn sparklers ignited, shooting off colorful light streams in all directions.

Her human wall spun—with her in his arms—and put his back to the flames. "You were saying?"

Temper flared higher than the damn cake flames and, primed to give Mr. Sarcasm a piece of her mind, Addie snapped her gaze northbound—because damn, the man was tall. The second her gaze locked on his hazel eyes, her mind temporarily blanked.

Addie had lived in New York City her entire life. There was no shortage of gorgeous individuals, and she'd never been the type to go gaga over a pretty face . . . but this guy wasn't pretty.

Or gorgeous.

He was . . . *hum*-ina. So gorgeous the only acceptable response was a long, drawn-out hum of appreciation. *Hum*ina. Dressed in an open-shirted suit instead of a tux, and with no tie in sight, he looked like a wedding guest.

A closely trimmed beard of light brown scruff covered an otherwise angular, square jaw, and almost hid a left-cheek dimple. *Almost*. His made-for-kissing lips quirked into a deeper smirk, and that dimple practically said, *Hello there. Were your undies already damp and uncomfortable, or are you just happy to see me?*

But it was the eyes that should be registered as lethal weapons. A pure mixture of green, blue, and brown, they damn near twinkled not only with mischief, but with an internal glow that—

Strike that.

That glow was a reflection from the now fully engulfed cake table.

Bailey sprinted back into the nearly deserted ballroom, fire blanket in one hand and extinguisher in the other, and gawked at the cake. "Uh, I think we'll need a bigger blanket."

"Just stay back." Addie grabbed the blanket and shot Mr. Sarcasm a hard glare. "And that includes you."

"I'm no stranger to putting out fires," Mr. Sarcasm announced.

"Unfortunately, neither am I," Addie muttered under her breath. "Do you mind?"

She gestured to his arms still locked solidly around her waist, and with a smirk, he relinquished his hold.

Fire blanket in hand, she edged closer to the growing inferno and tossed the fabric over the worst area. *Please let this work.*

"Here. Let me." Mr. Sarcasm stepped alongside her with the fire extinguisher he must have snatched from Bailey.

"Wait." She stepped in front of him, a hand braced on his arm. "The blanket just takes a few seconds to—"

Too late.

Mr. Sarcasm pulled the pin and squeezed. A thick mist of chemical-smelling powder burst from the nozzle, invading both her mouth and nose, and assaulting her outfit, whose once-beautiful midnight-blue color now appeared a muted, *wet* gray.

Mr. Sarcasm's mouth dropped open and closed a few times before shooting her a sheepish smile. "Sorry. You kind of got in the line of fire."

She cocked a single eyebrow. "You think?"

"But look." He nudged his chin toward the cake table. "The fire is out . . . and before the indoor sprinklers—"

A click sounded a second before the rain started, and then Mr. Sarcasm's words melted away along with the extinguisher muck and all of Addie's dignity. The ballroom door burst open and an army of firemen stormed into the room, all decked out in heavy gear as they spread out and canvassed the room looking for any leftover sparks.

The only ones they'd find were from her career going up in flames.

They'd been inches from crossing the finish line. The mix-up with the flowers had been averted—although narrowly, and thanks to Bailey's connections in the music world and some quick favor-pulling, the DJ pulling a no-show didn't dampen the mood on the dance floor. Hell, Addie had even thwarted a boxing match between the bride's divorced parents, who decided their daughter's wedding was the perfect opportunity to introduce their brand-spanking-new significant others.

One cake-cutting, a final toast, and a handful of dances had been all that stood between Addie and a much-needed hitch-free wedding event, and it was all thwarted by a damn pillar candle.

"Look at this disaster! Everything. Ruined." The bride's mother stepped into the room, her sobbing daughter at her side, both looking as soggy as Addie. The older woman drilled an angry glare toward the man trailing behind them. "Do you see this, Roger? I hope you're happy now that you completely ruined our daughter's special day."

The man's eyes narrowed, his round face reddening. "Me? What the hell did I do? There's no way you can pin this shit show on me, Darla."

"You're the one who insisted that we have that open bar because . . . 'appearances.'" She swung a manicured hand toward the chaos around them. "Now look what happened."

"If you want to blame someone, look in the mirror. You and Karleigh are the ones that demanded we have those ridiculous candles the size of my damn head."

"Because they create the perfect romantic ambiance," the bride interjected.

"Yeah? And how's that ambiance working for you now, huh?"

The bride sobbed louder, her cries mixing with the shrill alarm.

Addie worked to pull herself together as she muttered to Bailey, "We need to get the bride away from them and find her husband. I'll take the parental units . . . unless you want to switch."

Bailey snorted. "Absolutely not. I paid my dues in preventing them from killing each other during pictures. Good luck."

Bailey went into cleanup mode, immediately approaching the wilted bride. "Karleigh, why don't we find that new husband of yours while the firemen finish their job? The last time I saw him, he was by the ice sculpture."

The bride sniffled and let Bailey wrap her up in their arms. "This isn't an omen from the gods, right? It doesn't mean that my marriage is doomed to go up in smoke."

"Actually, there's an old saying about fire-blessed nuptials signifying high passion in one's marriage."

"Really?" The bride looked up at Bailey hopefully.

"Absolutely! We're in the happily-ever-forever business. It's our job to know such facts."

Addie nearly swallowed her tongue on a snort as her cousin talked straight out of their ass, leaving her alone with the parental units, who were less than three inches from each other, shouting in each other's faces.

"Excuse me . . ." Addie cleared her throat, unsuccessful in getting their attention. "If I could just have a moment . . ."

More hurled insults.

She waved her hand. "Pardon me for just one . . ."

The couple volleyed accusations back and forth like a badminton birdie, ignoring everyone around them. A professional whistler thanks to years of watching baseball with her father,

Addie slipped her fingers into the corners of her mouth and blew.

Loudly.

Everyone stopped. The mother and father of the bride. A handful of nearby firemen and hotel staff. And Mr. Sarcasm, who'd irritatingly stood off to the side, talking to three other guys she hadn't seen before.

"Not you." Addie waved the firefighters off and focused on the parents. "I understand this isn't what you envisioned for your daughter's special day, but I need the two of you to pull it together. No one could've foreseen this—open bar and pillar candles or not."

The mother scoffed, looking down her nose at Addie. "Actually, I worried something like this would happen, which is why I told Karleigh I'd be willing to eat the contract cancellation fees if she wanted to go with another event planner. Tell me, Ms. Whitlock, your last *how* many weddings had 'unforeseen' circumstances?"

Truthfully, she didn't know. The last six. Maybe eight.

She'd hoped this one would start a fresh without-a-hitch streak, but nope. Back to square one. Or negative one billion.

Addie smiled and affected her best customer service voice. "Again, unforeseen circumstances happen, and when they do, the only thing in your control is your reaction to them."

"I think I'm reacting justly to the fact that the biggest day of my baby's life has been ruined. The trauma. The humiliation."

"Okay, but let's look on the brighter side of things." Addie summoned her patience. "The ceremony was absolutely gorgeous, and your daughter married the love of her life."

The father scoffed. "The kid's a dipshit. I already slipped the name of my divorce attorney into Karleigh's purse during the first dance."

The ex-wife snapped her gaze to her ex. "Your divorce attorney? Roger, you didn't!"

Addie interjected, "If we could—"

"Hell yeah, I did," the father added.

"Please, let's just—"

"There is no way Karleigh will be using your attorney." The mother of the bride rolled her eyes. "Your lawyer couldn't find his way through divorce proceedings with a flashlight and a *Law for Dummies* textbook in his hands. No, she'll use my lawyer . . . the one who actually knows what they're doing."

"Oh, the one that you're fucking? Is that what you mean?"

Addie slowly watched what little handle she had on the situation melt away. The only saving grace was that things couldn't possibly get any worse.

Bailey, nervously biting their lower lip, burst around the corner. "Don't freak out. But we may have a problem."

"Gee. You think?" Addie flailed her hands toward the remaining firefighters currently searching for a suspected second fire.

Bailey grimaced. "Okay, yeah. This is bad, but I'm talking about one that is currently wearing a facial expression most often used by our cousins."

Addie froze, dropping her voice as she pulled Bails farther away from the still-arguing parents. "*Which* cousins?"

"Miss Whitlock." Addie's name, said in a terse, furious tone, answered her own question before she even turned.

The hotel manager stormed their way, smoke spewing from her ears that had nothing to do with the fire. Pure *fury*. So much that Addie sent a brief glance around the room, making sure that her Fury cousins hadn't made a cameo.

"Tina. Hey, I'm so sorry about—"

The manager waved off her apology. "I probably don't need

to tell you this, but I just want to make myself perfectly clear. Happily Ever Forever will never do another wedding here at the Golden Crown. N.E.V.E.R."

Bailey grinned anxiously. "So what you're saying is that you're up for negotiations?"

The manager shot them a hard glare.

Where was a portal to the Underworld when a demigoddess needed one?

2

NIPPLE PIERCINGS FOR THE WIN!

Addie

Multiple hours, two buses, and an overcrowded subway train later, Addie finally stood outside her Brooklyn apartment. The lock temporarily held her key hostage and she jimmied it harder, cursing with each attempted turn. On the other side of the door, Do-Re-Mi barked knowingly, losing their fool heads over their impending treats.

"I'm trying, guys. I'm trying."

Another finger-bruising twist, and the lock finally disengaged. Addie opened the door an inch and Do stuck his snout against the crack, his nostrils flaring as his big body blocked her way. "I can't get inside unless you three move back, and if I don't get inside, guess who doesn't get their evening treat?"

Do barked once, followed by Re, and they stepped back, allowing Addie to enter. All big ears and drooling tongues, Do-Re-Mi jumped up, large fuzzy paws easily landing on her shoulders as they licked her from all angles.

Coming from one of Cerberus's latest litters, Do-Re-Mi looked like a slightly larger cross between a German shepherd and a black Lab—except for the three heads and the fuzzy snakelike tail. Each pup had their own personality, but one thing shared was their love of bacon treats.

Who could blame them? Bacon was life.

They scarfed their treats in record time and then demanded a quick potty break. In all reality, they could blink out of the apartment and do their business whenever they wanted, a product of being from the Underworld, but the neighbors tended to get antsy when an unsupervised three-headed dog ran about the block chasing pigeons.

Now both fed and pottied, the trio fought good-naturedly over their rawhide bone and curled up on their favorite side of the couch as Addie beelined for the bathroom.

She needed nothing more than to watch the memories of the day—and the fire-extinguisher chemicals still on her skin—swirl down her bathtub drain.

As the tub filled with hot water, she searched for her new bath bombs. Her phone, sitting on the sink ledge, erupted into a Darth Vader ringtone that made her grin.

"Hey, Pop." Addie yanked her favorite lavender bath bomb out from the cabinet and tossed it into the rising water.

"Hey, cupcake. How did the big wedding go?"

"Oh, you know . . . same old, same old. Flowers were sniffed, vows were exchanged . . . and then fire sprinklers were set off, the NYFD busted in with their big hoses, and HEF was banned from yet another hotel."

"I'm not even sure if you're pulling my leg right now or if you're being serious."

"I couldn't find a joke right now if I pulled a joke book off the shelf and read it cover to cover."

She could practically see her father's wince over the phone. "That bad?"

"Bad would be an improvement. So would horrendous. Atrociously horrendous would barely be on the right track. Maybe the Fates are trying to tell me something."

Her father scoffed. "Like you'd let the Fates decide anything about your future."

Addie cracked a smile. Her father knew her so well.

Fates. Destinies. Gods and goddesses and societal expectations to go along with their familial lines. She shirked it all, and even made it her life motto to stay clear of all the drama. And while growing up, her father had worked damn hard to make that happen as best he could, too.

Sometimes it worked. Other times it didn't.

He started, "Have you thought about seeing if your mom—"

"No." Addie dropped a second scented bomb into the water.

"It couldn't hurt to see if—"

"Not in a million years or with a threat of apocalypse."

He sighed, his concern palpable even through the phone line. "Adalyn . . ."

"*Father.*" Flipping on her flame-free candles, she dimmed the overhead lights.

"Fine. I'll keep my yap-trap shut, but you know that if you ask Aphro—"

"Do *not* say her name. Please. She's like freaking Beetlejuice. Say her name too many times in a row, and she appears. Besides, if I ask her for assistance, she'll make things ten times more complicated and turn everything into a twelve-ring circus. I don't need that unnecessary drama in my life, not to mention that I don't have the patience for it. Only Maxi has that superpower," she said, mentioning her sister.

He chuckled. "Fair enough. I guess I'll let you get back to your plans for the rest of the night."

Addie snorted at the not-so-subtle info-digging for any hint of relationship news. "Yeah, I probably should. I'll see you at dinner on Sunday night, yeah?"

"As always, and there will be plenty of food if you want to bring someone . . . extra."

"And share your barbeque? Not likely. Love you, Pop."

"Love you, buttercup."

Addie hung up and quickly evicted her bra, shed her clothes, and sank into blissful oblivion, the hot water instantly easing her sore muscles.

With a breathy sigh, she picked her book off the tub-side table and dove into her story about sexy alpha wolf shifters. Fictional significant others far surpassed real ones. If they did or said something annoying, you could smash them between the pages of the book and not feel guilty about it.

Addie read until her eyelids drooped for the third time, signaling a shift into nap-mode.

She set aside her book before it took a swim, and nestled into her warm water blanket for a refreshing snooze. Her dreams quickly pulled her into a beach scene where she traipsed slowly into the ocean with a tall, hazel-eyed stranger, first to her knees, and then waist deep.

A dream wave rolled in quickly, taller than expected, and knocked her back, loosening her handhold with the sexy, mysterious stranger.

Another wave struck and ripped the beach babe away completely.

One more hit and Addie bolted awake, her heart lodged in her throat. Her knee smacked her reading table and the shifter romance plunged into the now cool depths of the tub. Cursing, she fished out the soggy mess and searched for whatever had startled her awake.

Boom . . .

Thud . . .

Bang-bang-bang . . .

At nearly midnight, both the walls and floor shook from the pulsating rhythm coming from next door. A guitar—and a loud one—strummed to a heavy thumping beat, adding to the monstrous cacophony that infiltrated her peaceful oasis and ruined her chances of relaxation.

Only fitting since the jerk had also beat her out for the best apartment in the building.

He hadn't even been a previous tenant, just showed up one day and sweet-talked the building manager into giving him the space, the very same apartment for which she'd placed her name months prior. Hell, the manager all but told her that it was hers . . . until it wasn't.

And now the obnoxiously loud, tattooed man next door enjoyed the extra two hundred square feet of space and two spacious walk-in closets. She'd only ever laid eyes on the backside of him as he left the building or walked down the hall, but even his nice ass wasn't enough to stop her from wishing he'd fall into a curse-filled viper pit—or into Medusa's sightline.

Fueled by exhaustion, sadness for her now soggy book, and an absolutely shitastic day, she climbed out from the tub and wrapped her curvy body in one of her favorite oversized towels before stuffing her feet into her unicorn slippers.

Her normal tactic of smacking her shoe against the wall wouldn't cut it this time.

Letting her anger brew to a steamy boil, she stormed from her apartment and headed next door. Dripping in the hall, she pounded once, then twice. With no answer, she knocked and didn't stop, her hand hurting more with each hammer of her fist.

What felt like an eon later, the guitar ceased, and the backup "music" lowered to a dull roar. Muffled footsteps headed toward the door, but Addie kept knocking until the wood disappeared beneath her hand.

She sucked in an unexpected, audible breath as her eyes connected with her brain and she slowly linked the dots.

"*You!*" She drilled her mystery neighbor with a hard glare. "What the hell are you doing here?"

Familiar hazel eyes beamed brightly as he leaned—shirtless—against the jamb of the doorway, his surprise slowly transforming into cocky recognition. "Pretty certain that should be my line because I live here. What's your reason? Did you feel our connection earlier, too, and follow me home? It's a little creepy if you did, but sometimes creepy is a good thing."

She snorted. "The only connection I felt was when you sprayed me with a fire extinguisher."

The gorgeous guy from the day's earlier catastrophic wedding grinned. "You were the one that stepped in the way when I was trying to save the day—and your pretty little hide."

"I didn't need you to save the day or my hide. I had everything well under control," Addie smarted back.

Mr. Sarcasm's smirk remained in place as he tilted his head. "Were we at the same wedding? Gaudy affair with ridiculous candles all over the place and over-the-top foliage?"

"That was what the bride wanted."

"Did she want her wedding cake to go up like a Roman candle, too?"

Addie bit the side of her tongue to keep from retorting. If she thought Mr. Sarcasm looked distractingly gorgeous in his slightly wrinkled suit jacket and undone shirt, he was mouthwateringly sexy now.

In the dimmed hallway lighting, his eyes appeared more soft gray than blue or brown, and his light brown hair hung over his left eye in pure disarray. He was taller than she'd first thought, at least a foot taller than her own five foot two inches, and broad-shouldered with nearly 80 percent of his exposed skin covered in a beautiful array of colorfully inked artwork.

And nipple piercings for the win!

Addie very nearly drooled, but the sight of his twisted little smirk snapped her out of her admiration. "What?"

His gaze slowly trailed to her open apartment door. "Am I to guess from the casual ensemble that you're my neighbor? Did you stop by to ask for a cup of sugar? Because I'm sorry to say that I don't usually keep the stuff on hand. I drink my coffee black as a starless night."

"I'm not here for sugar."

"Then what exactly are you here for?" His gaze slid down her body. "Unless that daydream I've been having since running into you at the wedding is finally coming true."

She realized the error in her thinking, not having taken the time to at least pull on a pair of sweats. It was too late now. By the time his gaze dropped to her rainbow unicorn slippers, Addie had stiffened her shoulders and forced her back straight.

"You wish."

"Yeah, actually, I do."

She ignored the interest glimmering in his eye. "Look, I realize you're not around all that much—"

"Aw, did you miss me?"

"I missed the *quiet* . . . which leads me to the reason I'm pounding on your door at close to midnight in my bath towel. Not everyone in the building needs—nor wants—to listen to your *music*. So if you'd be so kind as to turn it off, or at least *way* down, it would be greatly appreciated."

He cocked a single dark eyebrow, the one with a pierced hoop. "Maybe I'm not kind."

Addie copied his one-eyebrow lift, making his smirk broaden. "Maybe?"

"I'll tell you what, sparkles." His gaze momentarily dropped to her slippers. "I'll stifle the *music* just for you, but since you're asking me to give up my inspiration, I'll need to find another. You up for the position?"

Addie rolled her eyes, unable to withhold her groan. "Do lines like that usually work for you? Tell me there aren't people out there who fall for all your . . . bad-boy charm."

"Bad-boy charm?" Mr. Sarcasm chuckled. The sound did funny things to her decommissioned lady bits. "I'm sure there are others out there who have more game, but I don't do too bad. And I'm not trying to sound conceited or anything, but I usually don't need to dish out lines. People flock to me naturally . . . but something tells me you're not the flocking type."

"That's something you would be right about. Just please keep the noise down to a dull roar this time of night. Not everyone in the building keeps rock star hours."

He nodded, amused by what she said. "I'll do my best."

She ignored his come-hither stare and headed back to her door, which she'd left open in her haste to achieve quiet.

"So, can I get a name for my new muse?" One broad shoulder leaning against his open door, he flashed a megawatt smile. "It feels like something I should know, considering I have this innate feeling that you—and those pretty eyes of yours—will be my best one yet."

"Sorry, it wasn't a job that I applied for, so no."

"Ouch." He clutched his chest. "You wound me, sparkles."

She threw him one last glare and escaped back into her

apartment. A few minutes later, the music came back on, this time dialed down to a faint hum.

Addie smiled, and that one split-second moment of weakness was all her mother needed to pop into existence.

Literally.

"Hello, daughter of mine." The goddess smiled, the action lighting up the entire room.

"Dim the glow, Ma," she pleaded, shielding her eyes.

"Oops. Sorry." In a flash, Aphrodite's light diminished and there stood Addie's mother in all her goddess glory.

People everywhere had heard the Goddess of Love's name, and many knew at least something about Greek mythology. Some gossip was true. Most wasn't. Statues sculpted in Aphrodite's image stood all over the world, but most depicted her wearing a signature white linen toga and floral crown.

This Aphrodite wore black skinny jeans, a cashmere sweater, and six-inch stilettos. An expensive pair of Jimmy Choo sunglasses sat propped on her head of curls despite it not being the least bit sunny.

"Before we talk about today's little wedding mishap, tell me all about Mr. Tall, Dark, and Delicious next door? Whoever he is, whatever he does for a living, I approve. Wholeheartedly."

Addie scoffed. "He could probably be a puppy unaliver and you'd still approve."

At that comment, Do-Re-Mi picked their heads off their front paws, letting out a little trio of whines before settling back down.

"It's my role as your mother to want to see you happy, healthy, and in love." Aphrodite sat on the end of the couch.

"I'm not discussing what happened at the wedding—which apparently you've already heard about, and I'm definitely not talking about Mr. Sarcasm."

Her mother smirked. "You gave him a nickname already? This is promising. Maybe Maxi is right and you're finally starting to come around."

"No." Addie threw a finger at her life-giver. "No, I am not coming around, especially if to you that means me going on some great love quest. It's not happening. Not now. Not ever. It's not needed because it doesn't truly exist."

Love.

Sparkling unicorns had more chance of being real than that four-letter word that never ceased to send people into a tizzy.

Her mother's face fell in sheer disappointment. "It's not natural, Adalyn. My daughter is meant to *love* love. It's quite literally in both yours and Maxine's DNA."

She shrugged. "Don't know what to say except that she must have gotten the love gene, and I got the practical one. And my practical one is telling me that I've been up for way too long and this day from hell needs to come to an end. Thanks for checking in, but I'm good."

Her mother sighed and stood. "Fine. Ignore me. But you won't be able to do that forever. I'm quite literally everywhere. There is no escape."

"That's not as comforting as you think it may sound. It screams stalking kidnapper—which is, ironically, pretty on the mark."

"My sweet Adalyn . . ."

"My overreaching mother . . ."

Her mother squeezed her hand. "I only want your happiness, sweetheart."

"Then you've gotten what you want, Ma, because I'm very happy with my life right now," Addie said adamantly.

And she meant it wholeheartedly.

Not only did Adalyn Whitlock own and run a business

alongside her sister and cousin, but she lived in a building she'd loved since she was a child, and was seriously contemplating adding another plant to the little family on her windowsill.

She was also the daughter of Aphrodite . . . and *Love* was—most unfortunately—her middle name.

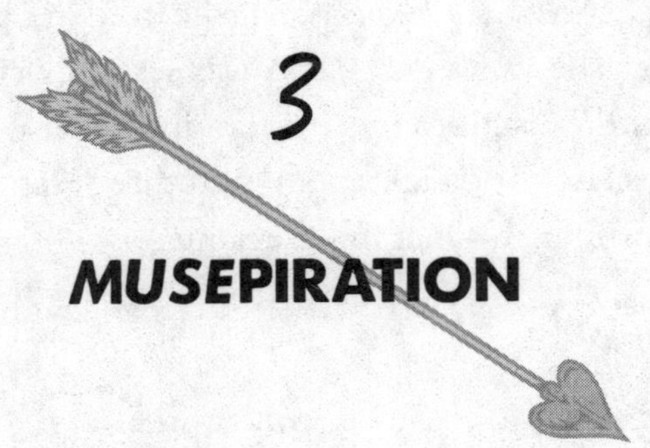

3

MUSEPIRATION

Addie

Addie dropped her head to her desk and willed the aching throb behind her eyes to go away. "I'm ten seconds and one more phone call away from running away from the city and joining an acrobatic circus."

Sitting comfortably in the chair on the other side of the desk and scrolling on their laptop, Bailey snorted. "Since when do you do acrobatics?"

"I practice every time I put on my brown knee-high boots. I can learn the rest."

Worried about the nightmare situation waiting for her at the office, Addie had put off showing her face today. She'd scoured her closet for the skirt she hadn't seen in months, and decided waiting in a long-ass line for overpriced coffee was better than using her travel mug or hitting up the always efficient Java the Hut.

She should've found something else to delay her. Where was a late train or broken bus when a girl needed one?

After walking through the Happily Ever Forever door,

it took five seconds to realize that not only were her fears about office chaos warranted, but it was much worse than anticipated.

Karleigh Kinkaid-Fink was a freaking society influencer, and she'd made good on her threat to share with the world—and her five million followers—about the "tragedy" that had transpired at her wedding, complete with sobbing testimonials.

Calls flooded in nonstop from all avenues. Karleigh's outraged fans issued veiled threats, and wedding bloggers and local news outlets zeroed in on Evelyn Sinclair's "exposé," seeking statements.

The most concerning calls came from worried current clients, one of whom canceled their event entirely, and most baffling was from someone inquiring if they handled anti-love ceremonies.

What. The. Fuck.

"Let's look at this in a positive light," Bailey suggested. "We've never been more popular than we are right now. Our DMs are bursting. We're being tagged left, right, and center. Once the dust settles, this could be a blessing in disguise. You know what they say . . . any press is—"

"If you say *good press*, I will show you how acrobatic I am by hurtling myself over this desk." Addie picked her head up and shot her cousin a look. "How is *this* good press?"

She pointed to her screen, which framed the latest *Wedding Woes* article, "Happily Ever For-Never."

An online publication with a significant following, *Woes* documented "wedding blunders, woes, and faux pas," and had featured Happily Ever Forever in their column not once but now three times and counting. Addie wasn't sure what she—or HEF—had done to piss in Evelyn Sinclair's cereal bowl, but it was clear the journalist had it out for them.

"Where's the Pepto?" Addie yanked open her desk drawers,

prepping to down the pink liquid like a college student with a string of all-nighter study sessions ahead of her.

"Knock, knock." Maxi stood in Addie's office doorway, her smile firmly in place.

Of the two of them, Maxine not only looked most like their mother, but she loved the idea of love, and had yet to meet a stranger, making friends wherever she went.

Addie's perfect opposite. Not that Addie was a total grumpy introvert. She ran a business, which required that she people on the daily. But after she turned off the customer service persona, she was usually decked out in her favorite pj's and sitting on her couch, only braving the public when dragged by either Max or Bailey.

Addie and Max's differences were what made Happily Ever Forever work. Max ran the matchmaking side of HEF, playing Cupid and helping clients find The One, and Addie handled the logistical side.

The numbers.

The schedules.

The event planning.

"Most people physically knock instead of saying the words." Addie leaned back in her chair, giving her tired eyes a break from reading yet more bad news.

Her sister's gaze dropped to the computer screen. "You saw it already. Crap. I was hoping to distract you enough this morning that you wouldn't."

"Kinda hard to miss it when our biggest fan, Evelyn, emails me a direct link to the article," Addie quipped dryly.

"Son-of-a—"

Addie cocked an eyebrow, the move effectively silencing her usually optimistic sibling.

Maxi dropped into the seat next to Bailey with a heavy sigh. "Things will pick back up. I mean, they have to, right?"

"One would hope, but it better happen soon. The Braxtons just canceled their wedding, saying they decided to go 'another route,' and I've fielded two other phone calls threatening to do the same. I had to make a few concessions to keep them from going somewhere else."

Maxi winced, knowing that meant discounts. Deep, deep discounts that wouldn't help their bottom line in the least.

"I'm so sorry, Addie," Maxi apologized.

"What are you sorry about? I'm pretty sure all the mess-ups that happened, happened on my end."

"Eh. That's one way to look at it. But if you really think about it, most of what happened on your end was just the fallout of improper matches." Maxi shifted uncomfortably in her seat as she avoided eye contact. "I've been having some . . . matching issues recently."

Addie waited for her sister to elaborate.

The two of them had always been opposites. As kids, Maxi always tended toward the fantastical and Addie toward the logical. Where Maxi had always dreamed and played the part of the princess in the ivory tower awaiting her one true love to rescue her from the fire-breathing dragon, Addie had played the part of the dragon.

And she'd played it well.

Maxi believed in the power of love sonnets and heartfelt devotionals, and the magic of a true soul match. She was a true daughter of Aphrodite, making their mother proud with her keen ability to find someone's soul match.

A Cupid.

It's what made Happily Ever Forever so lucrative in the

beginning. With Maxi's matchmaking superpower, the online-dating-app half of the business flourished with people flocking to find their soulmates. More and more happily engaged couples returned, all begging for wedding planning recommendations. So many they expanded HEF into an all-inclusive, one-stop shop for their success stories.

Only two short years ago, they'd been forced to turn people away, their waiting list years long. Now, Addie considered standing on the sidewalk twirling a sign next to one of those blowing squiggly-armed banners and offering their services for free.

"Have you talked to her about it?" Addie asked casually, knowing her sister would know about whom she spoke. "She's been all about the suggestions and advice lately. I'm sure she'll have something in mind."

"She said it's probably a phase, and that I'll outgrow it sooner rather than later, but . . ." Maxi sighed. "I don't know if I can handle it being later. My last match—by far—was the worst yet. And I've had some doozies."

"It couldn't have been that bad."

It was Maxi's turn to lift a brow. "Would you care to place a bet on that? Because I saw this pair of shoes I'd really like . . ."

"No . . . ? But now you have my attention."

"It all started well and good. They both went through the app's survey and their answers melded to form a perfect union on paper, and so I brought them in for a link check." Max winced, obviously picturing the moment when she'd brought in two potentials and put them in separate rooms. "And I felt it . . . a perfect, although a little roughened, link."

"So you not only found a good match but a soul tether. I'm not seeing the problem here, sis."

"Turns out that they'd already tried the marriage thing to one another. Their divorce became finalized less than three months ago and it was most definitely not amicable. At some point during the intro, something about a murder plot was screamed, but by that point I had blacked out."

Addie heaved out a slow breath. "Okay, so that's definitely not good . . . but hey, they didn't make it down the aisle again for things to blow up over the cake cutting . . . so *plus*!"

They shared a look, both bursting into laughter.

Bailey's gaze bounced between them, always calculating things much like their mother, Athena. "See. Things aren't as bad as you all previously thought."

"Oh, no." Addie wheezed, drying her tears. "Things are atrocious, but it's either laugh about it or go into the fetal position under my desk and never come out."

Bailey smirked. "I'm glad you're thinking positively. Maybe you'll be more receptive to my idea, because I've been thinking . . ."

"Gods help us," Addie and Maxi said in unison.

"We need clients who are walking around with hearts in their eyes and spewing love sonnets, ready to say those two little words, right?" Bailey glanced at Maxi apologetically. "Sorry, babe, but time is of the essence and waiting for you to do your Cupidess thing will just take too long."

"No apology needed." Maxi waved it off. "Weddings are what bring in the green. What's your idea to bring in sonnet-spewing love clients?"

"We need a rebrand. A *big* one, way more than a color scheme and updated logo. I'm talking a massive social media campaign, testimonials, a big-ass client with a big, nosy following . . . and a big celebrity endorsement. Someone everyone knows, regardless of how deep in the hole they stick their heads."

"And where are we supposed to find this celebrity endorsement?" Addie asked. "And not to mention, how would we even convince them to do it? It's not like we can pay them."

"Which is why it's such a good thing that you two have a link to one of the best endorsements Happily Ever Forever could ever hope to have." Bailey bit their lip. "I know the two of you have been adamant about keeping your relationship to Aunt Aphro—"

"No," Addie and Max said in unison.

"Just hear me out!" Baily cried.

"I've heard enough." Addie shook her head. "And it's not happening."

"But who wouldn't want to be 'matched' by the daughter of Aphrodite? And can you imagine what people would pay to have her other daughter plan their perfect wedding?"

"It all sounds good in theory, but it's the execution where it will all fall apart. It would come with so many strings, and I don't know about you two, but I'm too clumsy to navigate them without falling flat on my face."

"But—"

"She's not wrong, Bailey," Maxi agreed. "While Mom would jump at the chance to help us out, everything we're trying to do with Happily Ever Forever would get strangled in all the strings that come with dealing with the gods. There'd be way more negative fallout than positive in the long run."

"But it was a good idea," Addie quickly added. "Unfortunately, we just can't use it. At least not that part of it."

Bailey sighed. "Yeah, I already figured that would be your response, but that makes it even more important to bring in a big-name client. I'm not even talking about one with deep pockets. Someone everyone is watching right now. Someone who would benefit from all the extra attention of a social media campaign as much as we would."

"And where exactly are we supposed to find this miracle celebrity?" Addie asked.

Bailey shrugged. "I'm just an idea person. You two are the ones who execute the plans . . . so get planning."

A big client. A big PR campaign. And magazine-worthy nuptials that happen without so much as a flower out of place, no oversized cake s'mores, and definitely no Furies executing a revenge plot on behalf of scorned lovers everywhere.

In other words, they needed nothing short of a miracle.

Phoenix

Growing up, their neighbors called them trouble. Now, Phoenix and his best friends were the Stone Talons, a rock band formed in his parents' garage what felt like a million years ago and who were now, according to the national music magazines, upcoming rock gods ready to break records along with the hearts of adoring fans.

But right now, the only thing Phoenix envisioned breaking was the glass box currently protecting their snide-comment-hurling producer.

"Let's break for fifteen." Indy, the producer, released a shifter-like growl. "In the meantime, everyone needs to get their shit together. And Nix?"

Phoenix glanced up, already knowing what was coming. "Yeah?"

"Spend those fifteen thinking up lyrics that we can actually fucking use."

Phoenix's hands twitched on his sticks as he contemplated hurling them straight through the soundproof window.

"Ignore him." Easton's beefy hand transformed from gargoyle stone to flesh and bone, and landed on his shoulder. "He's had a stick up his ass all morning."

"If he doesn't shut down the attitude, he's about to have another one," Phoenix quipped to his best friend.

The four bandmates headed to the corner couches where they'd stashed their gear.

"Just give the cranky man what he wants." Gavin, their lead singer, threw himself onto the overstuffed chair, legs draped over the massive arm.

Phoenix shot the griffon shifter a glare. "How can you seriously be okay with more of the same? Parties. Girls. Sex. Repeat. You realize there are other things to sing about besides those three things, right?"

"Yeah. But it's not what the label wants to hear from us and the last time I checked, they're the ones throwing all the green our way."

Gavin wasn't wrong, but that didn't mean Phoenix had to like it—and he didn't.

Their debut single, "Flying Undies," had been a song he'd written as a joke, but that their new label announced was "their breakout." Now, with every *panty party* song written, a musician lost his soul—or at least Phoenix did.

He hadn't written anything notable for months, unless you counted the two lines of potentially lyrical genius that came into his head following a brief hallway encounter with a certain gorgeous redhead. Something about his feisty neighbor sparked something in him, and he hoped it was the end of his lyrical dry spell.

Only time would tell.

Xavier, a Titan descendant who played bass guitar, sat on the other end of the couch and tossed them each a water bottle. "I saw an advertisement for that *Muse*piration service on the subway. They match up creatives with their ideal Muse. They supposedly have a high success rate. If you're that down about things, maybe give it a try."

Gavin smirked. "I saw that, too. They're trained at that fancy-ass Muse Academy in Olympus. It's not a bad idea."

"I'm not renting a Muse." Phoenix glowered. Picking up his guitar, he played around with a few chords. "It'll happen when it happens."

"Then expect Indy and Marcus to be on your ass until it does."

A commotion sounded from the other side of the box. The label owner, Roger Kinkaid, stood in front of their manager, red-faced with his hands flailing wildly. They volleyed back and forth, the exchange looking more heated by the second.

"What the hell is going on out there?" Xavier asked.

Gavin grunted and played on his phone. "Fuck only knows with those two."

East, his eyes narrowed in concentration, put his lip-reading skills to use. "Someone did something that the label doesn't like and they're blaming Marcus for falling asleep on the job and letting it happen." East paused. "He needs to fix it." He paused again. "And quick."

Xavier smacked Gavin's booted foot. "What the fuck did you do now, man?"

"Nothing. I've been a fucking angel."

"Not Gavin," Easton added before his eyes snapped to Phoenix. "What the hell did you do to make Kinkaid throw an aneurysm?"

Phoenix's head shot up. "Me? Nothing. When I'm not with you assholes, I'm at home. How could I have done something?"

The label head stormed off, and Marcus turned toward them, shooting a lethal glare right through the window—at Phoenix.

A tablet in hand and smoke spewing from his ears, he barged into the booth.

"What the ever-loving fuck is the meaning of this, Cross?" Marcus waved the tablet before tossing it onto the couch between him and Easton. "Please. Explain it to me. So that I can then go back to the label and convince them that you're not shitting on everything they've done for you four."

"I seriously don't know what the fuck you're talking about, Marcus." Phoenix gestured to his guitar and his notebook. "It's coming. It's a work in progress, and it's not coming as fast as I'd like, but it's coming."

"What's coming is the label terminating your contract if you don't deliver the types of songs you promised." He waved his tablet, showing an open email. "This drivel is not what you promised them!"

"I know it's not exactly what the label expected, but it's not *that* bad."

"Your eyes sent a dart to my heart."

Phoenix felt the rest of the band watching the back-and-forth like a table tennis match. "It's more than I had last week."

"Listen up, and listen good." The vein in Marcus's temple throbbed. "Nix from the Stone Talons does not write about *hearts*, or anything close to feelings—unless that feeling is—"

"Horny?"

Marcus's eyes narrowed. "You're skating on thin ice, Nix. Get with the program—and quick. You need to start taking this seriously."

"I am. I think I may have recently found my Muse." The words left Phoenix's lips before he could contain them, and damn if they didn't sound true.

"Since when?"

"Since recently."

"And why am I only hearing about this now?" Marcus demanded.

"Because it's new and I'm not sure where it'll go. I wanted to make sure there was some concrete progress before I brought it up."

Their manager looked like he was chewing his tongue as he played a mental Jenga game. "Fine. See where it goes . . . just don't go overboard."

Phoenix lifted an eyebrow. "What the hell does that mean?"

"No hearts, flowers, or feelings. Keep the love sonnets for your personal journal."

Marcus stormed off, slamming the studio door behind him.

East turned to him, smirk firmly in place. "You're royally screwed. A *Muse*? If you're gonna lie you could just say that you've been working on some new material."

"It's not a lie," Phoenix declared.

"Yeah? Then why haven't I heard about this creative Kickstarter before now?"

"Like I told Marcus, it's—"

"Recent," the guys finished in unison.

Indy dropped back into his seat on the other side of the recording booth and flipped on the intercom. "Let's get back to work, and this time, play it like there are half-naked people in the crowd slinging underwear at you with fucking slingshots."

Phoenix failed to swallow a groan.

When did his life start revolving around airborne panties?

4

THE STEALER OF APARTMENTS, DISTURBER OF PEACE & RUINER OF RELAXING BATHS

Addie

Addie longed for her pajamas and her television, which had a recently released true-crime drama already downloaded onto her home screen.

Her club phase had come and ended over a decade ago, proven by the curious looks tossed her, Bailey, and Maxi's way as they approached the bouncer at the front of Club Olympus, a new venue on the outskirts of Queens.

At Bailey's demand, they'd honed their inner Charlie's Angels—Maxi in a short, waist-hugging dress that flared out into a full skirt, and Addie in her favorite slightly-heeled knee-high leather boots, tight torture jeans found in the far back corner of her closet, and a skimpy, sequined, spaghetti-strapped tank top that required two rolls of boob tape to keep the girls from drooping to her waist.

"Remind me why I'm not sitting on my couch with a bowl of popcorn and watching a documentary?" Addie eyed Bailey's outfit longingly, her cousin stunning in a fitted red suit that hugged the body, and a long, dangling, vintage bronze necklace that showcased the shirtless plunge pointing straight to the navel.

"Because it's sad, and a little unnerving, how much you like documentaries," Bailey answered. "You're thirty-two, Addie. Not three hundred and two."

"It's not sad if I'm happy while I'm watching them," Addie grumbled. "Sometimes I learn a lot of cool things."

Next to her, Max chuckled. "The documentary will still be there waiting for you when you get home."

"But it was actually blessedly quiet at my apartment for once. No neighbor playing loud music that shakes my walls and ruins my relaxing baths. Instead, the ones ruining my evening plans are my two formerly favorite people."

Bailey smirked. "We need a company bonding excursion and this is it, babe. Besides, I won these tickets—complete with backstage passes to meet the bands—and I never win anything. It's a sign we were meant to come tonight."

"Some people would think that the two closed subway stations, broken-down bus, and unexpected four-block detour were signs that maybe we weren't meant to show up," Addie challenged with a single look.

"You're so lucky I love you, Miss Curmudgeon." Bailey glared playfully. "But even your exceptionally curmudgeonly ways will not kill my happy buzz. And before you go on about this not being your 'type' of music, there is literally something for everyone here tonight. If one band isn't your jam, the next one might be."

Maxi chuckled mischievously. "Not to mention hot musicians."

"See!" Bailey pointed at her sister. "This one gets it! Hot rockers, Addie. Musicians who literally make musical magic with their hands."

"And mouths," Maxi added.

Addie whipped her head to her sister. "Who are you and who has body-snatched you?"

Maxi's lips tilted into a grin. "Guess there's just something in the air."

"That would be all the body odor from the sardine-packed venue," Addie muttered.

"Actually, that's why this place is so awesome." Bailey bounced with excitement. "It not only has a massive indoor space with a live DJ, but a backyard music garden with a stage for live performances, not to mention *multiple* kick-ass dance floors. There's nothing else like it in the tristate area."

Addie and Max followed as Bailey danced up to the security guard manning the door and flashed their all-access passes.

Inside, the club played up the factory-like interior with dimmed lighting and strobe lights while the DJ blasted music in front of an already large crowd. They grabbed drinks at the far bar and headed toward a bronze glowing sign that read MUSIC GARDEN.

Bailey was right. The outdoor area, although crowded, was a hell of a lot more tolerable. Spread throughout the massive yard, small fires lit up the night sky, creating a cozy atmosphere along with the thousands of little white twinkling lights artistically wrapped around a few trees. The focal point—by far—was the all-girl pop group belting out harmonious chords on a massive outdoor stage.

"Tell me this isn't great!" Bailey beamed wide, glancing around.

Honestly, Addie couldn't. Although a certified couch enthusiast, this was a night out that she could get behind. Despite all the people, it didn't feel crowded, and while the music was loud, the open stage gave it a magical backyard feel.

"Let's hear it again for Babes in the Wood!" An emcee jogged onto the stage and led a cheer as the all-girl group headed off. "How's everyone feeling after that great warm-up? Is everyone ready for more?"

The crowd roared.

"I can't hear you!"

The crowd yelled louder.

The emcee laughed. "Yeah, that's what I thought. Well, there's an incredible lineup for you tonight, including a special musical guest that's sure to . . . sink their talons into you."

The crowd went wild.

Less than three feet away, a woman released an eardrum-piercing squeal before swaying on her feet. Her friend, standing next to her, looped an arm around her waist and prevented her from a full-on collapse.

Addie leaned toward her sister. "What is everyone freaking out about?"

Max shrugged.

"No fucking way." Bailey's mouth dropped as they stood on their toes, peering up at the stage. "There was a rumor they'd show up tonight, but no way did I think it was true! See! Miracles really do happen!"

"You'll need to decipher all of this for me," Addie pleaded.

Bails rolled their eyes. "Seriously. Crawl out of your safe work bubble and into the real world every once in a while, Ads."

"I'll get right on that once you tell me why everyone is freaking out about getting mauled by talons."

"Because he was alluding to the fact that the Stone Talons are part of tonight's lineup."

"Oh-kay."

"The. Stone. Talons," Bailey elaborated slowly.

"Turning your words into one-word sentences won't do anything for my comprehension here, Bails."

"I deserve an award for surviving our bestie cousinship. Not to mention, a raise." Bailey pinched the bridge of their nose. "The Stone Talons is the hottest rock band on the rise right now. They haven't even released their first full album yet, and their songs are breaking records left, right, and center. Anyone who's ever laid eyes on them—or ears on their music—either wants to be best friends with them or fuck them. There is no in-between."

"Right," Addie scoffed.

"You'll see. If you don't fall into one of those categories after meeting them, I'll eat my underwear."

"Are you even wearing any underwear?"

Bailey smirked. "You won't find out because there's no way in hell I'm wrong."

"Everyone still going strong?" The emcee scanned the garden before glancing offstage. "Good! Because the Club Olympus Music Fest is about to sink their talons into you with our very special guest!"

"This is it! Let's go!" Bailey grabbed their hands and body-checked people off to the side until they stood pressed against the stage.

The emcee paused dramatically. "Let's welcome Xavier Knight, Easton Knox, Gavin Hastings, and everyone's favorite naughty drummer boy, Nix Cross! Let's hear it for the Stone Talons!"

The crowd erupted, Bailey adding to their screams as the rock band ran onto the stage. Bails wasn't wrong. Each one gorgeous, the four guys worked up the crowd with winks and waves. A pair of lacy red panties flew past Addie's head and landed by the lead singer's feet.

"How are you doing tonight, Queens?" the lead singer belted into the microphone. He laughed at the answered shouts, turning back toward where the drummer took his seat.

"I don't know, Nix. It kinda sounded like they were sleeping, didn't it? How did it sound back there?"

The floppy-haired drummer leaned forward and a low, familiar chuckle echoed through the microphone. "Pretty sure all I heard was snoring, man. I think you're right. Is this a music festival or a sleep-study lab?"

Addie froze.

That voice.

That sarcasm.

The Stone Talons's drummer stood, his drumsticks waving in the air, and Addie sucked in a breath.

It couldn't be . . .

She wasn't *that* unlucky . . .

Wearing low-slung, well-loved jeans, a buttoned shirt left open to reveal the wide expanse of a tattooed chest and chiseled abs, was the man who had starred in her dreams for the past few nights.

The Stealer of Apartments, Disturber of Peace, and Ruiner of Relaxing Baths . . .

Mr. Sarcasm smirked from behind the massive drum set, his gaze scanning over the crowd as he and his bandmates exchanged humorous banter.

Addie glanced around nervously, contemplating escape routes before that sexy hazel gaze landed on her. That delicious chuckle echoed through the mic again and the sound instantly sent a butterfly attack to her stomach.

The second he spotted her, Addie knew.

The butterflies turned into pterodactyls, and her hair lifted off her nape as a slight shiver rippled through her body.

As if pulled by a magnetic force, Addie slowly glanced up at the stage and . . . fuck.

Familiar hazel eyes glued her to the spot, widening slightly in a brief flicker of surprise before he smirked and the dimple popped into existence.

Nix Cross winked and her face heated hot enough to cook an egg as she wished for a hole to open beneath her feet, sending her to the Underworld. Hell, she was due for a visit to see her uncle Hades and aunt Persy.

Which Fate did she piss off? Addie really wanted to know so she could send some apology flowers or a box of chocolates.

Bailey, standing next to her, and oblivious to the exchange happening from the stage, floated on cloud nine. "I can't wait to meet them backstage. This is fucking awesome."

Addie snapped her attention to her cousin as a big ball of dread solidified in the pit of her stomach. "Say *what* now? Backstage?"

Bailey shushed her as the Stone Talons played their first song, and soon after, a second. With every minute that passed, it became crystal clear that neither flowers nor a box of chocolates would cut it as apology gifts.

She was solidly in blood oaths and left kidney territory.

Phoenix

"Thanks for coming out." Phoenix aimed a forced smile at the last two women in line, his already aching cheeks protesting the movement more with each slightly overzealous fan. "If one more person grabs my ass during a 'quick pic,' I'm wearing a barbed wire butt protector from here on out."

Phoenix shot a tired glance toward East, who was sitting on his left. The gargoyle, wearing his human skin suit since their last song, looked as thrilled to be there as he did.

"You good, man?" Phoenix asked East when his friend

glanced at his text screen for the fourth time since the meet-n-greet's start.

"Worried about Nai. Having a wedding so close to her finishing school wasn't the brilliant move we first thought it was."

"Anything I can do?"

"Nah. We got it. Just wish these vendors would call us back with updates."

Phoenix glanced around the room, searching for a certain gorgeous redhead. To say he'd been shocked seeing his neighbor pressed flush against the stage with a VIP badge around her neck would be an understatement.

More like stunned . . . and hopeful.

East paused to sign another autograph before shooting him a curious look. "Scoping out emergency exits? I'm pretty sure Marcus learned from the last time and has all routes blocked with security who could probably bench press two of you."

"He does. I already checked." Phoenix finally admitted, "So there's this woman . . ."

Easton howled in laughter. "I fucking knew it! I told Naiomi that you had a sex fog look in your eyes for the last few days. She said it was probably constipation."

Phoenix narrowed a glare at him. "It's not sex fog . . . or constipation."

"But you just said—"

"I met a woman. I'm not fucking her . . . or anyone." But it wasn't because invitations hadn't been dropped in his lap . . . or shoved into his pockets.

When the Stone Talons first started out, he'd been nearly as eager as Gavin to bask in the glorified title of rock stars. It's how he'd been slapped with the Naughty Nix persona. But unlike the griffon shifter, the label got old for him quick.

East smirked. "Okay, Sexless Nix. Who's the woman?"

"Woman? What woman?" Naiomi popped up like a jack-in-the-box, taking advantage of the brief lull in their line.

"Your sibling has been scanning the room looking for a certain woman." East studied his fiancée carefully and pulled her into a brief hug. "You okay, babe?"

"Yeah. Just wedding stuff." Her smile didn't quite reach her eyes. "We can talk about it later, at home. Right now, I want to hear more about this mystery woman."

Nai wouldn't let this go until Phoenix gave her what she wanted.

"You remember me telling you about the gorgeous redhead from the wedding a few nights ago?" Phoenix asked.

"The one you accidently doused with fire extinguisher muck," Nai reminded him. "Yep."

"That would be the part you remembered." Phoenix rolled his eyes. "I couldn't shake thoughts of her out of my head, and that night I went home, fully expecting never to lay eyes on her again, and guess who knocked on my door and told me to turn down my music?"

For a split second, both his sister and East looked confused, but his best friend put two and two together first. "No fucking way."

"Fucking way. I swear."

"What am I missing?" Naiomi's gaze bounced between them.

East draped his arm over his fiancée's shoulder. "Phoenix is saying that the hottie from the wedding is the neighbor who's been pounding shit against his walls, and whose ass he's been staring at walking out of their building."

Naiomi's eyes widened in realization. "Your building crush is also the wedding crush?"

"I wouldn't call it a *crush*, but—"

"Do you get all warm when you think about her?"

"I don't see how—"

"That's a yes. What about tongue-tied? Do you stumble over your words, nerves making you say stupid shit that you know will probably piss her off?"

"It's not stu—"

"That's also a yes," East added, Naiomi nodding in agreement.

Phoenix's sister grinned broadly. "That, my dear brother, is a crush."

Auburn, silky hair he could picture entwined between his fingers. Curves for fucking days and perfectly designed for a firm grip. And fucking-A, her mouth. Those sinfully kissable lips and the words that came flying out of them, all sassy snark with a bit of bite.

"Fuck," Phoenix cursed.

East chuckled. "He realizes it now . . . but a neighbor? Remember what happened when Gavin got friendly with that yoga instructor from his gym and it blew up in his face? He bitched for months about switching to the studio across town."

"First, I'm not Gavin. And second, it's just a fantasy because I'm pretty sure she can't stand me."

East clutched his chest in feigned shock. "You? Mr. Charismatic? How the hell is that possible?"

"I'll have you know that I can be a charismatic light show when I want to be."

His friend scoffed. "So you played your music too loud a few times? That's not completely irredeemable."

"It was more than a few times," Phoenix admitted with a wince. "At first, it happened by accident. Inspiration strikes when it strikes, you know? And then . . . I started pumping the volume up on my amp on purpose, hoping she'd either bang on the wall again or come over and yell at me in person."

"Wow." Easton smirked. "You just admitted to the adult equivalent of pulling a girl's pigtails on the playground. Even Gavin has more game than that, man."

Naiomi studied him carefully, her dark eyes narrowing. "But that's not everything, is it?"

Phoenix grimaced as he thought of what he considered the final nail in his crush coffin. "I'm pretty sure she was the 'other applicant' who wanted my apartment. The one the building manager told me not to worry about when I applied."

Easton whistled. "*And* you got the apartment she wanted? In New York City? Yeah, she's not getting over it. Ever. Congratulations, you now have an enemy for life."

"And she's here?" Naiomi's head swiveled. "I'll find her."

Nai was off on a mission, moving too quickly to be stopped.

Turning his back, Phoenix focused on anything other than his sister hunting down his mystery woman, even subjecting himself to a few more pictures and ass-grabs.

"Just out of curiosity, what does this sexy wedding neighbor with a hate-on for you look like?" East asked fifteen minutes later.

"Petite." Phoenix's lips twitched. "In heels, she'd probably come up to my chin. All curves. Dark red hair. Freckles. Fucking gorgeous."

Phoenix's cock twitched in his leather pants as the mental image of his neighbor infiltrated his imagination.

"Green eyes?" East asked.

"Yep. Like heated jade."

"A world-class glare with the ability to shoot daggers from across a room?"

"Definitely." Phoenix signed another autograph and sent the fan on their way before looking to his best friend. "Why?"

"Looks like Naiomi hunted her down—and they're coming this way."

Phoenix whipped around and sure enough, there *she* was. Walking alongside his sister, she looked anything but thrilled to be there, unlike the two others trailing behind them who flashed friendly smiles.

They came to a stop a few feet away, and Naiomi threw herself into East's arms. "Adalyn, Bailey, and Maxi . . . this statuesque stud is my talented fiancé, Easton Knox."

East, issuing a polite smile, nodded. "It's nice to meet the three of you."

Adalyn smiled politely at the gargoyle and waved awkwardly. "Hi."

Naiomi turned toward Phoenix. "And this is my brother, Phoenix."

There was no denying his sexy neighbor recognized him.

Instantly, his lips twitched into a smirk, and the second they did, Adalyn's frown dipped lower, her arms crossing over her lush chest that looked fucking spectacular in the low-cut tank.

Phoenix failed to contain a chuckle. "*Adalyn*. Finally. A name. It's very nice to *officially* meet you."

Adalyn's two friends gawked at her. *So she hadn't told them about him.*

He held out a hand, and she glanced at it like she expected it to bite her. When she didn't take it, he dropped it, chuckling. "Couldn't wait to see me when I got home later tonight, sparkles? I get it. I am pretty difficult to stay away from."

Nearby, Phoenix heard his sister mutter something about Gavin's lame-ass pickup lines rubbing off on him, and excused herself to answer her ringing cell.

Adalyn smiled sweetly. "Whoever told you that, fibbed. It would be quite easy to avoid you if you kept your music to polite decibel levels. Not everyone wants to live in a club every night."

Adalyn's friend with the stylish pixie cut and red suit—Bailey—cleared their throat. "I'm feeling a little lost right now, but you're the Stone Talons."

Phoenix flashed a genuine smile. "We're fifty percent of them."

Bailey's gaze bounced from him, to Easton, to Adalyn. "Addie . . . my dear cousin. *How* do you know the Stone Talons? And why wasn't I notified of that little tidbit? That seems like information that a cousin bestie should know."

"Or a sister," Maxi, the blond, added.

"Oh, we go way back, don't we, Addie?" Phoenix teased, relishing the redhead's glare.

"We don't go way back." Addie nudged her chin toward Phoenix. "*That* one is Mr. Sarcasm from the Kinkaid wedding. He's also the apartment-stealing neighbor who has absolutely zero regard for the sanctity of quiet-time hours in an apartment building."

"Definitely never forgiving or forgetting, man," Easton whispered to Phoenix before excusing himself to check on Nai.

Phoenix smirked. "Oh, come on, sparks. We're more than that, aren't we? I did offer you the role of my Muse, and I'm still hoping you'll reconsider and make me the happiest musician by saying yes."

Bailey's mouth opened and closed comically as she glanced toward Addie as if she'd sprouted a second head. "You turned him *down*?"

"It was probably the saddest day of my life," Phoenix added.

Addie rolled her eyes. "Something tells me that you'll get over it just fine."

"Then that something would be wrong. I don't make that offer to just anyone I meet off the streets, you know. It's a coveted honor."

"Then I'll gladly pass that honor to someone else."

Bailey looked flabbergasted. "Ads. This is inexcusable behavior."

Phoenix temporarily abandoned his stare-down with Addie and focused on his two potential new friends, holding out his hand. "And you are Bailey . . . ?"

"Bailey Vicks." Bailey's cheeks pinked. "Addie's former cousin bestie and business partner."

The blond smiled, taking his hand next. "Maxine Whitlock . . . but everyone calls me Max—or Maxi. Addie's sister and business partner."

Phoenix caught sight of East and Nai returning, his sister's face now red and splotchy with tear remnants running down her cheeks.

Protective Brother Mode Activated.

East caught his concerned gaze and mouthed a silent *Help me*, looking as if someone had kicked him between the legs.

"What's up, Nai?" Phoenix took a small, hesitant step closer. "Everything okay?"

"No! Everything is not okay!" Like a flipped switch, his little sister went from soppy sadness to fired up and ready to throttle someone. "If I ever get my hands on that low-life, money-swindling, no-good rat-bastard wedding planner, I'll fit him with a pair of cement shoes and drop him in the deep end of the Hudson!"

"That's . . . very *Godfather* of you. And why have you suddenly taken an interest in the Mafia?"

Nai shot a helpless look to Easton, who held her hand tightly, giving her a supportive nod. "Because evidently the man we hired to plan the biggest day of our lives is nothing but a con artist. Despite assuring me that he had everything handled, I called the hotel to double-check that they actually did have black tablecloths, and do you know what they told me?"

"That they didn't?"

She scoffed. "I fucking wish! They had no idea what I was talking about because they only have one event scheduled for that night, *and it isn't our wedding*!"

Phoenix blinked, confused. "I thought you booked the place months ago."

East nodded grimly. "So did we . . . and the venue isn't the only problem."

Naiomi wiped her nose on the hem of Easton's shirt. "Earlier today, I called Carter, sure he could clear up this misunderstanding, but he didn't answer. So then I followed my gut and I called and left messages with everyone—the florist, the caterer. *Everyone*. And do you know what *they* told me?"

Phoenix was starting to get it. "They had no record of—"

"None . . . but it wasn't until I called the bakery that I found out that they've had another client with the same problem. We were scammed. All those checks I wrote for Carter to give as deposits, and not a damn one went to those businesses. He pocketed all that money and now he's missing in action."

"Fuck."

"I feel so stupid." Naiomi groaned. "Why didn't I question things more? When the advertisement said that they handle all of the little things, I should've known it was too good to be true."

Easton hauled her in for a hug. "We'll figure something out, babe. We'll make sure you still get the wedding of your dreams."

"With what money? We've been saving up for this for over a year and a half. I know you're my gorgeous rock star, but you're not getting that kind of money yet, and I'm earning a teacher's salary with a shit-ton of student loans thanks to the doctoral program. We're still living paycheck to paycheck. Anything extra went to the wedding fund—which now has a big fat zero in it—and we're getting married in a month!"

"Babe, you know I don't need a big wedding to marry you. Hell, we can do it down at the courthouse. All that matters is that I see my ring on your finger, and yours on mine."

Naiomi stared up at East with hearts twinkling in her eyes as she rose onto her toes and kissed him. "That's why I love you, East. But . . ."

"You've been planning this for a long time." His friend nodded understandingly.

And he wasn't wrong. Naiomi had been planning her wedding day since they'd been kids, putting all her ideas and her entire wish list into a pink-and-white scrapbook that she'd squirreled away beneath her bed. Once upon a time, he'd hid it, and she'd cried as if their dog Sandy had died.

"We'll figure something out," Phoenix heard himself say. "You'll still get married in a month, and it'll be the wedding of your dreams."

His sister and best friend glanced his way, Easton giving him a *what-the-fuck* look.

"How are you going to make that happen?" Nai sniffled. "Even if we found vendors able to do something so last minute, they won't be able to do it for free, or for what little we'd be able to pull together."

Phoenix glanced left to see Addie deep in conversation with Bailey and Maxi. Bailey's hands moved animatedly as they spoke and Maxi nodded emphatically. Only Addie looked apprehensive, her bottom lip caught between her teeth.

"*We* can help you," Bailey announced with a dramatic turn, instantly commandeering everyone's attention.

"What?" Phoenix asked. "How?"

"We're co-owners of Happily Ever Forever. Maxi runs the

Happy Match portion of the company. I'm the marketing and PR brains, and Addie handles the Ever Forever events."

Silence hung heavy in the air until . . .

"You have got to be fucking kidding me?" Naiomi squealed, the sound piercing Phoenix's eardrums, and jumped excitedly in a very unlike-Nai way. "Tell me you're fucking kidding me. You three are Happily Ever Forever?"

Addie shifted on her feet. "Yes . . . ?"

Her hesitant answer put Phoenix on alert, but his sister, ignoring her new friend's awkwardness, pulled his neighbor into a breath-stealing hug. "This is fucking kismet! I can't believe it!"

"Uh, Nai?" Phoenix nudged his chin toward Addie's look of discomfort. "Maybe let her breathe a second."

"Oh. Sorry." She pulled back but still smiled from ear to ear. "Sorry, but I just can't wrap my head around the fact that my brother's building cr— Uh, that I've run into none other than *the* Adalyn Whitlock. I've followed HEF's event portfolio from your very first one. You are rock stars in the world of happily ever afters!"

Addie smiled. "That would be us."

"Happily ever afters, huh?" Phoenix asked curiously. "And that means that you—"

"Are known to match people with their perfect soulmates," Naiomi interjected with a look toward Maxi, then Addie. "And then design, plan, and pull off the most magical, spell-binding, and perfect vow-exchanging ceremonies. Your talents are seriously a gift from the gods."

Addie coughed, seemingly choking on thin air. Bailey and Maxi patted her back from either side, both smiling.

"We are pretty damn good at what we do," Bailey said with a smile. "So what do you say?"

Naiomi's wide smile slowly dimmed. "You heard about the lack of money, right? We sank everything we had into a con artist. There's no way I could afford to hire wedding rock stars like you, much less pay for the wedding itself."

"Don't worry about it." Bailey waved off the concern. "We'll use the event to add to our portfolio, and we have contacts and favors we can call in."

"It does feel like this is a sign," Nai agreed, tears in her eyes. "We needed a miracle, and then here you are, trying to avoid my brother at a meet-n-greet."

All eyes turned toward his sparkly little redhead, who seemed a significant shade paler than she had been a few moments ago. Her gaze went from her sister to her cousin, and then bounced off him before landing on a hopeful Naiomi.

"Then I guess we should set up a meeting to see how we can help," Addie suggested with a small, nervous smile. "How does tomorrow sound?"

"Yes!" Naiomi yanked the trio into a group hug. "Oh, wait. I have a meeting with my PhD advisor tomorrow, and I already rescheduled it twice. If I do it a third time, they probably won't give me my degree out of spite. East?"

"Tomorrow?" East yanked out his phone and checked his schedule. "Tomorrow I'm volunteering at the youth music school."

"How about I take the meeting instead?" Phoenix heard himself suggest.

Both Nai's and Addie's heads whipped toward him, the latter with a look of horror on her face, solidifying his impulsive plan.

"I'm sorry, what?" Addie asked.

"You'd do that for me?" Nai asked, getting teary.

"I happen to have some free time." Phoenix smiled. "Besides, there isn't a page of your wedding book that I didn't read growing up. I know what you want for your wedding day better than what I'd want for mine."

"Thank you so much, big brother." Nai threw her arms around him and squeezed him tight. "I don't know what I'd do without you."

"This isn't . . ." Addie stopped, thinking. ". . . I don't usually plan vow exchanges without at least one person who'll be exchanging the vows."

"But you can, right?" Nai asked hopefully. "Between the band and East's music school start-up at the youth center and my job and school, our schedules are so chaotic right now and in no way match up. I don't know how I'll be able to pull off regular meetings. But Phoenix is right. He's heard me talk about my wedding since I was six."

Addie looked poised to argue, but after small nudges from Maxi and Bailey, she smiled. "Sure. No. That's fine. We'll see what we can do and pivot if needed."

"Great!" Phoenix clapped his hands, more than a little excited. "Expect me at your office bright and early. What time? Seven? Eight?"

Addie snorted. "Let's aim for nine. I'm sure you'll have a long night tonight partying with all your . . . fans."

Easton slipped over to his side as Nai talked animatedly with Addie and the others. "Not that I don't appreciate the assist, but I hope like hell you know what you're doing, and you don't end up screwed in the not-fun way."

Screwed? Nah.

Phoenix actually felt like he'd just won the fucking Fated lottery.

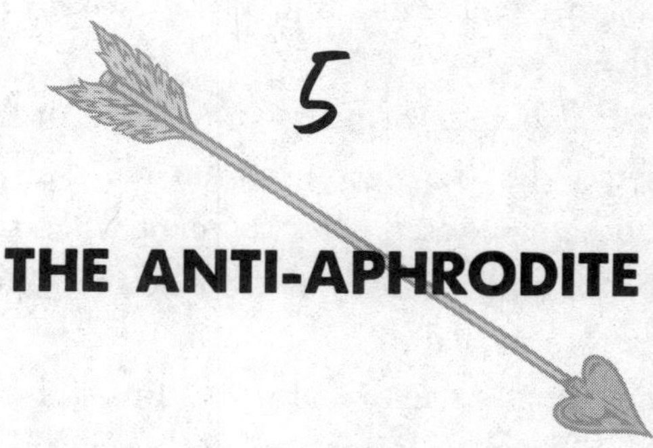

5

THE ANTI-APHRODITE

Addie

No less than a dozen times since waking at the ass-crack of dawn, Addie contemplated calling Maxi and Bailey and pleading *plague*. Not forever. Just long enough for the farce of that morning's "meeting" to pass, and then she'd be blessed with a miraculous immunity boost thanks to her super smoothie, and go on about her day.

Soon enough, reality sank its claws into her.

Seeing through the lie, Bailey wouldn't think twice before showing up at her door and dragging her ass through the streets of New York and into the office. A no-show also risked Mr. Rock God Cross thinking himself the reason, and the man already had a raging case of ego. There was no reason to add to it unnecessarily.

"Predictability and rock stars don't mix. He'll probably flake out on the meeting, right?" Addie asked Do-Re-Mi, and got three confused head tilts before she gave each their morning treats and ear scratches, and headed for the door. "Behave today, boys. If you need to stretch your legs, *poof* to the Underworld. You're still on probation for doing zoomies down Broadway."

They chuffed their agreements and settled in front of the bay window to watch the pigeon-fest outside.

Addie had barely locked her apartment when the door on the right opened and the man she'd hoped to avoid by leaving early stepped into the hall.

"Good morning, Adalyn." Phoenix's lips slid easily into a crooked smile. "Fancy seeing you out and about this early. Getting a jump start on the day, huh?"

Addie sighed internally. "Just getting in?"

His smirk broadened as he fell into step beside her on the way toward the elevator. "Since we're about to start working together closely to ensure my sister's dream wedding happens, we should probably get to know each other better, don't you think? What about a volleying game of twenty questions?"

"That's not really necessary."

"But it would probably make things run easier."

Addie jammed her finger into the down button and turned toward Mr. Rock God. "Look—"

"Phoenix. Although I'd be totally fine with you calling me whatever you'd like." He grinned.

Addie narrowed her glare, one that she reserved for the most difficult clients—and had inherited from her mother. "Do lines like that really work for you?"

"Truthfully? I don't know." His dimple popped into existence. "I've never been a corny-pickup-line kind of guy. That's usually Gavin's modus operandi."

The elevator dinged open and they rode it down to the street level in blessed silence, where the quiet ended the second they stepped outside.

Despite the early morning hour, people already packed the

sidewalks. Any hope that Phoenix would go on his separate way evaporated the moment she hung a left toward the nearest subway station, and he followed.

"We could share a cab or a Ryde." Keeping pace, he shoved his hands deep into his jeans pockets. "We are heading to the same place."

"I prefer the subway. Much more eco-friendly." And not to mention wallet-friendly. "But feel free to get a Ryde. I won't stop you. As a matter of fact, you should."

He smirked knowingly. "Then we can't get to know each other."

"What a tragic shame," Addie grumbled under her breath.

"We could always have this meeting over a cup of coffee and a bagel. My treat," Phoenix suggested.

"Initial meetings are always done in the office because that's where we keep our contacts catalogue."

"Right. Okay. Well, we wouldn't want to divert from the norm."

A bike messenger jumped the curb and hurtled down the sidewalk. Addie stared in horror, her joints frozen as the guy barreled straight toward her. The messenger's bag clipped her shoulder and she spun, the lid of her travel mug flying off her coffee.

Hot liquid splattered down the front of her blue-and-white sundress, quickly scalding her skin beneath. "Hot! Shit! Hot!"

"Watch it, asshole!" Phoenix shouted at the messenger, getting a shrug and a one-fingered salute as he continued onward. Phoenix turned to her and cursed, concern darkening his eyes. "Are you okay? How hot was that?"

Addie breathed through the worst of the pain. "Luckily, not scalding like Max takes hers. I usually put an ice cube in it before I snap on the lid."

He cocked a sexy eyebrow. "An ice cube?"

"Don't judge, okay? I don't like coffee I need to wait an hour to drink, and my mouth is too sensitive to drink it right out of the Keurig."

"Sensitive, huh? That's good to know." His gaze dropped quickly to her lips and then back up. "If you're sure you're okay, how about we replace what's all over the sidewalk? Unless you're not like Naiomi, who will turn into a fire-breathing dragon and chomp someone's head off their shoulders if she's not adequately caffeinated by ten in the morning."

Addie's lips twitched into a smirk. "My sister accuses me of the same thing."

He chuckled. "Then let's save some poor soul's head. I know just the place, and the baristas love me."

"Actually, I'll take a rain check on the coffee and risk a dragon transformation so I can run back up to my apartment and change. And *please* don't wait for me," Addie added when his mouth opened. "I'll see you at the office."

Surprising her, he nodded and stuffed his hands back into his pockets. "Sure thing, sparkles."

Breathing a little easier despite her sopping-wet clothes, Addie hustled back and changed in record time. She shot her favorite coffee shop, Java the Hut, a longing look, but bypassed it and hopped onto her train with seconds to spare.

As far as commutes went, hers wasn't too horrible, but she still took a deep inhale of fresh city air the second she hit the street and hustled around the corner of the HEF building.

She bumped into a burly guy blocking the sidewalk.

"Watch where the fuck you're going." The balding photographer whipped around, shooting her a hard glare before checking on the fancy camera in his hands.

A small media horde gridlocked the entrance to Happily Ever

Forever's building, and two more photographers hustled from across the street to join them, most likely documenting a celebrity sighting or film set. Definitely not unheard of in New York.

Addie squeezed around the perimeter, trying to camouflage herself into the background.

The photographer she'd bumped into suddenly whipped back around.

"It's you!" His camera three inches from her face, he snapped a rapid-fire series of pictures. "How does it feel being the Anti-Aphrodite? Don't you feel as though you're scamming your clients out of their hard-earned money? What do you say for yourself, Adalyn Whitlock?"

Addie's mind blanked. The anti-*who*?

More cameras flashed, and at least four more reporters shoved microphones into her face, hurling question after question that made her head spin.

"Excuse me. If you could just let me through . . ." Addie shouldered her way through the crowd, making it two feet before the horde swarmed, surrounding her on all sides.

The air thickened and Addie, struggling to suck in each breath, fought a losing battle against the tightness in her chest. Black dots swam across her vision, enlarging the harder she tried focusing. "Please, just let me . . ."

A strong arm wrapped tightly around her waist. "I got you, sparkles. Let's get some personal space here, okay?"

"What do you have to say about being called the Anti-Aphrodite?" someone shouted.

"What does your mother think about your stance on love?" another asked.

And yet another, "Hey, aren't you Nix Cross from the Stone Talons?" Flash. Click. Flash. "How do you know the Anti-Aphrodite? Are the two of you together, Nix?"

A photographer gripped Addie's forearm in a tight hold and yanked her left before sticking his camera in her face. In a split second, Phoenix was there, inserting himself between her and the paparazzi.

"Touch her again and see what happens," Phoenix growled threateningly right in the middle-aged guy's face.

"People have a right to know, man."

"People have the right to know jack shit." Phoenix threaded his fingers through hers and bulldozed through the bloodthirsty crowd. "Back the fuck off. Now. And get a life that doesn't revolve around someone else's."

Vidál, the building's head of security shot her a concerned look as they practically tumbled through the front door. "Are you okay, Adalyn? Shit. If I'd known that was you stuck in that madness out there I would've released the vulture spray."

"It's okay, Vidál." Damn, her voice shook too much for her liking.

"Tony. Ahmed." The head guard barked at two nearby uniformed security. "Make sure none of those assholes outside make their way inside. And if they do, hand over your key cards because you'll be fired."

Addie concentrated on breathing, her gaze fixed on the mystery white goo on top of her right sneaker as she waited for her heart to dislodge from her throat.

A gentle touch on her chin guided her gaze up.

Phoenix's thumb stroked a soothing path along her cheek as he studied her carefully. "Are you okay?"

"I'm fine," she heard herself say.

Phoenix's focus slid from her face to the arm that currently throbbed with its own heartbeat.

Eyes ablaze, he pushed her shirtsleeve above her elbow and

gently traced the reddening skin. "Fucking hell. I should have made that guy choke on his camera. That's probably going to bruise."

"I bruise when I even think about bumping into something . . ."

Her attempt at humor didn't work as he studied her arm a second longer before slowly guiding it back to her side. "Tell me the truth, Adalyn Whitlock. Are you a runaway princess looking for anonymity in the big city? Or an escaped convict?"

Addie snorted. "Nothing so exciting."

But now with space between her and the reporters, she distinctly remembered hearing another name attached to her own.

Her mother's.

"Shit, shit, shit." Addie hustled to the elevator banks and gestured toward Phoenix. "He's with me, Vidál!"

On the ten-floor elevator ride, Addie's mind focused on what had happened outside while Phoenix remained quiet at her side, but the second she threw open the door to Happily Ever Forever, the quiet shattered.

Maxi's and Bailey's heads snapped toward her.

"You saw." Maxi instantly read her annoyance.

"An army of grabby reporters was a little hard to miss," Addie quipped.

"Reporters are outside already?" Bailey's fingers flew over their phone screen. "Shit."

"Is someone going to tell me what the hell this is about? This can't all be because of some angry former bridezilla videos."

Maxi's mouth opened before her sister's gaze shifted toward a silent Phoenix. "You came! Great! Uh . . . Just have a seat, make a coffee or something, and we'll be with you in a minute."

"Maxi . . ."

Her sister grabbed her hand and dragged her to the back office, Bailey following close on their heels.

"You'll want to sit down for this," Maxi instructed.

"And remember that we're renting this space, and any major damage will not only hurt us in the long run but erase any chance of seeing that security deposit again," Bailey added, a grimace on their face.

"I really hate it when you guys say things like this." Addie tossed her bag onto the nearby chair, a headache already throbbing behind her eyes as she flopped onto her desk chair. "Okay. Hit me with it."

Maxi handed her the tablet and hit play on the latest uploaded *Wedding Woes* video.

Evelyn Sinclair's megawatt smile turned from the camera to someone standing out of frame. "I really appreciate you making time to speak with me, Dr. Parisi. And that you're willing to finally bring the truth to light."

The camera panned left . . .

Addie stiffened instantly. Hayden Parisi. Her *ex*. Talking to the president of Happily Ever Forever's nemesis club.

He flashed a beaming smile. "It's my pleasure, Evelyn. Stepping into the spotlight isn't quite me, but I feel as if it's my civic duty to speak up."

Evelyn Sinclair peered dramatically into the camera and paused. "For those just tuning in, I'm joined tonight by Dr. Hayden Parisi, a gifted surgeon who's saved countless lives."

"Saved by nose job, huh?" Bailey snorted.

"Dr. Parisi possesses intimate knowledge of the woman behind the notorious event planning agency, Happily Ever For-*Never*, Adalyn Whitlock." Evelyn turned to Hayden. "Hayden, tell our listeners about your connection to Miss Whitlock."

"Addie and I dated seriously for about six months." Hayden's face contorted into faux sadness. "I seriously considered making her my forever."

Addie snorted. "I wonder if he considered making all those other women he was seeing at the same time his forever, too."

"But you didn't end up getting that happily ever after, did you? Can you tell me what happened?" Sinclair asked.

"Honestly, I didn't know what happened—at first," Hayden replied. "For me, it was love at first sight. That's why I didn't see the warning signs before it was too late. I mean, who'd think it necessary to guard your heart against a daughter of Aphrodite?"

Addie's heartbeat skipped into another, stealing her breath.

Evelyn Sinclair's eyes gleamed as she pushed her microphone closer to Hayden. "Did you say 'daughter of Aphrodite'?"

"I did. Adalyn Whitlock, the owner of Happily Ever Forever, is the Goddess of Love's daughter, and she is staunchly, and will always be, *anti*-love. To her, it doesn't exist. It's a fleeting, temporary fascination that will eventually disappear. She's the Anti-Aphrodite."

Addie's stomach twisted into a boulder-sized knot as Maxi once again froze the screen.

"You know what? It's not as bad as I first thought." Bailey shrugged.

Addie looked at her cousin bestie as if they'd joined Cerberus in the land of three heads. "How in the hell do you not think this is bad?"

"I didn't say it wasn't bad. I said it wasn't *as* bad," Bailey corrected. Their gaze bounced from Maxi to Addie. "Am I the only one who sees it?"

"Evidently."

"Don't leave us in suspense. Please, share." Because at this point, she'd streak naked through Times Square if it somehow broke the curse.

"You have to fall in love."

Maxi, mid-swallow, choked on her cold-brew coffee, the liquid spraying.

Addie couldn't believe her ears. "Oh, just fall in love. Okay. And here I thought your idea would be ridiculous."

"Hear me out!" Bailey flung a ring-adorned hand toward a coughing Max. "We have our own certified Cupid right here. Maxi can find your perfect match. We'll make sure the cameras snatch some pics of your heart-shaped pupils and adoring looks, and voilà. No more Anti-Aphrodite."

Addie thunked her head onto her desk. "This can't be happening."

"Let's not forget that my Cupid mojo is on the fritz," Maxi pointed out. "I could very seriously end up matching her to a serial killer or something."

"Does anyone else have a better idea?" Bailey demanded.

"Why don't I just go full-blown rom-com and hire someone to have a spontaneous, wild fauxmance with me?" Addie muttered under her breath.

Silence wrapped around the room, so heavy Addie lifted her head to catch her sister and cousin exchanging looks.

"That's actually not a bad idea," Bailey admitted.

"I was kidding!"

"I'm not. We're in New York City. There's literally hundreds of acting hopefuls on any given square block."

"I am not hiring someone to play my boyfriend," Addie stated adamantly. "There's got to be another way out of this."

Phoenix

The Anti-Aphrodite. An ex. A fauxmance.

It sounded like the start of an interesting book, and yet

Phoenix heard it all with his own ears thanks to the amazing acoustics inside the Happily Ever Forever office space. The information whipped through his head like a bullet train, slowing only to form a half-assed idea and then scurrying away again.

But each time his thoughts raced, they swung back to one repetitive thought.

A fauxmance.

Hell if he knew what it was or how one worked, but he was known as a master at improvisation. You couldn't be in a band with Gavin Hastings and not be because you never knew what the hell the singer would do from one second to the next onstage.

Before he dwelled on any one thought too much longer, Phoenix doctored up a fresh cup of coffee from the waiting room machine, and headed toward the back office.

He knocked on the doorframe and was greeted with three head turns.

"Oh." Addie looked a little startled, as if she'd forgotten his presence. "Phoenix. Something came up out of the blue. We'll have to reschedule our meeting."

"Actually, I think I can help you with that out-of-the-blue thing." He held up the fresh cup of coffee. "Why don't we discuss it over some fresh caffeine? Sorry, but you didn't have ice cubes in your fridge out here, or I would've put one in for you."

Her plush pink lips twitched. "First you try and help your sister out of a bind, and now you're offering to help me? Don't tell me that Naughty Nix has a hero complex."

Did he? Maybe.

Outside, Phoenix had been a split second from leaning into his Naughty Nix reputation and shoving that photographer's precious camera up his nasal cavity. The image of Addie, quiet and pale, so unlike the snarky firecracker that banged on his door while wearing a bath towel and unicorn slippers, set him on edge.

"Look," Addie said, "I appreciate the offer, but—"

"It's not a hero complex if I get something in return, right?" His gaze flickered toward a curiously listening Bailey and Max. "But it is something I'd like to discuss in private . . . if we could."

Addie shared a glance with her sister and cousin, and then Bailey dragged Max out the door, closing it behind them.

Being in close confines, with Addie's gorgeous green eyes studying him warily, had him second-guessing his brilliant idea.

"You said something about fresh caffeine?" Addie's gaze dropped to the mug in his hand.

He slid the cup toward her before sitting down in one of the vacant seats. "Voices really travel in this office in case you weren't aware."

Addie grimaced as she took a sip of her coffee. "Look, I don't know what you think you heard bu—"

"All of it," he admitted. "The interview. The asshole ex—who sounded like a complete fuckwit by the way. And I learned that my gorgeous new neighbor is the daughter of Aphro—"

"Don't say her name aloud," Addie hissed, glancing around the empty office. "What is it with everyone always wanting to say her name aloud?"

"So you're really the Anti-Aphro—*her*?"

Addie groaned. "Please do not let that name become a thing."

"Sorry, but I'm pretty sure that boat has already sailed." Phoenix smirked. "Look, I know a thing or two about bad press. Gavin is always saying or doing something that gives our PR person a migraine. The truth will eventually come out and then people will get bored and move on."

"And therein lies my problem," Addie stated with a sigh. "Because the truth already came out—at least partially—and it's a shark fest outside."

"What do you mean by 'partially'?" Her admission piqued his interest, and watching her carefully, he slowly put two and two together.

"My mother *is* Aphro—*her*. And thinking everyone is meant to have one great, all-consuming love is to live in a fictional land called make-believe. It's a phase of heightened attraction, albeit for some, a happy one for however long it lasts. But that happiness doesn't last forever. It stales . . . until it eventually disintegrates."

"Whoa." Phoenix leaned back in his seat, letting her words sink in. "You're serious, aren't you?"

Addie tugged a bottle of pink Pepto from her desk drawer and took a deep swig. "You said something about needing to speak with me in private. Or maybe that's why you wanted to talk alone. You don't want the Anti-*her* to be the one planning your sister's big day."

"Actually, that's not it at all," Phoenix admitted, finalizing the last bits of his plan in his head.

A fauxmance.

A fake relationship meant time together, and more time meant not only the potential unlocking of musical genius, but helping his gorgeous neighbor out of a social media nightmare. If he ended up changing her views on love—and proved its very real existence, it was a big-ass bonus.

"You don't need to place any fake boyfriend ads or hire any wannabe actors," Phoenix heard himself say. "Fake date *me*."

Addie, about to dump some Pepto into her coffee, spilled the pink liquid on her desk. "I'm sorry . . . what?"

"You heard me." He became more determined with each word out of his mouth. "Fake date me and I'll give you a faux-mance that will not only make that fuckwit ex of yours sound like a fool, but will have people begging to have Happily Ever Forever plan their vow exchanges."

Addie's mouth opened and closed before her pretty eyes narrowed knowingly. "And what exactly would you want in return?"

He smirked. "Be my Muse."

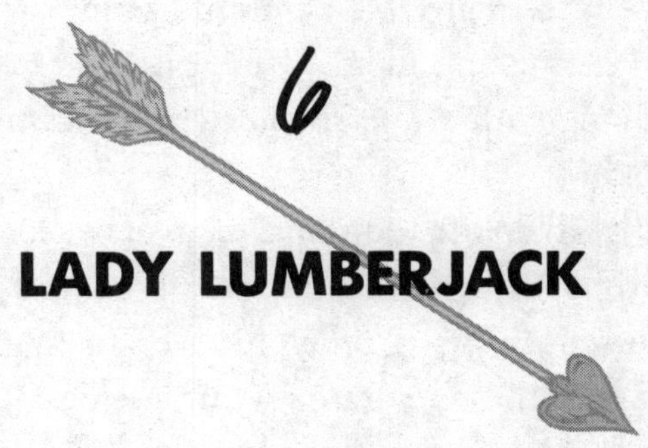

6

LADY LUMBERJACK

Addie

Maxi's Cupid mojo was most definitely on the fritz. Approximately half a minute into Addie's date from hell, she realized with 100 percent certainty that Peter Vanderhorn was in no danger of being her One True Love.

Actually, she'd known it less than three seconds after meeting him, when he'd spent that time ogling her boobs. Only desperation to fix this brewing shitstorm—and Maxi's earlier doe-eyed plea to let her try and find her soul tether—had her heading into the restaurant, Sense-Less.

Severely dimmed lighting made navigating the closely placed tables risky. The restaurant buzzed with a low hum of conversation as people found their spots. Peter had insisted on this place for their first date, stating that it was an "experience" that shouldn't be missed, one that everyone in attendance would encounter at the same time.

She didn't have a good feeling about this, already debating sending an SOS text to Bailey to come to her rescue.

Addie sat and mumbled a thank-you to the server who

showed them to their table before fluttering away to do the same to the next couple in line. Three plates sat in front of each of them, along with a tall, stemmed wineglass and a fancily folded napkin.

Addie picked up the additional scrap of black fabric and her stomach dropped. "Is this a blindfold?"

"Of course it is." Peter rolled his eyes, fueling more of her ire. "It's part of the restaurant's entire premise. I don't know how you haven't heard of this place. It's the hottest place in town and practically impossible to snatch a table. You have to know people, and even then, the waitlist is years long."

"And yet we're here . . . with only two days' notice." Addie couldn't have been less impressed if she tried.

Peter grinned smugly. "I happen to know the *right* people. That, and my name was already on the waitlist. I figured that I'd find that someone special to share the experience with by the time my turn came around. And I was right."

Addie bit the side of her tongue, holding back a retort when the maître d' tapped a microphone.

"If I could have everyone's attention, please?" The maître d' turned, gazing around the entire room. "Myself, and your facilitators here at Sense-Less, welcome you to a one-of-a-kind experience. We ask that once we begin, you allow both yourself and others to become fully immersed. That means no talking, no removing of your blindfolds, and you are to keep both your nose- and earplugs in place until instructed otherwise."

Addie glanced around the table. "Where is the silverware?"

A few people from surrounding tables chuckled.

Except Peter. His displeasure palpable, he glowered at her until she lifted an eyebrow in silent challenge. "What?"

"The entire point of Sense-Less is eating your meal without

the use of your five senses . . . hence the blindfold, and nose plugs, and—"

"And hands? But with no utensils and using your hands, aren't you using your sense of touch? And you're eating the food . . . so *taste*? So the senseless aspect deteriorates a little bit, doesn't it?" Addie asked, legitimately confused.

A red flush rose to Peter's cheeks as he scanned their surroundings before dropping his voice to an irritated whisper. "Let's just enjoy the experience, yeah?"

It took everything Addie had not to leave without a single look back, and if it wasn't for the fact that Happily Ever Forever's future hinged on this working, she would've been out the door faster than Peter could talk about himself yet again.

At least wearing earplugs and a blindfold meant she didn't have to talk to—or stare at—her date while they ate and she could enjoy her food in peace.

With a renewed, somewhat optimistic outlook on the rest of the evening, Addie was the first to shove the foamy earplugs into her ears. The blindfold was a little trickier, her hair getting caught up in the string.

Once she was sufficiently sightless, she sensed movement on her left. A hand caught her wrist and guided her hands in front of her where she felt a plate. This was the most challenging thing she'd ever done, and the second her hand dipped into something hot and sticky, she knew this wouldn't end well for her outfit.

It was the longest dinner date on record and by the third course, Addie wanted nothing more than to go home and spot-treat her favorite maxi wrap dress before the stains set in—and it would definitely need spot treatment. Possibly with the big guns and an extra-long pre-soak because she'd picked things up with her bare hands that most definitely weren't meant to be finger foods.

Throat clear—*soup*.

She'd fished food off her lap no fewer than a dozen times, and went searching in her cleavage at least four—*thank you, blindfolds, for no one seeing that fiasco*.

What felt like hours later, hands loosened the fabric binding her eyes, and the world—and her date—came back into view. She blinked, even the dim lighting taking a few seconds to adjust to as she removed the nose- and earplugs.

It didn't take long to register Peter's disappointed scowl from across the table as he ran his gaze over her and noted the obvious splatters down her favorite dress. His shirt—of course—was spotless.

"Well, that was . . . an experience." Addie forced a smile to her face.

"I'm glad you enjoyed it. Perhaps on our next date we'll keep food out of the equation." Peter smirked.

If said by anyone else, Addie may have laughed. Joked. But at that moment, she couldn't find a funny bone in her entire body. Peter droned on and on as they headed toward the exit with everyone else, the line slowing as they reached the foyer.

"So what do you think?" Peter asked.

So zoned out and plotting an escape, she hadn't heard a word he'd said. "What do I think about what?"

He sighed for probably the ten thousandth time that night. "What time of year were you hoping to have a ceremony? I'm partial to spring, but the weather can be very unpredictable. Not to mention that we'd have to wait nearly a whole year."

"I've always been partial to spring with all the blooming flowers." Addie tried to understand what he was alluding to, and failed. "I'm sorry. What ceremony are you talking about?"

Peter looked at her as if she'd sprouted Hydra heads. "Our. Ceremony."

Aw hell . . .

This was proof that Maxi's matchmaking mojo was on the fritz.

As they waited for the line to move closer to the door, Addie scanned the restaurant, looking for an emergency exit. A fire door. Hell, she'd take a window over a toilet at this point. The only thing she knew with 100 percent certainty was that she needed to get the hell out of there, and fast.

Phoenix

Phoenix leaned into the turn, making the right onto Prospect. The cab coming from the opposite direction slammed on his horn and the driver's arm came out the window and gifted him a one-fingered salute.

Phoenix waved back—the right way—and kept going when a call beeped from inside his helmet. He picked up the call without needing to look who was on the other end. "I'm on my way. Promise."

A siren wailed in the background, making his alibi ring true.

"East and I are heading inside and grabbing an aisle before they're all taken," Naiomi announced. "Better I start throwing pointy objects in a controlled atmosphere than toward any of my professors."

Phoenix chuckled. Visiting Sir Axe-A-Lot did a lot for working out aggression, and Nai needed it before she dove into the arduous task of finalizing and defending her PhD dissertation to the doctoral board. It would be one of only a few outings until after she and East officially tied the knot.

"Go hone your inner lumberjack, sis. I'll be there in a few." Phoenix disconnected the call and a few moments later, cursed as a road crew effectively siphoned three lanes of traffic into one.

Phoenix came to a full stop, his booted feet sliding off the footrest to hit the ground. An inch at a time, they slowly moved forward, and he let his mind wander with thoughts of a certain sexy neighbor.

He'd hurled out the fauxmance idea five long days ago, and hadn't seen—or heard—from her since. Not so much as a slipper slapped against their shared apartment wall, and her telling silence had him second-guessing everything.

And third-guessing.

And fourth.

But after each brief questioning moment, he came around to the same decision. *It was a damn good idea.*

A fauxmance not only got the media vultures off Addie's back, but Marcus and the music label off his. Writing two decent lyrical lines after meeting Adalyn Whitlock was not a random coincidence. It didn't matter he hadn't written a damn thing since.

Not so much as a *la-la-la*.

They hadn't spent any real time together, time that would be required to develop a whirlwind fauxmance. And keeping the sexy redhead close definitely wouldn't be a hardship.

It was a dangerous game and a big gamble, but he'd never been the guy to shy away from a challenge. Especially if the benefits outweighed the risks—and keeping Addie Whitlock close was one hell of a big bonus.

The line of cars inched up another foot before stalling and doing the same thing over and over. The road opened up once you passed the road crew. He just needed to get there.

Less than a hundred feet from the crew, movement on his right caught his attention. A couple deep in an animated conversation walked briskly down the sidewalk, hands flailing. The woman's body language screamed *get me out of here*, and Phoenix slowed his forward movement, much to the displeasure of the car behind him.

"Seriously. We tried. Let's just leave it at that and—" The woman's words were cut off when the guy, red-faced and obviously pissed, reached out and grabbed hold of her upper arm.

"You didn't *try*. And I didn't go through the pain of planning this night just so you could blow me off."

The redhead stiffened. "If you don't release my arm right now, I'll introduce you to a pain-filled night."

The guy dropped his grip, albeit reluctantly. "This isn't over."

"Oh, I think it is. I'd typically say the polite thing and quote that it isn't you, it's me, but it's totally you."

Phoenix choked on a laugh, the woman's snark reminding him of . . .

The woman turned, and Phoenix froze.

So did Addie Whitlock.

What were the fucking chances . . .

Phoenix snapped up his visor and shot the redhead a coy smirk. "Fancy running into you, sparkles. Not that I want to step on your very capable toes, but do you want a lift out of here?"

Addie's gaze slipped from the glowering man behind her to Phoenix's bike. "Abso-fucking-lutely."

Addie's date started ranting again, but she ignored him, stepping into the street and up to his bike. Phoenix held out a supportive hand, and she clutched it like a lifeline as she climbed unsteadily onto the back.

"Grab the spare helmet in the rear compartment," Phoenix instructed, revving the engine. The second she shoved it onto her head, he asked, "Where to?"

"Anywhere that isn't here." Her arms were wrapped around

his waist tightly before he could even suggest it, and after moving another few inches forward, they bypassed the road crew and he took off.

Addie's body pressed against him, the heat from her close proximity damn near melting through his leather jacket. As they turned a corner, he automatically dropped a hand to her outer thigh, giving it a small squeeze. "You good back there?"

She nodded and pushed her cheek against his back as close as the spare helmet allowed. Phoenix didn't really know where to go, so he kept heading toward Sir Axe-A-Lot and pulled over into a prime parking spot along the curb before cutting the engine.

Addie glanced up and looked up and down the street.

Phoenix apologized as he climbed off the bike. "I'll just be a second. I need to tell Naiomi and East that I'll have to take a rain check."

She pulled off the helmet, and damn it if her helmet hair didn't look fucking adorable. "Don't change your plans. You did me a favor by getting me out of that date from hell situation. I can call a Ryde, or jump on the nearest train."

"It's no biggie. Why deal with public transit when you don't have to?" Phoenix paused as he contemplated his next move. "Unless you want to picture your date standing in front of a target and hurl an axe toward his head? Naiomi's pictured it with a few of her professors throughout the years. She says it's pretty cathartic—hence why we're here."

Addie nibbled her bottom lip as she glanced toward the redbrick building. "I don't want to crash."

"Please." Phoenix waved off her worry. "She'll be ecstatic that you're here. Hell, she'd probably prefer your company to mine. Come in with me and say hello, and if you want to stay and throw some sharp shit, great. If you decide you want to head home, that's fine, too. Just say the word and we'll get the hell out of here."

Addie glanced down at her dress, which Phoenix just realized sported a few inconspicuous dark spots. "I'm not exactly fit for public viewing."

Phoenix lifted his brow. "Are you fucking kidding me? You're fucking gorgeous, sparkles. Of course, you look killer in a fluffy towel and unicorn slippers—and trust me, I know from firsthand experience."

Her lips twitched into a little grin and he counted that as a small win, mentally patting himself on the back.

"If you're really that worried about it, here." Phoenix slipped out of his leather jacket and with a twirl of his finger, gestured for her to turn around. She did, slowly, and he helped her slide into his favorite jacket before turning her back around.

He wasn't mentally or physically prepared to see her wearing something of his. His cock twitched in his jeans and his mouth went dry as the damn Sahara. She swam in the jacket, the sleeves obscuring her hands, but damn if it didn't look made for her.

"There you go." Phoenix cleared his parched throat and shifted his stance to try and make more room in his tightening pants. "Like I said . . . fucking gorgeous."

"Thank you, Phoenix." Addie gifted him a rare, almost shy smile. "And if you're sure that Easton and Naiomi wouldn't mind, I've always thought about going axe throwing. I just never worked up the nerve to do it. Thought I'd look ridiculous."

Phoenix chuckled. "No way could you look ridiculous, but it just so happens that I'm practically a professional axe-thrower, and I give a wicked tutorial."

He waited for her small nod of agreement, and the second it came, so did a small flutter in his chest.

Phoenix held the door open and gestured for her to go inside first. He hadn't been joking. Sir Axe-A-Lot had been a hot spot for their group for a while, one of the first axe-throwing locations in the country. The interior melded nature themes with a modern edge, a long row of log-lined throwing cages on one side and a dive bar—with a strict one-drink-limit-if-throwing policy—on the other.

As expected, the place was hopping. Phoenix briefly rested his hand on Addie's back and guided her toward the rear of the room where Naiomi looked to be six axes into her throw-fest. East watched intently as Phoenix's sister hurled another axe. It landed pretty damn close to the bull's-eye.

"Next one!" Naiomi spun, already reaching for the next axe when her gaze landed first on Phoenix, then the redhead at his side. A beaming smile erupted on her face. "Adalyn! What a surprise!"

Addie smiled awkwardly. "I hope it's okay I crashed your axe night."

"Are you kidding?" Nai pulled her into a firm hug. "Now we can make this a true competition."

Addie chuckled. "Oh, no, no. I've never done this before. You definitely don't want me on your team."

"Maybe I should teach her the mechanics first," Phoenix suggested, giving Addie a wink. "I'll have her competition ready in no time."

"Go for it . . . while I go for some wings." Naiomi turned a smile on her fiancé. "Let's go, stone man. Feed me."

Grin in place, East dipped his shoulder, easily hoisting Naiomi over it, and the two headed over to the bar side of the building.

"All right, you ready to get throwing?" Phoenix asked with a smirk.

"Teach me, Master Yoda." Addie pushed up the sleeves of his leather jacket.

"*Star Wars* references, Miss Whitlock?" Phoenix teased. "You just may be my soulmate."

She snorted, rolling her eyes as she picked up an axe from their lane's bin. "This isn't nearly as heavy as I expected."

Phoenix grabbed one for himself. "That's because they're specifically made for throwing. These aren't the axes you'd use to cut down a tree and build yourself a log cabin."

"Well, damn. There goes my idea for sliding one of these babies into my purse," she quipped dryly.

"Watch me first, and then you can go ahead and give it a try." He got into position at the line, holding the axe in a loose two-handed grip. "The key is not holding on to the axe too tightly. It's not like a baseball bat, and these axes are made to rotate, so there are no fancy spins to it. It's honestly all about timing. Release the axe when it's directly in front of your face. Not higher. Not lower."

Taking his time getting into position, he let her observe his stance and hand grip, and then with a flick, he lifted and released, the blade easily digging into the wood target—dead center bull's-eye.

"Wow." Addie applauded. "You weren't lying. You are a professional . . . but I am a little concerned with how easy you made that look."

"Just remember hand grip, distance, and release position. You'll be just fine."

"If you say so . . ." She took position a few steps behind the safety line, and with a mumbled, "Here's hoping," she released.

Her axe smacked against the board and dropped to the ground with a heavy clank.

"What the hell did I do wrong?" Addie frowned.

"I think you were too far back and released it a little too late. Do you mind?" He gestured, asking if she'd like help.

"Please tutor me."

He ushered her two steps closer, just behind the release line, and handed her another axe. Their fingers brushed when she took it from him, sending a little shock wave through his arm. Addie startled at the contact, telling him he wasn't the only one who'd felt it.

"Thank you." Whisper soft, Addie's voice caught, the sound kicking up his heart rate.

"Go ahead and grip the axe like you did before." Standing behind her, Phoenix's cheek brushed against hers, and damn if her skin wasn't the softest thing he'd ever touched. He coasted his fingers over the back of her knuckles and relished in the slight corresponding shiver. "Now gentle your grip."

She loosened her hold.

"May I?" Phoenix's lips hovered a millimeter away from the shell of her ear.

"Yep." Her breath stuttered slightly.

Sliding his hands over hers, he gently plucked her fingers, shifting them until she held the handle loose in her palm and her thumbs were braced along the back of the grip. "There you go. Gentle is key here. Lift the axe over your head"—he pulled her arms back—"and then when you bring it forward, you release it the moment it's in front of your face. Not chest level. Face. And you just release . . . no need to hurl or flick. Got it?"

She nodded, brushing her cheek against his. "Hold gentle. Pull back. Face release. And no fancy business."

"Got it. Now, let's see what you got, sparkles," Phoenix whispered, mouth hovering just over her ear.

He slowly stepped back and watched Addie talk herself through each step, releasing the axe at the sweet spot. The axe spun handle over blade a handful of times before thudding directly into the bull's-eye.

"Oh. My. Goddess." Eyes widened, Addie turned and hurtled into his arms. "I did it! I actually freaking did it!"

"Hell yeah you did, sparkles!" Phoenix whooped and twirled her into a quick spin that had them both laughing.

As her feet touched the ground again, she grinned teasingly. "Maybe you are good at this tutoring thing."

He chuckled. "Thanks for sounding so surprised, beautiful."

"What do we have here?" Naiomi shot Phoenix a coy smirk from over her plate of barbeque wings.

"Looks like we have a natural. Second throw. Bull's-eye." He shot a warning look to his sister and mouthed a quick *Behave* that he knew would go ignored.

The four of them fell into a groove, taking turns hurling a few axes while devouring the bottomless basket of wings and nachos they ordered for their table.

"You didn't tell me that you had Addie with you when I called you," Naiomi scolded Phoenix gently a while later as they all took a break to rest their hands.

"That's because she wasn't with me then," Phoenix said truthfully before shooting a glance at Addie. "I was stuck in traffic when I saw a pretty redhead tearing into someone on the sidewalk."

Naiomi shot a questioning look to Addie, who took a bite of a chicken wing and cleaned off her fingers with a napkin. "Story me, please."

"There's really not much of a story. Went on a blind date and it was a freaking fiasco." She opened Phoenix's jacket and gestured to the front of her dress. "His idea of a good time is a pretentious restaurant where you eat in earplugged silence—which honestly wasn't that bad because I wasn't forced to hear about the size of his bank account *again*. But it was the nose plug and no utensils that really brought it home. Finger foods are usually the way to my heart, but not with creamy soup."

"He took you to Sense-Less?" Naiomi swallowed a giggle. "I had a classmate who went there once and they kicked her out halfway through because her phone buzzed and 'broke the experience.'"

Addie snorted. "I would've paid big bucks to have gotten kicked out. And then he wanted to pin down a date."

"For a second date?"

Addie grimaced. "For our *ceremony*."

Naiomi's eyes widened. "No."

Phoenix glanced at Easton to see if his friend was following along with the conversation. When he shrugged, Phoenix's curiosity got the best of him. "So that grabby-handed ass from the sidewalk was a first date?"

A rush of something shot through Phoenix so fast he couldn't decipher it.

Jealousy? Maybe. It was a foreign feeling and it took a few moments for him to register it. And he didn't like it one damn bit.

Naiomi shifted her attention from him to Addie and back before clamping her hand around East's and hauling him off his chair. "I need to throw a few more axes. Come watch."

"I can watch you from here, babe," East complained, devouring a barbeque wing.

She shot him a silent glare that held an entire conversation as she tilted her head toward Phoenix and Addie. "But you'll have a better view of my ass from over there."

East smirked and dragged her to their lane. "Well, when you put it like that. Let's go."

Despite being surrounded by people, the only one Phoenix

could focus on was Addie. He watched her chase a jalapeño with a tortilla chip as he debated his next move.

Phoenix cleared his throat and gained her attention. "So I guess it's safe to assume that there won't be another date with Mr. Pretentious?"

"Hell no." Addie looked horrified. "But I need to figure out how to break it to Maxi. She's been so down on herself for creating these nightmare matches . . . but there is no way that guy will help me get Happily Ever Forever out of the gossip trenches."

"Will you let her try again?" Phoenix asked curiously, gently digging.

"I'm not sure it's worth it, honestly. Not only was it a long shot, but I think I need something a bit more . . . immediate." Her gaze traveled around the room before finally landing—and holding—on him.

His heart skipped as he waited for her to say something—*anything*.

"You know that idea you brought up in my office a few days ago has a ninety-percent chance of blowing up in our faces, right?" Addie lowered her voice. "It's ridiculous. Who on this earth would actually believe it? I mean, I was in a play in summer camp, and there's a reason why I wasn't given the lead. And be a Muse? I wouldn't have the first idea how to go about doing that."

"First, it's ridiculously genius, and I think so even more now than I did when I first proposed it," Phoenix admitted truthfully. He pulled out his phone and brought up one of the music mag articles Marcus had been sure to yell at him about a few days ago. "Summer play lead or not, the foundation is already set. All we have to do is have some fun . . . and that goes for the Muse thing, too. You don't need to do anything but be you."

"'Naughty Nix or Knightly Nix: Who Is Nix's Mystery Damsel?'" Addie read the article heading before her gaze snapped to his. "This was from outside the HEF building the other day."

He nodded. "Exactly. We can spin this however you want, but I think people will eat up the idea of us falling in love while planning my sister and best friend's vow ceremony."

Addie nibbled on her bottom lip, deep in thought. "How would something like this work? I mean, we'd have to set some kind of rules. Write up a contract."

Phoenix kicked up an eyebrow. "You want to write up a contract?"

"Don't laugh. We should have something that lays out all the expectations and limitations. That way there are no surprises for either party."

He failed to withhold a smirk and got a glare in return. "Fine. We'll draw up a contract."

"Good."

"Great." He paused before slowly sliding his open palm across the table and waited for her to slide her hand into his. "So we have a Fauxmance Arrangement and Muse Agreement? A FAMA?"

Addie snorted. "A FAMA?"

He shrugged. "It sounded better in my head."

The gorgeous demigoddess sighed and slid her hand into his. "I guess we have a deal."

A heated zing sparked on contact, bringing a smile to his lips and a pink blush to Addie's cheeks. Phoenix could practically hear the lyrics already jumping around in his head.

7

PORTAL PUKE

Addie

Addie, Max, and Bailey entered the New York Botanical Gardens conservatory, the gorgeous, open space, home to colorful flowers and thriving plants . . . and the Olympus Portal. For the regular citizen, the stone structure abutting the end of the reflection pool created the perfect ambiance and selfie background.

For Addie, it signaled the start of what would be a day filled with portal sickness—stomach cramps and nausea that made the worst food poisoning seem like a tropical beach vacation.

Addie dropped her tote bag on the nearby bench, and while a couple taking pictures near the portal finished up their photo session, pulled out the white linen dress she wore only when day-tripping to the land of the gods. Tossing it on over her clothes, she used the flowy fabric to camouflage her outfit change, and Maxi did the same.

"Freaking Olympian dress code," Bailey grumbled as they tugged their doctored wide-leg jumper over their running clothes. "What could they do if I show up wearing red? Take away my visitor badge? If they tried, my mom would start slinging arrows."

Addie chuckled, already imagining the bow-and-arrow-wielding Athena on the warpath. It didn't take much to set off the Goddess of War's temper, but messing with one of her children did it almost instantly.

The nearby couple murmured to each other while stealing curious, jealous glances at them.

"Think we could convince them to go in our place?" Addie murmured.

Maxi smirked. "Look at it this way. You show your face, let the aunts and uncles pinch your cheeks, commiserate with a few of the cousins, and then you'll be good for at least six months before Mom starts badgering you for another visit."

"If anyone comes at me for a pinch, I will sic Do-Re-Mi on them." Addie glanced down at her pups, whose tail wagged furiously, their gazes fixed longingly on the portal.

Bailey snorted. "Yeah, death by licking. What a way to go, am I right?"

"Can you three try and look a little more ferocious?" Addie rolled her eyes when their tail thumped wildly on the ground in response. "Guess not."

"You complain about visiting every time we go, but then when we get there, you end up having a good time," Maxi pointed out.

"I wouldn't say *good* . . ."

But it wasn't that far off.

After making the rounds and showing her face, she usually ended up at her favorite spot, a small out-of-the-way gazebo nestled along the perimeter of Fates Lake, which was coincidentally, her uncle Hades's favorite hiding location, too. Although far enough away from the Olympus hub to avoid most of the activity, it was close enough to serve as a prime viewing area as people made fools of themselves.

She and Hades usually recited play-by-plays that made even the most comical sports announcers pale in comparison.

Hopefully she'd at least get a little time at her spot, but she couldn't forget the reason she'd finally agreed to this day trip—other than getting her mother off her back.

Aunt Eunice.

The Muses.

Aka, she needed a Muse 101 lesson so she could hold up her end of the deal with Phoenix, a deal she still couldn't believe that she'd agreed to. A FAMA. Fauxmance Arrangement and Muse Agreement.

Addie didn't know the first thing about being a Muse and while Phoenix had told her to just be herself, she was pretty sure she'd need to do more than binge-watch her true-crime documentaries in her pj's. Once she had a basic idea of what to expect, she could formulate a plan . . . and then they could scratch each other's backs.

Not literally.

Well, maybe . . .

"You ready to get this over with?" Addie adjusted the gold rope belt around her waist and peeked over her shoulder to make sure her ass wasn't hanging out because the one time she didn't check after a quick-change would feed the fire for a lifetime of ridicule.

"Ready as I'll ever be." Maxi stepped up to the portal, taking her spot on the left while Addie took the right, with Bailey in the center.

With a quick glance in each other's direction, they simultaneously pressed their palms against the elaborate stone surface. At first touch, the cool rock elicited a wave of goose bumps, making Addie wish she was back in her clothes—and in a hoodie—instead of the light double-sleeved tank-toga. But the stone slowly warmed, the surface glowing brighter beneath their palms until the entire arch lit up.

If Addie didn't know what lay on the other side, she would've found the sight breathtaking, as did a few of the spectators hovering in the perimeter.

"State your line." The disembodied voice of one of the Fates drifted in on a nonexistent breeze.

Addie rolled her eyes at her aunt's attempt at humor. "Pretty sure you knew the second we placed our palms on the stone . . . but if you don't want to let us in, that's okay. You'll be the one to explain it to our mothers though."

To her left, Maxi snorted.

Her aunt sighed heavily. "It's bad enough I drew the short straw that put me on portal duty, but now you're taking away any potential fun that I can find, Adalyn Love Whitlock."

"Hey, hey. There's no need for full-name calling," Addie teased. "But fine . . . we'll play along." She cleared her throat and shot Maxi an amused glance before turning back to the portal. "The children of Aphrodite and Athena seek entrance into Olympus. Please light our way and guide our feet . . . oh Great Guardian of the Portal."

Maxi's and Bailey's laughs ended on a snort and the portal pulsed, signifying the impending opening.

Their aunt's voice invited, "You may enter, children of Aphrodite and Athena . . . and prepare your cheeks for pinching, smart-ass."

"Boys?" Addie tapped her leg and Do-Re-Mi bounded to her side, and as the pulsing glow held strong, signaling the opening, they leaped into the light first.

Maxi, Bailey, and Addie joined hands as they mentally and physically prepared for portal travel.

"Hold my hair back when I puke, okay?" Addie's stomach already churned.

"Ditto." Maxi grimaced. "Goddess, I hate puking."

"On the count of three?" Bailey suggested.

Maxi nodded. "One."

"Two."

"Oh, by the way," Addie interjected abruptly, "Phoenix Cross offered his fake boyfriend services, and I agreed. All I have to do in return is play at being his Muse."

"What?" Maxi and Bailey screeched simultaneously as Addie took the first step through the portal.

The gate sucked all three of them into the light.

Addie's curses fell away as the portal magic dropped over her like a heavy blanket, stealing both her words and her stomach. A dueling battle between a mega-force vacuuming your body forward and suction cups sealing your feet to the nonexistent ground, portal traveling elicited the oddest sensations.

Five seconds felt like a hundred until they reached the other end, stumbling through another golden haze and into the bright, Earthlike light of Mount Olympus.

Addie instantly regretted that morning's everything bagel as she leaned over and evacuated every ounce of her stomach contents, and quite possibly a few organs, onto the vivid green grass.

"I will never, in a million years, get used to that sensation." Addie deep-breathed through another rush of nausea, barely staving off a new round of gagging.

On her left, Maxi fared just as well, her usually pinkish glow a dimmed sallow green. Bailey, on the other hand, appeared unaffected, their arms crossed over their chest as they glowered directly at Addie.

"You do not blurt out things like 'Phoenix Cross offered his fake boyfriend services' moments before portal traveling," Bailey admonished, not looking the least bit amused. "And what the hell do you mean that you're going to be his Muse?"

Fighting through each deep breath, Addie stood. "He claims I'm his Muse, so in exchange for doing Muse things, he'll pretend to sweep me off my feet. Look, I have no idea how this will work, or if it even will."

"It will," Bailey stated adamantly.

"Then why is your Angry Athena Artery pulsating at your temple?"

Her cousin's lips slowly twitched into a smirk. "Because I'm a little pissed that I wasn't the one to think of it."

Maxi dry heaved one more time before joining the discussion. "So what does being his Muse entail?"

"No fucking clue." Addie shrugged. "That's why I finally caved to Mom's incessant badgering about the reunion. I hoped I could get some alone time with Aunt Eunice."

Bailey clapped their hands. "Then let's get this show on the road."

Thanks to contemporary art pieces, most people pictured Mount Olympus as open sky with a cloud-like ground, and while the sky—more often than not—was a gorgeous cerulean blue, Olympus itself looked a lot like Central Park.

Wide open spaces and lush green grass made it possible to frolic—if someone was the frolicking type. Like Do-Re-Mi. Their tongues lolled as their heads whipped toward Addie, silently asking for frolicking permission.

"Go. Stay out of trouble." She smirked as they took off, joyous barks alerting everyone nearby to their presence.

"Funny how you tell those mutts to stay out of trouble, but you, my dear niece, are the embodiment of it." Aunt Clotho, the youngest of the original Fates, stepped around the side of the portal, an exact copy of the one back in New York. "Are you prepared for cheek-pinching?"

"Are you prepared for a firsthand demonstration on just how *uncouth* we demigod New Yorkers can be?" Addie fired back, grinning as she used one of her aunt's favorite taunts.

As expected, Clotho laughed, taking time to give each of them a firm hug. "I'm glad the three of you could make it this time. It means a lot to your mothers."

"Yeah, well . . . we're doing our god-spawn duty."

Her aunt shot her a knowing look. "Spawn duty with some extracurriculars thrown into the mix, yes? Very efficient of you."

Addie narrowed a glare on her aunt. "It's not nice flaunting your all-knowing Fate-ness like that. Not unless you'll actually tell me what lies ahead."

Clotho patted her cheek. "And if I did that, Zeus would sentence me to a duty worse than manning the portal on reunion day. Go. Eunice is somewhere over by the pavilion . . . but do try and have fun while you're here."

With a wink, she urged them on their way, and they headed across the grassy knoll toward the pavilion. On the left, Do-Re-Mi played with their brothers and sisters—and Cerberus herself—chasing one another while yelping happily.

It quickly became obvious that the three of them were the last to arrive. Packed with gods and deities from all walks of life—even ones that according to human tales were blood-sworn enemies—laughter filled the vaulted gazebo.

Not that *everyone* got along, or that squabbles didn't pop up. You don't become as old as the gods without a few sporadic feuds, but most historical texts had been elaborated for wow factor and entertainment ratings.

"Well, well, well, and here I didn't think myself able to be shocked." Aphrodite, pausing her conversation with Persephone, pulled Addie and Max into a firm hug. "A visit from *both* of my loin-spring and their cousin bestie?"

Addie grimaced. "Let's not talk about your loins, Mom."

Aphrodite chuckled and wrapped Bailey in a welcoming hug, too. "Excuse my excitement. But I feel as though I won the goddess lottery. But you realize that I could've swung by your place and—"

"Goddess *poofed* us here?" Maxi's face turned a little green. "No, thank you. Portal travel is bad enough."

Aphrodite turned a knowing smile on Addie that had her squirming. "What?"

Her mother's smirk widened. "I heard from a little birdie that you're adding enamored Muse onto your résumé."

"Aunt Clotho can't tell me which subway train is running late, but she can tell you *that*?"

"One would think that my own daughter would tell me herself."

"It just happened," Addie said truthfully. "And while I did agree, I'm still not sure how I'll be able to pull it off. And no, I do not need any advice—or assistance—from you. Thank you for the almost-offer, but Phoenix and I will somehow muddle through."

Aphrodite patted her on the shoulder. "Well, you know where I am if you need me . . . but if I may say one thing—not advice, but a mere suggestion? Don't dawdle in the fauxmance department."

"Oh look," Maxi interjected, her gaze traveling to the other side of the gazebo. "There's Aunt Athena. Bailey, we should go and say hello to her. Right now."

"But I want to hear the adv—" Bailey's complaint was cut off with a stern look from Max as she dragged them away.

"Why would I dawdle, Mom?" Addie asked when they were alone. "The sooner people believe I'm not the Anti-You, the sooner I can get on with my life."

"Sweetheart, I love you. And I also know you better than you think I do."

"Meaning?"

"That I'm worried that you won't fully commit to this FAMA because you're either worried that it won't work, or that it will work too well. Phoenix Cross seems to be quite the specimen of—"

"Nope. Not having this conversation with you. We have an agreement, remember?"

Aphrodite frowned. "That silly thing? Sweetheart, I'm the Goddess of Love. You can't really expect me to stay out of your love life entirely."

"Oh, I can and I do. And that silly contract you signed was done on Olympus parchment, with Olympic ink. You break it and—"

"Yes. Yes. One of my sisters will put a damper on my day. I'm aware."

"You know I love you, Mom, but this?" Addie gestured around Olympus Field. "This isn't me. I'm not you. And I want my life to be affected by the gods as little as possible, and that's not a dig on who you are and what you do. It's just not me."

Aphrodite smiled warmly, her eyes a little glowy. "You are so much like your father—and I do mean that as a positive."

And that's what never made sense to Addie, and probably never would.

Her parents never fought or argued. Never spoke poorly about the other. Whenever they were face-to-face, it almost appeared as if they flirted, which never failed to freak Addie the fuck out. Their separation would almost be easier to understand if they railed and screamed and bad-mouthed one another.

But when asked, both parents would say that the love was still there. Still vibrant and thriving. And that it was simply in a new form.

In Addie.

And Max.

To Addie, it was basically a flowery way to say, *Once upon a time, we thought we loved each other, but nope. We were wrong—but at least got two amazing children out of our little experiment.* Did that make her a pessimist? Maybe. But that didn't mean it wasn't true.

"If it isn't one of my favorite demigods!" Eunice, the original Muse of Art, strolled over, her dark hair in a gorgeous display of loose, artfully swirled braids that crowned her head. "Someone told me that you were looking for me."

Aphrodite winked at Addie and sashayed over to where Hades manned the BBQ pit, Persephone watching closely over his shoulder while dishing out directions.

"Come, niece." Eunice linked their arms and guided them away from prying eyes and ears. "Tell me, have you finally run out of excuses to avoid visiting Olympus, or have you come across a need that far outweighs your desire to avoid all the dramatics?"

"Something tells me that you already know. Aunt Clotho—it appears—is chatty with everyone but me," Addie quipped.

"The only thing I was told was that today's festivities were ones that should not be missed. So enlighten me as to why I braved the rumblings of my siblings."

Addie nibbled her bottom lip as they climbed the gazebo steps. "What's involved in being a Muse?"

"How much time do you have?" Eunice teased, getting comfortable on the cushioned bench as she patted the spot next to her.

"Till I head back to the Land of Humans and iced mocha Frappuccinos."

"Oh, my . . . there's far too much information to fit into one Olympus afternoon."

Addie's heart plummeted. "How in-depth can it be? Can't you give me the CliffsNotes version?"

"I'll pretend you didn't mean that to sound insulting." Eunice cocked a sculpted eyebrow.

"No! No. I didn't mean—"

"Relax, child. I'm teasing." Eunice covered her hand, smirking. "You aren't the first to question the tasks of a Muse, and you most certainly won't be the last. But unfortunately, there is no one clear direction. It's why my sisters and I founded Muse Academy so long ago. The process is much more involved than many think, and its techniques are as vast as the Elysian Fields."

"So you're saying no to the CliffsNotes version." Addie's shoulders drooped.

Eunice chuckled. "How about you tell me what you're hoping to achieve, and perhaps I can give you a few ideas."

"Really?"

"There are no guarantees that anything I say will work. Keep in mind, my Muses attend the Academy for years before we deem them sufficiently trained enough to take on their own clients."

Addie purged it all. Her deal with Phoenix Cross. What she knew of his problems and how he hoped she could help him with them. A few short hours later, armed with a few more ideas than she'd had before, Addie felt only slightly better prepared to hold up her end of the deal with the rock star.

She just hoped she didn't make a fool of herself in the process.

Hours—and a second portal jump—later, Addie was still digesting Eunice's fountain of Muse knowledge . . . and would hopefully soon be ingesting a slice of steaming hot pizza.

Longing to shed the white toga and climb into her pj's, she wrestled with her apartment lock. The second she won the front door battle, Do-Re-Mi pushed past and did a spin by their dog bed before curling up and promptly falling asleep.

"Looks like I'm not the only one who's had a day, huh?" Addie quipped just as the elevator doors opened and Phoenix stepped into the hall.

His gaze drifted over her, still in her Olympus toga, and he whistled. "Damn. You make bedsheets look good, love."

Her gaze fell on the pizza box in his hands. "Is that—"

"From Soprano's around the corner. Extra cheese. Drippy grease." Phoenix grinned coyly. "For the right price, I might be persuaded to share."

Addie's stomach growled loudly. "What's considered the right price?"

"Honestly, I'm not sure there is a monetary value. Do you have any idea how long I had to stand in line to get my hands on this baby?"

Addie leaned closer to the box and sniffed the culinary masterpiece. "Fine. Forget money. I'll give you my apartment—oh wait, you already have that."

Phoenix's cheeks reddened as he chuckled. "Be my date for the Indie Awards."

Addie's gaze snapped to his. "What?"

He smiled sheepishly. "The Stone Talons are both performing and up for an award at the Indie Rock Awards in a few weeks, and I thought we could make it a date."

"A date?"

"A date. You know . . . *a public outing*."

"A public outing . . . with you?"

Phoenix chuckled. The dimple popped into existence and temporarily squashed whatever brain cells remained in her head. "You do remember our FAMA, right? Fauxmance Arrangement and Muse Agreement? They both typically require spending time together, and for the fauxmance portion, publicly."

Dates. Public outings.

What the hell did she get herself into?

"I'll share the pizza with you even if you decline to be my plus-one," Phoenix added with a grin. "I can hear your stomach growling from here."

Phoenix

He couldn't have planned this better if he'd tried, and yet as he stepped into Adalyn Whitlock's domain, he second-guessed his entire strategy—which wasn't so much a strategy as it was a cross-your-fingers-and-hope-for-the-best mindset.

Not a single article of clothing lay on the floor. Not a speck of dust on any surface or a takeout container to be seen. Hell, even her bookshelf, framing both sides of a modest television, rippled in a near-perfect color-coded rainbow effect.

Addie, stepping out from her bedroom dressed in her flannel

little-duck pj's and sparkling unicorn slippers, caught him smirking.

One sexy eyebrow lifted. "What?"

"I didn't take you for the rainbow bookshelf type. Don't get me wrong, it's aesthetically pleasing, but I would've guessed you to be more into alphabetized organization. You seem the type to . . ." His voice trailed off as her eyebrow rose higher.

"The type to what?"

"To want things in a precise spot."

She drilled him with a hard look that nearly broke him into a sweat before her lips twitched. "Actually, I do usually alphabetize them. I left Bailey and Max unsupervised one afternoon and when I came home, rainbow."

"And you didn't change it back?"

"It grew on me." She shrugged, and after grabbing some plates and napkins from the kitchen, claimed a seat on the far end of the red couch. "And finding certain books wasn't as difficult as I thought it would be. It turns out I remember cover colors better than I do book titles or author names . . . unless they're one of my auto-buys."

Phoenix plopped a slice of pizza on a plate and handed it to Addie before grabbing one for himself. A few cushions down, her dogs' snores rumbled through the room, front feet kicking as they chased something in their dreams.

He chuckled. "Looks like they had a good day."

"They always enjoy their visits to Olympus. They're spoiled with treats and extra attention, and they also get to see Cerberus and their littermates."

"And did you have a good day?"

Addie paused with a bite of cheese escaping the corner of her mouth. "Well . . ."

"Was that a trick question?" Phoenix teased. "Or maybe just a loaded one."

"Visiting my family is . . . a lot. Drama mixed in with more drama, and while I love them all, after visits, I always feel like some energy-sucking vampire used me as their walking buffet."

"Energy-sucking vampires. That definitely sounds like a good time," Phoenix joked dryly.

Addie burst into laughter and a cute little snort escaped her nose. "Tell me more about the award show. It sounds like a big deal."

"Truth?"

She nodded.

"I'd rather go anywhere else, and that includes the dentist to undergo a root canal without anesthesia." He developed a migraine with each of Marcus's event reminders. "But it's one of those necessary evils of the business. It's great exposure for the band, and exposure is practically currency in the music industry."

Addie watched him astutely. "I sense a *but* in there."

He shrugged. "I loved the scene and everything that came with it when we were teenagers playing in my parents' garage, but the longer we stay in the business and the more noticed we get, the more things like the award shows lose their luster. I'd much prefer being off center stage."

"Writing music."

"Writing the music."

"So why not do that instead?" Addie asked innocently.

That was the million-dollar question, and one Phoenix had asked himself many times over the last two years. "For one, it's not reliable. If the creative mojo is on the fritz—like mine is now—then you've got problems."

"True."

"It also doesn't feel right to pull back from the Stone Talons just because my dreams have shifted," Phoenix surprised himself by admitting. "Making a name for the group is still important to people I care about, and by extension, me."

Addie stared at him, and after a pronounced stretch of silence, he squirmed. "Do I have pizza sauce all over my face or something?"

"No. Sorry." She shook her head, still looking contemplative. "It's just that I know how that feels. I'm proud of what Max, Bailey, and I have accomplished with Happily Ever Forever, but it's something that I fell into because of my mother. As her daughters, there'd always been an unspoken expectation that we'd go into the 'family business.'"

"Damn obligations," Phoenix joked dryly. "Both a blessing and a curse."

"Speaking of obligations . . ." Addie wiped her hands on a napkin before glancing around the room and grabbing a Sharpie and one of the spare napkins. "Let's talk contract."

"You were serious about that?"

"Absolutely. That way we can make sure we're both on the same page and know what's expected of each other. No surprises."

"Sometimes surprises are the best thing."

"We're talking about a Fauxmance Arrangement and Muse Agreement, not finding an extra chicken nugget in your Happy Meal."

He set aside his empty plate and shifted closer to her on the couch. "Okay, so FAMA."

She shot him a look. "Do we really have to call it that?"

"Do you have a better title in mind?" At her silence, he chuckled. "Yeah, didn't think so. What do you think we should include in this agreement?"

She shrugged. "This is my first foray into both Museship and fake dating, so I have absolutely no idea."

"Let's talk about our fauxmance first," Phoenix suggested. "What do you think you'll need?"

Her eyes, wide like a doe caught in high-beam headlights, blinked. "Need?"

"How many public appearances do we make a week? And what constitutes public? Paparazzi-followed walks in the park? Quick-pic coffee grabs? Or are we only counting formal events—like the upcoming award ceremony?"

"Walks in the park and coffee?"

Smirking, Phoenix playfully bumped his shoulder into hers. "This would probably work better if you did more than repeat what I say, sparkles."

Addie cleared her throat, a pretty pink blush forming on her cheeks. "Are people really snapping pics of you walking around the corner to grab a coffee?"

"It's not always a full-blown paparazzi horde. Sometimes it's an excited fan or two, but pics are pretty much guaranteed if I go anywhere but from my couch to my bed."

"That's . . ."

"Stifling? Intrusive? Tiring?" He nodded. "Yes to all."

"Well, I don't know if there's a magic number for joint appearances, or a grandeur scale. Maybe we should start with a number and adjust it as we go? If we plan smart, we can get double use from each appearance. It can both help feed into our fauxmance storyline and fuel your musical inspiration."

"Efficiency. I love it." She shot him an annoyed look, and he laughed. "I'm not teasing. It not only makes sense, but sounds totally doable."

"Should we say one public outing a week?"

Phoenix lifted a brow. "That's not exactly a big splash in the deep end. That's more like someone dripping on you when they climb out of the pool. How quickly do you want your business back on track?"

"Months ago," Addie joked.

"So let's start with three appearances a week, and like you said, we can always reevaluate and adjust."

"Won't that be too big a commitment for you with everything you need to do with the Stone Talons?"

"Typically, yes. But considering Marcus and the label want music out of me sooner rather than later, they can't jump down my throat too much. Plus, we can use some TST events as Adix sightings."

Her brow furrowed in an adorably confused expression. "Adix?"

"*Ad*alyn. Phoen*ix*." He smirked. "It can be our ship name."

"We're not calling ourselves Adix."

"Why not? It's cute and catchy."

"It sounds like a heartburn medication."

His shoulders shook from barely withheld laughter. "Fine. No cute ship name."

On the napkin, Addie jotted down everything they'd agreed to in her small, neat print.

"We should probably discuss physical expectations and limitations, too," Phoenix added.

Addie's marker slipped across the napkin, a black line streaking over her pajama pants as her head snapped up. "Physical expectations?"

"There you go repeating me again. Public displays of affection. On a scale of one pearl to an entire string, how many pearls do we want people clutching when they see us?" He grinned wickedly, grin broadening as she registered his meaning. "Put your mind at ease, sparkles. I don't think public sex will be necessary for people to believe we're falling head over heels in love."

Addie snorted. "I would hope not . . . but don't they call you Naughty Nix? Wouldn't it look odd for the Stone Talons's bad boy to suddenly not participate in at least a few public pearl-clutching activities?"

"That's a *them* problem, not an *us* problem." Phoenix shrugged. "We'll do what you're comfortable doing. Not a pearl more. You just need to decide how many pearls that is."

"What the hell is one pearl versus a half- or full-strand?"

"Full-strand should be obvious, but we've already agreed that public sex is probably a bit overkill. One pearl would be equal to public handholding. Two pearls, some arms around waists and adoring looks. Three, a no-licking peck on the cheek. A half-strand is when things get . . . spicy."

"Spicy." Addie nibbled on the marker cap. "Basically more handsy, and more mouth action."

"Precisely." In an attempt to hide a smirk, Phoenix took a sip of water.

"I'd be okay with half-strand spicy action if the situation called for it, but it shouldn't be the default."

Phoenix choked, water occluding his airway. "Sorry, but *what*?"

With a severe eye roll, she wrote *half-strand PDA* on their napkin contract. "You talked about what I'm okay with—which is a half-strand of pearls, but what's your comfort limit?"

Brain temporarily misfiring, he replayed her casual statement about more hands and mouth action. "I'm good with a half-strand."

He'd be good with a hell of a lot more.

"Maybe we should have some kind of code word," Phoenix suggested. "Like a safe word, to signal to the other that we're okay with taking things one pearl further." Because the last thing he wanted was to ever cross a line Addie wasn't comfortable crossing. "What about *sparkles*? Obviously, I'll have to give you another nickname."

"Sparkles? You can't be serious."

"I take consent very seriously." He grinned mischievously. "So? Do we have our safe word? *Sparkles* for the all-clear?"

"Fine. *Sparkles.*" She jotted it on the napkin and caught him smirking. "But you can forget about that Adix thing. I won't be caving on that, Mr. Rock Star."

"We'll see. I bet it'll grow on you."

"Like a fungus," Addie muttered under her breath.

"What's your middle name?" Phoenix couldn't help asking.

Addie paled, a pizza slice halfway to her mouth. "Why?"

He shrugged. "Just figured I'd ask since you're in the market for a new nickname."

"Yeah, you're not using that."

That piqued his curiosity. "And why not?"

"You're just not and leave it at that." Realizing he wasn't about to give up, she sighed. "Fine. But it stays in this room, do you understand?"

"Cross my heart."

"My full name is Adalyn . . . Love . . . Whitlock."

Phoenix waited for the punch line, and when it didn't come, he laughed anyway, tears springing to his eyes. Addie sat across from him looking less than amused, which only made him laugh harder.

"The Anti-Aphrodite's middle name is *Love*? Shit. This stuff is too good."

"Get it all out of your system now, music man, because you're never mentioning it to anyone ever again."

He waved off her warning, wiping the tears from the corners

of his eyes. "Yeah, sure. Not a peep . . . but you did just get a new nickname so I hope you weren't too attached to *sparkles*."

She narrowed her eyes on him. "What are you talking about?"

"Well, we're meant to be falling in love, right?" He grinned mischievously. "I may have to adopt a little British terminology."

"No."

"Oh, yes . . . and it can be a sweet little inside joke between just the two of us . . . *love*."

Phoenix wasn't sure which of the gods he'd made happy in a previous life, but whoever it was, he hoped that he kept doing it. This day just went from shitastic to fan-fucking-tastic in the blink of an eye.

With a smile on his face, he helped himself to another slice of pizza. He didn't know if any of this would help him regain his musical magic, but at least he'd be entertained while he figured it out.

8

BRIDEZILLA STRIKES AGAIN

Addie

Addie read Naiomi Cross's intake questionnaire for the sixth time and hoped an idea would spring into her head. *Any* idea. At this point, she'd take a bad one over a good one because at least with a bad one, she could take it to Maxi or Bails with a doe-eyed, *Help me make it better.*

Formulating an attack plan shouldn't be this difficult. She'd orchestrated countless vow exchanges, and Nai's list, although slim, didn't include any bizarre requests. No performing aerialists. No guest photo with a Hydra. Everything appeared basic and straightforward.

And that was the damn problem.

Nothing about the intake form screamed *Naiomi Cross*, the woman who'd created a wedding journal before she even hit double digits, and trying to solve the puzzle brought on a pounding headache that ibuprofen didn't touch.

Her lack of sleep the night before sure as hell didn't help. Despite drinking a gallon of Sleepytime tea, taking a lavender-infused bath, and turning her sound machine onto the ultra-sleep setting, sleep still evaded her.

What she hadn't dodged were her thoughts of a certain sexy drummer and the ridiculous FAMA contract still sitting on her coffee table. She'd thought the fauxmance thing a bad idea right from the start, but the second they started talking about public dates and pearls, the idea morphed from bad to potentially volatile.

Kids drama camp aside, where she'd been relegated to Tree #3, she hadn't acted a day in her life. Hell, her father claimed she was the least talented liar he'd ever come across when she once feigned a stomachache with the hope of getting out of a math test. If she couldn't fake food poisoning, what made her think she could fake being in love?

"A chamomile tea with lemon for you." Bailey slid a tall mug across the table toward Addie and took the empty seat on Maxi's left. "And vanilla mocha fraps with four extra espresso shots for me and Max."

Addie frowned. "I need caffeine. Not relaxation."

"Pretty sure you've hit your daily caffeine limit." Bailey shot a pointed look to her knee, bouncing beneath the table.

"Last meeting for tomorrow rescheduled, and to say the clients weren't happy would be an understatement." Maxi groaned from behind her laptop. "I still don't understand how we missed the landlord's fumigation notice."

Addie shrugged. "It happens. We've all been a little preoccupied."

When they found out they needed to vacate the HEF building for two days, Bailey sweet-talked the coffee shop owner around the block into letting them commandeer one of their back corner tables. But despite the hipster ambiance and flowing caffeine stream, work progress dragged at a snail's pace.

In deep concentration, Maxi stared toward the massive line of waiting customers, her lower lip caught between her teeth. Her eyes narrowed and widened before narrowing again as if trying to summon some kind of X-ray vision.

"Keep thinking that hard and we'll be asking the baristas where they keep the fire extinguisher," Addie joked.

Bailey snorted as they scanned through the business's social media accounts. "Or start bringing the fire blanket everywhere we go."

A little growl escaped Max's lips as she slouched in her chair with a massive sigh. "I can practically feel flickers of a soul connection just beneath the surface, and the second I try to pull it forward, it disappears."

"Maybe you're trying too hard."

"Once upon a time, I didn't have to try at *all*. If two people were a match, I felt it instantly. Mom thinks it's performance anxiety."

Addie studied her sister over Naiomi's questionnaire. "What do you think it is?"

"Hell if I know. But it would almost be easier to deal with if I stopped feeling soul tethers altogether. Not this . . . slow erosion." Maxi shot Addie a warning look. "And it's not because true love doesn't exist."

"I wasn't about to say that."

"Really?"

"Maybe the thought crossed my mind, but I wouldn't say it aloud because you're already having a crappy day," Addie teased.

Maxi glanced back at the line. "Take that blond woman in the red dress and the guy standing next to her. I swear I felt a connection between them a few minutes ago, but now there's nothing."

Bailey and Addie both glanced toward the talking couple, and Addie did a double-take. Not only was there no luminescent love connection linking the two, but the tether appeared tarnished and rusted.

Sick.

"They're definitely not a match," Addie heard herself say.

"How do you know?" Maxi studied the couple harder, her eyes narrowing.

Addie shrugged. "Theoretically, they could get together, but the relationship would definitely end—and definitely not in a happily-ever-forever way."

Bailey and Maxi fastened their gazes on her, questions forming in their eyes.

Maxi asked first. "Again, how do you know?"

"It looks . . . rusty."

"What looks rusty?"

"Their link. The tether. The cord. Whatever you call it." At Maxi's confused look, Addie sighed. "You're the one Mom Cupid-trained. I don't know how it works." Addie glanced back at the couple and the rusted link was gone. "I'm both overdue a prescription update and caffeine deficient. Ignore everything I've said."

The coffee shop door opened and a stunning woman with long, cascading onyx braids entered, a box of art supplies clutched in her hands. The woman in red glanced her way while speaking to the man at her side, and stumbled over her words.

The air shifted. Addie glanced around for the open window or rotating ceiling fan, but when she didn't find either, she looked back toward the two women and nearly fell out of her seat.

Another link slowly flickered into existence, its golden glow at first faint and gradually becoming more intense the longer they exchanged small, sweet smiles.

Addie's heart rate kicked up. "Do you see that?"

"See what?" Maxi asked with a glance toward the counter. "You mean the daily special? I don't think it's much of a special deal."

Careful not to dislodge her contacts, Addie rubbed her eyes and looked again. The pretty gold link between the two women was gone.

No link.

No golden glow.

Nothing.

She exhaled heavily. For one very brief, panic-filled second, she'd thought she'd seen a soul tether. The Anti-Aphrodite morphing into a Cupid and seeing soul connections all throughout Manhattan. Goddess, wouldn't that be karma biting her on the ass?

Max glanced at Nai's questionnaire. "How are things moving along with Naiomi and Easton's ceremony?"

"They're not. And it's not like she's asking for the moon. Red and white roses. Silk aisle runner. Orchestral processional. It just all feels very—"

"Ordinary," Maxi finished.

"Exactly."

"Sometimes what people think they want isn't actually what they want, but what others expect."

Addie glanced from her sister to the list and back. "You don't think this is her actual wish list?"

Maxi shrugged, but the more Addie thought about it, the more she wondered if that was the case and why what she knew of the bubbly brunette didn't match what was written on the form. She replayed some of their earlier conversations and kept rewinding back to their first one when she mentioned her childhood wedding journal.

"Son-of-a-bi—" Bailey jolted in their seat as they flipped their phone toward her and shoved it across the table. "Bridezilla Kinkaid strikes again."

A red blinking LIVE notice flashed in the top right corner as Karleigh Kinkaid-Fink stared into the camera, tears catching in her eyelashes. The number of people watching her quickly grew from a hundred, to over a thousand . . . and more.

Bailey bumped up the volume.

"I want to thank my followers who've reached out and who've showed me so much support in this dark time," Karleigh gushed. "If there's one good thing to have come from my encounter with the Anti-Aphrodite, it's realizing that love—my love for all of you—can help me overcome any obstacle. We are stronger together. Thank you, everyone."

Karleigh blew a kiss into the screen, and her tears miraculously dried up. "And don't forget to hit the follow button if you want to see what's coming next."

"Oh. My. Fucking. Goddess." Addie stared at the video, literally feeling the color drain from her face as the comments flooded in, one after another, so fast she couldn't read them all, and after catching one that didn't paint Happily Ever Forever in the best light, she didn't want to.

Bailey cursed. "It's going fucking viral."

Maxi paled. "What the hell are we going to do? She's got over a million followers, and unlike our summer drama experience, hers was evidently spot-on."

Addie closed her eyes and released a slow breath as she rummaged through their options.

It didn't take long because she didn't have any.

Except one.

She needed to talk to a rock star about a first date.

She pulled out her phone, fingers hovering over the text screen, when it rang with an unknown number. She debated letting it go to voicemail, but picked up anyway. "Happily Ever Forever . . . how can we make your forever happen?"

"Adalyn, babe," came a familiar, unexpected voice. "You asked me to touch base if I ever had a last-minute opening, and guess what?"

Addie sat upright in her seat. "Are you serious?"

The voice on the other end of the line laughed. "You know I don't joke about event planning. How soon can you get here?"

"Let me make one quick call to my co-planner, and we'll swing right over." Addie hung up, smile firmly in place as she shot off a quick text to Phoenix.

Received exciting venue
news. You free to see a place?
ASAP?

"Who was that?" Maxi asked, curious.

"The Globe has a last-minute opening, and we have to jump on it now if we have any hopes of securing it."

I'm right around the corner
from your building. It's kismet.
Will swing by and pick you up
in 5. –P

"You guys hold down the fort here. Hopefully when I come back, I'll have secured the venue for Naiomi and East's ceremony." Addie quickly tossed her notepad, pen, and a few other odds and ends into her leather satchel. Realizing she hadn't told Phoenix about working out of the café, she hightailed it toward the HEF building.

Already parked out front when she turned the corner, Phoenix leaned casually against his motorcycle, legs crossed at the ankle and looking too sexy for his own good. Dark sunglasses covered his eyes, but it didn't shield her from his weighted gaze as he watched her approach.

He grinned. "Good morning, love. Didn't expect you to come from that direction."

"Building woes. Don't ask."

Bright lights flashed on her left. At least three photographers began instantly snapping pictures. "You weren't kidding about the stepping-outside photo thing, were you?"

After taking her bag and tucking it into the storage compartment, Phoenix turned to her with a chuckle—and a helmet. "I didn't even realize they were there. All I could see was you."

Addie kicked up an eyebrow and snorted. "Sure."

"So where are we off to this fine morning?"

"I'll tell you when we're in motion."

"A surprise. One of my favorite things."

Of course it was.

Phoenix climbed effortlessly onto the bike and crooked his finger in a playful *come-hither* motion. Struggling not to let her forced smile turn into a glare, she slowly closed the distance and stopped right next to him.

He tucked a stray lock of hair behind her ear, his fingers trailing along her cheek a little longer than necessary as his gaze roamed over her face. "Hate to cover these pretty eyes, but safety first."

He expertly slid his spare helmet onto her head and took his time fastening the buckle beneath her chin, his eyes remaining fixed on hers the entire time. Her skin stayed warm every place he touched her, even after he snapped the strap and claimed her ready to ride.

"Your chariot of steel and power awaits. Pretty sure you remember how to climb onto one of these babies, right?" Phoenix held out a supportive hand.

Ignoring the resurgence of camera flashes and hurled questions, she slid her hand into his and climbed on behind him. The second her ass touched the seat, Phoenix reached back and gripped her thighs, tugging her front flush against his back.

"Much better." He gave her right knee a faint squeeze and revved the bike's engine. "So where are we off to?"

She rested her chin on his broad shoulder. "The Globe—and while I'm not usually a fan of speeding while riding on the back of a two-wheeled death stick, the space won't stay open for long."

"Fast requires extra safety measures. Can't have you flying off at the first turn." Phoenix gently unhooked her fingers from his belt loops and laid them flat against his hard abs, the snug embrace smooshing her breasts against his back. "Hang on."

Addie expected weaving and questionable cutoffs, but Phoenix stayed in his lane and used his blinkers to signal each move well before he actually made it. Whether it was for her benefit or his usual style, she didn't know, but she appreciated it. Before long, she sank into the warmth of his leather jacket and enjoyed the passing scenery.

"You okay back there?" Phoenix's question startled her an indeterminate number of minutes later.

She'd damn near fallen asleep.

"Sorry." Cringing, she wiped what looked suspiciously like a drool spot off the back of his jacket. "I hope this has been waterproofed."

"Use me as your pillow anytime, love. I don't mind." They pulled up to the Globe five minutes later, Phoenix holding tightly onto her hand as she climbed off the back and got feeling back in her legs.

The Globe, a New York City historical landmark, hosted celebrity events and had served as a hot spot film location in more than one movie in its one-hundred-and-five-year existence. Booking an event at The Globe didn't happen without ten years' notice and Olympus intervention, and never out of the blue and last minute, but the new—and temporary—event coordinator owed her a favor. After seven years, she was finally about to cash it in.

Priceless artwork decorated the lavish lobby, and crystal sculptures, suspended by nearly invisible wires, hung from the ceiling. Artists from all over the world salivated at the opportunity to display one of their pieces here.

And Phoenix didn't look the least bit impressed. Hands shoved into his jeans pockets, he eyed the massive room with a critical eye, his face a blank slate.

"Adalyn! It's marvelous to see you!" Roman ate up the distance between them and pulled her into a tight embrace. "Someone said something to me the other day and it made me realize how long it's been since we've gotten together."

She smiled, just imagining how her name had come up. "Then it must be kismet."

Roman's gaze flicked to Phoenix. "Is this your new assistant?"

"Phoenix Cross." Phoenix held out his hand. "I'm actually the brother of the bride, and best man to the groom. Just tagging along to make sure the happy couple gets the day of their dreams."

"They'll definitely get that here at The Globe. Let's take a tour of the available space and then we can talk logistics." Roman gestured for them to follow.

The place was gorgeous, the open hall large enough to easily fit five hundred guests or more. Already set up for another event, it was easy to picture the limitless possibilities.

The more Roman showed them, the deeper Phoenix's frown dipped until his silence became like the fourth person in the room.

"So?" Roman turned toward Addie at the end of the tour. "Perfectly divine, isn't it?"

A small snort came from Phoenix's direction.

"It's a stunning space, Ro." She tried hiding her annoyance with the gorgeous rock star next to her with a smile. "Do you mind giving me a moment alone with the best man?"

"Absolutely. I'll just be over there checking in with the florist."

"Thank you." Addie waited for him to be out of hearing distance before spinning on the man next to her. "What the hell is wrong with you?"

"What?"

"*What?* You've been snorting and eye-rolling and chuffing like a damn horse since we arrived. What could you have possibly disliked about *The Globe*? Do you have any idea how sought-after this venue is?"

"Yes. I do. Because *Roman* mentioned it no less than fifty times within the first ten minutes. The rest of that time was spent ogling your breasts and giving you come-hither looks."

This time, Addie rolled her eyes. "Roman is a *friend*. There was definitely no ogling or come-hither looks."

"I doth think you don't have your eyes open, love. I know come-hither looks, and that guy was dishing them out like dessert, hoping you'd spoon them up."

Ignoring the insinuation, she focused on the reason they were there. "And what don't you like about The Globe?"

"Just about everything."

She folded her arms over her chest. "Such as?"

"First, it's too big. Even with East being forced to invite a few of the music execs, they're probably looking at a hundred people maximum."

Addie shifted on her feet. "Okay, well, I can see your point there."

"And it's not . . . *them*." He looked around the lavish space, frowning. "East is a jeans and T-shirt guy, and even though Nai likes to dress up on occasion, she almost always bitches about it first. Don't get me wrong, this place would be perfect for someone else. But they'll want to celebrate the day, let loose, and have fun with friends and family. Not worry about spilling something on a thousand-dollar tablecloth."

As much as she hated to admit it, he had a point. So wrapped up in The Globe's availability, she hadn't thought about anything else.

"If not The Globe, what type of venue did you have in mind?"

His slow grin put her on instant alert. "If your calendar is clear, we can head out now and take a look at the place."

Roman approached, and this time she caught the subtle glance toward her cleavage. "Should we head back to my office and go over some logistics?"

Addie turned a smile toward her friend and ignored Phoenix's one hundredth eye roll. "Actually, Roman, as exceptional as this space is, I'm not one-hundred-percent certain that it's the right one for our happy couple."

Roman looked taken back. "The Globe is the right venue for every couple."

Phoenix snorted.

Addie not so gently shoved an elbow into his side and heard him grunt. "I'm sorry, but we'll have to keep looking. But I'll definitely keep this in mind for any future clients."

"You know it won't be open long. I held it an extra few hours just because it's you, but there's a massive waiting list of people to be called."

"Thank you for doing that for me, but I understand you can't hold it. I wouldn't expect that of you."

He frowned but nodded, guiding them back to the lobby where they said goodbye.

She and Phoenix walked silently back to his motorcycle, where he handed her the helmet.

"Up for a little drive?" Phoenix smirked coyly.

"A drive *where*?"

"Where is your spontaneity, Addie Whitlock?"

"I must have left it in my other bag." She slipped on behind him and her arms immediately wrapped snugly around his waist. "But seriously . . . where are we going?"

"You'll see as soon as we get there . . . but it's perfect."

She'd reserve judgement until seeing his "perfect" location for herself, but when they left the city limits, whatever hope she'd had shrank until it—and the city—were a small speck on the horizon.

Phoenix

The second they left the city, a weight fell off Phoenix's shoulders. That's how it always felt when he visited Emilio's. Lighter load. Insignificant worries. And now with Addie tucked close behind him, her arms wrapped snugly around his waist, he couldn't imagine a more perfect escape.

Except if he'd had his guitar and music journal with him.

He didn't need a GPS to guide him to his destination, able to make the trek with his eyes closed. Busy suburbs turned into small towns, then small towns into a single two-lane road nestled on either side by open grassy fields as far as the eye could see.

He glanced over his shoulder to see Addie soaking in their surroundings and could only imagine the thoughts going through her head.

Her helmet bumped against his as she leaned over his shoulder and shouted, "Please tell me your perfect venue isn't in the middle of a cow pasture."

"Technically, no. Just do me a favor and keep an open mind." He smiled at her indecipherable mumble and slowed his speed as a familiar white farmhouse came into view.

He hung a left at the private driveway. Addie's fingers tightened around his waist as he slowly rolled the bike down the gravel lane. As they reached the house, a familiar figure stepped onto the porch, and next to him, an exceptionally excited black-and-white sheepdog.

"Figured that engine belonged to you when Dottie started pawing at the back door, begging to be let out." Emilio Santiago, a longtime friend of Phoenix's parents, smiled warmly as he approached. His gaze shifted toward Addie as she climbed off the bike. "And you brought a beautiful lady friend with you. Should I be worried that you kidnapped her?"

"Wouldn't be far from the truth," Addie quipped, sexy grin in place.

Phoenix chuckled and accepted the older man's bone-crushing hug. "Emilio, this is Adalyn Whitlock. Addie, this is Emilio Santiago, renowned horse trainer and resident comedian."

"It's nice to meet you, Mr. Santiago." Addie smiled.

"Just Emilio, please." Emilio turned toward Phoenix. "Not that you need a reason to visit, but I can't help but be curious what brought the surprise. Everything okay with your folks?"

"They're happy and in love and about to hit another milestone anniversary. I know this will come out of left field, but can I show Addie the barn? She's helping pull off the impossible for Nai and East's vow exchange and I had an idea."

Emilio scratched his white beard and chuckled. "You kids and that old barn. Sure. You know the way. But if this idea is what I think it may be, you should know that space has been a catchall for all the odds and ends around here. Anything we don't know what to do with gets put in there."

"I'm sure it's not that bad but consider me warned. We'll swing back up to the house before we head out."

"Make sure that you do." Emilio clapped him on the shoulder before calling Dottie and heading back inside.

Phoenix led the way down toward the back barn, counting to ten before Addie opened her mouth.

"You get an A-plus for mystique, Mr. Rock Star. Consider me intrigued. Now it's time to tell me what we're doing here," Addie demanded.

"Nai and I practically lived here in the summer when we were growing up, helping Emilio around the farm and with the horses. Nai deemed this barn her magical spot." He nudged his chin toward the looming building that, judging from the exterior, had definitely seen better days. "It was her quiet place to think. An escape. And when East came out here on the weekends, they disappeared into the barn to . . . *you know*."

She rolled her eyes. "And we're here because . . . ?"

"Because *this* is where East and Nai became *East and Nai*." Phoenix stopped at the barn door and turned toward her, more than a little nervous as he waited for her response. "Is it a bad idea?"

A soft smile gently curved the corners of Addie's mouth, and the sight of it sent his heart into a gallop. "No, it's not a bad idea. It's actually—"

"Romantic?" Phoenix grinned knowingly. "Perfect? Perfectly romantic?"

Addie rolled her eyes, but chuckled softly. "And you really think your sister would prefer this place to somewhere like The Globe?"

"Without a doubt."

Addie turned a thoughtful look to the barn door. "Some of the most magical ceremonies happen in the unlikeliest of places."

He clutched his chest in mock surprise. "Was that you telling me in a roundabout way that I'm *right*?"

Her lips twitched. "I'll reserve judgment until we see what lies on the other side of these doors. Let's not forget Emilio's warning."

Phoenix shrugged. "It can't be in that much disarray."

Red flakes sprinkled to the ground as he lifted the rusted barrel latch and yanked the door open.

Addie stepped next to him, mouth slightly agape. "You're right. This isn't in disarray. This is—"

"Pure chaos."

Old tack and rusted machinery filled the large space, mixed in with discarded furniture and stacks of boxes that nearly reached the rafters.

Phoenix's bright idea was mangled in an overabundance of cobwebs. "Guess this was a bust. Back to square one."

"Not necessarily." Addie stepped deeper into the barn, her gaze swiveling.

"Do you see what I see?"

"Dirt and muck can be cleaned." She peeked under the tarp and found a rusted tractor that definitely hadn't been moved in years. "And objects can be relocated."

Phoenix arched an eyebrow. "What are you saying?"

She turned toward him with a coy smile that quickly stole his breath as it broadened. "I'm saying that you better have been serious about helping with the planning, and that help better include physical labor. We just found our venue. Let's go talk to Emilio. I'd like to run some ideas by him and see what he thinks."

"You're serious."

"Absolutely. Now, if only I could get my hands on Naiomi's wedding journal, then things will have completely turned in the right direction."

Addie turned and headed toward the house, giving Phoenix a prime view of her perfectly lush ass. He let himself admire it for a few moments before shifting his focus back to the present and jogging to catch up with her.

Nai's wedding journal.

Hell, it had been years since he'd laid eyes on it, but he'd always been able to find it no matter where she hid it when they were kids. It shouldn't be too damn difficult to find it now.

And if having it put another smile on Addie's face like the one she'd just flashed him, he'd gladly tear through his parents' place.

9

CUPID CAM

Addie

Phoenix's mysterious directive had played on a loop in her head ever since he asked her if she was free for their first official public FAMA appearance, and he wouldn't tell her what he had planned. The only clue he'd given?

Wear your team pride.

Addie stared at the items laid out on her bed and groaned at the impossibility. Not owning Yankees merch wasn't the issue, but choosing select items from her extensive collection, which rivaled Bailey's ring assortment, definitely was.

T-shirts in different sizes, colors, and cuts. Long-sleeve shirts. Hoodies. Beanies. Even undies, a prank gift that turned out to be the most comfortable she owned. Any serious fan also had gear specifically designated for both in-person stadium games, and couch-watching.

Not knowing Phoenix's plans made choosing unbearable.

Whether Bronx-bound or hitting a local sports bar, Addie hoped Phoenix had prepared himself for meeting her father's daughter. In the Whitlock house, little was taken as seriously as family, food, and Yankees baseball.

Addie cursed at the time and pulled on her favorite soft, curve-hugging jeans before closing her eyes and choosing a shirt at random. She picked one of her favorites, the short-sleeved tee with a frayed, deep V-neck plunge that framed her cleavage perfectly. And with a minute to spare, she tugged her baseball cap into position and grabbed her crossbody bag before heading out the door.

Butterflies attacked her stomach as she rode the elevator to the ground floor. First dates and her didn't mix. To be more accurate, Addie and dating of any kind didn't mesh well. There was no reason to think fake dating would be any different.

Hayden had only been the latest ex who suffered from a case of Oily Zipper Syndrome.

Before him, there'd been Romeo—the name should have warned her instantly.

Then Colton. Mateo. Sam. Et al.

They'd all ended for various reasons, but one thing in common was that they'd ended with fanfare. But it was after Hayden that she vowed *never again*, and not because he'd broken her heart when she found him balls deep in someone he'd claimed was "only a coworker."

Never again would she waste time, energy, and thoughts on someone who didn't understand that sometimes after a long workday, a girl just needed to climb into her pj's and binge-watch crime dramas with her three-headed dog, not club-hop all over the city until her feet barked.

And here she was about to break her no-first-dates rule—*again*.

She glanced in the reflective wall and second-guessed her

pigtail braids, but Phoenix had said team pride, and one game day tradition she never broke was braided piggies.

The elevator opened into the lobby, and Addie spotted Phoenix instantly. Holding two travel coffee mugs, he leaned against the far wall, a baseball cap covering his wavy locks. He glanced up when she approached, eyes damn near twinkling as his twitching grin turned into a full-blown laugh.

Addie froze, mouth agape as she grappled with the sight in front of her. "No fucking way."

"And here I thought you were certifiably perfect. I knew you had to have a flaw. Looks like I found it," Phoenix teased.

Arms folded over her chest, she drilled Phoenix Cross with a narrow-eyed glare. "*My* flaw? Oh, I don't think so, buddy. The shortcoming is entirely on your end. The *Mets*? Seriously?"

"A Cross may joke about a lot of things, love, but baseball isn't one of them." He pushed off the wall and slowly closed the distance, his lips a bit higher on his dimpled side.

Addie visually drank him in as if she'd just finished a hot yoga class in the Sahara. Faded light-blue denim jeans hung off his trim waist, and his signature leather jacket hung open to reveal a gray Mets T-shirt. The baseball cap—which he wore backward and which threatened the vitality of her ovaries—no doubt also supported his preferred team.

Addie subtly checked for drool, happy when her hand came back dry.

"I should probably keep this second coffee for myself." Phoenix's boots bumped hers as he stopped right in front of her.

She lifted her eyebrows. "And I should probably cancel this date. I don't think being seen with an outright Mets fan will do anything to boost my public image. Not to mention that if my father ever found out, I may be disowned."

"Ditto." With a chuckle, he held out the second mug. "Eh,

what the hell. I love living dangerously. I am Naughty Nix, after all."

She accepted the coffee with a small snort. "So now that we each know the other's most shameful secret, what are these plans?"

"I'm so glad you asked." Phoenix draped his arm over her shoulder and steered them toward the front door. "How do you feel about funnel cakes, Ferris wheels, and rigged carnival games?"

"I feel like that could be a trick question," Addie answered carefully.

It wasn't. An hour and a packed subway ride later, they stood outside Coney Island's Luna Park, the rides already motoring and people milling about the walkways.

She caught Phoenix watching her carefully, wearing a look that almost looked nervous. "Coney Island, huh?"

He stuffed his hands deep into his pockets and smirked coyly. "This is Wave One of Date Day. Unless you completely hate the idea, in which case, give me a few minutes with my phone and I'll figure something else out."

She fought against a grin and lost. "How many waves are in this Date Day?"

"Two. Maybe three. We'll see where the day leads us." He glanced toward the rotating Ferris wheel. "So yea or nay?"

She instinctively reached out and squeezed his hand. The only one more surprised by the contact than her, was Phoenix. They both glanced down at their hands, where a soothing warmth traveled up her arm.

"I actually love Coney Island," Addie admitted. "And I haven't come here in *years*."

"Yeah?" Phoenix's eyes snapped up while his fingers slowly threaded with hers.

"This is a great Wave One, Phoenix." Her cheeks heated. "So what's first on the agenda? Rides, games, or food?"

His grin stretched. "Fried fucking Oreos."

His hand anchored to hers, he led them directly to the Better Fried food stand, leaving Addie to believe that it definitely hadn't been years since his last Coney Island visit.

"Is fried food the best decision before rides?" Addie teased as he paid the attendant and eagerly accepted the paper dish of fried gooeyness. "And first thing in the morning?"

"There is *never* a wrong time for fried Oreos." He held one out to her and waited patiently for her to accept it. "Breakfast of fucking champions."

She took a tentative bite and instantly moaned at the burst of flavor that danced on her tongue. A quick glance at Phoenix's darkening gaze and Addie covered her mouth while she finished the rest of the cookie. "Sorry . . . that was just unexpectedly delicious."

"So was that little moan." Phoenix grinned wickedly.

Addie should've worn her industrial-strength Yankees panties, if for no other reason than to give her the mental fortitude not to let Phoenix Cross's naughty thoughts conjure her own.

They walked along the boardwalk and formed a game plan as they snacked on the fried cookies. Phoenix being a game guy didn't come as a surprise, but what did was his avoidance of the carousel. Going from destination to destination, he guided them the long way around to avoid walking past it, and while on top of the Ferris wheel, didn't glance even once in its direction.

Finally, Addie asked, "Do you have something against the carousel?"

Phoenix, his arm draped behind Addie's shoulder, broke into a nervous chuckle. "You could say that. A school field trip back in the day turned us into mortal enemies. I can do literally anything else. The Zipper that continuously flips you upside down over and over? All good. Coasters that require signed liability waivers? Cool. But the carousel?" He shivered in revulsion. "Nope. Not if I was an adrenaline junkie and it was the only ride open."

"That must have been some childhood trauma."

"You have no idea, and considering we just ate fried Oreos, we probably shouldn't relive it now. Especially if you have a sensitive stomach."

She grimaced, already imagining. "I don't, but yeah, let's not go there. I'll get my carousel-pony fix another day."

"You like the carousel?"

She shrugged. "Honestly, it's one of my favorites, right up there with the Ferris wheel."

He threw an inquisitive look toward the rotating pony ride down below, and gulped. "Favorite, huh?"

She reached next to her and gently patted his leg. "It's not a big deal. I can forgo the carousel *if* you promise we can do the go-kart raceway."

A slow grin slid onto his face. "Fuck yeah we can."

She studied him carefully, and the longer she did, the stronger her stomach butterflies became. Not once could she remember ever feeling the odd sensation, and yet it seemed like a repetitive occurrence when in Phoenix Cross's presence.

In a last-ditch effort to evict the butterflies, she pulled her gaze away from his and flicked it to his mouth. An overwhelming desire to see if his lips were as soft as they looked washed over her. It wouldn't take much . . . a little lean, a slight pucker.

Kiss.

But unless someone hid nearby with a telescopic camera and

a hell of a lot of free time, there was no reason to go up a pearl level, and her own curiosity sure as hell didn't qualify.

The wheel jerked to a stop at the ground ramp, yanking their bodies—which had somehow gotten closer—apart. Oblivious to the sudden pronounced silence, the attendant released their lock and ushered them off the bench.

Phoenix's fingers interlocked with hers as they navigated the busy walkway, occasionally sneaking each other secret glances. They bought—and devoured—cookies-and-cream-flavored cotton candy, and after a twelve-year-old beat them both in go-karts, they moved systematically from ride to ride.

Phoenix was right. He loved them all, taking great enjoyment in her every squeal, curse, and threat to his manhood. During the course of the morning and afternoon, she lost track of both the time and how often she laughed, knowing only that her sides ached every time she did.

Armed with the last bite of her ice cream cone and the stuffed unicorn she'd won at the balloon dart game, Addie glanced up and was surprised to see the sun setting on the horizon. "I can't believe we've spent all day riding rides, eating, and playing games."

Phoenix gently pulled her into his side. "Great way to spend our first official Date Day?"

Date. *Shit.*

Did she seriously enjoy a first date? One that lasted an entire day without a single thought of losing Phoenix in the crowd or claiming food poisoning with the hope of cutting it short?

Addie cleared her suddenly dry throat. "I've definitely had worse."

"And it's far from over." He glanced at his watch and cursed. "But we need to move so we don't miss the start of Wave Two."

"What's Wave Two?"

He wagged his eyebrows teasingly. "If I told you, it wouldn't be a surprise. But there's one thing we need to do before we head out."

"Get more deep-fried Oreos?" Addie hoped.

He guided her to a gentle stop in front of the carousel. "It doesn't feel right not to jump on your favorite ride."

Her eyes widened and she shook her head. "No, no. I told you. It's fine. It's not like I can't come back anytime and ride it."

"Which pony is your favorite?" Phoenix was already heading to the entrance.

Addie hustled, hot on his heels as he greeted the attendant and circled the platform. "Phoenix, seriously. I'm fine without riding the carousel. Let's move on to Wave Two. Didn't you say something about being late?"

"A few rotations won't make a difference." He jumped on the platform and scanned the ponies, his gaze landing on one that looked a lot like the stuffed unicorn in her arms . . . and her slippers at home.

Its mane flowed with shades of pinks, purples, and blues, both its harness and saddle sparkling with faux diamonds.

He turned toward her knowingly, a grin plastered on his face. "It's this one, isn't it?"

"How did you—"

"Just an educated guess." He tugged her closer. "Are you climbing up into that seat on your own or do you need a boost?"

"I get on the back of your bike just fine." Short all her life, she'd learned to improvise.

"Yeah. With the help of the curb. This baby is in the up position."

Shit. It was.

She eyed the height suspiciously. "Maybe we can sit in one of those stationary seats."

"If my girl wants to ride the unicorn, she'll ride the unicorn." He eased her in front of him, his broad chest brushing her back as his hands settled low on her hips. Addie's breath stalled as his lips faintly touched the outer shell of her ear. "But this will probably go smoother if you stick that gorgeous foot of yours in the stirrup."

"Right. Yeah. Sorry." Thankful to be facing away from him so he didn't see her reddened face—or sense her inappropriate thoughts—she used his body for leverage as she slid her foot in the hold and grabbed the pole.

Phoenix's hands slid from her hips to her ass, his wide palms bracing both cheeks as she hoisted herself up.

Embarrassment and something else she couldn't pin down flushed her cheeks more than they already were. "Sorry for sticking my ass in your face."

"That's definitely not something you need to apologize about, babe." Phoenix waited until she was safely situated in her saddle before he easily climbed onto the horse next to her.

The ride lurched forward, and Addie smiled, tilting her face into the cool breeze. Two revolutions later, a soft groan turned her attention to Phoenix.

Face devoid of all color, he held the glittery gold pole in a white-knuckled grip.

"Are you okay?" Addie watched, concerned.

He nodded faintly, eyes tightly closed. With each rotation, his face lost more color, sweat dotting his forehead. The second the ride stopped, he was off the horse and through the exit, a man on a mission as he veered to the bushes.

Addie caught up to him moments after he'd purged everything he'd consumed throughout the day. She laid her hand on his damp back and rubbed small, soothing circles. "Take deep breaths when you can. In for three, out for four."

He followed her directions with an occasional gag but eventually worked some color back into his cheeks.

Addie passed him a napkin from her pocket and he took it, shooting her an embarrassed look. "How many cool points did I just lose with that little show?"

"None. We've all been there," Addie said truthfully with a grin. She brushed a strand of hair by his eye that had escaped from his baseball cap. "School field trip repeat?"

He grimaced. "Except back then, there was a lot more in my stomach to purge."

Phoenix

So fucking suave. That was Phoenix Cross. Share the finest carnival foods with a gorgeous woman, and then spew them all into a fucking bush like a drunk frat boy during pledge week.

But damn, the smile on her face when she sat atop that carousel horse? Breathtaking, and totally worth the humiliation.

An hour—and a quick bodega side trip for some travel mouthwash—later, they climbed the 161st Street subway station stairs and walked toward Yankee Stadium with thousands of other baseball fans.

"You okay with Wave Two?" Phoenix snuck a quick glance to Addie.

"I should probably give you time to change your mind." Addie threw him a teasing smile, green eyes glimmering like jewels from the overhead stadium lights.

"It'll be a little embarrassing standing next to you while you're wearing all that, but I'll manage." He scanned her head-to-toe Yankees gear, pausing on the fucking adorable braids. "Maybe we'll get lucky and there won't be any picture-taking paparazzi."

"I wasn't talking about my love for the best New York team."

"No? Then what were you talking about?" Phoenix held up his phone and let the attendant scan their tickets.

"After the first pitch, I don't usually sit in my seat very much. I can get a little excited during games."

"Then we'll be excited together, because I don't do much sitting, either."

Addie had clearly understated her warning, something Phoenix realized two hours later, when she jumped to her feet in the middle of the fifth inning after the umpire called a third strike.

"What the hell was that, ump?" Addie cupped her hands around her delectable mouth and shouted, nearly dropping her slice of pizza. "Do you need me to draw you a picture of what a ball looks like?"

Addie and Phoenix's seat neighbors chimed in, a few loudly voicing their firm agreements along with high-fives.

A nearby couple wearing Mets hats shot Phoenix a look, and he shrugged, smirking. "What can I say? She's gorgeous and opinionated."

The teams traded positions for the start of the sixth inning.

"*Excited*, huh?" Phoenix teased.

A beautiful pink flush rose high on her cheeks.

"I did warn you. It's on you if you didn't take it seriously." Addie brought her pizza to her lips, and keeping it level, nibbled the corner tip. "Yum. This is good."

Phoenix watched in unabashed horror. "What are you doing?"

Chewing, she shot him a curious look. "Eating this very overpriced pizza? Was I not supposed to? Did you just give it to me to hold?"

"Yeah, *eat it* the right way." At her confusion, he folded it lengthwise, and ripped off a large piece with his teeth. "Right way."

"You took a bite just like me." Addie still looked confused.

"Uh, no. Definitely not like you. I ate it like a New Yorker. You took a bite like someone from upstate," Phoenix added coyly. "How did I miss this with the Soprano's?"

Truth was, he'd probably been too busy ogling her in the sexy bedsheet to critique her pizza-eating skills.

"I had a plate, table, and plenty of napkins. I didn't need to be all that careful. Now, I do," Addie admitted.

"Overlooking you rooting for the wrong team is one thing, but I'm not sure I can overlook this pizza-eating tragedy. It's *criminal* . . . and a much more serious offense than wearing the wrong T-shirt. How have you not been run out of New York yet?"

Addie chuckled, the sound ending on a fucking adorable snort. "Is this the end of our whirlwind romance?"

"I'll have to give it some serious thought."

They stared at each other, both grinning like fools when the people around them hooped and hollered. The guy behind him—on his fifth or sixth beer—slammed his hand down on Phoenix's shoulder repeatedly before whipping out an arm and pointing to the jumbo screen.

Zoomed in and dead center of a cartoon frame decorated with dancing hearts and a half-naked Cupid, was a live video-stream image of Phoenix and Addie.

The Cupid Cam.

Addie spun around as she searched for the camera angle. "Nope. No, no. Go to the next person."

Phoenix chuckled and earned himself a hard glare.

"You can't seriously find this funny!" She turned back toward the camera and waved her hands in a *shoo* gesture, groaning when the cameraman zoomed even closer. "This is archaic and not to mention, not happening."

A low chant started somewhere in the stadium and slowly gained momentum. *Kiss. Kiss. Kiss.*

"Can you really deny the people what they want?" Phoenix teased.

"Yes. Yes, I absolutely can."

Phoenix turned toward the camera with a shrug and a smile. Loud, echoing boos filled the stadium, and an older woman—somewhere in her eighties—shouted, "I'll take her place, handsome!"

"Oh, for crying out loud." Addie sighed, and cheers erupted.

Phoenix glanced toward the petite redhead just as someone freed him of his pizza. "What are you—?"

Addie bunched the front of his T-shirt in her hand and dragged him closer until the tips of their shoes bumped. This close, her green eyes glittered like emeralds as she peered up at him, her pink lips barely parted and less than an inch away.

He stared so long at her mouth it took him a moment to realize she'd said something. "What?"

"Sparkles?" Uncertainty shifted over his face as she waited for him to register her words.

And then they clobbered him up the back of his head. "Oh, *sparkles*. Uh . . . fuck yeah."

"Then kiss me, rock star." A gentle tug and their lips met to a chorus of screams and cheers.

Phoenix's lips zinged on contact, and after restarting his heart, he looped an arm around her lower back and dragged her even closer. He tilted her face up and playfully brushed the tip of his tongue against her lips, silently asking for permission to enter. She gifted it immediately, the kiss instantly shifting from sweet, slow seduction to an all-consuming devouring.

Their surroundings fell away, leaving only the two of them, and Addie's fingers gently slid into his hair. Each brush of her tongue conjured a slow, sultry scale, and as the kiss went on and every lush curve of her body melted into his, a beautiful melody echoed in the distance.

Phoenix didn't want it to end.

But regretfully, Addie's lips slowly retracted, and taking her cue, he anchored his arms tightly around her waist and slowly tilted her backward into a rom-com-worthy dip. She giggled against his mouth as he trailed a series of playful kisses from her jaw, down her neck, until he brought her upright.

Eyes bright, face flushed, and lips pink and swollen, Addie's gaze flickered to him bashfully as he mentally patted himself on the back for a kiss well done.

Satisfied with their performance, the Cupid Cam moved on to their next victims. Neither Addie nor Phoenix moved, their breathing still slightly labored.

"Do you think that kiss will be televised?" Addie's innocent question yanked Phoenix—and his raging libido—back into the moment.

Cameras. Fauxmance.

Fuck. He tried not to mourn their first kiss happening on a massive jumbo screen and not in private, but now that he knew how it felt having Adalyn Whitlock in his arms, he was determined to experience both again.

A lot.

He mournfully dropped his hands and hoped she didn't notice the hard bulge currently pressing against his zipper. "Probably, but if it's not, I'm sure more than one person will post it to their social media."

"Great. Good." Addie straightened her hat and braids,

which he'd somehow shifted askew during their embrace. "Then I guess that kiss will have been worth it."

A serrated knife to the gut was less painful than hearing Addie play off the kiss that had just tilted his world on its axis and quite literally knocked a sweet melody into his head.

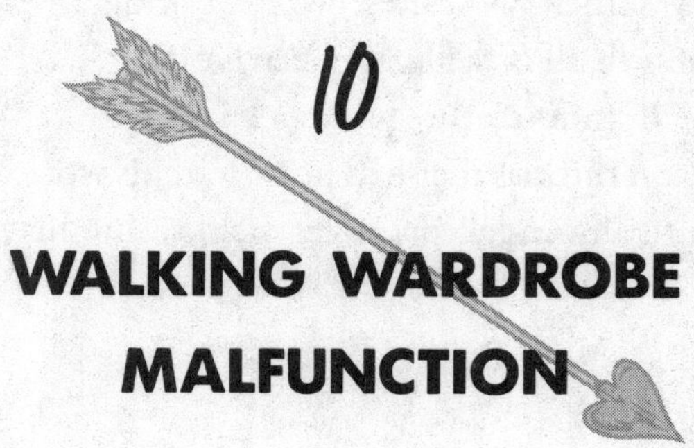

10

WALKING WARDROBE MALFUNCTION

Addie

She spent the better part of her morning going up and down, and not only because of Bounce House—Maxi, Bailey, and Addie's current exercise destination for low-impact endorphin release.

While performing aerial leaps thanks to the sturdy shock cord attached to the ceiling, she contemplated the intelligence of a fauxmance with Phoenix Cross.

And replayed the mental image of their Cupid Cam kiss.

What had seemed like a good idea at the time, quickly turned, the wickedly grinning drummer sweeping her legs out from beneath her, not to mention stealing her breath. If she hadn't been holding on to him, her buckling knees would've sent her into a swoon.

Adalyn Whitlock didn't swoon.

And that was the cause of the matted knot of nerves growing at an exponential rate in the pit of her stomach. Thinking about their lip-lock paved the way for imagining the locking of other parts, embedding itself so deep in her psyche that she'd experienced her first-ever sex dream the night before.

In surround sound.

She'd woken that morning sweaty, horny, and unfocused, weaving right in bungee class and nearly colliding with Bailey when she should've dodged left. It was only a matter of time and opportunity before Bailey and Max pinned her in a corner and demanded answers.

"Okay, spill it." Maxi barely waited for the fitness instructor to announce the end of class. "You've been glaringly groodier than normal, and I want to know why."

"Groodier?" Addie shimmied out of her harness and led the way toward their water bottles.

"It's a mashup of grumpy and broody—which you've been since we got here." Max watched her with all the knowingness that came from a lifetime together. "Start talking."

Addie glanced to Bailey for support and received a shrug in response. "Don't look at me. She wanted to give you the chance to fess up on your own. I said we should withhold coffee and wait it out until you break."

Addie really needed new friends. "It's this agreement with Phoenix."

"You said your talk with Aunt Eunice went well," Max reminded her.

"It did. She had a lot of good suggestions. It's not actually the Muse thing I'm worried about." Addie dropped to the floor by her bag. "It's this fauxmance thing."

"You mean what if it doesn't work and everything you've built through the years comes crumbling down around you like an old Greek temple?" Bailey asked.

"Or," Maxi added, "it works too well, and despite reminding

yourself on the daily that it's not real, you somehow trick yourself into thinking it is and end up with a broken heart?"

Bailey grimaced. "Ooh. Yeah. That would suck, too. And after that kiss, I can see why that would be a concern."

"Kiss? *What* kiss?" Maxi's head snapped toward their cousin.

Addie groaned. "It was for the camera!"

Bailey's brows lifted. "But was it really?"

Yanking their phone from their bag—because of course they'd already seen and downloaded it—Bails tilted the screen toward Maxi. "It may have started for the camera, but—"

"Whoa." Maxi's eyes widened.

"Right? And watch this upcoming back and forth . . ."

"The hand placement!"

"That's not the only thing about to be placed." Bailey pointed to something in the top right corner and Maxi gasped. "*Yep.*"

Addie glared at them both. "Are you done?"

Maxi, her gaze still focused on the phone, held up a finger in a *wait a second* gesture. "And this was the first date? Okay, yeah. I take back what I said. This fauxmance is totally working. If this is his level of commitment during date one, can you imagine what the next one will be like?"

"That's it. I'm breaking the FAMA with Phoenix," Addie stated with a heavy sigh. "He'll just have to find another Muse to take to that award ceremony and I'll live the rest of my life as a hermit on my couch."

"Award ceremony?" Bailey asked, attention shifted. "What awards?"

"Some music award thing in a few weeks." Addie shrugged. "The Stone Talons are nominated in a few categories and they're also performing during the show."

"He's taking you to the fucking Indie Rock Awards?"

"Is that a music award thing that's being held in a few weeks?"

"Yes!"

"Then that's probably it."

Bailey's mouth opened and closed. "Why the hell do I hang out with someone who doesn't know the—never mind. What are you wearing?"

"I haven't really thought about it. Maybe that black pencil skirt suit that I wore to the—"

"Absolutely not." Bailey was already shaking their head. "You cannot wear one of your work outfits to the *Indie Awards*, and definitely not when you'll be walking the blue carpet with a member of the Stone Talons! For the love of the gods, Addie!"

"Then what do you suggest I wear? Because all I own are jeans, yoga pants, and work outfits."

"We'll swing around to how sad that is later. Right now, we're shifting into emergency mode." Bailey sprang to their feet and grabbed their bag, then Addie's, then Max's. "Chop-chop, you two. I'm good, but our time constraint pushes even my limits. Let's go."

"It's weeks away." Addie let herself be yanked to her feet with a groan. "Can't we run home and showe—"

"Absolutely not. Spritz some good-smelling shit on your pits and bits and let's get the hell out of here."

Bailey in go-mode never boded well for the person being hustled, bustled, and tussled. Three and a half hours, four boutiques, and zero bathroom breaks later, Addie's feet sported Grand Canyon blisters and her bladder prepared for rupture.

"I have a good feeling about this place." Bailey tugged open the door of boutique number five, not looking the least bit winded from their shopping marathon.

"The only thing I can feel right about now is my bladder about to explode." Addie earned a sympathetic smile from her sister.

"Less whining, more trying things on." Bailey approached the first dress rack and immediately riffled through it, pausing on a flashy sequin gown before eventually shoving it aside. "Are you sure you can't ring your rock star to see what he's wearing to this thing? Knowing the color palette would help narrow things down."

"Absolutely not," Addie said emphatically. "This isn't prom, Bails. We don't need to color match."

Bailey shot her a stern look. "You won't be saying that if you end up in a red gown and he's in a green suit."

"As far as I know, Phoenix doesn't even own a suit."

Bailey grumbled but continued shopping as Addie slinked through the boutique.

Their collection consisted of simplistic everyday wear to chic cocktail dresses and lavish, stunning gowns. Noting a few she wouldn't mind looking at a little closer, she skirted the room and kept out of Bailey's way.

A slinky black dress caught her eye and she stepped over to give it a closer look when a familiar voice anchored her to the spot.

"I don't know why this is so difficult for you to understand." High-pitched and getting higher, the customer repeated herself. "Any boutique worth anything offers this service, but you're telling me that you can't."

"Like I said, we do alterations, but with our regular seamster out on paternity leave, we're outsourcing, and there's no way we'd be able to do the amount of alterations you need within your timeline." Red-faced and flustered, the boutique hostess faced off with a tall, lithe blond whose back was turned toward Addie. "We could look for some pieces that wouldn't require as many alterations, and if you don't find something here, we have a sister store on the other side of the city."

"I am not trekking downtown for something that you can do here. Call Julien. Tell him that the alteration is for me. I'm sure he'd happily take a break from his diaper-changing vacation."

The snide tone. The entitled expectations. That way-too-familiar and overwhelming scent of privilege and overpriced perfume. Addie recognized Karleigh Kinkaid-Fink's voice before the influencer even turned the corner.

Karleigh's eyes narrowed into accusing slits when she spied Addie. "You."

"Me." Addie straightened her posture as much as her sore back would allow. "And you're you."

"What the hell are you doing here?"

"I'd imagine the same thing that brought you here." Addie slid a supportive look to the hostess. "Although our methods of execution are obviously different."

"What's that supposed to mean?"

"It means that sometimes you catch more flies with honey than vinegar. This lovely stylist is trying to help you, but you're not quite hearing her suggestions."

"Because none of them are acceptable," Karleigh snapped.

"Then maybe you should change what you consider acceptable. People can only adapt to what's within their power, and like . . . Gen . . . said, their current seamster is on paternity leave."

Addie's former client crossed her arms over her chest before bouncing her glare between Addie and Gen. "Then I suppose I'll be forced to take my business—and my substantial budget—elsewhere." She turned toward Gen. "And you won't be seeing me again."

Karleigh shot a menacing grin Addie's way. "But you'll definitely be hearing from both me and my followers. For a moment, I contemplated forgiving you for the debacle that you made of my wedding, but running into you has now firmed my resolve to bury you—and your sad excuse of a business—under six feet of bad press and monetary debt."

"There you go threatening me with a good time," Addie quipped dryly. "Didn't you say you were leaving?"

With a huffed growl, Karleigh stormed out of the boutique.

Addie turned to apologize to Gen, but instead, got hugged.

"Thank you so much." Gen squeezed her tighter before embarrassment flooded her cheeks and she let go. "I hate when she comes into the shop. Usually, I try to hide in the back storeroom when I see her walk in, but it's just me here this afternoon and—"

"Say no more. Trust me, I get it. She's a breath of vile air and putrid enough to make anyone sick to their stomach. I know her father has deep pockets. I hope you won't get in trouble for losing her business."

"Even the owner has been hoping she'd sink her claws into another store. How can I repay you for sticking up for me?"

"That's really not necessary."

"Actually . . ." Bailey stepped up with at least a dozen dresses flung over their arm, obviously overhearing. "If you could hook us up with a dressing room."

"Absolutely." Gen eagerly nodded, quickly taking the stack of dresses from Bailey, her eyes lingering on the various fabrics and styles. "If you don't mind my asking, what type of event are you looking to be outfitted for? Maybe I could help."

"She's the plus-one of an Indie Rock Awards nominee and will be walking the blue carpet in a few weeks," Bailey answered for her.

Gen's mouth dropped. "Did you say the Indie Rock Awards?"

Addie grimaced. "Yeah. I know the chances that I'll find something in my size in stock without any alterations would take a miracle."

"Actually, I have a few pieces already in mind, and if you find something that you love, we'll figure out the alterations if needed."

"But your seamster—"

"Yeah, Julien's knee-deep in diapers with the twins, but I have a backup on speed dial that I can call for my special rescuers."

It was a whirlwind of fabric, dresses, and disappointment as Addie tried on dress after dress, with Max, Bailey, and Gen sprinting from the boutique racks to the dressing room. Long dresses. Short dresses. Fitted dresses and airy dresses. Nothing seemed right. Addie silently began rehearsing a conversation with Phoenix where she *regretfully* backed out of the appearance.

"Try this one." Bailey tossed a swatch of fabric over the top of the dressing room door and it fell onto Addie's head. "I have a good feeling about it."

"As good as the last one you had me try?" Addie mentally cringed. The copious white feathers had made her look like a human-sized swan.

"Just shut up and try it on . . . and don't even think about taking it off before we've had a chance to see it."

Knowing her cousin wouldn't be above scaling over the top of the door like a zombie from *World War Z*, she slipped the dress off the hanger and eyed the minuscule fabric. "Uh, is this supposed to be a two-piece? Because there's not enough fabric to cover a stick scarecrow, much less me."

The fabric—silky, gorgeous, and iridescent, devoid of any one color—reminded her of a mermaid's tail. The metallic beading changed hues depending on the way the light hit, from one direction appearing silver, and with a slight turn, glowing like a colorful rainbow.

"Try it on," Bailey ordered. "And don't worry about the bra situation. We can tape the boobs into compliance."

Addie held up the "dress" in front of her. "And what about my ass situation? Because mine will make an appearance the second I do more than breathe. Strike that—breathing might be off the table, too."

"Put it on and just show us, Ads." Maxi sighed. "You know Bailey isn't leaving until you do."

Wishing it was possible to swap out family like underwear, Addie slipped out of the last dress and into the new one, although *slip* was an exaggeration. She shimmied, contorted her body, and broke into a cold sweat, but eventually, she smoothed the sleek fabric over her hips and braved a look in the mirror.

Although not as bad as she feared, it definitely didn't sit in her comfort zone, hugging her curves in a way that emphasized the steep plunge into her cleavage. She slipped a hand beneath her left boob and hoisted it into proper position, mimicking the effects of boob tape.

With the twins in proper alignment, she looked—and felt—pretty damn sexy . . . but she wasn't wrong about the hemline. Standing upright, the dress ended around her upper thigh, which, for short girls, meant only a few inches from the bottom curve of her ass cheek.

"Well?" Bailey asked impatiently.

Addie inspected herself from different angles. "It's not as bad as I thought it would be, but it's a risk."

"Let me determine if the risk is worth it."

"Maybe I should just wear a parka. Can't they be considered in fashion?" Addie opened the dressing room door and mentally prepared herself for the incoming comments.

Bailey's and Maxi's eyes widened.

"Holy—" Maxi started.

"Hotness," Bailey interjected.

Addie snorted. "Right. When was the last time you saw your optometrist?"

"Seriously, Addie," her sister added. "You look—"

"Like a walking wardrobe malfunction?"

"Stunning."

"She's not wrong." Looking smug, Bailey buffed their dark polished nails on the front of their shirt. "Damn, I'm good. That's the dress."

"I don't know." Addie glanced down, smoothing the already seamless fabric.

"Well, I did the moment I laid eyes on it. *That's* the dress that needs to be worn down the Indie Rock Awards carpet. It says, *I love life, love love, and I'd love for you all to take my picture so that I can shove it up the uptight behinds of every ex who dared call me the Anti-Aphrodite.*"

"This dress talks a lot. Maybe I should pick something a little quieter."

"You put this back on the rack and I will disown you, and considering I'm the only one who knows how to work the office coffee machine, you definitely don't want that happening."

"Are you sure this isn't too much?"

"Absolutely not," Bailey answered.

"Not at all," Maxi chirped.

Gen appeared from around the corner and instantly broke into a wide smile. "That's the dress. And it looks like it only needs an extra stitch or two to really snatch in the waist."

Addie's eyes bugged. "Bring *in* the waist? It already fits like a freaking corset!"

"Trust me. Dresses are what I do. Whoever is escorting you to the Indie Rock Awards will be *your* plus-one when we get everything fitted."

As much as Addie wished she could believe them, she wouldn't know without a doubt until it was too late to do anything about it.

Phoenix

Phoenix erased the last line written in his journal, the eraser flakes joining the mountain of others spread across his coffee table. Different keys. Altered tempos. He played with his guitar, determined to find the ones that closely matched the stomach flutters that happened whenever he mentally pictured Adalyn Whitlock in all her Yankees baseball lovin' glory, but just when the lyrics were within reach, they danced away, not sounding right on paper or falling off his lips.

He'd been at it all morning and *almost* had a melody. Not actual words, but playable music that didn't resemble nails on a chalkboard or drumming on a metal trash can lid—and it wasn't even close to the Stone Talons's sound. That's probably why he loved it, physically unable to abandon it and shift into party, panty, and pussy mode.

Now, if he could only nail down the words, he'd be on a hot streak.

"What do you think about *branded like a tattoo on my mind*?" Phoenix strummed the chords and hummed the words out loud before glancing to his audience for their feedback. "Stupid? Genius? Don't hold back. Be brutal."

Addie's dogs lay curled up on the end of his couch, their heads resting on their front paws. They'd shown up in his apartment the second he'd thrown popcorn in the microwave, and after making a second bag for himself, he didn't have the heart to tell them to leave.

Do watched him, eyebrows raised in a confused look while Re huffed out a low grumble. Mi, by far the most laid-back of the trio, didn't even budge, obviously not easily impressed.

"I'm not so sure about it, either." Instead of crossing out the line or erasing it altogether, he put it in parentheses and inserted a question mark.

It wasn't *horrible*. It just wasn't meant to be part of a repetitive chorus.

Eyes closed, he time-traveled back to their first Date Day, replaying everything but his post-carousel puking session. They'd joked and laughed, her hand feeling natural and at home in his.

And don't get him started on the baseball game.

When she showed up in her Yankees gear and braids, he'd known he was in for a treat, but not even in his wildest dreams had he expected her to jump from her seat, lush ass swaying in front of him, as she yelled down onto the field.

Damn if he couldn't wait to find out more of what made Adalyn Whitlock tick.

His cell buzzed on the coffee table, but he ignored it, jotting down a few lyric ideas before sharing them with his lounging co-writers for additional input. A minute later, his cell vibrated again.

And again.

Only Naiomi, currently burrowed in a study room at the library, and one other person, dared contact him this late at night.

Marcus.

M: Kinkaid wants to see progress on the new song ASAP. ETA?

Phoenix sighed. It never fucking ended.

Not showing until it's done

M: He won't like that

He'll deal
It's my process

M: I'll try and stall. GET. IT. DONE.

Working on it.

Phoenix silenced his phone and glanced to his critique partners, who all looked at him curiously. "Well, fellas, it looks like I'm switching back to parties, panties, and pussies."

Mi growled low in his throat before setting his head back on his massive paws . . . and hell if Phoenix didn't feel the same way.

11

BOXED CHICKEN *IS* FOOD

Addie

Addie spelunked through her father's freezer trunk, wishing she had one of those helmets with a flashlight. She shifted things, and went deeper, her feet coming off the ground before she realized the truth.

"Pops!" Addie turned a harsh glare on Simon Whitlock. "You said you had food and that I didn't need to make a grocery trip!"

Lying down, back flat on a rolling cart, only her father's lower half stuck out from under the rusted mass of steel he'd "rescued" from the nearby dump. "I do have food. You've been digging through it all for the last forty minutes."

"No, I've been searching through all these boxes of frozen fried chicken trying to find it."

"Is chicken not food?"

Addie took a deep, mental breath. "You're killing me here, Pops. And yourself with all that instant stuff. Where are the vegetables? And what about a salad?"

"That stuff goes bad too fast."

"Not if you actually eat it and don't let it sit around forever."

Her father rolled out from under the car and shot her a look. "Who's the parent here? Me or you?"

"I don't know. Who has to make sure you eat something other than boxed fried chicken?" Addie cocked a hip and dared him to challenge her.

"Sometimes I throw some French fries into that fancy air fryer thing you got me."

"I bought that to make it easier for you to roast vegetables, not French fries!" The landline phone rang in the house, giving her an opportunity to make some kind of grocery list. "This discussion isn't over. I'll see who's on the phone, and then I'll head to the store and get you some healthier meal options.

"Hello?" Addie picked up the wall-mounted phone, an ancient relic she'd tried convincing her father to give up years ago, and waited a beat, fully expecting a scam phone call.

"Hi." The woman's soft Irish accent sounded surprised. "Sorry, I wasn't expecting someone to answer the phone other than Simon. Is this Maxine? Or Adalyn?"

Not a telemarketer then . . .

"This is Addie," she answered, curiosity piqued.

"I'll take a wild guess and say that Simon is currently buried under that scrap-metal project of his?"

"Sounds like you know my father. Would you like me to go get him?"

"No, no. I don't want to interrupt him. But could you give him a message for me?"

"Absolutely." Addie pulled a pen and paper out of the junk drawer.

"This is Caroline. Could you let him know that I'll be watching my grandson a little longer than I anticipated, so we can either reschedule, or maybe try and catch a later movie."

"A later movie. Sure." Addie's pen hovered over the paper a second before she scrambled to write everything down. "I'll make sure he gets the message. And he knows how to get back to you?"

"Absolutely."

"Okay. Good."

"It was nice finally getting to talk to you, Addie. I've heard so much about you and your sister that it's nice to finally put a voice with the stories."

"Same." Or it would've been nice to hear stories or a name, but that was a conversation to be had with her father.

She hung up the phone and leaned against the counter, first pausing to digest the information that her father had just received a call from a *lady friend*. Not only that, but they'd clearly made date-type plans, and from the sound of it, not for the first time. She couldn't recall her father going on even one date since her parents' split.

Not a group date. Not a blind date. Definitely not a movie date.

Addie debated next tactics and dialed her sister.

"Does the name Caroline mean anything to you?" Addie asked the second Maxi picked up the call.

"Should it? Please don't tell me it's another disgruntled former client because we have all of those that we can handle at the moment."

"Definitely not."

"Good." Max hummed, deep in thought. "I vaguely remember booking Pop a haircut a few months ago, and I *think* the stylist's name was Caroline. Although I could totally be pulling that out of my ass. Why?"

"Because I just played secretary for our father, and it was *Caroline* needing to change the time of their *movie date*."

Maxi gasped. "You did not."

"Why would I lie about that?"

"That's . . . wow." Maxi paused. "Wait. If he was ready to date, why didn't he ask me to match him? I could save him from kissing a lot of toads."

Could she have though? Her matchmaking track record had definitely plummeted recently.

"Or maybe not." Maxi sighed as if reading her mind. "What did you say when you asked him about her?"

"I haven't yet." Her father's tools clanked in the garage and a moment later, his footsteps slapped against the cement floor as he walked toward the house. "Shit. He's coming."

"Play it cool. Be subtle."

"Subtle. Right." No one who knew her had ever accused her of being subtle, but how difficult could it be? "Gotta go."

"Who was on the phone?" Her father stepped into the kitchen and scrubbed his hands at the sink. "Another salesperson bribing me to add all those streaming services?"

"Not unless their name was Caroline and you have a movie date with them," Addie joked.

Guess she couldn't do subtle after all.

Her father froze like a deer in headlights before wiping his still greasy hands on his pants and turning toward her. "It was . . . uh . . . Caroline?"

"Yep. And just so I'm passing the message on correctly"—she held the note in front of her and cleared her throat—"she's watching her grandson later than expected. Either reschedule or catch a later movie. Let her know."

They stared at each other in awkwardly growing silence, a stubborn battle of wills.

Neither wanted to cave first, but Addie's curiosity eventually surpassed her stubbornness. "Know what I find funny? I'll tell you. She said she was thrilled to put a voice to all the stories she's been told about me and Max, but I couldn't return the sentiment because this was the first I've heard the name *Caroline*."

"It's not what you think." Pink stained her father's whiskered cheeks.

"I *think* it's a date, and from the sound of it, tonight wouldn't be the first one with her."

He bristled. "I'm a grown man, Adalyn Whitlock. I'm allowed to date. Hell, haven't you and your sister been begging me to do so for years?"

"It's not that you have a girlfriend, Pops. It's that this is the first time we've heard of it, and her, while Caroline seems to know all about us."

He scraped his palm over his face before sighing. "I'm not good at dating. Never was. Never will be. There was no point in telling you girls about Caroline until there was a marginal chance that I wouldn't fuck it all to high holy Hades."

"So you've dated before Caroline?" Addie couldn't keep the hurt out of her voice.

"Only a couple times, and none went past the first."

Now *that* Addie understood well.

"It may come as a shock to you," her father added, "but I'm not very good at it. Guess I'm too old and too gruff for some. What do they call it? A fixer-upper?"

"Bullshit." Addie's defenses rose. "Anyone you date should feel honored to do so, and if they don't, that's on them. Not you. There's no fixing necessary."

He leaned his ass against the counter, his lips pulled into a small smile. "All right then. Yes. I've gone out a few times with Caroline and she's . . . nice. Definitely doesn't scare off easily, so that's saying something. We've gone out a handful of times."

"A handful?"

He shrugged. "Maybe six."

"Six dates is technically two handfuls."

Her father shot her an amused look and she lifted her hands in mock surrender. "Okay. So six dates with a seventh up in the air. I guess I'll call Maxi back and tell her that our father hasn't been body-snatched after all."

"As long as we're on the subject of mystery dates . . ."

Addie's fingers paused on her cell. "Actually, they're not considered mystery dates anymore because I know about them."

"Yeah, I'm not talking about *my* mystery dates." Her father hesitated, watching her intently. "The oddest thing happened during the Yankees-Mets game the other night."

Addie's heart went from a normal rhythm to a quickened staccato as she slowly turned to face the music. "Really?"

"Yeah. Damnedest thing." He crossed his arms over his broad chest. "Needed a fifth-inning snack and was in the kitchen for maybe ten seconds and came back to dozens of texts from Zee, from down at the rec center."

"Sounds pretty run-of-the-mill to me. Pretty sure the two of you shit-talk during every game," Addie said of her father's longtime Mets rival.

"Except he wasn't texting about the game. He swore up and down he'd seen you on the Cupid Cam, and according to his daughter, the guy you were lip-locked with was some bad-boy rock star."

Addie feigned innocence. "Huh. That *is* odd."

"Told him he'd fallen off his rocker and hit his head too hard, but I found the replay so I could see for myself. You either have a doppelgänger with your exact baseball wardrobe, or that was you being dipped and kissed *by a Mets fan*."

"Okay, it's not what it looks like." Addie mirrored his words by way of defense.

"You're telling me that he's not a Mets fan?" Her father tilted his head, the move emphasizing his disappointed glower. "Because I can overlook the musician thing, but rooting for those other guys? Not sure that's something I can condone."

Addie struggled for words, the entire situation so ridiculous that she couldn't do anything but chuckle, and once she started, she couldn't stop. Tears leaked from her eyes as she struggled to breathe.

"I'm glad you find this humorous," her father grumbled.

"You find out that I'm dating a drummer, and yet all you're worried about is his favorite baseball team? For most parents, it would be the other way around. You know that, right?"

"Well, I'm not most parents. And you know how to take care of yourself when it comes to all those other dating things. But those fans? They're ruthless. It wouldn't surprise me if he had an ulterior motive and plans to lure you over to the dark side."

She wiped away tears of laughter. "He's a Mets fan, Pops. Not a member of a doomsday cult."

He grunted. "Pretty much the same if you ask me. So . . . you're dating?"

"Yes. No. I mean . . ." Addie wheezed, reining in her breathing. "Kind of? But not really. He and I are helping each other out."

"Am I supposed to know what that means?"

"He's helping me with the whole Anti-Aphro-Mom thing, and I'm helping him get in touch with his musical Muse." She paused. "Fuel some inspiration."

He studied her without saying a word, his silence pregnant.

"What?" Addie finally asked awkwardly.

"What type of music are you inspiring?"

Addie opened her mouth to answer, but quickly realized she didn't have one. "I don't know. I didn't really ask."

"If it's cynical funk, or something like that, yeah, I get that . . . but if it's . . ." He trailed off.

"If it's what?" Addie already knew what he was about to say. "Are you saying I can't inspire him to write a love ballad?"

"Sweetheart, I love you more than my next breath, but you know what I'm saying here, right?"

She heaved out a heavy sigh. "Yeah. I know. And honestly, I have no idea how to help him, but he claims that I do. The point I'm trying to make is that what you saw on the Cupid Cam wasn't real. It's a fauxmance."

He stared blankly.

"Like a fake romance," she added.

"Okay. Sure. I get it."

He didn't look like he got it.

"You know what it reminds me of?" Her father rubbed a palm over his bearded jaw as she began writing a grocery list.

"What's that?"

"This rom-com Caroline and I saw last week. The main characters started off a lot like you just mentioned. With an I'll-scratch-your-back, you-scratch-mine arrangement. Hell, they even wrote a contract. But it didn't go the way either of them expected."

Her father's not-so-subtle warning didn't come as a surprise, except for the info that he'd willingly watched a rom-com. But she didn't have any other options. All she could do was hold on tight and wish for the best.

And hope her life didn't turn into some ill-fated rom-com.

12

CROSS HIDEAWAY

Phoenix

Phoenix subconsciously pushed his motorcycle faster the closer he and Addie got to his parents' place. Redbrick homes, abutted by large, weathered sidewalks, lined both sides of the street, and oversized trees created vast pockets of cool shade. Dogs barked in backyards and children played tag, running from one front yard to the next while their parents shouted warnings for them to be careful.

The second his parents' house came into view, Phoenix slowed.

Home sweet home—and birthplace of the Stone Talons. Color burst from his mom's overstuffed flower boxes, and a massive WELCOME sign hung prominently on the bright red door. Every holiday, the manicured yard would be lit with lights and blow-up figures, but in the summer months, the only thing decorating the front of the house were lots of cars.

Phoenix counted them as he pulled the bike to the curb and cursed.

"Do all of these cars belong to your parents?" Addie climbed off the bike with a hesitant glance toward the house.

"Not exactly." He grimaced. "It looks like when I told Mom that we'd be stopping by to grab the wedding journal, she took it upon herself to turn the visit into a family gathering."

Addie turned around, pure panic all over her face as she headed back to the bike. "I should stay out here while you go look for the journal."

He caught her elbow and veered her right back into his arms, smirking knowingly. "Are you afraid of a little domesticity, Adalyn Whitlock?"

"No." She played off his obvious dare with a soft scoff. "But *manners*. And dropping in unannounced is societal faux pas number one."

"I told her you'd be with me."

"Okay, but . . . I didn't get an invitation. And societal faux pas number two—"

"Doesn't apply either because I'm ninety-percent sure she threw this little shindig because you were coming."

Addie's jewellike eyes narrowed on him. "And why would she do that?"

"Because you're the person saving her daughter's special day." The admission took a little of the annoyance out of Addie's sails.

Her shoulders sank with a deep exhale as she glanced toward the very full house and accepted her fate. "Okay."

He tugged her gently toward the house, not disguising his laughter. "It's not like you're about to step into the wolves' den. No one will take a bite out of you. Well, except little Jordie. He's teething and has been gumming up everything."

Less than four feet from the house, two familiar little boys and a smaller girl who fought hard to keep up, tore around the corner.

"I'm going to get you," Samantha bellowed.

"Not unless you drink a speed potion," Blake, the oldest boy at eight years old, taunted.

All three kids came to a screeching halt when they saw them standing there, but it was Sam who squealed and launched herself toward Phoenix first. "Nixxy!"

"Hey there, Tails." Phoenix effortlessly whipped her around in a spin that had her giggling. Once she was sufficiently giddy, he set her on her feet and performed complicated handshakes with the two boys.

"Who are you?" Samantha—aka Tails—studied Addie as if she were a bug under a microscope.

"Hi." Addie waved awkwardly. "I'm Addie. I'm—"

"Addie's a good friend of mine." Phoenix casually draped an arm over her shoulder and pulled her a little closer. "Addie, these three are the youngest Cross cousins: Blake, River, and Samantha—aka, Tails."

"Only Phoenix can call me Tails," Samantha warned.

Addie pushed a nervous smile onto her face. "Got it."

Phoenix cleared his throat, barely stifling a chuckle. "Well, we'll leave you three to whatever it was you were doing."

"Can we have a game tournament tonight?" Blake asked eagerly.

"Oh. Uh . . ." Phoenix glanced down at his little cousin. "Actually, I'm not sure how long Addie and I are staying."

Samantha's lower lip trembled, obviously not liking the answer.

"Hey now." Phoenix dropped into a crouch. "None of that."

"But you haven't come to a game night in *so long*, and I've been practicing all the games. I'm so good now, you wouldn't even believe it!"

"Why don't you stay for game night, grab the journal while

you're here, and then just drop it by the office? I can catch a bus home," Addie offered.

"You could always play, too," River offered. "But tonight's *Mario Kart* racing night, and this family is cutthroat. It's basically the *Game of Thrones'* Red Wedding."

Addie blinked, obviously not knowing what to do with that information.

"Do you even know what the Red Wedding or *Game of Thrones* is, big man?" Phoenix laughed and ruffled River's already messy curls.

The kid smirked, shrugging. "No, but I heard my mom and dad talking about it. Is what I said not true though?"

Phoenix threw Addie a devilish smirk. "Actually, he's not too far off the mark. Game nights are known to be a little cutthroat. If you don't think you can take the heat, I can always take you home before things get serious and swing back here afterward."

Addie narrowed a glare on him. "I know what you're doing."

His smirk twitched. "And what's that?"

"You're preying on my competitive nature . . . issuing a challenge you don't think I'll be able to resist."

"Is it working?" he asked wickedly.

"Yes." Addie tossed him a challenging look. "Looks like we're both staying for *Mario Kart*."

"Yay!" the kids cheered in unison, tearing into the house and leaving the door wide open.

"Are you sure it's okay if I crash family game night?" Addie asked.

"One thing you should know about the Cross family is that we love surprises." Phoenix wrapped his hand around hers and headed to the side gate that would take them around back.

The chaos of a Stone Talons concert had nothing on a Cross-hosted barbeque. Children raced around the yard playing a make-your-own-rules version of tag while the adults laughed, and the smell of his father's grill permeated the air.

It didn't take long to find the man himself. Commanding his pride and joy, a slow-cooker smoker and old-school charcoal grill, Judd Cross stood just off the end of the brick patio, his favorite Kiss the Cook apron tied around his waist and his favorite Mets baseball cap on backward, covering his balding head.

A pair of tongs in each hand, his father bounced his attention from grill to smoker, an image of profound concentration.

The sight pulled Phoenix's lips into a smile. "You've done this enough times to know that staring at the meat won't make it cook any faster, old man."

"Who the hell are you calling *old*, kid?" His father pulled him into a hug. "Although you're not wrong . . . just don't tell your mother in case it gives her an idea to leave me for a younger model."

Phoenix snorted. The idea of his parents—ridiculously in love since middle school—splitting was hilarious. He'd heard the story so often growing up. New boy on the block meets quiet girl on her bike. Quiet girl literally runs her bike into new boy.

It was love at first collision, and before they'd finished grade seven, his mother, Lani, had told her parents that she would "marry that Cross boy one day."

That day happened almost forty years ago.

Phoenix clapped his father on the back and chuckled. "We both know if Mom leaves you for any reason, it's because you lit another grill on fire and she had to bake another half-dozen lasagna casseroles for the fire department as a thank-you."

"Grills are meant to be fired up," his father teased back.

"Yeah. Not the way you do it. So did you give the station a heads-up that you were having a barbeque today?"

"He didn't, but I did." Phoenix's mother came out the back door holding a tray of corn on the cob. She leaned in, giving him a kiss on the cheek. "How are you doing, baby? Everything going okay with you? We listened to that new song of yours on the radio yesterday. I like it."

The hidden meaning beneath her tone was unmistakable. "It's the sound that the record label wants to hear from us, Mom."

"Oh, I'm sure it is, and it was definitely memorable. Guess I was hoping that we'd hear some of *your* songs."

"They are my songs, Mom." But he knew what she meant and he couldn't fault her for it because he felt the same way.

He longed to write songs that spoke of love and loss. Songs that elicited feelings and stirred emotion. The only *stirring* lyrics the label wanted described loins. Did he like it? No. But most people's childhood dreams didn't come true. His did. And he couldn't toss the opportunity away because he didn't like damn photo ops and the long studio hours that came with it.

Phoenix's mom looked past him to where Addie did her best to hide behind his back. "Hello there. Since my oldest has forgotten all the manners that my husband and I tried to ingrain in him, I'm Lani. And this is my husband, Judd."

"Nice to meet you . . . ?" Judd coaxed.

"Addie." Addie stepped hesitantly next to Phoenix. "It's nice to meet the both of you, too."

"Addie. *Oh!*" Lani's eyes widened. "You're the one that's—"

"Helping Nai and East with their ceremony. Yep. That's Addie." Phoenix drilled his mother with a silent plea to behave. He'd regretfully told her his suspicion about Addie being his Muse and she hadn't stopped gushing since. "I told you that we'd stop by to pick up Nai's wedding book. Hopefully Little Naiomi will give us some ideas."

"That's right. And it's a wonderful idea, but I've already searched this place from top to bottom and I couldn't find it. I swear that girl can create pocket dimensions and squirrel things away never to be seen again."

"Actually, I'm pretty sure I know exactly where it is. It's not a pocket dimension, but it's pretty damn close. We'll be back in a second." Phoenix took Addie's hand and headed toward the back corner of the yard where there were nothing but trees.

"You think she buried it?" Addie asked curiously.

"Nope. Not buried." He brushed his thumb along the back of her hand and her fingers tightened around his as he stopped in front of a massive oak, its branches looming high into the sky and housing a child-sized fort.

Nailed into the bark at odd angles, crude steps staggered up to the slightly saggy aerial deck, and for anyone who wanted an extra challenge, a thick knotted rope dangled from the small opening above.

"Welcome to Cross Hideaway," Phoenix announced. "Anything worth hiding, we hid here. Not only because Dad's fear of heights prevented him from climbing a foot off the ground, but Mom's spider phobia had her avoiding the tree house at all costs."

Phoenix shot her a wicked grin. "Want to come up?"

Addie shook her head. "Not in the least. What goes up must come down, and knowing me, I'd land on my head. Or my ass. I'll stay safe and sound on the ground."

"You sure? We also used Cross Hideaway as a secret rendezvous spot." Phoenix wiggled his eyebrows, not able to help himself. "Nai used it for that more than me, but I'd be up for closing the distance a little more."

"Considering that we are neither rendez-ing or vous-ing, I'll stick with my plan to stay right here."

Phoenix laughed. "Suit yourself, but you're missing a great view."

He grabbed the knotted rope and, using mostly his arms, hoisted himself up, hand over hand, and prayed he didn't make an ass of himself by stalling halfway there, or worse, falling on his ass.

He breathed a little sigh of relief when he made it to the top and glanced down, catching Addie mid-ogle.

"Did you enjoy the view, love?" He smirked, flashing her a coy wink. "Give me a second and I'll give you another one on my way down."

She rolled her eyes, but stayed put as he headed into the tree house and went right to the old antique trunk they'd used not only for storage but as a game board and dinner table. Wedged between two slightly musty blankets, its bright purple cover and bedazzled *Nai's Happily Ever After* made the book instantly recognizable.

"Bingo." He grabbed one of the smaller blankets and wrapped it around the journal protectively before sticking his head out of one of the windows. "Ready to catch?"

"You found it?" Addie opened her hands and prepared for the drop.

"Of course." He let go and she caught it perfectly, cradling it protectively in her arms as he climbed back down to the ground. "Do you think it will help?"

Addie carefully flipped from page to page, her smile growing. "I think it'll give us one hell of a good start."

***

"No way! How do you know where the secret boxes are? I didn't even know those were a thing and I read all the cheat mags!" James, Phoenix's sixteen-year-old cousin, accused a grinning Addie, who simply shrugged and kept her character, Princess Peach, motoring along the rainbow highway.

In first place.

Phoenix's souped-up Yoshi Bike lasted ten minutes and approximately three heats until he got booted from the tournament, but Addie steadily remained in the top spot despite his cousin's tricks to divert her attention.

They'd pulled out the distraction big guns and sent in Samantha, but their usual tactic backfired and now the four-year-old sat on Addie's lap and gleefully "helped" her guide the kart around the track. Every time they intercepted a flashing yellow star and plowed through their opponent, Samantha giggled and begged her to do it again.

James looked seconds away from spontaneously combusting.

"How's it going in here?" Phoenix's parents stepped into the room, his father's arm linked snugly around his mom's waist. "Wait . . . is James . . . ?"

"In last place?" Phoenix chuckled, getting up to stand next to them. "Abso-fucking-lutely," he whispered.

"Never thought I'd see the day." Judd laughed. "You picked good, kid. Anyone who can hold their own during a Cross family game night is made of hearty stuff."

Phoenix reluctantly dragged his eyes away from the sight of Addie sitting between his cousins, and focused on his parents.

His mom's smile practically stretched her face to its breaking point. "She's lovely, Nixxy."

"It's not what you both think," Phoenix hated saying.

"No?" his dad questioned. "Because I think you brought

someone to the house—if my memory is correct—for the first time in . . . ever."

"It is," Lani interjected with a nod. "Very first. He didn't even bring his prom date home for pictures."

"Because I didn't *have* a prom date," Phoenix clarified. "The Stone Talons played at the prom."

His dad's eyes damn near twinkled. "There's also the fact that you haven't taken your eyes off her since you got here."

Fuck. He wasn't wrong, and judging by the growing smirk, his father knew it, too.

Phoenix struggled to find the words—or any excuse—that steered away from the truth:

Adalyn Love Whitlock fascinated him like no one ever had.

Her sassy obstinance and grumpy, uncaffeinated self charmed him as much as the video game shark–slash–carousel lover. Despite her "love is a sham" outlook, she cherished her friends and family, not to mention her pups. She worked too much. Didn't play enough. Cheered for the wrong baseball team. And ate pizza wrong.

But hell if he didn't like all of it.

Phoenix caught his parents' knowing gazes. "I brought her here to look for Nai's journal. It's not like I could just leave her to fend for herself with the Cross heathens."

"Yes, because they look like they're eating her alive," Lani teased. "Pretty sure Blake and River have a crush now, and she earned Samantha's approval. And that little one is a tough nut to crack."

Hell, she wasn't wrong, either.

"But if it's any consolation," Phoenix's mom leaned closer and whispered, "I'm pretty sure she watches you as much as you watch her."

On cue, Addie's gaze shifted his way and her lips twitched into a small smile before Sam patted her leg in a bid for her attention. Something about seeing her comfortable with his little cousins, and joking with his family warmed a spot in his chest, and when she glanced his way and gifted him that subtle smile, that warm spot burned hot.

Thirty minutes later and Cross family game night came to a disappointing end—if your last name was Cross.

"No hard feelings, James?" Addie stuck out her hand to the teen, who took it with a grumble. "I don't remember the name of the gaming blog I read, but I'll look it up when I get home and have Phoenix tell you, okay? Maybe you'll be able to find some more secret boxes."

The teen looked a little more upbeat. "Deal."

"You can call me Tails," Samantha announced seriously, her little arms folded over her chest as she glanced up at Addie. "If you want."

"I'd like that very much. After all, I couldn't have won without you." Addie pulled the gift card, a coveted Cross game night prize, from her pocket, and handed it to the four-year-old. "That's why I think you should have this. Special helpers deserve special prizes."

Samantha's eyes widened as she took the card. "Really?"

"Really. Just make sure you get a really good book."

"I know the exact one I'm getting! It's about a unicorn with sparkly hair!"

"That sounds like an *amazing* choice."

Goodbyes alone took a solid thirty minutes, which was pretty short based on typical Cross departures. The sky looked like a dark, star-laden blanket as they walked down the lit walkway toward the bike.

"Sorry about bombarding you with all of that." Phoenix gently bumped his shoulder into hers. "Crosses are not for the fainthearted. Thankfully, that was only one small branch of the family tree. Basically a twig."

Addie's eyes widened before she broke into laughter. "I won't lie, I was a little freaked out in the beginning. Our family gatherings usually total three—four if Bailey hitches along."

"So your mother's side . . ."

"Is a fifty-ring circus." Addie quickly added, "I adore my aunts and uncles, and my cousins, too, but they're a lot. And I can only tolerate Olympus shenanigans in very small doses. I have very little patience and no tolerance for drama."

Phoenix grinned. "And yet you won over Samantha, and trust me, she's difficult to impress."

"She's a little sweetheart underneath all that sass."

"Sounds a lot like someone else I know." He shot her a teasing look and she laughed, rolling her eyes.

"And your parents are great," Addie added, smiling. "Your dad actually reminds me a lot of mine."

"Maybe we can get them together for a playdate or something." The words left Phoenix's lips before he really considered how they'd sound—or how she'd take them.

As they reached the bike, Addie turned toward him. "That sounds like something a couple who *isn't* fake-dating would do."

Phoenix rubbed the back of his neck as he felt the heat creep into his face. "Yeah, I guess you're right."

They'd spent four hours at his parents' place. They'd glanced through Nai's journal, and joked around with his family. Addie even joined them more than once to tease his face red. He couldn't recollect a single moment when something felt fake.

13

A HYPER-EMOTIONAL STATE

Addie

A cool breeze lifted Addie's hair from her shoulders, left bare from her sleeveless tee, and her pores soaked it in in a valiant attempt to bring down her body temperature. Present Addie needed to give Past Addie—who'd erroneously thought the fresh, open air of Central Park would help spark event planning ideas—a stern talking-to.

Heat and Addie didn't mix well. The shade that the nearby tree had provided an hour ago disappeared as the sun shifted in the sky. She grabbed an iced lemonade from the cooler and flipped through Naiomi Cross's wedding book, occasionally jotting an idea on the tablet sitting on the blanket next to her.

She had a few . . . but she needed more. And then there was figuring out the logistics. A good idea wasn't good unless you figured out how to execute it. A lot of great ideas failed due to poor implementation.

Familiar overexcited dog barks yanked Addie's head from her work and directly to Do-Re-Mi. They stood beneath a tall tree, all three sets of eyes locked on a humongous squirrel holding an acorn. The gray creature twittered and shifted. Each move sent her pooches into a tizzy . . . and then it dropped an acorn right onto Do's head.

Do's big eyes blinked in confusion, and both Re and Mi whimpered pathetically.

"Will the cute squirrel not play with you three brutes? Gee, I wonder why." Addie snorted.

Re's and Mi's heads swiveled her way, and the squirrel took that moment to launch itself onto their back, riding them like a furry surfboard. All three pooches jumped and ran in a circle, but the squirrel held on tighter, having the time of its life before vaulting onto Umpire Rock and skittering away.

Do-Re-Mi looked forlornly at the spot it disappeared from.

"If you really just wanted to play, you should've been nicer," Addie tutted.

"Let's turn those frowns upside down, boys. Look what I got," Phoenix's deep, sultry voice announced. If Addie wasn't overheated before, she was now.

Black T-shirt pulled tight across his chest and showing off his colorful tattoos, Phoenix walked toward her, muscles rippling as he held to-go boxes in each hand. Well-worn, faded jeans hugged his legs. He didn't have on his signature leather jacket, but his wicked smirk traveled everywhere, broadening when she caught sight of what he'd brought.

"Iced caramel mocha something for my demigoddess Muse." Phoenix grinned knowingly before shooting a glance at Do-Re-Mi. "And chilled pup cups for the good boy hellhounds."

Addie chuckled but eagerly accepted the supercharged beverage. "Hellhounds are actually Underworld-born shifters. Think bigger, grumpier, and with more fang than a mortal-born wolf shifter. They don't leave the Underworld too often. Something about the poor air quality here."

"Really?" Phoenix dropped down next to her, instantly reclining onto the blanket while Do-Re-Mi devoured not only the whipped cream from their treats, but the cups, too. "I learn something new every time we hang out." He nudged his chin toward his sister's book. "How's it coming? Any genius ideas sparked?"

"I don't know about genius, but I've definitely gotten a few." She handed him her tablet and nervously watched as he read through the list.

She didn't realize until that moment how much his opinion mattered to her. Of the ideas she'd written down, at least 50 percent of them were pretty good—or at least she hoped. And she hoped Naiomi loved them. They were all a million miles away from the Globe, and the more she got to know Nai and East, she realized that was actually a good thing.

Finished with their treats, Do-Re-Mi circled the blanket twice before commandeering a back corner and closing their eyes. Their soft snores came a few seconds later.

Waiting for Phoenix to glance through her ideas, Addie scanned the park. They weren't the only people taking advantage of the gorgeous day. People pushed strollers and walked their pets, and an outdoor yoga class stretched into downward dog on the grassy patch a hundred feet away.

An excited laugh drew Addie's attention to the bike path and the older couple wobbling on Rollerblades. The taller of the two chuckled, his legs locked as his partner held on to his arms for dear life in an obvious attempt not to fall on his ass. They shared a sweet kiss before laughing again, eyes twinkling as they stared adoringly into each other's eyes.

A smile blossomed on Addie's face as she watched the exchange . . . and her vision blurred.

She rubbed her eyes to wipe away the sweat she'd thought

had dripped down, but surprisingly enough, found none thanks to the iced caramel mocha frap.

Another glance at the couple and Addie felt the color drain from her face.

The air shimmered around the couple as a gold glow slowly eased into existence. Wrapping around their bodies before fusing in the center, it pulsed gently and became more solidified the longer Addie concentrated.

A gold cord, this one more real and elaborate than the one from the coffee shop a few days ago. Hell, delicately threaded, it looked a lot like the one she used as a belt with her Olympus toga.

Except this one *glowed*.

"You okay?" Phoenix's concerned gaze went from her to the Rollerbladers. "You look a little pale."

"I'm fine." She glanced toward the couple and the link was gone. "Just mentally reminded myself to make an eye doctor appointment. So what do you think?"

"These are some solid suggestions." Phoenix circled more than half of them. "I especially love the idea of using the white fairy lights in the barn and hanging glowing orbs from the rafters. Nai actually keeps little lights lit in her apartment all year round. She'll love it."

"Then we're a go on overhead lights . . . and what do you think about the tables?"

Phoenix chuckled. "Artificially lit lanterns? Yeah, great idea. Pretty sure Emilio wouldn't like his soon-to-be cleaned-out barn to be burned to ash."

Addie snorted on a laugh, adding the table lanterns to the Green to Go column. After they cleared out the barn tomorrow, she hoped more ideas would spark to life.

"I have a question for you." Phoenix hijacked her attention.

"And I may or may not have an answer."

He lay back, elbows propping his upper body off the blanket and his gaze locked on her. "Do you really believe love doesn't exist, or do you tell yourself that to avoid any potential heartbreak?"

Addie groaned. "That's your question?"

"That's my question." He smirked. "Are you answering?"

She considered not, but what the hell . . .

Legs folded comfortably, she turned toward Phoenix and waited for the shocked reaction that always came when she laid it all out there. "Love is nothing more than a hyper-emotional state of either selfish interest or attraction. Let me explain."

"Please do." Phoenix sat up and mimicked her pose, touching his knees against hers as he shifted closer.

"Before you can claim to love someone, that person sparks your interest, or maybe you're attracted to them," Addie pointed out. "Whatever the initial meet-cute is, you're curious enough to want to spend more time around them."

"Okay . . ." Phoenix studied her carefully.

"So you spend more time together. You . . . *date*."

"Right."

"And then that interest either fades away, or maybe it intensifies and turns into the hyper-emotional construct called *love*."

Phoenix's eyes narrowed in clear challenge. "What about love at first sight?"

"Doesn't exist."

His eyebrows lifted. "It doesn't?"

"Nope." She shook her head. "Attraction at first sight? Absolutely. Not love. In very simplified terms, what people call *love* is just intensified attraction—or interest."

"Then how do you explain the people that sacrifice things for the people they love?"

"They do it for themselves, not love. Humans are innately selfish. That's just the way it's always been. If they do something, or risk something for the other person, it's because in doing so, that person will stick around. If they stick around, their bond grows. And if the bond grows, they never feel the pain of not having them close by. Selfish hyper-emotional state."

"That's . . ." Phoenix's brow furrowed as he struggled to form words. "Wow."

"You asked. I answered."

"You definitely did." He studied her a few beats longer before lying back in his earlier position and flipping to the next page of Nai's wedding journal.

The iced caramel mocha frap turned sour in Addie's stomach. It wasn't the first time she'd admitted her love theories, but the low-key unease she felt this time around was definitely new.

This time, she felt like the Anti-Aphrodite.

And she didn't like it in the least.

14

THE KISSING TREE

Addie

Addie's hair escaped her messy bun and whipped around her head, the breeze from the open windows and sunroof creating a mini-nado in the cab of her dad's truck. A road trip meant blaring music, an achy back, and a grumbling Bailey sitting sandwiched between Addie and Max on the truck's bench seat.

"You know I can hear you muttering, right?" Addie smirked as she slid her cousin a side-eye. "You're not as quiet as you think you are."

"I wasn't trying to be," Bailey grumbled. "When did I sign up for this? I'm an office rat. I scroll through social media posts and dissect algorithm analytics on best posting strategies. I don't do physical labor."

"If this vow exchange doesn't go off without a hitch and get us in the spotlight for a *good* reason, you won't have any labor because we'll be out jobs," Addie pointed out.

Bailey folded their arms over their chest. "Fine. Point made. But I still don't like it."

"I think it's refreshing," Maxi added, her gaze scouring Naiomi's wedding scrapbook for more ideas. "Everything about this entire plan screams romance. It makes my heart happy. I can't begin to tell you how proud I am that you came up with it, Ads. And you thought you sucked at event planning."

"Phoenix definitely helped the idea along. And just wait until you see the barn! By the time we're done giving it a little TLC, it'll look like a venue straight out of a wedding magazine. Actually, it'll look even more breathtaking."

Bailey studied her profile, burning a hole in the side of her head. "Exactly how much TLC are we talking about?"

"An average amount."

"And that means . . . ?" Her cousin's eyes narrowed.

"Promise me you'll keep an open mind . . . and wear gloves at all times."

Max's amused snort turned to low chuckles. "Where's your sense of adventure, Bails?"

"Back in civilization."

"It's not like we'll be doing this alone." Addie defended herself and the idea. "Phoenix is meeting us there with Easton and the rest of the band."

Bailey perked up. "Really?"

"That's what it took to turn your grumpy frown upside down? Dangle musicians in front of you?" Addie teased.

For the first time in a while, Addie felt pretty damn good about this wedding-planning thing, her excitement growing the closer they got to Emilio's place. She turned onto the farm's gravel lane and they bounced their way toward the main house.

Bailey and Maxi stared at the horses in the fields as they passed. Two more stood alongside Emilio, who stood next to another truck and Phoenix's motorcycle as they pulled up to the house.

Phoenix popped open the driver's door and helped Addie down the second she'd parked and shut off the engine. "Perfect timing. How was the ride out?"

"Bumpy," Bailey answered. "I didn't know there was still such a thing as unpaved roads."

Phoenix chuckled and gestured to the truck. "Rental wheels or . . . ?"

"My dad's. I figured it wouldn't hurt to have it in case we need to haul things around."

"Exactly why Xavier brought his pickup." He gestured to a much newer white truck that obviously had all the bells and whistles and glinted in the sunlight. "Pretty sure Beast can haul a Mack Truck without breaking a sweat."

"Still going through with it, huh?" Emilio walked up to them with a broad smile.

"Absolutely." Addie introduced the horse trainer to Bailey and Max. "So my plan—if you're up to it—is for us to clear the entire barn so it's easier for you to lay eyes on everything that was inside, and then we can divide it into three groups. Store it. Donate it. Or toss it."

"Sounds good and efficient to me. I don't think I've ever seen that barn cleaned out."

Bailey muttered something under their breath, earning an elbow to the side from Max.

"Is there anything you don't want us touching?" Addie asked.

Emilio snorted. "Honestly, I couldn't even begin to imagine all the stuff that's in there, so if you all haul it out, I'll do my best to start purging. Fair warning though, nothing in there has been touched in *years*."

"Consider us warned. And you are not to lift a finger. This was our bright idea, so we'll do all the heavy lifting. We're bringing enough chaos into your life."

"Yeah, but I'll also have a nice clean barn after you're through, so the least I can do is maybe feed and hydrate you all while you're here."

"We definitely won't say no to that," Phoenix cut in. "Especially if your enchiladas are on the menu."

Emilio chuckled. "Pretty sure I can swing that. Let me know if you have any questions, and grab me when you're ready for me to start purging."

As Emilio headed back to the house, Addie and Phoenix led the group down to the barn, the front door latch as rusted as it was last time.

"Maxi?" Addie asked.

"On it." Her sister whipped out a notepad from her back pocket and plucked the pen tucked through her ponytail.

"What do you have there, beautiful?" Gavin shifted close to Max, peering over her shoulder.

Addie's sister stopped writing their to-do list and shot the Stone Talon's lead singer an annoyed glare. "A pen and a piece of paper. Have you never seen one before?"

Addie and Phoenix choked on barely controlled laughter.

The griffon shifter's startled shock morphed into a cocky grin. "I've been known to dabble here and there. But seriously, what are you doing?"

"Keeping track of anything that needs to be done besides cleaning the place out. Replacements. Repairs. That kind of thing."

"And what will we do once you write it down in your little notebook?"

Max smiled way too innocently. "Hopefully you tinker

with a hammer and nails as much as you dabble with the ladies because when everything is all cleaned out, we'll start with the repairs needed to make this place beautiful *and* safe."

Max's sass didn't deter the singer one bit, judging by his growing grin.

"On that note," Phoenix interjected, clearing his throat, "we should probably divide into teams and give each group a specific task. Emilio wasn't joking when he said there's a lot of shit. I'm thinking East, Max, and Gavin are crew one. Crew two is Bailey and Xavier. And then Addie and myself make three."

Maxi's panicked expression at being on Gavin's team had Addie adding, "Or we can split into team Happily Ever Forever and team Talons."

Phoenix turned her way, a knowing tilt to his lips. "Except there's bound to be some pretty hefty things hiding in this mess, and it makes sense to spread out the supernatural mojo. In their gargoyle and griffon forms, East and Gavin could probably bench press Xavier's truck."

East snorted. "I could do that in my skin suit, too."

Addie shot her sister an apologetic look because the man spoke sense. "Yeah. All right. In that case, I think crews one and three should begin emptying the space, and crew two can group what we haul out into categories so it's easier for Emilio."

"And then once everything is cleared, it's all hands in for cleanup," Phoenix added.

"Exactly."

They assigned rooms and got down to work, Addie and Phoenix starting in the tack room.

If the main barn area was a disaster zone, the tack room was ground zero. Everything except actual tack filled the space, and in some places, nearly reached the ceiling. Boxes. Farm equipment. Old furniture long feasted on by termites and other creatures.

Addie went dry as she realized she'd completely underestimated this chore. "Maybe we should've hired an actual crew."

"Nah. We got this, love." Phoenix stepped into the room and missed the shovel lying on the floor. His boot hit the curved metal and the handle whipped up, slamming into his face with a loud *wack*. "Fuck!"

"Shit." Addie ran over to him and tossed the shovel to the side before cupping his face and tilting it down toward her. "Let me see. Did it break anything?"

"I think it broke my entire face." Tears slipped from the corners of his eyes as he let her inspect, wincing when she prodded a little too hard. "How bad is it? Is my nose still attached? Hit me with the truth."

Addie gently brushed her finger over his cheek, tracing the red line just to the left of his nose. "You'll definitely have a significant bruise."

"Nothing a few days of not shaving won't hide. Plus, I'm Naughty Nix. I'll claim bar fight and no one will question it," Phoenix joked dryly. He rubbed his face and made a series of funny faces, stretching out his facial muscles.

Addie's stomach fluttered when she realized she still cupped his jaw, thumb stroking over his cheek. She pulled it back, but Phoenix slid his hand over hers, holding her hostage.

The stomach flutters kicked up another few notches as he leaned his scruff-laden cheek into her palm, emitting something that almost sounded like a low, rumbling purr. "I will never get over how soft your hands are. Not a damn callus in sight."

"I moisturize." At that moment, her mouth, dry as the Sahara the longer he kept his gaze locked on hers, sure as hell needed a little moisture.

Phoenix's gaze dipped to her mouth and caught the unconscious nibble of her bottom lip. His eyes filled with a surge of heat that nearly melted her knees.

"We should probably start moving things out." Addie took a regretful step back, and immediately missed his closeness.

He stared at her for another beat before nodding and turning toward the packed room. "Do you really need this room for the ceremony? We could just slap a sign on the door that says Do Not Enter For Your Own Safety, and call it a day."

"Yes, we'll need it." Addie's laugh sounded awkward and strained even to her own ears. "This will be Nai and the girls' dressing room. Emilio offered the main house for the guys."

"Then we should probably get started. If you see anything furry with a naked tail, you should know ahead of time that I will be of no help and will be the first one jumping on the nearest piece of furniture."

Smirking, Addie shot him a coy glance and she wasn't sure if he was joking or not.

Phoenix

Phoenix joked about a lot of things. His fear of mice wasn't one of them. Mice. Rats. Gerbils. Anything with a furry body and un-furry tail freaked him the fuck out—except, for some reason, Do-Re-Mi. He blamed Naiomi and a prank she'd played on him with her second-grade class pet.

With a shared goal in mind, he and Addie worked efficiently, keeping one ear open to ensure Max didn't murder Gavin on the other side of the barn. It wasn't long before they'd cleared out about 90 percent of the tack room, leaving behind an antique desk that had somehow remained standing despite the amount of shit that had been stacked on it.

"This desk is gorgeous." Addie stared at it in awe as she ran a hand over the deeply pockmarked surface. "Can you imagine all the things and experiences this desk has seen?"

"Definitely can." He grimaced, trying to see the beauty in it that she did, but failing. "Probably saw a lot of mice taking a dump in those drawers, too."

Addie chuckled at his look of disgust. "You don't like antiques?"

"Antiques—to me—are just germ-ridden old things."

Addie rolled her eyes. "Spoken like someone whose apartment is sparse and industrial."

"I think you mean easy to clean."

"I said what I meant." She headed to one end of the desk. "All right. Let's go ahead and take this out to Xavier and Bailey, and then we can see how the others are faring."

As it turned out, everyone had fared pretty well, and by the time lunch rolled around, all that needed emptying was the loft. They worked up a modified bucket system to move everything down and then it was time for the fun part.

Making the place sparkle.

Phoenix couldn't help but smile as he snuck yet another glance at Addie as she finished sweeping up the far back corner. She smiled wistfully, her gaze occasionally glancing around at everything they'd accomplished.

And they'd accomplished a hell of a lot, the barn nearly unrecognizable.

So mesmerized by the soft, gorgeous, upward tilt of Addie's lush lips, Phoenix didn't see the incoming projectile until it scurried over the top of his boot. He glanced down and froze, his heart leaping into his throat.

The barn mouse stared at him with beady, judgmental eyes, its faint squeak sounding like a lion's roar before it scrambled up his jeans.

"Fuck!" Phoenix squealed and kicked air before leaping into an empty wheelbarrow and riding it like a damn surfboard. "Not today, you furry little Satan!"

"What are you doing?" Leaning on her broom, Addie watched him as if he'd sprouted a Hydra head.

"There was a . . ." He glanced around the room and didn't see the little fucker anywhere. "It was here a second ago."

"Whatever it was, I'm pretty sure you scared it away." Addie's lips twitched as she tried—and failed—to withhold a laugh. "Either that, or it's biding its time and waiting for you to come back down to earth before it makes a calculated move."

"Fuck." Phoenix gulped. "Do you really think it's lying in wait?"

Addie burst into laughter, and he didn't even care that it was at his expense. "No, Phoenix, I don't think it's waiting in the wings staging its attack. It was probably more scared of you than you were of it."

He snorted. "Yeah, pretty sure you got it reversed, love."

Addie, still smiling, approached his elevated wheelbarrow position with an extended hand. "I, Adalyn Love Whitlock, promise not to let the big scary mouse hurt you. Also, I'm fairly certain the wheelbarrow you're standing in once held horse poop, and it's so rusted, the bottom will probably fall out in about five more seconds. Unless you want to add a tetanus shot to today's agenda, you may want to climb down."

"Hey, did I hear Phoen—" East's words were cut off a moment before he and the others stepped into the barn. The gargoyle smirked. "Let me guess . . . mouse?"

"It wasn't *just* a mouse," Phoenix defended himself and

jumped down. "The thing was fucking massive. It could've worn a fucking saddle it was that big. The city monsters have nothing on that country fucker."

East rolled his eyes. "If you're done scaring the local wildlife, Emilio said that dinner is ready to be devoured, and I don't know about everyone else, but I am fucking hungry as hell."

They all headed up to the main house, Phoenix and Addie bringing up the rear. Her gaze kept sliding toward her sister.

"What do you think is going on there?" Phoenix watched his friend and Maxi closely.

They snuck glances at each other, but where the other daughter of Aphrodite looked murderous, Gavin looked confused. Maybe even somber. Phoenix couldn't remember a somber day in his friend's life. Nothing fazed the Stone Talons's lead singer, everything rolling off his back as if he were a seal shifter instead of a griffon.

"I was about to ask you the same thing," Addie admitted sheepishly. "I've never seen Maxi act so openly hostile to anyone before. That's always been my forte."

To the left of the back porch, one of Emilio's ATVs sat parked and gave Phoenix an idea. "How hungry are you right now?"

"Moderately," she answered carefully. "Why?"

"Think you can hold out for forty-fiveish minutes?"

"Maybe?"

"Wait here." Phoenix jogged into the house and grabbed the ATV keys before warning the others that there better be food left when they got back. He walked back to Addie and caught her looking out into the fields, a small smile playing on her lips. "You ready for a ride? I want to show you something."

"And that something would be . . . ?"

He chuckled. "You really hate surprises, don't you? Fine. I thought we'd run out to the kissing tree Nai mentioned in her wedding journal and we can see if it's as magical a spot as she claims."

"Abso-fucking-lutely." Excitement sparkled in Addie's eyes as she snatched the ATV keys from his hands. "But this time, I'm driving."

He paused by the vehicle as she climbed up and inched forward. "Do you know how to drive one of these things?"

"How hard can it be?" With a menacing grin that instantly stirred his cock to life, she patted the seat behind her. "Now it's your turn to hold on tight, and don't forget to scootch in nice and close. We wouldn't want you to fall into any cow patties."

"You mean horse patties?" Phoenix chuckled as she used his words against him.

In a role reversal, he climbed behind her onto the ATV and immediately inched forward until his chest brushed her back. One arm banded snugly around her waist, and he settled the other hand low on her hip.

"Ready whenever you are." His lips skimmed her ear, and hell if she didn't shiver in his arms, making him want to do it all over again. "Head left and keep going until our only options are to stop or swim in the creek."

She turned the ignition, and they jetted forward, the ATV's headlight growing brighter the more the sun sank into the horizon. Ten minutes later, the massive willow loomed in front of them, a natural monument in an open field of green.

"Oh, wow." Mouth agape, Addie's gaze slid over the nearby bubbling creek before tracking the movements of a gentle swarm of fireflies as they made themselves known.

Phoenix jumped from the ATV and helped her off.

Her knees buckled and he quickly braced his hands on her waist, holding her upright. "You good?"

A pretty pink blush rose high on her cheeks. "Sea legs."

"Here to catch you whenever you need, love."

She rolled her eyes, but smiled.

He counted that as a win as he regretfully moved aside to let her take in the kissing tree and its surroundings. "What do you think?"

She tilted her face toward the clear, starry night sky before closing her eyes with a small sigh and letting the moonbeams soak into her skin. "No wonder Naiomi called this place magical. I feel it in *everything*."

Addie stole the breath from Phoenix's lungs and he wasn't sure if he wanted her to give it back. He'd always thought this spot enchanted, too, but it paled in comparison to the magic emanating from the woman standing in front of him. She inspired feelings he'd never felt before.

Things he couldn't decipher, and the more he tried, the more impossible it seemed. It had physically pained him when she'd explained her views on love, and even though she did make a few valid points, he'd made a promise to himself.

To prove to Adalyn Whitlock that she was wrong.

If anyone deserved to possess someone's whole mind, body, and soul, it was her. He didn't know if he was the right man for the job, but he damn sure wished he could be.

"This is the place," Addie announced in a soft whisper, her eyes opening and immediately landing on him. "We'll ask Emilio about logistics for transporting guests out here for a sunset ceremony. Hopefully, if we time things right and luck is on our side, when East and Nai exchange vows, the fireflies will come out to play and it'll be—"

"Beautiful," Phoenix finished.

"Exactly." She beamed excitedly, emitting a quiet giggle. "So we're in agreement. This is the place?"

"No. I mean, yes. I mean . . ." Phoenix mentally smacked the back of his head in the hopes it got his mouth and brain working in tandem again. "Yes, you're right. This is definitely where they should have the ceremony, and it *is* beautiful."

With an agreeing nod, she glanced toward the slowly trickling creek.

Phoenix took a deep breath and took the plunge. "But the *beautiful* I was talking about just then was actually you."

Her head whipped toward him, gaze scanning every inch of his face as if judging the sincerity of his words.

She'd find nothing but truth. The woman was so damn beautiful it sometimes hurt to look at her directly, almost as if she exuded a goddess's golden glow. If that was even a thing.

"You know people don't say stuff like that, right? At least not without it being a pickup line and expecting something in return." Addie shifted awkwardly on her feet and trapped—and nibbled—the bottom corner of her lip between her teeth.

"Well, it's not a line. It's the truth." His body gravitated toward her and he took one slow, small step forward. "And in case you haven't realized it yet, I've never much liked doing as others do."

"I'm starting to get that." Addie mirrored his movement. Her gaze, glittering in the moonlight, flickered to his mouth and back. "You're definitely not like anyone I've ever met before, Phoenix Cross."

He smirked smugly. "I'll take that as a compliment."

"It is."

Another step closer for each of them.

Addie's flowery scent wrapped around him, invading all his senses. His *everything*. With less than an inch separating them, Phoenix visually stumbled into her beautiful green eyes—eyes flecked with mesmerizing golden starbursts.

Giving her time to pull away or step back, Phoenix trailed

his fingers in a featherlight touch until he cupped the side of her face. His thumb caressed her cheek, and she leaned into his touch, eyes fluttering.

Addie's hands, braced on his lower abdomen, slowly slid up his chest, which moved with each quick breath. "Phoenix . . ."

"Can I be brutally honest with you right now?" Phoenix asked, his voice a low, husky rumble.

"Yes?"

"Is that a question or an answer?" he teased, unable to help himself.

"Both?" Fingers flexing nervously in the front of his shirt, she teased. "What's on your mind, rock star?"

"Our first kiss."

A little, nearly inaudible gasp left Addie's lips. "The kiss?"

"As lovely as it was, all I've been able to think about since is how much I wished our first time had been just for us." He gently tilted her chin up. "Not in front of a crowd of thousands. Not for the benefit of a cover story. And with no polite pearl limitations."

"An entire strand?" Addie asked in a whisper.

"An entire strand." His lips danced into a smirk. "A kiss that would imprint on us both for a damn long time if not forever."

Addie lifted a single eyebrow. "You think a lot of your kissing skills. You really have that kind of ability?"

He leaned in, brushing the tip of his nose against hers. "Is that a dare, love?"

"Not a dare. But if you come out of the gate making big promises like that, you better be prepared to prove it."

"Proving it would require a one-on-one demonstration." His gaze dropped to her mouth. "You think you're up for that?"

She hummed in agreement, the edges of her lips twisted into a small, coy grin. "*Sparkles.*"

Phoenix's mind blanked—and then the word smacked him in the face. *Sparkles.*

Sliding his hand into her hair, he hauled her mouth to his. Her body melted against him instantly, lush lips parting on a breathy sigh that he used to deepen the kiss. Addie's fingers, anchored around the back of his neck, tugged him closer.

Tongues dancing. Breath mingling. Phoenix lost track of where he ended and she began as their bodies moved, propelled by the need for more.

More of *everything*.

Addie's back gently bumped into the trunk of the flowering willow tree, but it didn't dislodge their kiss. Her hands slipped beneath the hem of his T-shirt and ran over his abdomen before rising to his chest. Phoenix, palms practically itching with the need to feel her, cupped her lush rear end, and with one firm squeeze, guided her legs around his waist.

The height shift put her mound directly against his massive erection. Addie slowly rolled her hips, the movement dragging a groan from each of their throats.

Fuck. What he'd give to take her right there against the kissing tree . . . under the stars and surrounded by fireflies. Just them. No clothes. And all the time in the world to explore—and devour—each other fully.

A vaguely familiar sound shattered the charged quiet.

"Please tell me you don't need to get that?" Addie murmured against his lips before plunging right back into their heated kiss.

It took Phoenix another few moments to recognize East's ringtone. "Bastard can wait a few minutes."

One hand protecting the back of Addie's head from the tree, Phoenix dragged a series of open-mouthed kisses and gentle nips down her neck. "Fuck. You taste as sweet as sugar."

He skimmed her tank top strap down her arm and continued his feast along her shoulder and across her collarbone.

Xavier's ringtone blared loudly from his back pocket.

Then Gavin's.

Five brief seconds later, Addie's cell chimed, too.

"I really hate our friends right now." She pulled her mouth away with a groan and dropped her head onto his shoulder, panting nearly as heavily as he was. "They won't stop until one of us answers."

"It's time to get new friends."

She giggled as he ruefully loosened his hold and forced himself to step back.

Phoenix yanked his phone from his pocket. "What?"

"Dude, if you and Addie want any food, you better get your asses back to the house pronto. I can only hold Xavier back from the homemade guac for so long without risking life and limb."

"We'll be back in a few." He hung up East's call and found Addie smirking as she leaned against the ATV. He stepped right up to her and slowly brushed his lips against hers in a silent promise. "To be continued."

"We'll see, rock star." She smiled mischievously.

Oh, they would . . . because now that he'd gotten a taste of what it was like to really have Adalyn Whitlock in his arms—and beneath his hands—he already couldn't wait to experience it all over again.

After he kicked his friends' asses.

15

BEANBAG BANGIN'

Addie

Addie wasn't a pacer, but she'd also never been this conflicted over a guy, equal parts thankful and pissed that she and Phoenix had been interrupted by their friends' phone calls a few hours ago.

Would she have really stripped down and allowed Phoenix to have his way with her against a damn tree? Even when fully clothed and wearing multiple layers, mosquitoes still managed to suck the blood from her body, but if she'd been completely naked?

An all-you-can-eat Addie buffet.

Talk about communing with nature—not to mention the potential breach in their napkin contract.

But Holy Hellscape, the man's kiss left her weak-kneed and horny as hell. *Still*. Hours after they got back to the main house and ate an unhealthy amount of enchiladas and guac. To say it had been an awkward ride back to the city—with both Bailey and Maxi watching her every move—was a big understatement.

But now Addie stood in her apartment—alone and all too

aware—that Phoenix Cross was right on the other side of the wall.

"I can't believe I'm debating this." Addie threw a questioning glance at Do-Re-Mi, who warily watched her pace from the safety of their corner bed. "Getting physical would be a monumentally bad idea. Right?"

Do and Re cocked their heads as if contemplating, while Mi chuffed and lay his head down like he didn't care in the least.

"It's a horrible idea. Atrocious. Whatever momentary pleasure happened would evaporate the second it was over, and then there'd be nothing but a brewing shitstorm of complications." Addie ignored the uncertainty in her words—and tone—as she flopped onto her couch. "I just need something to distract me. There's got to be some kind of documentary on or something."

She flipped through all the streaming services and finding nothing she hadn't already watched, turned off the TV to scroll the HEF social media account. She quickly regretted that and tossed her phone onto the coffee table with an annoyed huff.

Staring at the ceiling and contemplating a bubble bath, Addie startled at an abrupt pulse of music. Heavy bass reverberated under her feet, moving upward, the words only slightly muffled as the culprit turned up the volume just as the singer belted out something about sleepless nights.

Phoenix.

A minute later, the song shifted to another. This one—if she remembered correctly—boasted about horny thoughts and some kind of sex drought. It played through the refrain before transitioning to a smooth, velvety voice expressively describing his inability to get someone off his mind.

Addie chuckled, her cheeks aching a bit from her grin.

No way he didn't play those songs on purpose, and her suspicion was confirmed another minute later when the slow ballad went silent and an upbeat chorus detailing the intricacies of a midnight booty call took its place.

For thirty minutes, songs bounced back and forth from naked-themed lyrics to tales of love and sonnets. At thirty-one minutes, Addie resigned herself to her fate—and her persistent next-door neighbor.

When executing a bad idea, do it with a bang.

Literally.

She didn't bother changing out of her flannels. She marched to Phoenix's door and, unlike the first hallway encounter, knocked once before the damn thing flew open and the man himself stood in front of her in all his shirtless glory.

Addie's brain froze, but her eyes freely roamed over his tattooed chest and eight-pack abs. Abs she wanted to lick.

And touch.

And maybe try to bounce a quarter off of later if he was game.

Her tongue, dry and sticking to the roof of her mouth, failed to cooperate with the rampant thoughts running through her head.

"Hello there, neighbor." Phoenix leaned casually against the frame of his door, much like the first time she'd stalked over to his place. "Did you finally come over to borrow that cup of sugar? I actually bought some to make sure I had it on hand—just for you."

Addie's nerves slowly melted away and she bit her bottom lip to keep from laughing at his attempt to replay their first encounter.

"Actually, I'm here to complain about the music. Again. You do realize that there are people trying to sleep in this building, right?"

"Sleep is highly overrated." Hazel eyes twinkling, Phoenix crossed his arms over his chest, forearm porn in full effect as his muscles rippled. "And evidently impossible when you've been mentally replaying a run-in with a really fucking sexy redhead."

"A run-in, huh?"

"More like my biggest dream come to life. Or it would've been if we hadn't been interrupted by my asshole friends." Phoenix amped up the sad, wistful look on his face. "Now the only thing I can do to prevent my imagination from wandering is distract myself with loud, obnoxious music."

His heated, lust-filled gaze glided down Addie's body, and instead of annoyance or irritation—her typical go-to emotions when dealing with corny one-liners and verbal games—had goose bumps erupting all over her skin. Phoenix's gaze alone was like an intimate touch and it lit something inside her she couldn't remember feeling before.

"Is the distraction working?" Addie teased.

"Not in the fucking least."

Addie fought—and failed—to keep her voice even as she continued the game a bit longer. "It's odd. I also can't get someone out of my head. And I really, really should for a whole laundry list of reasons."

"Yeah? And what's on that list?"

She ticked them off on her fingers. "To name just a few? We are absolutely nothing alike, and I do mean *nothing*."

He shrugged. "Opposites have been known to attract since the dawn of time."

Another tick . . . "My focus needs to be on saving my business, not naked fun times with a sexy musician."

"All work and no naked fun times aren't really conducive to a good work-life balance. Burnout is a real thing. And combating it with a musician? Not trying to sway you either way, but I hear they're good with both their mouths and their hands."

Addie barely swallowed an amused chuckle and counted another tick . . .

"Physical intimacy always leads to complications and the potential for—"

"Feelings?" Phoenix's weighted gaze held Addie's next breath hostage. "Catching feelings doesn't seem like something the Anti-Aphrodite would be too concerned about."

Bracing her hands on her hips, she struggled to bring some reality to the forefront. "It's not me I'm concerned about, Phoenix."

Liar, liar, panties on fire . . .

Something—a lot of somethings—all pointed to one thing.

Of all the people on this planet, the man standing in front of her with a determined glint in his gorgeous eye was the one with whom she should be most concerned about catching feelings.

Phoenix pushed off from the door and inched forward, a predator keeping his prey in sight—and that prey was *her*.

Not in a creepy way, or one found only on Animal Planet.

In a sexy *Phoenix* way.

Addie's heart thumped wildly as she countered his movements. In two steps, her back was pressed against the wall, and Phoenix's body hovered less than an inch away. He slowly tucked a loose strand of hair behind her ear and gave her all the time in the world to turn away before bracing his hand on the wall inches shy of her head . . . and leaning in.

Fuck. The sexy wall-lean. Her body all but spontaneously combusted right on the spot. Hell, she still might if he stayed in that position much longer.

"Are you really worried about me catching feelings, love?"

Phoenix's mouth—a breath away from touching her skin—hovered just over the sensitive spot below her ear. "Or are you actually worried that it might be *you*?"

A denial rested on the tip of her tongue, but she couldn't say it aloud. Releasing a shaky breath, she struggled between what her head demanded she do and what her body craved.

And damn it. Addie didn't like anyone bossing her around—not even herself.

"This is a really bad idea, Phoenix," Addie whispered, her voice scratchy.

"On average, I'm a big fan of them. They usually lead to the most fun." The colors in his hazel eyes warred for dominance, but it was desire that won out, overtaking them all as his heated gaze melted into hers. "Tell me you're not the least bit curious what it would be like between us and I'll back off right now. But if you can't stop thinking about it, and want it more than you want your next breath—just like me . . . then say so. And then the next music genre that will be spilling from my apartment will be your pleasure-filled moans."

Addie's knees would've disappeared if she hadn't been leaning against the wall for support. "I don't think I've listened to that genre in . . . ever."

Phoenix commanded her attention with the softest chin tilt. "What will it be, Addie? Want to experience some bad ideas with me?"

Neither scuba gear nor a life preserver could have prevented her from drowning in desire. And instead of a frigid wave of dread that normally came with this level of intimacy, a warm, tingling blanket of excitement settled over not just her body, but her mind and all her chronic doubts.

"They do say bad ideas are best executed while naked,"

Addie heard her breathless voice counter. "And no regrets, right? No strings. No expectations. No—"

"No worries." Phoenix's thumb brushed against her lower lip. "Just you and me, and quite possibly every surface of my apartment."

Her lips twitched, and before she could talk herself out of it, she nodded. "Lead the way, rock star."

Phoenix's gaze dropped to her mouth a split second before he released a low growl. "I can do better than that."

His mouth claimed hers in a searing kiss, one hand delving into her hair to hold her close while the other slid up her thigh and toward her ass, giving it a firm squeeze. "Up."

"But I—"

He released her mouth with a small groan. "Get your gorgeous legs around my waist right the fuck now, Addie."

He gently pushed her against the wall, using her back as leverage as his hands slid down her body and over her backside until he reached the backs of her thighs. He dragged each leg up, waited until her hands clamped onto his shoulders, and spun them right through his open apartment door.

He kicked it closed the second they stepped through, mouths still fused.

Addie ground her mound against the very obvious erection trapped between their bodies and beneath their clothes.

Phoenix's grip on her ass tightened. "Keep doing that and I'll be forced into ripping off your clothes and devouring every inch of you."

"Won't hear a complaint out of me." She rolled her hips again, a tease that instantly backfired when her already aching clit throbbed. "Here. I'll get us started."

She yanked off her shirt and tossed it aside.

Phoenix's gaze dropped to the sight of her exposed breasts,

nipples already hardened both from chill and excitement. A brief flicker of self-consciousness zipped her because she wasn't small. Not her hips or her ass. And definitely not her boobs.

"Fuck." Phoenix cupped a heavy breast, gaze hungry as his thumb gently swiped over an aching nipple. "I could drown in these perfect breasts and die a happy man. Fucking perfect. Let's see if they taste as good as they look."

His hazel eyes lifted toward her face as he slowly licked the tip of her left nipple. At her shudder, he went back a second time, kissing and sucking until it looked like a cherry about to burst.

And then he did the same with the other one, his gaze never leaving her face.

With a heady moan, Addie sank her fingers into his hair and held him close. "More."

"Bed." His mouth and hands still anchored on her body, Phoenix stepped farther into the apartment, a man on a mission as he headed toward the back hall.

Two steps into the bedroom—and four away from the very sturdy-looking bed—Phoenix tripped. "Shit."

"Oh no." Addie's fingers tightened on Phoenix reflexively as she prepped for a pain-filled fall, but Phoenix spun, putting himself beneath her as gravity dragged them to the ground.

She waited for the hard impact.

And waited.

When it didn't come, she opened one eye at a time and slowly registered the leathery mound of softness cushioning their still conjoined bodies.

Addie, sitting astride his waist, erupted into a giggle. "You have a beanbag chair in your bedroom?"

"Hey." Phoenix's lips twitched with feigned indignation.

"It's one of those mega-beans, and it's probably more comfortable than my bed."

"Oh yeah? Want to test it out?"

Reading the challenge in her face, Phoenix chuckled. "Your mind is just as gorgeous as your body."

He fisted her hair and dragged her mouth back down to his. It wasn't long before they both drowned in desire—and each other—despite shedding every article of clothing.

Blissfully naked and with nothing between them, Addie used her upright position to her advantage. Palms exploring Phoenix's upper body, she nibbled and kissed her way over his chest and down his abs, exploring—and tasting—every colorful tattoo. His hard cock twitched each time it brushed along her wetness, and soon she did it on purpose.

"Fuck." Head tilted back, Phoenix groaned with the effort to hold back. "Do that much longer and I'll come before I'm even inside you, and I need to watch you fall apart before that happens."

Addie opened her mouth to ask him about his plans when his hands, anchored on her hips, effortlessly lifted her up the beanbag while he slid down.

Her bare pussy now hovered less than an inch above his face.

She comprehended his plan instantly. Excitement mixed with an acute case of fear as she prepared to move.

"Where do you think you're going?" Phoenix's eyes snapped to her, his hands holding her firmly in place above him.

"Somewhere that's less likely to smother you? Maybe the bed we didn't quite make it to."

"Don't worry about my safety, love." Phoenix's mischievous smirk buckled her knees. "If tasting you is how I go out, then at least I'll have glimpsed heaven before I do. Now lower that pretty pussy so I can get my first taste of nirvana."

Addie's chuckle transformed to a low, needy groan the second Phoenix guided her hips down to his mouth. Knee-quaking pleasure rolled through her with the first leisurely swipe of his tongue. By the second, Addie questioned how long she'd be able to remain upright.

Fingers flexed in the beanbag chair beneath her, and fighting not to pass out from the pleasure, her head lolled to the side. Phoenix hummed against her sensitive center, and when her gaze caught his, she nearly combusted on the spot.

Addie had never considered herself a big fan of oral stimulation. A few lackluster experiences had left her ambivalent to the act. But Phoenix was on a one-man mission to change her outlook. He played her body like a musical instrument, and she was more than ready to sing.

"Phoenix." Addie panted, battling to keep her eyes open as she swiveled her hips in time with his tongue. "It feels too good. I'm going to come if you keep going."

He hummed against her center, and without seeing them, she knew his lips twisted into a satisfied grin. "That's kinda what I'm going for here, love."

He held her tighter against his mouth as he feasted, and soon she forgot all about her smothering concern. Her body chased each swipe of his tongue, pleasure coming in quick, surging waves. Phoenix picked up his pace, and then slowed it down, alternating between slow licks and gentle sucks to her clit. Addie loved it all, both her knees and her arms trembling with the struggle to remain upright.

"I'm coming." Addie's gaze dropped to Phoenix to find his gaze already locked solidly on hers. "Fuck. I'm coming. *Phoenix*."

Her body erupted, morphing into a quivering ball of sensation.

And most certainly filled his apartment—and probably their entire floor—with her pleasure-filled music.

Phoenix

Seeing Adalyn Whitlock come and knowing he'd been the one to make it happen was Phoenix's new favorite thing. With gentle swipes of his tongue, he eased her through one orgasm and into another, and already couldn't wait to witness it again.

And again.

Hell, if he had his way, she'd come so often and so hard, she'd be too wrung out and weak-kneed to leave his bed in the morning.

As a last, wispy little sigh escaped Addie's lips, Phoenix grinned in satisfaction. "Like I said . . . heaven."

Addie's hooded gaze fixed on his as her chest heaved. "You look awfully smug, rock star."

"I am."

"You have every right to be."

He chuckled. His rock-hard cock glided through her dampness as he shifted them back to their original position, his ass planted firmly in the beanbag and her sitting on his lap. He slowly pulled her mouth into a kiss that zinged straight to his core. They each pillaged and plundered. Addie reached between them and wrapped one soft palm around his already throbbing cock.

He groaned on contact, aching to be inside her as she gave his length a firm tug. He quickly settled his hand on hers, preventing a second pump, and got a questioning look.

"I am dangerously close to coming in your hand, gorgeous, and while I might be up for that some other time, this first one I want to be inside you," Phoenix clarified.

Her subtle nod sent him reaching for his discarded pants and he quickly grabbed the condom from his wallet.

"Too slow." Addie plucked the foil from his fingers, ripped the package open with her teeth, and slid the latex down his dancing cock. It twitched with every stroke of her fingers, an involuntary reaction that had her giggling by the time he was completely sheathed.

"Tell me you're okay with this." Phoenix nudged her chin toward him. For his own peace of mind, he needed to ensure she was really consenting. "No regrets. No worries."

"Only regretting how long it's taking until you're inside of me," Addie teased breathlessly, her desire mirroring his.

"Then let's not waste another second." Guiding her hips back over his straining cock, he let her take it—and him—the rest of the way.

Groans ripped from their throats as she sank down on him to the hilt, her lush body wrapping around him like a tight glove. No working up to it. Not easing in an inch at a time. One moment, his cock was outside of her pliant body, and the next, he was fully seated.

This was what euphoria felt like—at least, that's what he thought until she pulled nearly all the way back, and did it again.

Addie set the pace, hips—at first—swiveling in a slow rocking movement that built up to a speed that had them both breathless and sweaty in seconds. Phoenix clamped a hand on her hip and thrust up from below. His other hand slid up her soft belly and along her torso until he cupped a lush, delectable breast in his palm.

He brushed his thumb over her erect nipple, smirking as it pebbled on contact. "You're so fucking responsive."

As she rode him, he leaned forward and took the reddened

bud into his mouth. If anyone would have told him a month ago that he'd be fucking his gorgeous neighbor on his oversized beanbag chair, he'd have called them ridiculous.

It didn't feel so ridiculous now.

It actually felt way too fucking good to be real.

"Phoenix." His name falling from Addie's lips in a soft beg sounded like music to his ears.

"Take what you need from me, love." Phoenix slipped a hand between them and found her clit as she rocked over him, her gorgeous breasts swaying back and forth. "That's it. Take it all. Everything I have. Just let me feel you come around my cock."

Addie's pussy quivered around him, signaling her impending orgasm. It was a race to the finish line as his own release grew more imminent with each passing second, but fuck if he'd let go before her.

Addie's fingers dug slightly into his chest as she leaned forward.

"Keep those beautiful greens on me," Phoenix demanded gently and she followed direction instantly, eyes locked on his. "I want to devour every inch of your expression when you come around me."

He gripped her hip even tighter and thrust into her pussy with more snap. Addie whimpered and rocked faster, her body trembling.

Phoenix sat up and took a hardened nipple into his mouth. Now, with his mouth on her breast, his finger on her clit, and his cock damn near throbbing in her pussy, it was just a matter of time.

"Phoenix!" His name fell off her lips like a plea.

"Let go, baby." Phoenix momentarily released his hold on her hip to slip his fingers into her hair and then he guided her into a deep, sensuous kiss that pushed them both over the edge.

The walls of Addie's pussy rippled around his cock as she came—hard—and the sensation opened the floodgates of his own release. Kissing her through the euphoria, their bodies lost their sync, working hard to keep the pleasure going for as long as possible.

It felt like he came forever, no doubt filling the condom with the first wave of cum. He already knew one time with Adalyn Whitlock wouldn't be enough.

He already needed her again.

As many times as she was up for it, and as Addie slowly sank into his arms in a breathless, fully spent afterglow, he ignored the little voice in his head saying that this was the very opposite of *no strings*.

16

OH. MY. GODDESS.

Addie

Sitting in the waiting room, Addie scrolled through social media, searching the Happily Ever Forever hashtag with wary—but hopeful—anticipation.

The results were a mixed bag. There were a lot of comments supporting HEF, and a few who cheered on Karleigh Kinkaid, but not nearly as many as there'd been a week ago, which she considered a small win.

She'd strictly stayed away from all media forms for the past few weeks, trusting Bailey's words—and a few occasional headline glimpses—that the FAMA with Phoenix was doing what they hoped.

But now?

She typed Phoenix's name into the search engine, erased it, and retyped it again before working up the nerve to hit the Enter key.

"Whoa." She wasn't sure what she'd expected, but this hadn't been it.

He'd warned her that both paparazzi and random people

photographed him nearly everywhere he went, but a small part of her thought he'd been exaggerating just the tiniest bit.

He hadn't.

Images of Phoenix flooded the results page, some from tabloid articles like the one claiming that Naughty Nix was an alien prince sent to Earth for his own safety. Others originated from random social media accounts and fan feeds. A bunch came from music magazines and other sources—like the paparazzi.

It didn't take long to find the images of him and Addie.

The two of them, shoulders brushing, as they walked down the street. Standing in line for coffee. Unsurprisingly, she lost count of how many highlighted the Cupid Cam kiss, but was shocked to see nearly as many taken during their impromptu Central Park coffee break. There were pics taken in different locations all over the city, but whether fan pics or paparazzi, they all had one thing in common.

They looked . . . cozy.

Soft smiles. Laughs. She and Phoenix either stared at one another simultaneously, or when the other wasn't paying attention. It was *those* pics that had her shifting uncomfortably in her plastic chair . . . because Phoenix Cross wasn't the only one sneaking shy little glances and timid smiles.

By mistake, Addie ended up in someone's comment section.

She fumbled her phone, and before she backed out, glanced at the first post and flinched. "Well, hell . . ."

The man had more offers to kick Addie out of his bed and fill the spot themselves than she had hair on her head. Occasionally, one popped up in support, but most were uber fans who claimed they felt robbed of the chance to be with Naughty Nix.

Sensing a brewing headache, she quickly stuffed her phone

deep into the abyss of her purse and eyeballed the clock. The two women sitting across from her in the waiting room continued their stare fest, one of whom snapped a very indiscreet picture.

It wasn't lost on Addie that she wished she was tucked back in Phoenix's bed, all warm and toasty, and away from prying eyes.

Last night, he'd made good on his promise to devour every inch of her, first trying out a few new positions on the beanbag chair, then the floor. Bent over his dresser. She'd lost track of the time—and her orgasm count—by the time they reached the bed, and had both, at some point, passed out with smiles on their faces.

The only reason she woke up hours later was thanks to her screaming, full bladder—and this doctor's appointment. An appointment she'd nearly been late for because Phoenix had bribed her with a parting orgasm in the hopes that she'd cancel it altogether in favor of an all-day sex-fest.

He'd almost succeeded, but she needed answers about the damn vanishing glowing rope. Every time it appeared and disappeared, she got a headache that ibuprofen wouldn't touch.

The office door opened, and Dr. Ashad's assistant poked her head through. "Adalyn? He's ready for you now."

Addie grabbed her things and hustled to the back. Dr. Ashad had been her ophthalmologist for years, a kind, grandfatherly figure with graying hair and a perpetual smile. The second she sat down in the patient's seat, she told him about the visual disturbances, and he listened raptly, deep in thought and occasionally interjecting with a question or two.

But after almost two hours, copious tests, eye dilation, and more tests, Dr. Ashad's expression didn't give Addie the warm fuzzies.

"I won't lie to you, Adalyn," Dr. Ashad started off. "I'm a little perplexed. As far as I can tell, nothing has changed since your last visit. Your pressures are the same, as are your peripheral views. There's no corneal lacerations or inflammation. I'm . . . stumped."

He pulled up multiple images on different screens and placed them side by side. Even she, with no medical knowledge, could see how similar each image looked to the one next to it.

Addie's shoulders slumped. "I don't understand . . ."

"I wish I had answers for you, but I don't see anything that would be causing the symptoms you're experiencing," Dr. Ashad said sincerely. "The only thing I can think of for us to try is to give your eyes a rest from contacts for a few weeks, and then to swap them for another batch in case the one you're currently using is defective."

"Yeah. I guess that makes sense."

"Give it two weeks, and then shoot me an email to tell me how things are going. Then we'll go from there, okay?"

"Sure. I can do that." Addie headed out into the warm Manhattan air and into the heavy throngs of midday rush.

In desperate need of caffeinated pep, she hooked left and searched for the nearest coffee spot, finding Buzzed just across the street. She lost herself in the crowd and nearly walked past the coffee shop before making a quick U-turn and yanking open the door.

Trendy and modern with sleek, industrial silver accents and a ceiling with open duct views and wooden beams, Buzzed had everything from regular coffee to currently viral drinks and a breakfast sandwich that looked like a simple egg and cheese but was called Eggstra EZ.

Addie was glancing over the menu choices on the wall when a familiar low chuckle turned her head to the corner seating area. She opened her mouth to call out to her father and question why he was in Midtown—a place he avoided at all costs—when she realized he wasn't alone.

Dressed in what Addie considered office chic, the woman sitting across from him, her dark brown hair intermixed with stylish wisps of delicate silver, tossed her head back in laughter at something Simon said. In response, her father's lips twisted into a small smirk.

And he *blushed*.

Addie's father actually *blushed*, his full cheeks pinking as his gaze focused intently on the beauty reaching across the table to touch his hand. A noise escaped Addie's throat.

Her father's head turned in her direction. Addie dodged behind the stand-up travel mug display, knocking a few metal tumblers to the ground in the process.

Eyes closed, she counted to ten and hoped to hell she hadn't been spotted. When nothing happened, she opened her eyes and felt her heart stop in her chest.

"What the hell are you doing here?" Addie demanded.

Her mother, crouched down to her level a few scant inches away, shared Addie's hiding spot.

"Who are we hiding from?" Aphrodite's voice dropped to a low whisper.

"*Mom*," Addie demanded. "Why are you here?"

"Very genuinely asking you the same thing, sweetheart. These appear to be lovely travel mugs. Which one has caught your fancy?" Aphrodite knowingly rose to her feet, her gaze drifting across the room toward Addie's father. "Oh, look. Your father is braving Midtown."

"Don't let him see you!" Addie clenched her mother's hand and tried pulling her back behind the display. She moved, but only barely.

"Sweetheart, he won't see me. His focus is on that lovely woman in front of him." Aphrodite glanced at her, still practically sitting on the floor. "Why are you hiding from your father and his date?"

Date?

Addie's brain slowly caught up. "Oh. My. Goddess. He *is* on a date, isn't he?"

"It would appear so. Good for him. They both look quite smitten."

Addie peered around the tower to look for herself, and she had to admit that her mother was right. Simon did look smitten, and so did the woman across from him. She laughed at something he said—again.

Oh, it was definitely a date. Her father wasn't that funny.

"I wonder if this is Caroline," Addie murmured absent-mindedly.

"That's a lovely name," Aphrodite gushed warmly. "Really, sweetie. Your legs will cramp if you stay down there too long."

Fuck. She was right. A cramp had already formed in her left calf. Using the display shelf to help her up, she stood and snuck a glance toward her father's table. All his attention remained focused on the dark-haired beauty in front of him.

She studied them a bit longer when her vision blurred. "Fucking hell . . . not again."

Yep, again.

That familiar gold shimmer blurred its way into existence before wrapping around her father and his conversation partner like a damn boa.

"Everything okay, sweetheart?" Aphrodite's concern had the visual apparition disappearing in a snap.

Addie muttered a curse and rubbed her aching eyes. "Yeah. I just need to get to the office and get these contacts out of my eyes." She snuck a glance at her mother's knowing gaze. "Why are you looking at me like that?"

"There's something different about you today."

"Other than being woefully un-caffeinated, things have been pretty much the same," Addie lied. She kept her face passive, blinking innocently, and silently hoping her mother moved on.

"The same, huh?" Aphrodite's eyes narrowed on her.

"Pretty much." Addie caught herself fidgeting with her satchel zipper, and stopped. "Except that Dad's obviously dating again. I mean, I already knew it, but it just hits a little different seeing it in person."

Was she proud to throw her father under the bus? No.

But her mother's notorious meddling left her with no other choice.

"How is that rock star romance of yours going?" Aphrodite surprised Addie by shifting into another topic altogether.

Addie's eye twitched, a small, nearly microscopic movement, and yet it was the only tell her mother needed.

A knowing smile slid onto the goddess's face. "That good, huh?"

"It seems to be doing the job." Addie pushed through the lump forming in her throat. "One step forward and then two back."

"Maybe you should up the stakes a bit. In this day and age, subtlety isn't so much a human trait. Who knows, maybe mixing a little pleasure with your work is just the missing ingredient that you need."

"Phoenix and I are mixing things just fine, Mom."

"It was only a suggestion."

"Thanks, but we've got things covered."

"Okay. You know how to reach me if you need me." Aphrodite *poofed* into the ether.

"Addie?" Her father walked toward her, now standing alone by the display, one hand resting low on the mystery woman's back. "I thought that was you, kiddo."

He pulled her into a hug, and she gave an awkward one in return, her gaze landing on his date. "You're in Midtown."

Her father chuckled. "Yeah, but don't get used to it."

"That was my fault, I'm afraid," the woman interjected with a smile, holding her hand out. "I'm Caroline. It's nice to meet you face-to-face, Addie. I feel as though we've already met. Your father talks so proudly about you and your sister. Thank you for giving your father my message the other day. I hated rescheduling, but if I didn't watch the grandbaby, it would have put my daughter and her wife in a bit of a bind. Luckily, your father is a gem and didn't mind in the least."

"Yeah, he's a great guy like that." Addie slid her gaze toward her father, taking great enjoyment in his new pink flush. "So . . . Midtown on a weekday? You've always said it would be the coming apocalypse if you ever got within a twelve-block radius of Times Square."

Her father snuck a quick glance at the woman next to him. "I don't recall saying *apocalypse*."

"Oh, I do. As a matter of fact, I think your exact words were 'couldn't open up in the city, threatening an apocalypse, with me the only person possessing the ability to close it, and I still wouldn't set foot within twelve blocks of the Times Square circus.'"

"*Simon*." Caroline playfully swatted his arm. "You told me it wasn't a big deal to meet here. If I'd known you didn't like traveling to Midtown, I wouldn't have suggested this place for my lunch break."

"No, no. It's just . . . I mean, yeah . . . I've never been a fan, but it's probably high time I stepped out of my comfort zone."

Addie snorted, earning herself a glare from her father.

Caroline smiled warmly at him, her arm wrapping affectionately through his. "Well, I'm very honored that you stepped out of your comfort zone for me."

Her father's face flushed bright red.

Addie could not wait to tell Maxi about this entire encounter. "Well, my doctor's appointment has me running a bit late this morning. I need to get into the office."

Her father's attention snapped to her. "Doctor's appointment? Are you feeling okay? Everything all right?"

"Just an eye exam." Addie waved off his concern, planting a kiss on his cheek before flashing them both a small wave. "See you later."

Without a caffeine fix in hand, Addie hustled to the exit, and took one last glance at her father and Caroline.

That faint golden rope flickered into existence yet again, and with almost all inexplicable certainty, Addie knew Caroline wouldn't be going anywhere.

Her father very well may have found himself a keeper.

17

NIX IN SHINING ARMOR

Phoenix

Sweat stuck his sleeveless shirt to his back like a second skin. He shrugged it off and tossed it onto one of the nearby chairs in the corner of the mobile changing room before reaching for another.

"Leave it." The record label's stylist appeared out of nowhere, her gaze running over him from head to toe in a calculated assessment. She frowned at his much-loved biker boots, but nodded approvingly at his ripped jeans, and paused at the area of his chest—and nipple piercings. "Yeah. Definitely leave it."

"Leave my shirt?" Phoenix shot her a questioning look.

She shot him a *duh* look in return. "Will being shirtless infringe on your ability to bang on drums?"

"I do a little more than bang on drums."

She shrugged, obviously not caring in the least. "Whatever. Consider this your new look."

The stylist—Brit—shifted her attention off him and quickly

hustled over toward Gavin and Xavier, already yelling at the griffon shifter to put something back *on*.

"Consider yourself lucky," East growled next to him. "I'd much rather strut naked onstage than wear this fucking clown outfit."

Phoenix turned toward his best friend and laughed at the gargoyle's pained expression. In all honesty, he looked damn good in the button-down shirt, half open and with the sleeves rolled up. But it was a far cry from the typical T-shirt and leather vest he preferred.

Phoenix smirked. "Just think of it as practice for the wedding day, man."

East's face paled, and already in his gargoyle form, that said a lot. "Fuck. I need to wear a shirt with fucking buttons for our ceremony?"

Phoenix laughed at his friend's horror-stricken expression. "Actually, I don't know what we're all wearing. I'll have to ask Addie what she found in the book."

"Aren't you planning the thing with her? Shouldn't you already know?"

"Tell me what you want to wear, and I'll see if I can put that bug in her ear . . . and just know that I'm pretty sure she won't go for the leather vest."

East sighed. "Honestly, I don't care. I'll wear a fucking clown suit if it'll make Naiomi happy. Whatever she has in that little book of hers, I'll suck it up for a few hours."

"Good man, East." Phoenix clapped his best friend on the back, smirking.

"Good start to Bands at the Beach, guys." Roger Kinkaid strolled into their mobile changing room, Marcus hot on his heels. "You four had the crowd going wild, and things are only getting warmed up. By the time your second set rolls around, there won't be a panty-wearing individual in the crowd!"

Hoping to avoid a direct confrontation, Phoenix feigned looking for his favorite drumsticks.

It didn't work; Kinkaid headed right for him. "Nix, if I could have a word?"

Fuck. "About?"

The older man cocked an eyebrow, and Phoenix reined in the attitude—a little. "Marcus sent me a screenshot of some of the new music you're working on and I'm a bit concerned."

Phoenix shot an accusing glare at his manager, who strategically found something else to look at, heading over toward Gavin. He obviously needed to do better hiding his music journal.

He turned his full attention to Kinkaid. "And what exactly are you concerned about?"

"Don't get me wrong, what I saw wasn't bad for some other band. But it's definitely not worthy of the Stone Talons. Not even remotely close to your brand."

"I'm not exactly sure what Marcus shared with you, but—"

"Something about butterflies and sonnets or lyrics or some shit." Roger chuckled. "So you can see why I'm concerned. I also know that the label okayed you keeping close ties to that Muse chick, but if that's the music she's inspiring in you, we may have to rethink that agreement."

Phoenix blinked.

Rethink the agreement that kept Adalyn Whitlock nice and close, in his bed, not to mention fueling the best music he's written in forever? Not a fucking chance.

"Like I said," Phoenix said calmly, "I'm not sure what Marcus showed you, but I'm more than aware what music is on-brand for the Stone Talons. You'll get more songs, and Adalyn will be the sole reason for it."

Kinkaid watched him carefully before nodding. "Okay then. Good. Because you know how much I'd hate to dim your creative light."

Phoenix barely withheld a snort. The man couldn't identify something creative if it bit him on the ass and left a permanent mark.

"I'll let you guys warm up for your next set." Kinkaid beckoned to Marcus across the trailer, and the two left as abruptly as they'd arrived.

"You handled that pretty well," East commented. "You know you'll have to give him something soon, right?"

"Yeah." But that didn't mean he had to like it, and he sure as hell didn't like Marcus digging through his shit.

Everyone knew his music journal was off-limits and the fact the ass had gone searching through it for something to show Kinkaid pissed him the fuck off. The second Bands at the Beach was done, they'd have words.

As he and the guys warmed up and got ready for their next set of songs, his phone buzzed with an incoming text.

Muse-alicious: We finally got up front. I'll be the one spinning my undies around my finger.

A smile worked its way onto Phoenix's face as he typed back.

And I'll be the shirtless drummer god with exposed nipple piercings

Muse-alicious: 😮

East chuckled as he read the texts from over his shoulder. "You're never to make fun of me for my *heart-eyes* when you look like that doe-eyed emoji come to life. I'm guessing Musealicious is Addie?"

Phoenix tried to look affronted, but couldn't stop his smile from peeking through. "Yeah. And?"

East shrugged. "And nothing. It's just good to see you smile, man. It's been a while."

"Yeah." Phoenix sighed, pocketing his phone. "And the music? I don't know what it is about her, but it comes so damn easy with her—especially in the last few days. Hell, and not just the music. Being *with* her is pretty damn effortless, too."

East kicked up an eyebrow. "You sure that you're having a fauxmance? Because that sounds like the exact opposite of faux."

He couldn't disagree. Hell, the more time they spent together, the more Phoenix's feelings grew. And after their night together? And morning? *Fuck*. He'd promised uncomplicated and no strings or worries, but he'd be lying to himself if he didn't admit that he wasn't worried about catching real feelings.

Or concerned that he already had.

Addie was the first thing to pop into his mind when he woke up and the last to leave it when he fell asleep. Hell, thoughts of her worked their way into his dreams, too.

East's full-blown laughter pulled him out of his mental gymnastics, the gargoyle clamping a stony hand on his shoulder. "Welcome to the club, man. Your life will never be the same."

Phoenix played off his friend's comment with an eye roll and acted as if it hadn't just rocked his fucking world.

One of the backstage managers stuck their head into the trailer. "The Stone Talons in ten!"

They all hustled out, Phoenix grabbing his sticks on the way toward the stage. Nestled along the Atlantic and well-known for their summer concerts, Jones Beach's amphitheater held fifteen thousand music lovers, both in the stands and far out on the grass, and that day was no exception.

Due to a last-minute performer cancellation, the band scored an invite to play at the festival of all festivals, and Marcus jumped on the opportunity like Gavin on fucking hotcakes.

Phoenix climbed the backstage stairs and stayed hidden from view as they waited for the band ahead of them to finish their last song. The sun sank on the horizon, lighting up the sky in a gorgeous display of pinks and oranges.

But Phoenix scanned the crowd for something infinitely more stunning.

The second his eyes landed on Addie, his entire body hummed. Arm linked with Bailey's on her right, she talked animatedly with Naiomi, standing on her left. Behind Nai, Max's gaze swiveled around the massively growing crowd.

Roger Kinkaid hadn't been wrong. The crowd had practically doubled in size since their first set hours ago, and the more time that passed, the more people partied. Some massive guy behind the quad stumbled and knocked into Addie, ramming her into the nearby speaker. Both Bailey's and Naiomi's fast reflexes prevented her from hitting the ground.

His sister turned to the guy with a glare and gave him an obvious earful.

East came up next to him. "Nai's got your girl covered. She won't let any assholes get too close and personal."

Phoenix unclenched his grip on his drumsticks, which he hadn't realized had been digging into his palms, and took a few deep breaths.

His girl.

Fuck. He really did like the sound of that way too much for his own good.

Addie

Being the event coordinator at Happily Ever Forever, Addie thought she'd known pure chaos, but the Kinkaid wedding debacle didn't hold a candle to Bands at the Beach. Bailey had tried relentlessly for years to coerce Addie into attending, but she always came up with an excuse.

Not this time.

This time she'd suggested attending to Bailey, and the complimentary tickets Phoenix offered them nearly put her cousin into a frenzy.

Thanks to the stifling heat, it felt like they were on hour one-million of the all-day event. Her airy flutter-sleeved tank top helped to keep her marginally cool, but her jeans, at this point, had basically become a second layer of skin. They'd started the morning in the back, sticking closer to the shaded areas, and slowly inched their way closer to the stage throughout the day.

"They're up next!" Naiomi shouted in Addie's ear.

Addie nodded. "Phoenix said something about his nipples making an appearance. What's that about?"

"Hell if I know. I've been so out of the loop with school. All I know is that it'll be a miracle if I survive long enough to get my doctorate."

"You got this, Nai." She squeezed the other woman's hand. "If I've learned anything in the short time we've known each other, it's that you don't let anything get in the way of something you want."

Nai chuckled. "That's a nice way of putting it. I just wish my brother had the same philosophy. He's been trudging along, writing all these panty party songs instead of focusing on the type of music that he really wants to write . . . and all because the label is full of assholes who want to box them into a corner."

Addie winced. "Yeah, Phoenix mentioned something about that."

"Personally, I think both he and East are wasting their talents jumping all these hurdles . . . but I'll never say that to them." At Addie's inquisitive look, Nai added, "East loves teaching guitar to the neighborhood kids. It's been his dream for a long time to open his own music school. And Phoenix? He's never really liked all the attention that comes with going up onstage. He's a good actor when he has to be but he'd—"

"Rather be the one making the music," Addie finished.

"Exactly." Nai nodded and sighed. "But it's my job to be the supportive fiancée and sister, so whatever they think they need to do, I'll support."

Addie chewed on those words while the current band finished their last song. The emcee danced onto the stage and immediately plunged into a mini-monologue to keep the crowd pumped and excited while sets swapped out.

"Oh, I almost forgot!" Addie dug into her jeans pocket and pulled out a lacy red thong.

"What the hell?" Maxi and Bailey exclaimed simultaneously while Nai threw her head back and laughed.

"I need a picture of his reaction." Phoenix's sister whipped her phone from her back pocket, solidifying Addie's decision to do it.

Were the panties hers?

Yes . . . *technically*.

She'd dug them out from the back of her drawer earlier that morning.

Had she ever worn them? *Nope*.

And she had no intention of putting something on that could floss her ass crack. Hence why she'd be flinging them at a certain sinfully sexy drummer.

The emcee introduced the Stone Talons and the guys ran onto the stage to a loud chorus of shouts and cheers. Nearby, two girls broke into sobbing tears, brimming with excitement as they screamed for Gavin to look their way.

Phoenix's gaze landed on her as if he'd already known where she stood. Addie lost herself in the excitement, and lifting her red thong in the air, spun the swatch of lace around on her pointer finger.

Phoenix laughed and flashed her a wink as he climbed behind his drum set. Settled onto his seat, he crooked his finger in her direction.

Glad she'd picked the high-elasticity thong, Addie stretched the fabric between her fingers and sling-shot the undies onto the stage.

Phoenix stood and leaned over his drums, catching them on his extended drumstick.

His text message finally made sense.

Instead of a well-loved T-shirt, his gorgeously tattooed chest—and piercings—were on full shirtless display. Her mouth damn near watered at the sight. But she became momentarily distracted when a shirtless Phoenix perched her red thong on his head like a freaking headband, keeping his hair from dangling into his eyes.

Heat flooded Addie's cheeks as she laughed, and the Stone Talons belted out their first song. Addie, Nai, Bailey, and Max sang along with the chorus as they bounced to the steady beat. More than once—or a dozen times—her gaze caught a smirking Phoenix looking ridiculous—and somehow still sexy—while wearing her underwear on his head.

They finished Flying Undies and dipped right into another song. Addie's smile never left her face.

"Who are you and what have you done with my cousin bestie?" Bailey demanded, all smirk and humor.

"What?" Addie shrugged. "You're right. It's fun. I'm not saying it's not a lot, and I'll gladly hermit for about a month after this, but I'm having a good time."

Bailey inspected her critically, eyeing every inch of her face through narrowed eyes.

"What?" Addie's self-consciousness grew the longer they stared. "Do I have something on my face?"

"You have something, but it's not just on your face." Bailey shared a loaded look with Maxi.

"Yeah, I see it, too." Her sister nodded.

"What are we seeing?" Nai leaned in for a closer look before breaking into a knowing smirk. "Oh yeah. Now I see it. Who would've thought?"

"I did," Bailey answered. "But I thought it would take a little longer. Unless . . ."

"What the hell did the three of you smoke before we came here?" Addie demanded. "And what are you talking about? What would take a little longer?"

"I thought it would take longer for this *fauxmance* to start getting blurry." Bailey smugly folded their arms over their chest. "Especially with your relationship track record and being the Anti-Aphrodite and all."

Maxi nodded in agreement. "We said it would take a month, maybe two."

"Unless there was a magical penis involved," Bailey added.

At the mention—and insinuation—of Phoenix's penis, Addie lost her train of thought . . . and her words. It was all the ammunition they needed. All three of them burst out with questions, demanding answers . . . and in Bailey's case, explicit details. When she'd fielded one question, someone blurted out another, and soon she didn't know who was asking what, or even what answers she was giving.

"You like magical penises?" A broad palm landed on her ass—and squeezed—hard. "I have a magical penis right here I'd like to introduce you to."

The grip tightened again, and Addie whirled around to find the asshole who'd bumped into her earlier. "Hands off the ass, buddy."

He swayed on his feet, clearly inebriated and exuding some strong beer breath as he stepped way too far into her personal space. "Oh, come on. You like big cocks, yeah? It happens that I have a massive one, and it's definitely capable of some magic tricks."

He made a clumsy attempt to grab her again, and she knocked his hand away. "It would need to be magical if you got it up with how plastered you are. Why don't you go find some coffee and contemplate ways to approach women that don't involve groping them without consent?"

"What did you expect to happen with you wiggling that ass in front of me? And why act all prim and proper now? I saw you throw that thong onto the stage."

The asshole's friends, nearly as drunk as him, but with more sense, attempted to rein their buddy in. He shook them off and leered down at her. It was a clusterfuck with Maxi, Bailey, and Nai attempting to intervene, but they were thwarted by both the guy and the growing crowd.

"Come on, baby." He grabbed himself through his pants. "What do you say about getting acquainted with my magic cock?"

Chaos broke out around them, bodies shifting, people

shouting. Someone knocked into Addie from the left, and then a familiar tattooed body was stepping in front of her, blocking the drunk asshole's advance.

"Touch her one more fucking time, and you'll be acquainted with my magic right hook," Phoenix warned, his voice a low, deadly growl.

Addie blinked, glancing at the stage—which was minus a Stone Talons drummer—and glanced back to the shirtless man in front of her. East stood on the edge of the stage barking orders at nearby security.

"This doesn't have anything to do with you, drummer boy." Mr. Grabby puffed out his barrel chest. "This is between me and the underwear-flinging bitch standing behind you."

"Say that again, I dare you." Phoenix stepped closer, fists balled at his side.

This was getting out of hand quickly.

"Just let it go." Addie gripped Phoenix's tightened bicep in a failed attempt to hold him back. "Phoenix. He's drunk. It's not worth it."

"Yeah. Let it go, *Phoenix*," the guy mocked. "That way I can show her how a magical cock really works."

The guy reached around Phoenix and grabbed her wrist with a surprisingly tight grip. A surprised, pain-filled gasp escaped her lips.

Phoenix moved instantly, so fast he blurred. Someone shouted. Addie lost her balance. This time, there was no Bailey or Nai to prevent her fall. She tripped over someone's feet and went down in the crowd, glancing up just in time to see Phoenix land a swift—and hard—punch to the asshole's jaw.

Addie placed a hand on the ground as leverage to climb back to her feet, but someone stepped on it. Some people moved toward the brawl, and some shifted, trying to move away. A knee knocked into the side of her head and sent her right back onto her ass.

What felt like a million years later—or maybe only a split second—gentle hands slid down her arms. "Hey there, love. I need you to open those gorgeous eyes and look at me so I know you're okay."

Addie pried her eyes open—not even realizing she'd closed them, and immediately locked them onto Phoenix. Crouched down to her level, he studied every inch of her face before moving down her body, his jaw tightening as he reached her sore wrist. A vein pulsed at his temple.

There was a little more space around them than before, East, Xavier, and Gavin at some point having jumped off the stage, providing a muscle-barrier while security hauled away the drunk jerk and kept the rest of the crowd at bay.

"Addie?" Cupping her cheek, Phoenix gently eased her gaze up to his. "Talk to me, baby." He glanced at someone over her shoulder and barked, "Where the hell are the medics?"

"I'm okay." Her voice sounded scratchy even to her own ears.

"No offense, but you don't look okay." Phoenix tucked a stray hair behind her ear, and cursed. "Fuck it. The medics are taking too long. We're going to them."

"What do you mean—"

Her question was cut off as he slipped his arms around her back and beneath her legs, and lifted her into his arms from a crouch as if she weighed nothing more than a feather.

"Phoenix!" Addie's eyes widened. "Put me down!"

"I'll put you down when we reach a medical bed and not a second before."

"But what about your performance?"

"Fuck the performance. It's not like they don't have other bands waiting in the wings." With a silent nod to East, they were off, the band paving the way through the crowd and Bailey and the others following closely on their heels.

A little woozy from the gentle sway of Phoenix's gait, Addie tucked her head into the groove of his neck and listened to the thundering stampede of his heart. Both the steady beat and his familiar scent comforted her like a warm blanket and she sank deeper into his embrace.

Phoenix exchanged a few words with someone next to him, and they changed direction as her head started spinning. The more time that passed, the more her head spun, taking her stomach along for the ride.

"I don't feel too good," Addie murmured.

Someone shouted "grab the trash can" a second before a plastic bucket hovered in front of her with not a moment to spare.

She retched, each nausea-inducing wave bringing a fresh surge of hell. Once her stomach was sufficiently emptied, the trash can disappeared and a wet washcloth took its place. She grimaced as she pressed the cool cloth to her face and willed the world to stop spinning.

People in scrubs walked in and out of what looked to be a tent, and other than the obvious medical personnel, the only person there besides her was Phoenix. He stood directly in front of her while she sat on what she now realized was a gurney.

"Bailey, Max, and the others are waiting outside," Phoenix stated. "They don't let anyone but patients in here."

"And you, obviously," Addie joked dryly.

He smirked, but the worry never left his eyes. "Well, I was literally carrying the patient, so they made some allowances. Plus, they couldn't get me to leave even if they used a fucking bulldozer."

"This seems like overkill. I got knocked down. I'm fine."

"Sorry, babe, but I'll need to hear that from the medical professionals before I actually believe it. And even then, we'll see."

Her gaze caught his and the continued worry etched on his face nearly undid her. She opened her mouth to say something when an older woman in dark blue scrubs and a stethoscope tucked into her pocket stepped forward.

"Hey there." She smiled warmly. "I'm Dr. Sethi. What's this I hear about a ruckus up by the stage?"

"Some guy got too handsy," Phoenix answered. "He gripped her wrist way too hard, and when things went to hell, she was knocked to the ground."

"All right, well, let's check you out . . ."

"Addie." Addie smiled wanly.

She lifted her left arm, noticing the very obvious bracelet bruise forming around her wrist. Phoenix's gaze dropped to it, too, and he cursed under his breath, muttering something about finding the asshole and punching him again.

Dr. Sethi poked and prodded, moving to her other hand to inspect her fingers that had been stepped on, and then she shone a ridiculously bright light into her eyes.

"Did you hit your head when you fell, Addie?" Dr. Sethi asked.

Phoenix remained deathly still at her side.

"Um . . . not when I fell."

"But you did hit your head?"

"I think so . . . ? It was pretty crowded, and I'm pretty sure someone accidentally kicked me in the head. I saw stars for a few minutes."

"And she threw up the second we got into the med tent," Phoenix added.

Dr. Sethi smiled in grim understanding. "It wouldn't be a surprise if you had a minor concussion."

"Should I take her to the hospital?"

The doctor glanced at Addie. "Did you lose consciousness?"

She shook her head and immediately regretted it. "No."

"Then I don't think you need an emergency room visit, but I do want you to treat yourself as if you have a concussion. We'll give you some acetaminophen right now, and you'll take it every six hours for any remaining headache. Do you have anyone to stay the night with you?"

"She does." Phoenix drilled Addie with a *try to argue with me* look that sent her eyes into a roll.

"Apparently I do, yes."

Dr. Sethi chuckled. "Then you'll need to be woken up every hour for the next twenty-four. If at any time you become confused, or unarousable, or if your headache worsens instead of improving, then it's time for that ER visit, okay?"

"Okay."

"Any questions?" Dr. Sethi glanced from Addie to Phoenix. "All right. Then I'll have a nurse bring over that acetaminophen and then we'll let you get home to rest. And that's a doctor's order, Addie. *Rest.*"

Phoenix chuckled. "It's like she knows you."

Addie grumbled under her breath, glad someone was having a good time. It didn't take long for the nurse to bring over the pain medicine, and then after a few signed papers, they stepped out of the medical tent and into a swarm of worried friends.

Maxi, Nai, and Bailey instantly wrapped her into a group hug.

"I'm okay. Seriously." Addie attempted to reassure them. "Just a few bumps and bruises."

Phoenix snorted. "And a concussion. I'm taking her home so she can rest."

"Are you sure you'll be okay?" Max nibbled her bottom lip, a nervous habit she'd had since they were kids. "Do you want me to go home with you?"

"I'm sure. And evidently I already have a babysitter for the night." Addie, more than ready to climb into her pj's and into her bed, kissed her sister on the cheek. "I'll call you in the morning and let you know when I'll be in the office."

"How about at not-happening-o'clock?" Phoenix accepted the shirt Easton tossed his way and tugged it on.

She shot him a glare but ignored the comment, too distracted—and bummed—about the disappearance of his nipple piercings.

Witnessing the disappointment on her face, Phoenix wrapped an arm around her waist and whispered seductively in her ear, "If you're a good patient, you'll see them again later."

Addie was determined to be the best patient ever.

18
PRETTY KITTY

Phoenix

Not trusting Addie wouldn't slip off the back of his bike, Phoenix exchanged keys with Xavier before heading home with a slightly loopy Addie tucked in his arms. She'd fallen asleep the second he buckled her into the passenger seat, her soft snores filling the truck's cab the entire ride to their building. He snuck incessant glimpses of her, making sure she was okay.

He now knew what people meant when they said they saw red.

From the moment that asshole first bumped into her, he'd been hyperaware and watching the guy's every move. The only reason he didn't hop off the stage at that first contact was because Addie was more than capable of putting that jerk in his place.

And she did . . . until things got out of hand and one thing led to another.

Phoenix wanted to kick his own ass for not acting sooner. If he had, he could've prevented not only the concussion, but the bruised wrist. He still silently berated himself as he parked in his garage spot and closed the driver's side door a little too hard.

The heavy thud woke a groggy Addie.

She unbuckled herself and was fumbling for the handle when he opened the door and held out his arms expectantly. "Your carriage awaits, princess."

"I'm perfectly fine walking." A hand to his chest, she gently pushed him backward and walked to the building entrance slowly, but on her own two feet.

He stayed close, prepped to catch her if she went down. "Definitely not rushing, but if you let me carry you, you'll get me shirtless again a lot quicker."

She chuckled and immediately groaned, rubbing her temple. "Don't make me laugh."

"Can't do. I love hearing it," he said honestly.

And truthfully, there was little he loved more.

"While tempting, I'll hoof it myself." Her small smile stole his breath nearly as much as her fingers sliding through his as she held his hand. "There was too much to-and-fro before, and I already threw up once tonight."

Phoenix tucked her in his arms, chin resting on the top of her head, as they rode the elevator up to their floor in companionable silence. They headed for Addie's apartment automatically, and Do-Re-Mi, as if sensing she didn't feel well, waited patiently for them to step inside.

"Go get into something comfortable," Phoenix ordered gently, "and once I feed the terrifying triplets here, I'll come and help you."

She rolled her eyes, but did as he requested. "I'm more than capable of putting on my own pajamas, rock star."

"I know. But if you do it by yourself, I don't get the pleasure of seeing if that red lacy thong really did come off your hot body." He winked, unable to help himself.

"You mean the red panties still on your head?" Her gaze gently lifted and a soft smirk raised the corners of her mouth.

Phoenix paused while filling the dog bowls and slipped his fingers through his hair before finding—and yanking—the sexy garment off his head. "No wonder I was getting looks every time we stopped at a red light."

Addie's soft laughter filled the apartment as she headed toward her bedroom. "Sorry to disappoint you, but those panties have never touched this body."

"Let me fantasize, okay?" Phoenix called out.

Phoenix quickly finished feeding the dogs and filled their water before digging through the fridge and grabbing something to make for Addie. By the time he finished a kick-ass PB&J, she'd stepped into the living room wearing cute fuzzy shorts and an oversized sweatshirt.

Looking fucking gorgeous, she settled on one end of the couch and pulled one of those gigantic knit blankets over her lap.

"You sure you don't want to climb into bed and get some sleep?" Phoenix eased into the spot next to her, careful not to jostle her too much as he handed her the plated sandwich.

"Not gonna lie. That thought crossed my mind, but I'm not quite ready for bed." She cast him a coy grin. "Why? Are you ready to call it a night already?"

"With you right next to me? Not in the least." He rested his arm on the couch, right behind her shoulders, and she nestled closer, tucking snugly into his side. "So what's on the agenda? Fireside stories without the campfire? A game of truth or dare? Although I should warn you, I almost always choose dare."

"Why does that not surprise me?" She giggled sleepily.

"I don't know. I've always thought myself a man of mystery." He grinned wickedly, waggling his eyebrows.

"No truth or dare, but I do have a question for you."

"Ask away."

"You seem to love pushing the limits. Why haven't you tried doing more with your music?" She glanced up at him with genuine curiosity shining in her eyes. "I don't mean the Stone Talons's music, I mean—"

"I know what you mean." He shrugged and took a nervous sip from his water. "You've obviously been talking to my sister."

"Maybe a little, but you mentioned before that you didn't really care for the rock star life and all the panty party songs. Why don't you step back from performing to focus on songwriting?"

"It's not like I haven't thought about it, but there's a couple reasons."

"Like?"

"Like I'd be letting the guys down, and those assholes are my family in every sense of the word. We all made a commitment to each other when we decided to go for it, and now that we're finally on the verge of making it big, I can't just walk away." He studied her expression as she listened intently. "Then there's also the fact that songwriting isn't a guarantee. When inspiration hits and the music flows, it's great. When everything is stagnant, it's . . . less great."

"And then you're forced to ask your neighbor—a publicly denounced Anti-Aphrodite—to play the part of your Muse so you can bust out some lyrics," Addie teased wryly.

"Exactly." Phoenix's fingertips absentmindedly stroked her arm. "The other risk of songwriting is that no one in the business will feel the same connection to your words as you do. It's a risky gamble in multiple ways."

"I get it. It's a little like how I feel about Happily Ever Forever."

His interest piqued, he tipped a glance in her direction and caught her nervously nibbling her bottom lip. "What do you mean?"

"In case you didn't already know, love and I have a love-hate relationship," Addie joked.

"*No*. Really?" Phoenix gasped. "I never would've guessed."

She smacked his chest playfully, making him chuckle. "But Max loves everything about love. It practically oozes from her pores. It's why we came up with the concept for Happily Ever Forever."

"You started it for Maxi."

"I didn't have anything else I wanted to do." She nodded. "But I've felt like imposter ever since. Sometimes I think all this bad luck we've been having—the catastrophic events and botched matches—is karma punishing me for trying to be something I'm not. Yet in a weird twist of fate, I still can't think of anything else I'd rather do."

"Maybe the two of you should switch roles," Phoenix suggested mischievously. "Shake things up."

"Put me in charge of finding someone's love match?" An open-mouthed, horror-struck look transformed Addie's face. "That would be worse than working with ten Karleigh Kinkaid-Finks."

They burst into laughter. Addie regretfully clutched her head with a groan, but giggles still slipped out. They temporarily tucked the serious question aside and turned on the TV before playing a round of rock-paper-scissors to pick their movie. Addie won and picked a horror flick. Before a massive boat anchor impaled the second victim, her soft snores filled the room.

Phoenix kept her close and finished the movie, waking her

once an hour as instructed by the doc. She grumbled adorably while he settled her down on the couch and tucked the soft blanket around her. Only when she fell back fast asleep did he glance at his phone.

A billion notifications lit up his screen, most tagged videos of him punching the asshole from Bands on the Beach. He didn't regret it one damn bit, except maybe not taking another swing. But the guy had been all talk, no bulk. Like most guys who pulled that macho shit.

Phoenix shut down his phone and tossed it aside.

The label would spin this one of two ways. They'd either celebrate him leaning into his Naughty Nix persona, or be pissed because it was a punch thrown defending someone. Phoenix couldn't give a rat's ass which path they chose. All that mattered was protecting Addie, and if Roger Kinkaid had an issue with it, he—and Marcus—could kiss his ass.

Addie

Addie winced as the throbbing headache from her dreams slowly followed her to waking life. She pried her eyes open one lid at a time, thankful for the room's relative darkness.

Her bedroom.

For the life of her, she couldn't remember how she'd gotten here because the last thing she remembered was telling the woman on the television screen to look behind her and not in the closet. Then, nothing.

Bits and pieces gradually returned.

Phoenix's arm wrapping beneath her legs—yet again. Him gently laying her on her bed and tucking the blankets around her as she burrowed into them like a caterpillar wrapped in its cocoon.

Not that she'd mind a few months' nap. That sounded pretty ideal right about now, exhaustion making it difficult to climb from bed and get her legs beneath her. She glanced at the bedside table, smiling when she saw the bottle of acetaminophen and a water bottle, little Post-its that said *swallow me* and *drink me* stuck to them.

Something about Phoenix Cross was so damn disarming, and she both relished it and feared it at the same time. He'd come to her defense, metaphorical—and literal—fists swinging, and then handled her with such gentle care as he shuttled her to the medical tent.

Before Phoenix Cross, no one carried her anywhere—except her father when she'd been five and in serious danger of peeing her pants because she'd downed three large ices and then they couldn't find the public restroom. In movies and books, nothing sent her eyes into a deeper eye roll than a *damsel* being swept off their feet by their muscled love interest.

Now?

She could almost see the appeal.

Almost.

Addie downed the medicine, hoping it worked fast, and padded barefoot into the short hall. A sweet, soothingly low hum drew her into the living room. Phoenix sat at her bay window, one knee propped on a cushion as he played his guitar. Sleeves rolled up, his tattooed arms flexed and bunched as he strummed the strings in an effortless motion.

She couldn't tear her eyes away from him.

Body relaxed, and a soft smile on his face, he obviously assumed he was alone. He stopped humming and jotted something in the book lying open in front of him, and then started again, an entire onslaught of emotions swimming over his face.

"That was beautiful." Addie announced her presence softly. "Is that one of the new Talons songs?"

Phoenix sat up straight instantly and eyed her from head to toe as she approached. "I was feeling a little antsy, but I didn't want to leave you alone tonight, so I went next door and got my guitar. I didn't wake you, did I?"

"Nope."

Phoenix closed the notebook and set his guitar aside as he opened his legs and crooked a finger. "How are you feeling? How's the head?"

He drew her into the open V of his thighs and pulled her close, hand resting low on her hip. Being in this position felt natural, her body content as his hand slowly slid up her arm and cupped her cheek.

Phoenix searched deeply into her eyes. "I was about to wake you up in ten minutes to make sure you're still you, and to take some more pain medicine."

"I saw your notes, and I already took them." She rested her hands and gently rubbed over his tensed muscles. "Now that my brain doesn't feel sludgy, I realized I forgot to thank you for diving into that mosh pit. And for getting me into the medical tent. And getting me home. And for staying with me tonight."

"What else would I do, and where else would I be?" He smiled at her, expression soft, and tucked a stray lock of hair behind her ear. "I'm just glad you're okay—as a whole."

"Will you get in trouble with Marcus for leaving the concert? And for punching a member of the audience?"

He shrugged. "First, that guy deserved so much more than the one single punch. Second, it doesn't matter if Marcus—or anyone else—has an issue with cutting things short. The moment that asshole laid hands on you, there was only one course of action."

His words warmed something inside, helping her see the appeal of the touch-her-and-die micro-trope found in a lot of romance novels.

Addie ran her fingers softly over his stubble. "You never answered my first question."

"Which was what?" He gently grabbed her hand, and kissed her palm before entwining their fingers.

"That pretty song you were just humming. Is that one of the new Stone Talons songs? Will you play it for me?"

He snorted. "No, and no."

"No?"

"It's definitely not on-brand for the Stone Talons, and as for playing it for you, it's not fit for anyone's ears just yet."

"What are the benefits of having a fauxmance if my fake boyfriend won't serenade me?" She pouted exaggeratedly and he chuckled.

"Once you're no longer concussed, I'll give you a firsthand demonstration of one of the perks of having a fauxmance with me as your fake boyfriend. But until then, remember the doctor's order? *Rest.*"

"You know," Addie leaned closer as she summoned her inner vixen, "Dr. Sethi said 'probably' concussed. There wasn't a definitive diagnosis."

Phoenix's lips twitched into a knowing grin. "Go twenty-four hours without a headache, and you're on."

"Really?" Addie began calculating hours.

"Really. A *non*-medicated twenty-four hours," he added.

And there went her idea of popping acetaminophen like Tic Tacs.

"Let's get the patient back to bed." Phoenix wrapped her legs around his waist and took her to the bedroom where he gently laid her on the center of her mattress.

"You know, they say orgasms are a great non-medicated form of pain relief," Addie said coyly.

"They say that, huh?"

"Yep. It works for cramps, too, and headaches are basically cramps of the head, right? I mean, you've already been so helpful today, it would be a shame not to keep the streak going."

He laughed, and much to Addie's excitement, slowly crawled onto the bed and over her until his arms and legs bracketed each side of her body. "That would be a real shame."

"Absolutely."

"Maybe I should give it some serious consideration."

"I would if I were in your shoes."

He brushed his mouth over hers in a soft caress of her lips, once, then twice. The third time, he deepened the kiss until her entire body breathed an excited sigh of relief. Slipping her fingers into his hair, she held him close and let her tongue play with his in an intimate give and take that had her quickly begging for more.

She emitted a little growl of frustration when he slowly pulled away.

Until he dragged his mouth down the curve of her neck . . .

Over her chest . . .

His hand, calloused from the guitar and drums, flirted with the bottom edge of her pajama top before sliding beneath and gently palming a heavy breast. Her body arched into his touch.

"No moving, love," Phoenix directed softly but firmly, his gaze locked on hers. "I'll give you that non-medicated orgasmic pain relief, but you better not move from this position. Got it?"

She bit her bottom lip to keep from whimpering, and nodded. "Yep."

He waited a beat, and then her shirt was pushed up and his mouth ghosted over her skin and down to her torso. He made quick work of her panties, sliding them down her legs and flinging them across the room.

"Such a pretty pussy," Phoenix murmured a second before he lowered his mouth and kissed her inner thigh. He slowly inched his way closer to where she wanted him, no doubt dragging the act out on purpose to make her squirm.

And she was squirming—or trying not to as he'd ordered.

He teased, kissing every inch of skin while carefully avoiding where she needed him most. And she did need him. More than her next breath. More than her next dose of pain meds.

When the tip of his tongue finally caressed over her clit, Addie saw stars, all air instantly sucked from her lungs.

He did it again and again, and soon it was nearly impossible for Addie to remain still. With Phoenix's head between her legs, she didn't once think about her headache. She rolled her hips, searching for more. More of Phoenix. More pleasure. More everything.

And she never wanted it to stop.

Phoenix devoured her, his desire-filled gaze locked on her as he nudged her closer to the edge. Her knees shook from her impending release, each breath more labored than the next as she slipped her fingers into his hair and pleaded for more.

With his mouth fused to her clit, he slid two fingers into her already quivering pussy and pushed her right over that cliff.

Addie fell apart.

And as Phoenix pushed her from one orgasm into another, prolonging her release just a little bit more, she felt him putting her right back together.

19

THE MAGIC PENIS

Addie

For the first time in a long time, the phones' constant ringing and the flood of incoming social media notifications didn't give Addie a headache, and that was saying something, since for the last three days, anything louder than a whisper seemed to bring one to the forefront.

But no headache. Lots of calls. And Addie couldn't help thinking things had finally turned a corner—and for once, *without* a head-on collision. The media pounced on the Jones Beach incident, most outlets dubbing Phoenix "the Nix in Shining Armor" for saving a damsel in distress, and while the entire blowup would normally send her sarcasm meter soaring to astronomical levels, it was exactly what they'd needed for this fauxmance to take off.

Love made people do the unexpected—according to the article title she'd read on her commute into the office, the article that *finally*—and blatantly—linked the Stone Talons's bad-boy drummer to the Anti-Aphrodite. Those very same people who'd chomped at the bit to kick her out of Nix's bed now loudly questioned how anyone *couldn't* believe them madly in love.

But the best news yet?

Crickets from Evelyn Sinclair.

Not a post. Nary a comment.

Intrusive photos aside, Addie finally didn't feel like hiding beneath her desk in the fetal position, and focused everything she had on the last-minute, magic-making plans for East and Naiomi's vow exchange. The fairy lights she planned on hanging in the barn and around the kissing tree had arrived earlier that morning, and thanks to Emilio's friend a few farms down, they'd secured more than enough wildflowers to not only create a gorgeous bridal bouquet, but bring a little of the outdoors into the barn.

Life was good.

"This day couldn't get any worse." Maxi burst into her office and dropped face-first onto the corner couch. "Fire me. Because at this point, you'd be better off having one of the Fury cousins take my place because I'm obviously not meant for it."

Addie sent her sister a supportive smile. "It can't be that b—"

"Bad?" Max's head swiveled to her and Addie fought not to wince.

Her sister's typically flawless, creamy complexion was splotchy and red, covered in what looked to be stress hives.

Maxi sat up with a huff. "You're right. It's not *bad*. It's appalling. Horrendous. Epically atrocious. Give me a thesaurus and I'll come up with more words for really, *really* bad."

"So the brunch cocktail hour isn't going well?" Addie guessed warily.

She'd thought it was a good idea, inviting a few current clients to a HEF-sponsored brunch and letting them mingle.

Low stress. No fuss. And by having everyone in one space, it would hopefully be easier to read the room and link any possible matches.

"Well, they say it's not a party unless the cops are called, so in that case it would be deemed a success," Max said dryly.

Addie's eyes popped. "Uh, excuse me?!"

Her sister waved her off. "It's fine now, but evidently client two-five-seven is a known felon with multiple aliases who's been scamming people out of their money for years and has somehow eluded authorities—until about fifteen minutes ago."

"At least they were caught?"

"Sure. And now the remaining clients—the ones who didn't leave—are trauma-bonding over the experience."

"At least that's . . . wait." Addie glanced at the open door. "If you're here, who's overseeing the brunch?"

Her sister avoided eye contact. "I may have told Bailey I had a DEFCON-1 bathroom situation."

"Was that the smartest idea, leaving them alone with clients, unsupervised? There's a reason why Bails is the person *behind* the socials."

"Fine." Max sighed. "But come with me and tell me that this brunch isn't a complete lost cause."

She wasn't sure how she'd do that, but in sister solidarity, she slipped her arm through Max's and they headed toward the small event space down the hall. It was basically a meeting room, but they'd pushed the long tables to the side and created a makeshift buffet station. There was coffee and juice, and a mini-mimosa fountain for those who needed a little extra kick to be social.

Addie realized what her sister meant by *atrocious* the second they stepped into the room.

It was *quiet*.

Like hear-a-pin-drop silent, so much so that Bailey's clunky platform boots sounded like thunder as they sauntered over. "Four more people left since you pretended to empty your bladder. Is it a bad sign when food and alcohol can't get people to stick around?"

"What about them?" Max nudged her chin toward a dark-haired duo off to the left. They both reached for a muffin and chuckled awkwardly . . . and started talking. "That looks promising. They look cute together."

Addie was already shaking her head. It didn't feel . . . right.

She scanned the clients. Most stood alone in the far corners of the room. One guy, leaning stiffly against the wall with his arms crossed, exuded grumpy pheromones and checked his phone approximately every five seconds.

Addie opened her mouth to suggest they shut things down and try another day with another group, when her eyes watered.

"No. No, no, no." She whipped off her glasses and pressed her palms to her eyes, already knowing it wouldn't help.

"Are you okay?" Maxi asked worriedly.

"No, I am definitely not okay." With a heavy sigh, she mentally prepared for what she already knew would be there, and looked over the room again.

And yep.

A glimmering gold toga cord encircled Mr. Grumpy Phone Watcher and stretched across the room, winding past two others before playfully wrapping around the ankle of the quiet dark-haired woman standing in front of the mimosa fountain.

Mr. Grumpy watched her for a few heart-pounding seconds before dipping his nose right back into his phone.

"Those two," Addie reluctantly admitted. "They'd be a good match."

"The muffin couple?" Maxi smiled. "I thought so!"

"No. Sir Grump-A-Lot and the Mimosa Lady."

"What about them?"

"See if they'll be interested in a one-on-one meeting."

Max's face twisted into a look of pure horror. "Why in the loving hell would I do that? They haven't so much as taken one look at each other, much less exchanged pleasantries. That's not exactly the actions of a soul tether."

"I don't know, Max." Addie sighed, mentally and physically drained. "I don't know what to tell you except that I think you should give it a try. What do we have to lose?"

"Not much." Max glanced from Grumpy to the Mimosa Lady. "I'll see what I can do and hope for the best."

"It'll be fine, sis." Addie pulled her sister into a side-hug and fought to get back her earlier positivity. "Good things are on the horizon."

"What good things?"

Addie shrugged. "Hell if I know."

Both Max's and Bailey's questioning gazes fell on her simultaneously.

"It must be the magic penis," Bailey said first. "I'm not sure what else would have had you doing a personality one-eighty."

Phoenix

When Phoenix woke up with a text from Marcus telling him about the meeting with Roger Kinkaid, he delayed the inevitable for as long as he could. Hell, he even contemplated claiming he'd lost his phone and not showing up at all, but reality settled in and he walked into the offices of NAS Records.

Albeit thirty minutes later than summoned.

"About damn time." Marcus strode across the lobby, his

usual mask of frustration and annoyance firmly in place. "I told you I'd send a car to pick you up. That way you wouldn't have to worry about finding parking for the bike."

"I didn't have a problem finding a spot."

"Then why the fuck are you a half hour late?"

"Don't you and Roger want me to start acting more like Naughty Nix? Time doesn't seem like something he'd be worried about." Phoenix shrugged, acting like an ass and not really caring. He glanced around the room, noting it was just him and Marcus, no other members of the Stone Talons present. "If this meeting is about what I think it is then it's pointless. I have better things to do than rehash the same old shit, Marcus."

"At this very moment, the label owns your ass, Phoenix. Your ass, your hands, and they have a firm grip on your balls, too. Regardless of how many times they want to rehash the same old shit, you'll do it. Without them, all those dreams of yours and the band go up in smoke."

Jaw clenched, Phoenix nodded noncommittally and followed his manager to the receptionist's desk. He verified their appointment and took them down a familiar hall. Usually, they met in one of the many meeting rooms, but they bypassed them all and were ushered through the last door.

Loud and imposing as the man himself, Roger Kinkaid's office screamed arrogance and wealth. Framed records and awards littered every inch of the bloodred walls, and what wasn't an award was a framed photo of him standing next to famous musicians.

Roger sat behind a massive black lacquer desk and glanced pointedly at the massive gold watch around his wrist. "Considering the lateness of your arrival, I'll get right down to it."

"Please do," Phoenix said, getting a stern look from his manager.

Kinkaid tossed a handful of article printouts and pictures onto his desk, a few of the larger headlines catching his attention. Phoenix had already seen most of them that morning, noting that most—if not all—in some way mentioned the altercation at Bands on the Beach.

"Headlines like these—if they continue—will undoubtedly affect promo for the upcoming album." Kinkaid leaned back in his seat, his gaze drilled on Phoenix.

"Aren't these the types of headlines that publicists salivate over? Punches were thrown."

"And a concert cut short because the drummer—and then the entire damn band—jumped into the fucking audience because some chick couldn't stand someone getting a little too close to her at a damn rock concert!"

Phoenix was ready to retort, but got jabbed in the ribs by Marcus.

"We know it wasn't an ideal situation," Marcus interjected, "but it was most definitely a onetime thing."

"Is it though?" Kinkaid questioned. "Because there's been an influx of reports coming in to the label, and they all revolve around Nix and one additional person. Adalyn Whitlock. There's actually quite an impressive amount of them."

Phoenix's spine stiffened as his asshole alert blared. "Did you mean for that to sound so stalkerish?"

Kinkaid flashed a forced smile. "NAS Records throws a lot into our investments, and whether or not you choose to believe that, that includes you, Phoenix, and your bandmates. I'd hate to see you squander all the opportunities for a piece of ass."

Jaw clenched so tightly his teeth ached, Phoenix crossed his arms over his chest and glared at the man behind the desk.

"Do not fuck this up, Nix," Marcus hissed under his breath.

Phoenix ignored him, matching Roger Kinkaid glare for glare. "You may have made an investment, but the last time I read through our contract—and yes, I do actually read them—there's no mention about the label—or you—having a say in who any of us date."

Next to him, Marcus muttered a string of curses, pinching the bridge of his nose.

Kinkaid raised his eyebrows. "*Dating*. The last update I received from Marcus on the situation indicated that what you shared with Ms. Whitlock was a Muse and Musician agreement. Is that no longer the case?"

Phoenix cursed under his breath . . . because yes, that's exactly what he'd told himself, too—and the label. But now? Now it felt like so much more.

It felt like . . . *everything*?

With no time to fully process his emotions—much less try to feel out Addie's—he was basically flying by the seat of his leather pants.

"Using her as your Muse, dating her, or fucking her. I don't give a shit." Kinkaid came around the desk, red-faced and fuming. "It's in your best interest to end it. As far as I'm concerned, she's not fulfilling her end of the agreement. Cut all ties now and the label will think about fronting the money to get someone straight from Muse Academy. Someone legitimate."

"Not interested."

"*Phoenix*," Marcus hissed.

"Not interested in what, exactly?" Kinkaid demanded.

"Ending it. Cutting ties. Muse Academy." Phoenix looked the exec dead in the eye. "Is that all? Because I have somewhere else I'd rather be."

Roger Kinkaid looked ten seconds away from blowing his

top. "Contract or not, Phoenix, you should remember that the label won't hesitate to do what's necessary to protect its interests."

Phoenix didn't hang around to listen to more. He stalked from the office and went straight for the elevator, Marcus catching up to him right when the doors opened.

"What the fuck—" Marcus started.

Phoenix snapped.

Fisting his manager's shirt, he pushed him hard against the wall, making sure he had his attention. "If you ever—and I mean *ever*—touch my shit without express permission, I will make you swallow your own fucking teeth. Do you get me?"

"You weren't exactly being forthcoming about the new music," Marcus blustered. "I had to—"

"Never. Again."

"Fine. Whatever." Phoenix released Marcus and his feet dropped back to the ground. "Fucking hell. Hope you know that Kinkaid was serious back there. He and his people will do anything to protect their investments—and like it or not, that includes you."

The second the elevator door opened, Phoenix stepped inside and counted down the floors until he could get the hell out of there.

Kinkaid could kiss his backside.

He may have invested in the Stone Talons and Naughty Nix, but he sure as hell had no rights to Phoenix Cross.

That bastard wasn't giving up Adalyn Whitlock without one hell of a fucking fight.

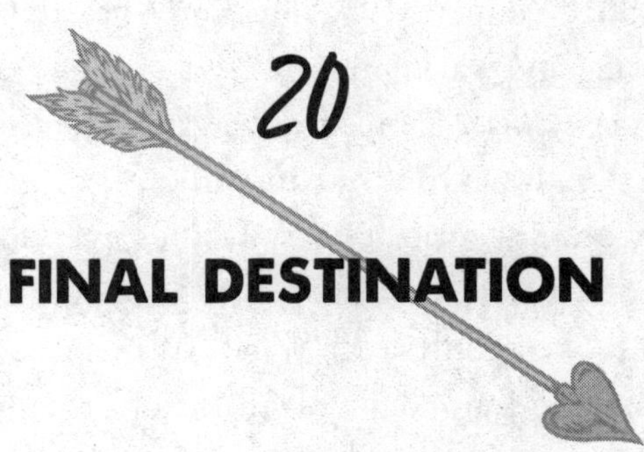

20 FINAL DESTINATION

Addie

Addie had gotten too many odd requests from bridal parties through the years to count them on her two hands, much less the hands of a Times Square crowd on New Year's Eve. If someone could think it up, it had probably been requested.

She learned to go with the flow, indulge when she could, and tactfully redirect when she couldn't—like the couple who wanted to parachute off the Empire State Building for their reception entrance. Neither groom took too kindly to the fact that the city had ordinances that prevented that kind of thing, and the person they saw do it in a movie had—in fact—not actually performed the act.

But for some reason, Naiomi's request to meet up at a little coffee shop just off Columbus Circle—in comfy shoes—topped even the parachuters. Maybe she just wanted an update on preparations—which were actually going well. Or maybe she'd changed her mind about having the Anti-Aphrodite plan her special day.

The worries tore through Addie's stomach until she stepped

into the coffee shop and was instantly greeted by Naiomi's beaming smile and warm hug.

The other woman glanced down at her sneaker-clad feet. "Oh, good. You wore your moving shoes."

"I also wore my curiosity cap. It's not every day I'm given absolutely no details about my plans for an evening."

Naiomi looked confused. "What? When I called the HEF office and offered it up, Bailey said you'd be totally thrilled."

Addie's confusion morphed into slow wariness. "Thrilled about . . . ?"

Naiomi's mouth opened to answer when the coffee shop doors opened, and Phoenix strode inside. His mouth pulled up into something of a smile, but it was far from the broad panty-melting, mischievous version that Addie had grown to expect.

"Got your message, sis." Phoenix stopped next to them, his hands shoved deep in his pockets. "What's up?"

Addie glanced at Naiomi expectantly.

"Okay, him I didn't tell," Nai admitted.

"Tell me what? You know I don't like guessing games, Naiomi." Phoenix's out-of-character grumpiness earned him looks from both Addie and Nai. "What?"

"Want to try that again, big brother? Maybe without the pointy spear up your ass?"

He threw out a heavy sigh, the tenseness of his muscles slowly relaxing. "Sorry. Just . . . shit happening at the label."

"Apology accepted." Naiomi's smile returned quickly as she lifted a black book bag from a chair and shoved it into his chest. "This is for the two of you. There's water, sunscreen, and some snacks. And a map of the park just in case you need it."

Phoenix blinked in confusion. "What the hell are you talking about?"

"A few months back, I signed East and me up for this Great

Amazing Hunt: Central Park thing, and as it turns out, I underestimated how much free time I'd have leading up to my presentation."

"What does this have to do with me and Addie?"

Addie nodded. "What he asked."

"Because it's a fun early evening of hilarity and fresh air, and ends with a romantic movie under the stars." Nai rested her hands on her hips. "And I already paid for it and there are no refunds, and if I can't enjoy it, then I want people I love to do so. Is that a sufficient enough answer?"

Addie recognized a bride close to the edge, and Naiomi Cross's balance was close to teetering.

"Absolutely." She took the book bag from Phoenix and flung it onto her back. "Thank you for thinking of us. As it turns out, I've wanted to do this scavenger hunt for a few years now, and I somehow always manage to miss the registration date."

"Liar," Phoenix mumbled under his breath, his mouth twitching at the corners.

Addie nibbled on her lower lip to keep from grinning back.

Nai was already collecting her purse, her job obviously done. "Great. So have fun. Make sure you put the sunscreen on since there's at least another hour of harsh rays ahead, and don't forget to take lots of pictures. And enjoy the movie, too—if you make it to the end. There's a picnic blanket in the bottom of the bag. Oh, and meet-up is by the statue outside in five!"

She waved and with a dramatically blown air kiss, left the two of them alone.

"So you had no idea about this, either?" Addie turned toward a too-quiet Phoenix.

His silence was a little disconcerting, but his lips twitched again slightly as he shook his head. "Not a damn thing."

"We could always tell her that we went and stalk the hunt's

social media accounts, so we know enough to answer any questions if she asks later," Addie suggested.

Phoenix laughed as he took the backpack off her shoulders and threw it onto his. "Knowing my sister, she'll use the Family Locator app to check our GPS coordinates, and even if she doesn't, she'll figure it out somehow. It's best to just do it and hope for the best. How difficult could it be? It's Central Park. As long as they don't make us do it on bikes, we'll be fine."

Fifteen minutes later, and Addie couldn't restrain her laughter at Phoenix's horror-stricken face. Not only did the organizers have bikes waiting for all the scavenger-hunt attendees, but they were two-person cycles, and required to travel from point A to point B.

Clearing her throat, Addie struggled to keep her voice neutral. "It won't be that bad. You ride a Harley, for crying out loud."

Phoenix's gaze snapped to hers. "Totally different machines, babe."

"Yeah, this one can't kill you if you fall off and it runs over you." Addie snorted at his unamused look and got onto the front bike. "This isn't a problem. I'll do the steering, and you just help pedal the damn thing. The rest will come naturally."

He grumbled, but climbed onto the rear seat before ripping open the clue envelope they'd been handed at the registration table. "'It's no Yankee Stadium, but . . .'"

Addie's brow furrowed. "No Yankee Stadium? The Mets Stadium?"

"Ha. Ha." Phoenix glanced around the area where they waited with all the other participants who were also trying to decipher their first clue.

Not all groups received the same one, the event coordinators staggering the locations so people didn't just follow the crowd, with the exception being the final destination. Everyone ended at the same location.

Suddenly, the clue hit Addie. "The ball fields. Unless you can think of something else. They said our track was the lower half of the park so that would make it—"

"The softball fields." Phoenix gripped his handlebars tight. "Lead the way, love."

They each pushed off the ground, and came to an immediate stop as the bike teetered precariously, unable to find their balance. They tried again, and again. After the sixth attempt, Phoenix cursed the tandem bike while Addie snorted with laughter at his frustration. The seventh time was the charm, and they wobbled their way in a somewhat steady path toward the softball fields.

With at least five fields in close proximity and all in tree-lined areas with bleachers, there was no telling where they'd find the next clue. Literally. On the left field, a group of young girls in mid-game huddled around their coach as their crowd of spectators cheered loudly from the bleachers.

Addie shifted her sunglasses and squinted against the fading sun until she saw a guy sitting among the crowd wearing the bright orange GAH T-shirt that matched the rest of the event staff.

Addie took hold of Phoenix's hand and pointed at the bleachers. "How much do you want to bet that's where we'll find the next clue?"

Phoenix spotted the guy instantly. "At least they're giving us hints to help us along the way."

Addie circled the bleachers while Phoenix looked underneath.

They met around the side where he climbed out, holding

another orange envelope and wearing a grin. "Want to perform the honors?"

She ripped into it and his hands wrapped around her waist from behind, chin propped on her shoulder. "'Take your stinking paws off me, you damned dirty ape.'"

Phoenix groaned. "That's too damn easy. They couldn't challenge us a little?"

Addie read the clue again, still confused.

"Wait. Don't you know what that quote's from?" Phoenix stared at her as if she'd sprouted a second head. "First you don't do the classic rom-com movies, and now you don't know this? Adalyn Love. Maybe we should rethink this romance."

His words, although said innocently, hit something that sent a painful zing through her chest. She rubbed the spot and breathed through the sting.

Romance. *Faux*mance.

It had been an innocent slip. Not even worth mentioning. But the longer she thought about it, the more difficult it became to suck in her next breath. Bailey's earlier teasing about blurred lines immediately surged to the front of Addie's mind.

No strings was never no strings.

Not in books or movies. And real life rarely followed the path you expected it to take, Fate loving nothing more than to shake things up with a quick, sharp veer to the right. And Addie knew that for a fact, considering her mother belonged to a book club with Clotho, Lachesis, and Atropos.

Fuck.

When did her path go rogue without her realizing?

"Hey." Concern shone from Phoenix's eyes as he cupped her face and steered it toward him. "You okay?"

"Yeah. No. I'm fine." She shrugged off the panic and dragged her focus back to the moment and the clue in her hands. "I have no idea where this is from, so do you want to enlighten me, or do you want to continue picking apart my movie choices?"

He repeated the clue in an obvious impersonation of someone else that didn't help in the least bit, and at her continued silence, he laughed. "My celebrity impersonations lack a little something to be desired, but come on. It's one of the most famous quotes from *Planet of the Apes*."

"And we do what with that clue? Charter a bus to take us there?" Addie asked sarcastically.

"I'm assuming it's telling us to go to the monkey exhibit at the Central Park Zoo." A grin in place, Phoenix gently pinched her chin and dragged her mouth to his for a soft, knee-quaking kiss. It stopped way too soon, and she groaned in protest. "You're so fucking adorable . . . and definitely getting a crash course in movie classics the second our asses are back on a couch."

They climbed back onto their bike and headed the half-mile toward the zoo, going straight to the monkey exhibit where they came across another Great Amazing Hunt organizer—and another clue. That clue led them toward Bethesda Fountain, where hordes of people mobbed the patio and more than four proposals were in process.

But no event organizer.

"Maybe it's not Bethesda Fountain." Addie turned in a slow, three-sixty spin, scanning the area. "Could we have gotten it wrong?"

"No, it's got to be here." Determination narrowed Phoenix's eyes as he looked around, too. "We're just not seeing it from the right view."

"Well, it's not like we have a hot-air balloon or a sky lift to change that and get an aerial view."

"Maybe not a hot-air balloon, but . . ." Phoenix shifted toward the fountain, the angel's wings expanded far behind their back. He grabbed her hand. "Come with me . . . and stay on the lookout."

"The lookout for what?"

"Park police."

"What?!" He dragged her to the edge of the fountain and kicked off his shoes.

It wasn't until he stepped onto the ledge of the fountain that she realized what he intended.

"Phoenix!" Addie gasped. "You cannot climb into the fountain!"

"Watch me. Besides, that's not all I'm climbing." With a grin and a quick kiss, he jumped into the fountain and waded through the water until he got to the base of the angel statue.

People stopped and stared, some murmuring to one another, which was saying something for New York. Typically it was eyes straight ahead and don't gawk, but people gawked and pointed, and a few pulled cameras from their pockets.

Addie already saw tomorrow's headlines: NAUGHTY NIX SWIMS WITH ANGELS.

She watched for the park police while Phoenix climbed on Bethesda Fountain's angel as if asking her for a piggyback ride. If someone didn't end the day in jail, or an emergency room, she'd call it a win.

"Sneaky fuckers." Phoenix, arm draped around the angel's shoulders, pointed toward the two-story archway. "Over there—under the tree."

"Okay. Good. Now get down before the cops come and arrest you or—" Her next words died on her lips as Phoenix's bare left foot slipped.

He hit the water ass-first, his massive body forming the mother of all cannonball splashes.

She ran to the fountain's edge as he wiped the water from his face and eyes.

His gaze caught hers before he broke out into typical-Phoenix laughter and opened his arms. "Come on, love. Want to come in and join me? The water's quite refreshing."

"No, thank you. I'll stay right here. Nice and dry." She giggled and shook her head, laughing harder when she realized that the tourists surrounding them were giving them a wide berth.

Phoenix got to his feet and Addie completely forgot about her scouting responsibilities.

His once-white T-shirt was now see-through and plastered to his body, both nipple piercings and tattoos on prominent display. More than a few people stopped to join in her ogle-fest, but Phoenix was oblivious to them all—except her.

His hazel eyes heated with unspoken promises as he stalked to the side of the fountain. "See something you like, love? Because I sure as hell do."

"Sir, step out of the fountain." A stern-faced park police officer prowled over. "Now."

"Sorry about that." Phoenix stepped out and grabbed his shoes. "Just needed a little refresh from the warm day."

The officer's gaze dropped to the envelope in Addie's hand and he scowled. "Damn fucking scavenger hunt. Every damn year."

He tromped away, muttering under his breath.

"Guess we're not the only ones who took a dip." Phoenix chuckled.

"Uh, *you* took a dip," Addie corrected. Phoenix shifted as if to draw her into a hug. "Touch me right now and I'll throw you back into the fountain. I don't want to spend the rest of the day wet and chafing."

A wicked grin slid onto Phoenix's face as he leaned closer and whispered, "But I like you when you're all wet, love."

Addie's mouth dried up and her mind instantly blanked to everything but the sway of Phoenix's ass as he headed toward the final clue.

"Let's go, love." He tossed a wink over his shoulder. "There's not much time left for you to claim your reward."

For some reason, Addie felt like she already had.

And that fucking scared the crap out of her.

Phoenix

His quick dip in Bethesda Fountain efficiently washed his bad mood away.

Actually, that wasn't true.

Laying eyes on Addie in that café did it.

Little snippets of his interaction with Kinkaid and Marcus had tried pushing their way through, but the more Phoenix focused on Addie and the present, the more his mood improved.

Now, with Belvedere Castle looming in the distance and the Shakespeare Garden set up for a movie under the stars—their reward for making it through the Great Amazing Hunt—Phoenix kept everything but Addie in the background.

She spread Nai's blanket from the backpack on the grass, far enough away from any other participants that they could pretend to have their own private viewing, and pulled out a few snacks as he walked up with cold water supplied by the event organizers.

"Sounds like we're in for a real treat for tonight's flick," Phoenix teased. "Talk about cinematic classic."

Addie looked wary as hell. "Please tell me it's not *Planet of the Apes*."

He chuckled. "Nope. But we are at a castle so it's *The Princess Bride*."

He waited for her reaction . . . and waited. He climbed behind her on the blanket and pulled her deep into the V of his thighs. His chest, still a little damp from his earlier swim, pressed against her warm back. "Please tell me you've—"

"Yes, I've seen *The Princess Bride*." She gifted him a smart-ass over-the-shoulder eye roll.

"Did you have a thing for the Dread Pirate Roberts? Because Naiomi sure did. Caught her kissing her pillow once and murmuring, 'Oh, Westley.'"

"Actually, I was more Team Fezzik. And Inigo Montoya. And I kinda rooted for the oversized rat things to eat Buttercup."

Phoenix enjoyed the way Addie melted into his hold as he pulled her closer. "Are you telling me that Adalyn Whitlock has always had a secret thing for *bad boys*? Wow. Just when I didn't think I was capable of being surprised, you manage to do it yet again."

"They weren't bad . . . they were just severely misunderstood."

"Fezzik and Inigo, sure. But the rats?" Phoenix tucked his nose into the curve of Addie's neck and ran a trail of kisses down to her shoulder.

If anyone asked him what bliss smelled like, it was Addie. Honeysuckle and sunshine. Even after their day biking around the park.

His fingers teased the bottom hem of her shirt, knuckles brushing against her soft skin. By the time the movie started, all he could focus on was the woman in his arms and his desperate desire to get her home and alone.

She tipped her head back and pulled him down for a slow, seductive kiss that brought his cock to life.

"Keep that up and you'll get me in trouble for public indecency and I've already had my one brush with the law today." Phoenix nipped her bottom lip playfully and got a naughty smirk in return.

"And here I thought you liked living dangerously," Addie teased.

"Point made." Cupping her cheek, he eased her mouth back toward him and kissed her until they both parted, breathless and panting.

"Well, you got your wish, rock star."

"What wish was that, love?"

Addie turned back toward the movie with a wicked grin. "Now we're both wet and uncomfortable."

21

SECRET TRIPS & SKINNY DIPS

Addie

Five days until Nai's (and East's) day.

Two till a promised Phoenix and Addie naked fun time.

Tomorrow, the Indie Rock Awards.

And now?

Attacking the to-do list from hell.

Every time Addie crossed one thing off, two more appeared. She and Phoenix, along with Bails and Maxi, showed up at Emilio's place ridiculously early to navigate deliveries and make final preparations in the barn.

Hours into the day and things were finally taking shape. White fairy lights wrapped around the banisters and Addie already had the lantern globes prepped and ready to hang from the rafters. When guests returned to the barn after the vow exchange, the place would be alight with a magical glow and ready to celebrate the happy couple.

Weather anchors predicted an unseasonably warm day for ceremony day, so Emilio suggested opening both ends of the barn to allow for a sweet cross breeze. Altering their original idea a smidge, they'd extend the seating to encompass both the indoor barn and outdoor area, allowing people to stretch their wings and dance under the stars.

Addie hung the last string light and climbed off the step stool to check her handiwork. "Damn, I'm good." She gifted herself a mental pat on the back for a job well done, and checked another item off her list. "We may actually get this done in time."

Phoenix stepped into the barn and immediately evaporated that optimism with a dour look.

"No." Addie shot him an only half-joking warning glare. "We can't afford any bad news. Make it go away."

Phoenix's lips quirked. "Before you panic, it's completely fixable."

A massive list of possible problems rushed to the forefront of her mind, making her head spin.

"Hey." Phoenix wrapped his arms around her waist and tugged her in for a warm, tight hug.

The man really had no business smelling as good as he did while standing in the middle of a barn after hard manual labor for half the day. Still, she wrapped her arms around him and inhaled his natural woodsy scent. Almost like catnip, it immediately settled her nerves.

"When you're done sniffing me like a weirdo, I'll tell you what we're dealing with here," Phoenix teased, chest rumbling with a deep chuckle.

Her head lolled backward to peer up at him. "Okay. Hit me with it. It's the wagons, isn't it?"

"Yeah. Emilio uses the one wagon routinely, so it was kept in pretty good shape, but the second? Not so much. In our eagerness to test out the wheels, the rusted axle shattered into red powder. We've got a dead wagon."

"And that's fixable how? Can we run to the hardware store and pick up another one?"

"Nope." Phoenix grinned. "But Emilio has a friend one town over that has a spare wagon that they already said we can use. He's heading over now to pick it up."

"That's great news. What's the downside?"

"The friend's a bit of a gabber, so it may be a while before Emilio can get back. When he does, we'll see what kind of repairs it might need, or what kind of makeup we'll have to slap on it to make it look rustic chic and not—"

"Rusted."

"Exactly. Emilio said we have at least two hours to kill."

"Oh. Okay." Addie glanced around the barn and the tables that had arrived earlier that day. "Honestly, there's not much else to do around here until the actual day."

Mischief glinted in Phoenix's hazel eyes as he slowly dropped his face down to hers. "That almost sounded like we have free time."

"It did, didn't it." Addie's heart pounded in her chest.

"Free *alone* time."

Nervous excitement warmed her from the inside out. "What do you want to do with all that alone time?"

He caressed his lips over hers in a faint touch that left her body tingling. "Do you want to drive the ATV again?"

Addie paused and laughed. "Okay, that's definitely not where I thought we were heading with this. Where are we taking the ATV?"

"To one of *my* favorite spots on the farm."

Eagerness to learn more about the complicated man in front of her had her already walking toward the ATV parked just outside the barn, Phoenix's chuckle following behind.

At their first meeting, he'd exuded cocky playfulness and

an I-take-nothing-seriously attitude. He'd joked—*a lot*. He'd leaned in to the Naughty Nix persona almost as if it were a crutch, a backup to use if things got a little too real.

And boy did she know how that felt.

But the more time they spent together, the more Addie saw *Phoenix Cross*. A man with an unhealthy attachment to eighties and nineties rom-coms. Talented songwriter and hopeless romantic. A guy willing to put his own dreams on indefinite hold to see his friends' dreams come to fruition. Doting son. Protective brother.

Amazing lover.

Phoenix Cross was what Aphrodite would call *a balm to the heart*.

Goddess knows he'd somehow brought calm and comfort to her own chaotic, view-distorted life.

With Phoenix's directions, Addie guided the four-wheeler in the opposite direction of the kissing tree. The farther they went, the closer they got to the heavy thicket of trees identifying the end of Emilio's property.

And a beautiful natural pond, its surface twinkling like diamonds sprinkled across its surface.

"Welcome to Lazy Lagoon." Phoenix jumped off first and easily lifted her off the seat. "At least that's what I call it. After finishing my daily chores, I came here. The amount of times this water has seen my naked ass may surprise you."

Addie snortled. "Probably not."

She turned and found Phoenix unbuttoning his pants.

"What are you doing?" Slight panic bulged her eyes.

"I know we're not completely done with today, but we almost are. I'd hate to break tradition."

"Break tradition by not getting a parasitic infection from

swimming naked in stagnant water?" Addie's gaze dropped along with his pants—and boxer briefs.

Phoenix kicked them away, grinning. Half-hard and with a little twitch, his cock bobbed heavily against his thigh before slowly rising the longer she stared. She'd been so mesmerized by what Bailey called his *magical penis* that she didn't realize he'd shed everything.

"I've swum naked in this pond dozens upon dozens of times and haven't gotten an infection of any kind."

He gave her ample ogle time as he slowly stalked her way, and the closer he got, the more her body hummed.

It physically pained her to back up a step, but she did. "You go ahead and live your best skinny-dipping-in-questionable-water life, and I'll stay here. Nice and dry. And parasite-free."

"Where's your sense of adventure? Didn't that adventure bug bite you during the scavenger hunt?"

"Sure. And I stayed clothed and dry. Come to think of it, you went diving into questionable water that day, too. I'm starting to think you're a daredevil under all those tattoos."

She took a final step back. Her heels hit the side of the ATV and brought her to an abrupt stop.

"Phoenix . . ." Hands raised, she warned him off with her palms as if she had the magical ability to create some kind of force field.

She did not.

He leaped and she squealed, making a mad dash around the four-wheeler, but barely skirted around the back end when his arms hauled her off the ground.

"Phoenix, please." Addie squirmed as he walked them to the edge of the swimming hole.

"This is your last chance, love." His mouth brushed against

her ear as he took the first step into the water. "Accept your fate and let's shimmy you out of these clothes, or you're going in—clothes and all."

"I am not spending the rest of the day in sopping-wet jeans," Addie insisted adamantly. "Okay. Fine. Put me back on dry ground and I'll get undressed."

He paused as if judging her sincerity before stepping back and putting her on dry land. "I'll be watching you . . ."

He stepped back toward the water and did just that, eyeing her with an unmistakable hungriness as she yanked off her shirt and bra and tossed it on top of his clothing.

When they both stood there naked, all sign of the playful Phoenix who'd threatened to toss her in the pond was gone, leaving behind nothing but desire and need.

Addie needed Phoenix Cross against her body—and inside it—more than she needed her next breath.

Phoenix hauled her into his arms and against his chest, trapping his cock between their bodies as his large palms gripped her ass in a silent demand. She locked her legs around his waist instantly, and he carried them back to the water.

Addie tried not thinking about the murky depths and focused on the man hotly pressed against her flesh, the one eliciting an entire onslaught of feelings she couldn't decipher without a few hours of serious reflection and a pitcher of frozen margaritas.

Water up to their waistlines, Phoenix took her mouth in a searing kiss that vibrated her body all the way to her toes. Hell, her hair felt it. Or that could be his hand, fisted in her messy ponytail as he angled her mouth in the best position to devour her.

"I need you, Phoenix," Addie murmured against his lips. "Fuck. I can't believe we're about to do this in a bacterial playland."

Phoenix rolled his hips and his engorged cock slid against her pussy entrance. "Do you want to do this on dry land?"

"I want to do this *now*."

Phoenix chuckled at her surliness and playfully nipped at her bottom lip. "Then I guess it's a good thing Emilio treats this water routinely in the summer months since he has campers who come for weekend events. This swimming hole is probably more hygienic than most public swimming pools."

Addie couldn't even chastise him for teasing her. She ached to be filled, and the longer they took, the worse that ache got. "We're covered on my end if you don't want to use a condom."

Phoenix's eyes darkened as he visually devoured every inch of her face. "I'm covered, too. But are you sure that you're okay with it?"

"I'm good. Perfect even." She dug her hands into his hair and yanked his mouth closer. "Now fuck me."

Phoenix grinned against her lips. "As you wish."

Phoenix thrust up as she sank down. They both groaned, and Addie's ache turned to full-blown pleasure.

No way could she ever get used to this. This *did* feel perfect.

Perfectly pleasureful.

Perfectly right.

Perfectly all-consuming.

And with perfect clarity, Addie Whitlock was falling for Phoenix Cross, and she was falling hard.

Phoenix

What once came in gradual, satisfying bursts since laying eyes on Adalyn Whitlock, now bombarded Phoenix from all angles.

Music.

Notes *and* lyrics, and so much more.

He hummed quietly in his head, fingers ghosting above his guitar strings. He didn't want to wake her where she slept in his bed, a gorgeous, peaceful smile gently tilting up the corners of her mouth. Common sense said he should go into the other room, but he couldn't. He couldn't take his eyes off her and completely accepted that it sounded a bit stalkerish.

Something that had hovered over them the entire day at Emilio's shifted back at the swimming hole. He didn't see it, but he could sure as hell feel it.

In the air. In his heart. In Addie.

In the *music*.

Phoenix's gaze strayed over Addie's naked body, wrapped up in his bedsheet, and the heavy rightness of it invited the music in as he grabbed his journal:

Before you, the world was dark and grim.
A quiet battlefield.
Loud with overwhelming silence.
My future dim.

Phoenix reread the newest bridge over and over before flipping the notebook and diving into the chorus and tweaking a few words. He played around with the intro and got so much closer to accurately depicting the storm of emotions rumbling inside.

He jotted down another change when Addie's green eyes fluttered open, heavy with sleep. "Were you just singing or did I dream that?"

"You may have heard a hum or two." He climbed back onto the bed and pulled her into his arms. She turned in to him instantly and nestled into the curve of his shoulder.

"Something . . . uncorked. It's like I can almost hear an entire song in the background."

Excitement snapped her eyes open a little wider. "Really?"

He stroked a finger down the length of her spine and savored her little shiver. "Really."

"Well, what I heard sounded peaceful. Beautiful."

"Most of it is."

"Only most?"

"It's a bit of a before-and-after glimpse. The *before* isn't quite so peaceful . . . but the *after*? Blissfully so."

A small smile worked its way onto her lips. "I like that."

"I do, too."

She sat up and swung a leg over his waist until she sat astride him. "So when am I allowed to hear this before-and-after for myself?"

"When it's done."

"Which will be . . . ?"

He chuckled. "Careful there, love. You almost sound like Marcus."

She smacked his chest playfully, and he caught her wrist before bringing it up to his mouth to kiss the sensitive skin inside.

"I want to make sure it's perfect before you hear it," Phoenix admitted. The song was still in fragments lined up in his journal and he already felt as if he was exposing a bit of his soul.

Making it perfect also meant untangling the rampant emotions surging through him, and then expressing them in a way that didn't send Addie screaming for the hills. The last thing he wanted was to chase her away with the depth of his feelings for her, which he'd come to realize were core-of-the-earth deep.

"Fine. I'll put on my patient pants." Addie trailed her mouth over his chest. Her pink tongue teasingly flicked his left piercing before sliding over to do the same to the right.

He smirked, adoring her playfulness. Actually, he adored all her sides.

He sank his fingers into her hair as she went lower, and lower, until her soft hand wrapped around his already hardening cock. "Fuck, love."

She hummed against his tip before brushing it with her cheek. "Is all of this for me?"

"Every inch. Think you can handle all of it?"

"Only one way to find out." No hesitation. No little licks. She took him into her mouth, practically taking his entire length in one go.

Phoenix threw his head back with a groan as she took more and more of him, her fist tightening around the base of his cock. She lifted and sank back down, setting a pace that quickly drove him to the edge of release.

"Fuck, baby." His grip on her hair tightened and her eyes snapped up to his. "Your mouth feels almost as good as your pussy."

She hummed around him and the vibrations sent a bolt of pleasure right to his aching balls. He panted, and Addie, encouraged by the sight, let him pop out of her mouth before she sank back down, taking him straight into the back of her throat.

She bobbed up and down, her eyes never leaving his as she read every one of his silent cues, giving him what he wanted before he even knew for himself what that something was. Precum leaked from his tip and she lapped it up, its appearance spurring her on.

"I want to be inside you when I come, and I want to feel your pussy coming around me when I do," Phoenix panted.

Addie immediately released him with a wet pop just as he yanked her up and tossed her onto her back. She giggled as she bounced, and the sound was like music to his ears.

Her eyes lit brightly with arousal as she opened her legs and exposed her already dripping pussy. "We really don't need any foreplay, so—"

He needed no further encouragement. Gripping her hips, Phoenix lifted her ass off the mattress and slammed into her in one thrust. Addie's pleasured shout echoed through the room as he bottomed out and did it again.

With every meeting of their bodies, Addie begged for more. For everything.

That's what he wanted, too.

To give her more pleasure.

More orgasms.

More laughter.

Bodies and gazes locked, Addie's pussy gripped him in a tight, pulsating vise and sent them over the edge together. Wave after all-consuming wave washed over them, and they held on to each other, barely keeping each other afloat.

When the last ripples eased away, Phoenix dropped to her side and tugged her into the protective circle of his arm. Sated and sleepy, she snuggled into his chest with a breathy sigh.

There was only one thing Phoenix couldn't give her.

His heart.

Because she already possessed it.

22

NERVOUS NIX

Phoenix

Nausea curled low in Phoenix's stomach, growing far beyond the motion sickness that usually plagued him when he sat in the back of big cars and limos. He also usually blamed big public appearances, and the Indie Awards was the biggest one for the Stone Talons yet. Hell, he could even blame the gas station breakfast burrito he'd devoured earlier that morning against his better judgement.

But the truth was he was seconds away from seeing Addie, and after the music-filled revelations last night, his jumbled feelings for the sassy demigoddess were a hell of a lot less tangled.

"Will you stop with the knee bouncing?" Naiomi stilled his leg. "You're acting like you've never been to one of these things before."

Next to her, Easton grinned wickedly. "He hasn't been to one with a certain gorgeous woman on his arm, so it's a little bit different. And because it is different, photographers are gonna throw a spotlight on him that's larger than the fucking Bat-Signal."

Phoenix stopped bouncing his leg and shot his friend a glare. "Seriously? That's not helping."

"I'm sorry, was I supposed to be helping?"

"I still don't know why you're so worked up," Naiomi interjected. "You handle the press probably better than anyone in the group. And you're not a monk who's never been on a da—" His sister's face slowly eased into a grin that matched her fiancé's. "*Oh*. Your stomach's doing the jig because the woman on your arm is *Addie*. Is Naughty Nix . . . *nervous*?"

Phoenix wouldn't confirm nor deny that statement because the second he denied it, his sister would call him out on his bullshit answer and he had enough on his mind to not want to add familial taunting to the evening.

Tonight needed to go well. No hiccups, fuckups, or muckups. And once the circus portion of the evening was done, he'd lay everything out there.

For him, this was no longer a fauxmance.

Maybe it never was. Maybe he'd tricked himself—and her—into thinking there wasn't something there from the very beginning. He wouldn't find out until he got this damn award show and after-party out of the way.

Ignoring the soft snickers from his sister and best friend, Phoenix glanced out the window as the limo slowed to a gradual stop in a Brooklyn neighborhood and compared it to the address she'd texted him earlier.

"This is it." Phoenix tossed Naiomi a warning look. "Are you going to be on your best behavior? If not, we're sending you right back to the library to continue your studying."

She stuck her tongue out at him and he climbed out from

the back. By the time he stepped onto the curb, the door of the single-story ranch home had opened.

Phoenix missed a step and stumbled, making a complete fool of himself.

"Have a nice trip?" Addie's peach-tinged lips curled into a teasing smirk.

"Adalyn." He detached his dry tongue from the roof of his mouth. "Fuck. You look incredible."

A blush rose up on her cheeks. "Thanks. You don't look too shabby yourself."

"Is this when I warn him that he better have you back by midnight?"

The redhead rolled her eyes and shifted, giving Phoenix a view of Maxi and an older man standing just behind. With matching auburn hair and familiar eyes, there was no doubt this was her father.

"Mr. Whitlock." Phoenix hustled up the steps, his hand extended. "It's nice to meet you, sir. I'm Phoenix."

"I know who you are. I googled you the second I saw your mouth attached to my daughter—along with thousands of other baseball fans." The elder Whitlock folded his massive arms over his chest. "You've been parading my girl all over this damn city and you're only now introducing yourself?"

"Pop!" Addie's wide eyes shot her father a warning look.

"No, he's right. We should've been introduced long before now. My parents would give me a hard time about it, too, if they knew this was the first time."

"Good." Addie's father took his hand in a firm grip. "You know there's a lot of information about you on the internet, right?"

Phoenix grimaced. "I'm sure it made for some entertaining reading."

Mr. Whitlock grunted. "It's a good thing I'm a man who likes making his own decisions. It's nice to meet you, Phoenix . . . and your manners."

Addie cleared her throat. "We should probably get going."

A wolf whistle pierced the air, and Naiomi, half-leaning out of the limo, waggled her eyebrows. "Damn, Addie! They won't need the smoke machine tonight because they can just use the smoke coming off you! Hubba-freaking-highway!"

Phoenix rolled his eyes, but Addie laughed. "We're sharing a limo with East and Nai, as you can tell," he said. "Hope you don't mind."

"A limo, huh? It kinda feels like prom."

After a round of goodbyes, they headed to the limo, Phoenix holding the door open and giving Addie his hand.

"Problem?" he asked when she paused.

She sighed. "Don't look down when I bend over to get in."

"Well, now that you told me *not* to . . ." Phoenix teased. She tossed him a heated glare and he laughed, raising his hands in surrender. "I kid! I kid!"

He glanced away and allowed her to slide in before following, and then they were off, Nai and Addie chatting like long-lost best friends. They talked about Nai's final presentation and Addie offered to give her a wedding update, to which Nai slapped her hands over her ears, begging not to know a thing.

They all laughed and chatted, and it damn near felt . . . normal.

"It's almost time to walk the plank and drop into shark-infested water," Nai grumbled out the window before sending Addie a warm look. "You sure about this? You can change your mind."

"Hey now." Phoenix dropped his arm over the back of Addie's seat. "Don't go scaring off my date. It's not that bad."

"You're right, it's worse." Nai nodded. "But it'll all be fine. Stick to Phoenix, smile like you just inhaled laughing gas, and just think of later tonight when you'll get to climb into your pj's."

"You make this sound like a big ball of fun." Addie's voice wavered slightly.

"The music part is fun. They really go all out for the performances, and then the after-party is always good for a few laughs—or so I'm told. Someone always ignores their Honey, No person, and does something stupid. With this group, it's usually Gavin."

"Honey, No person?"

"Honey, No." Phoenix chuckled. "It's the person who stops you from saying or doing something stupid in the heat of the moment. That last-minute-voice-of-reason person who poses the question, 'Maybe you should think twice before you do what you're about to do?' Easton is usually mine."

East snorts. "And he ignores me about eighty-five percent of the time."

"No, I don't. I hear you. I think about it. I just feel like going ahead and doing it anyway."

Everyone laughed, including Addie, which was what Phoenix wanted . . . to take her mind off what was about to happen in a few seconds. But as they pulled up in front of the concert hall and into the long line of waiting limousines, her gaze drifted to the horde of media on either side of the blue carpet.

"Holy shit," Addie whispered, her eyes transfixed on the massive gathering. "Bailey was right."

"It's not as bad as you think," Phoenix tried putting her mind at ease.

"So you're saying they're not as feral as a zombie horde anxiously looking for their next meal?"

"Nah."

"Really?"

"Nope. They're a feral zombie horde looking for their dessert," Phoenix added teasingly. "Big difference."

Addie fiddled with the hem of her gorgeous dress as an attendant opened the passenger door. Phoenix nodded for East and Nai to climb out first, and the second they did, cameras flashed and reporters called out to the soon-to-be-wed couple.

Phoenix dropped his hand to Addie's bare knee and her body froze, gaze snapping to meet his.

"Let me go first," he offered. "I can be your barrier wall while you get out."

She flashed him a breathtaking smile that sucker-punched him straight in the gut. "Thank you. There are enough stories floating around about me right now. I didn't really want to add thong-flasher to the mix."

Phoenix climbed over her to head out first and his dressy boot—not one of his preferred footwear—slipped. He plummeted into Addie's lap, the surprise eliciting a startled yelp from the sexy redhead. He tried righting himself and slipped again, this time with his face landing a mere inch from the deep plunge of her cleavage.

They both froze, Phoenix's hands planted on either side of her knees as he slowly tilted his gaze up and stared at her from between her luscious breasts.

A merging of reality and his fantasies temporarily stole his ability to move—or think of anything beyond Adalyn's sweet honseysuckle scent.

"That took an unexpected turn." A cute little snort escaped Addie's throat, and they both laughed.

"No way could I have pulled that off if I tried. Well, maybe if I *tried*. I mean, the second I laid eyes on you I imagined myself on my knees and between your—never mind."

Bright flashes snapped them back into the present—and to the photographers attempting to snap a few pics of their current conundrum.

"Fucking hell." With a growl, Phoenix climbed out of the limo and used his bigger body to push the assholes back, and in a blink, East and the event security were there helping to do the same.

Phoenix waited until the reporters had been pushed back behind the ropes, and held out his hand, doing as he'd promised and using his body to block her exit from the limo from prying eyes.

"Thanks." Her cheeks flushed as she slid her soft hand into his calloused one and joined him on the walkway.

Hand palming the small of her back, he stood close and let her eyes adjust to the bright flashes. "You okay?"

She nodded faintly, not meeting his gaze.

Phoenix gently pinched her chin and tilted her face up to his. Uncertainty was written all over it, emphasized by the slight dip of her pretty mouth. "If you've changed your mind, we'll climb right back into this limo and go home, or get Soprano's pizza. Whatever the hell you'd rather do."

"It'll be a little hard to accept your award, or perform, from the back of a limo," she stated wryly. "Or at Soprano's."

He shrugged. "Seems like a problem for Naughty Nix, not Phoenix. Right now, you're my only concern."

Her long lashes fluttered as she tried—and failed—to mask her surprise.

But damn it, he was serious. The last thing he wanted was to put her in an uncomfortable situation.

"I'm okay. Let's go and dive into the deep end." She patted his chest, and automatically he slid his palm over the back of her hand, holding it in place as he questioned her silently with another look. "Seriously, Phoenix. It's okay. Let's do this."

He waited a beat before nodding. "All right then. Let's do this."

He flashed her a wink and stepped to the side, keeping his arm around her waist. Lights flashed continuously, more abundantly the farther onto the blue carpet they walked. East and Nai waited for them a few feet away, Phoenix's sister flashing Addie a supportive smile and small nod.

Safety in numbers was definitely the way to go.

Addie

One foot in front of the other. Don't trip. Keep your gaze moving and never lock eyes.

All sage words of advice given to her by Naiomi, and Addie tried her best to do all of it, especially not tripping over her own feet and falling flat on her face. They walked slowly, Phoenix and East stopping occasionally to sign a few autographs for the eager fans lining the ropes. A few screamed so loud her ears rang, and she couldn't help but snort when one excited woman asked Phoenix to sign the top curve of her boob.

Phoenix always stopped and made sure she was okay before leaving her, and then quickly returned, his arm slipping effortlessly back around her waist. People called to him, asking if he really was taken—and he just smiled and winked, easing them farther down the carpet as the crowd went ballistic.

At the steps of the massive concert hall, a man she didn't recognize parted the sea of people and headed straight for them.

His dark eyes narrowed into a glare focused on Addie before shifting to Phoenix and East. "About damn time you two showed up."

"Hello to you, too, Marcus." Phoenix patted Marcus on the shoulder and he winced. "And we showed up exactly when we were supposed to. We strutted. We waved. We signed some autographs."

"Yeah? Did the two of you talk to *Music Entertainment* and *Mic Drop*?" As East and Phoenix exchanged looks, he sighed. "I thought not. East, go over to *Mic Drop*. Nix, you go to *ME*. Then get inside and find your seats with Gavin and Xavier. I want you all seated before the cameras start sweeping the audience."

"Will do." East nodded, and after shooting Phoenix a knowing smirk, led an eye-rolling Naiomi to the left.

Phoenix, his palm slowly traveling to the small of Addie's bare back, nudged them right. "Let's get this over with. The sooner we make Marcus happy, the sooner we can get away from these cameras."

"He's a warm ball of sunshine," Addie quipped, making Phoenix chuckle.

"As our manager, it's his job to be a ball of sunshine, and honestly, I don't blame him. It's not like we make his job particularly easy. He stuck with us through the garage band days, when we were getting paid in—sometimes literally—peanuts. He just doesn't want us to fuck this up."

"Still. There are ways to get things done without being . . . *dickish*."

Phoenix chuckled as they approached a tall, gorgeous woman holding a *Music Entertainment* mic. At their approach, her shoulders pushed back and she gestured to the cameraman at her side.

The second the middle-aged man propped his camera on his shoulder, the reporter's beaming white smile flashed. "Look what the navy-blue carpet brought our way! Naughty Nix, from the Stone Talons! How are you feeling tonight?"

"Pretty damn good, Carla." Phoenix grinned, not missing a beat. "It's a perfect night for music."

"The Stone Talons are performing tonight and the group is up for *three* awards: Hottest Upcoming Singer or Group, Most Viral Song, and Band of the Year. How do you feel about your chances of taking home a golden microphone?"

"I don't let myself worry about that because what will happen will happen. Better to focus on things I can control. Everyone nominated tonight deserves to bring home that mic, so I'm just here to have a good time and soak in the moment."

The brunette's gaze swung toward Addie, her ruby-red lips curling mischievously as she gave her an appraising glance from head to toe. Her eyes tightened, signaling the faux smile.

Addie had seen people like her do it a million times before. She steeled her spine and prepared for the incoming interrogation.

"And it appears that you're not walking the carpet alone." Carla's too-sweet voice could've given anyone a cavity. "You brought a lovely lady here with you tonight to share in your good time."

"I did." Phoenix's hazel eyes twinkled blue under all the flashing lights as he glanced to Addie, a warm smile curling his lips. "Don't think I'd want to share this night with anyone else."

Addie's heart fluttered, and it took a moment to put her head—and her other body parts—back to rights. The cameras were literally pointed in their faces. There was no need for excited little heart flips and stomach turns. This was quite literally what their FAMA was supposed to make happen.

And yet her heart still fluttered, and she couldn't take her eyes off Phoenix. This was definitely Naughty Nix, but she still saw the easygoing, kindhearted, sonnet-wielding version of him staring at her with those twinkling eyes.

Remembering her part to play, Addie let a sultry smile twist up her lips. "Sweet talk will get you everywhere, Nixxy."

Phoenix chuckled at the use of the nickname, and winked. "We'll test that theory later, love."

"Looking forward to it."

"All right, Nix," Carla interjected abruptly, "tell me and all your adoring fans . . . is Naughty Nix off the market? And just know, you have not only my heart in your hands but the heart of each and every *Nix Naughtigan*."

Addie choked on her own spit in an attempt to swallow a laugh. *Nix Naughtigans*.

As if sensing her internal struggle, Phoenix's fingers flexed on her hip knowingly, his eyes narrowing in amusement as he glanced her way.

Phoenix flashed a wicked smile toward Carla. "Then let this be a public service announcement that it's always a good thing to brush up on your CPR skills, Carla."

An overhead announcement gave a fifteen-minute warning to the start of the awards.

"Guess that's our sign to get moving," Phoenix added. "It's always good talking to you, Carla. Thank you."

"Absolutely, Nix . . . and good luck."

They climbed the stairs to where Easton and Nai stood waiting by the door, and Addie couldn't hold her laughter anymore.

"The Nix Naughtigans?" Addie gasped.

"Oh my goddess, right?" Naiomi burst into laughter, too. "And their slogan is "Naughty for Nix." Just in case it didn't sound ridiculous enough for you."

They both laughed until tears sprang to their eyes.

Addie gasped. "I can't breathe . . . I can't . . . Crap. This dress is too tight for me to laugh like this without risking splitting a seam."

"Keep laughing it up," Phoenix joked dryly, "but not everyone gets their very own fan club."

"It's not a real fan club unless there are T-shirts . . . tell me, are there T-shirts?"

"Actually, there are. Play your cards right and maybe I'll get you one." Phoenix tapped her gently on the nose and Nai and Addie chuckled some more.

They were ushered into the main theater and escorted to their seats close to the stage, where Xavier and Gavin were both already seated, the latter with a gorgeous blond sitting to his left, and a raven-haired beauty on his right.

Nai and Addie sat next to each other with East and Phoenix flanking them on either side. Addie glanced around, noting the celebrities and musicians that would've had Bailey freaking out if they'd been there. A few of their favorites sat only a few seats away.

Phoenix's warm hand slid over hers where it rested on her lap, his long, calloused fingers tangling with hers. "You doing okay?" He studied her carefully. "You did fantastic on the carpet, by the way. If I didn't know any better, I'd say that you walk those things every damn day."

"That's definitely not an everyday occurrence, and as exciting as all of this may be, I've never been more solid in my choice to stay out of the limelight. All of *this* is definitely not me."

Phoenix's smile slowly melted away. "It's not all me, either."

"No, but it is a large part of you. It's your job. And your hobby." She paused, trying to gauge his shift in mood. "I'm not saying that it's a bad thing. It's just not a thing that everyone enjoys. Like my mom? She would eat this stuff up like a hot-fudge sundae decked out with all the toppings. Me? Not so much."

He opened his mouth to say something when the house lights flickered. People hustled to their seats and the lights dimmed before the award host, a popular action-movie star, strutted onto the stage.

The night passed in a series of jokes, acceptance speeches, and heart-pounding performances. The closer it got to the Stone Talons's award categories, the tighter Phoenix squeezed Addie's fingers.

"You okay?" She slid her hand over his and leaned firmly into his side.

Phoenix looked nauseous and a little pale. "For the last seven years, the winner of this next award has gone on to win a Grammy during the following award season. I'm not usually superstitious, but that would be—"

"A lot of pressure?"

Phoenix huffed a short laugh. "A ridiculous amount of pressure."

The next two presenters walked onto the stage. Phoenix's fingers tightened around hers and she squeezed back, settling her other hand on his rock-hard forearm.

Hottest Upcoming Singer or Group.

The presenters took their time announcing each of the four nominees. As they announced the Stone Talons's nomination, a nearby cameraman swung around the corner, and slowly panned down their row. Addie's throat dried as she avoided looking at it and instead focused on the stage.

Seconds felt like hours, and before long, her knee bounced with her own rising nerves.

"And the winner of the Hottest Upcoming Singer or Group is . . ." The man paused dramatically and held the envelope open for his co-presenter to read.

"The Stone Talons!"

The crowd cheered and Addie squealed. Next to her, Phoenix blinked, seemingly frozen in position.

"Phoenix!" She squeezed and shook his arm until his gaze

snapped to her, lips spreading into a ridiculously wide smile. "You guys did it!"

Xavier and Gavin stood up next, and East followed suit, pulling Nai in for a hot and heavy kiss that would've made Addie blush if she didn't suddenly find herself yanked from her seat.

Blue eyes glittering, Phoenix twirled her around to face him and her breath caught at the excited, hungry look on his face. His gaze flickered from her eyes to her mouth, causing her to reflexively moisten it with her tongue.

"Sparkles?" she heard herself ask.

Phoenix blinked before his gaze drifted back down to her mouth, and nodded. "All the fucking sparkles."

Addie expected him to bend her over in a deep dip and devour her akin to something like East and Naiomi. Instead, he palmed her cheek, thumb caressing over her bottom lip in the gentlest of touches, and slowly brought their mouths together.

His thumb continued sweeping over her newly flushed skin as he gifted her the most delicate—and delectable—of kisses. It couldn't have stolen her breath any more than if he'd vacuumed the oxygen straight from her lungs.

Her body readily lifted onto her toes as she searched for more, not wanting it to end, but Phoenix slowly pulled away and his heated gaze turned her into a puddle of goo.

Breathless.

Boneless.

And speechless.

"Go get your award, rock star." Addie gently shoved him to where East and the others waited at the bottom of the stage.

He chuckled and jogged to catch up, hugging them all before they climbed the steps.

Naiomi linked her arm through hers. "I'm not trying to make this weird considering he's my brother and all, but holy Hades, that was some kiss."

Addie's cheeks warmed. "I don't know what you mean. It was barely a brush."

Naiomi snorted. "There's a whole lot more to a good kiss than lips, tongues, and teeth. But judging by your slightly erratic breathing pattern, I'd say you already know that."

Xavier took possession of the golden microphone award before giving a personal thank-you speech on behalf of the entire group. Addie couldn't take her eyes off Phoenix, and when his gaze found hers a few seconds later, he flashed her a cocky wink that would normally send her eyes into a roll, but instead sent a flurry of butterflies through her lower stomach.

Locked in Phoenix's gaze, it took her a moment to realize she'd missed what Naiomi had said to her as the guys finished their speech and headed backstage. "I'm sorry, what?"

"I said there's no getting out of the after-party now. Marcus will demand it. Although, I hear they go all out for the golden mic winners, so maybe it won't be so bad. Goddess knows I could use a little mindless fun."

Mindless fun.

That sounded way out of Addie's wheelhouse, but the excitement glinting from the other woman's eyes called to her own, and before she realized it, Addie couldn't wait to experience that thing called *fun*, either.

And who better to experience it with than a rock star?

23

BEST SEAT IN THE HOUSE

Phoenix

Three nominations. Three wins. And one hell of an after-party. Phoenix knew the music industry went all-out for the award after-party, but this was beyond anything he'd pictured in his head.

The two-story converted warehouse throbbed with a musical pulse, the tones from the in-house DJ reverberating off the vaulted ceiling to rain down onto the dance floor. Four massive screens, alight with high-definition pictures, flickered to the beat and added color to the otherwise dim space, and costumed people danced on high, vaulted mini-stages.

People packed the place from wall to wall and yet it somehow felt less stuffy than the award show itself.

Hand braced against the small of Addie's back where it had been since they arrived, Phoenix hovered his mouth over her ear. "It's a lot less crowded upstairs so we're heading up there."

"Well damn, and here I was enjoying the sardine-can atmosphere," she quipped.

He chuckled and led the way to the spiraling staircase that

would take them to the second floor's VIP area. The muscular security guards gave them a once-over before allowing them through.

The Lounge was a club within a club, the second story open and airy enough to people-watch from over the heavy iron railing. Plush couches and overstuffed chairs replaced the smaller conversation tables downstairs, and a miniature version of the main bar took up the far back corner. There was room to breathe and move without worry of colliding with someone—unless on purpose.

"So much better than downstairs." Naiomi looped an arm through Addie's as she shot Phoenix a warning look. "I'm stealing your girl for a second and we're getting drinks. Your job—because you have no choice but to accept it—is to keep the rock bunnies from climbing onto my fiancé's lap."

"Or Addie and I could go get everyone drinks, and you can guard your fiancé's crotch yourself," Phoenix quipped.

Nai rolled her eyes and dragged a highly amused Addie away.

Phoenix stared at the magical view of Addie's ass until she disappeared into the three-people-deep border surrounding the bar.

"They'll be fine." East steered him to one of the empty leather sofas. "But you, my friend, I'm not so sure about."

"Me? Why?" Phoenix commandeered one end of the long couch, and East took the other as they purposefully manspread to leave room for the girls' return. "I'm fine—unless one of these stage bunnies somehow manages a sneak lap attack and Nai kicks my ass."

East studied him before smirking. "I'm not sure if you're just in denial, or you're just a really good actor. You don't want to talk about it yet? Fine. Just know that you're playing with fire, my friend, and I'm not sure there are enough fire extinguishers to put it out when things explode."

"Oh my goddess, you really are Naughty Nix and Easton Knox." Two women stood in front of them, both looking as if they'd stepped off a Victoria's Secret runway. The brunette batted her heavily mascara'd eyes. "The guy over there said you'd be happy to take pictures with us."

Phoenix's gaze shifted in the direction she'd indicated and met Marcus's palpable glare from across the room.

East, seeing the silent ultimatum, too, sighed. "Yeah, we can take a picture."

With ear-piercing squeals, the girls immediately dove ass-first onto his and Easton's laps.

Phoenix burst into laughter at his friend's horrified expression until his own horror took over and the brunette on his lap threw her arms around his neck and planted a kiss on his cheek. A third groupie came from out of nowhere and snapped a pic.

It all happened so fast. A lap dive, kiss, and pic all in the span of an eyeblink.

Unfortunately, not quickly enough that the only woman Phoenix wouldn't mind on his lap didn't witness it. And then there was Naiomi, whose look contrasted Addie's curiosity with one of polite murder.

"Thank you for keeping my fiancé and brother entertained, girls, but we've got it from here." Nai's sweet tone barely contained her underlying meaning: Move or I will move you. "Now shoo. Photo ops are done for the night."

They jumped up immediately, giggling as they skipped away.

Nai took her rightful spot on East's lap. "Freaking groupies are like cockroaches. The second you step out of the room, they swarm. Not that I don't trust you completely, babe," she added quickly, dropping a kiss on his cheek. "My shy, gentle, gargoyle giant."

Nai's eyes twinkled as she glanced toward Addie. "Did I ever tell you that it took this man *months* to work up the courage to kiss me the first time . . . and that's after we basically grew up together?"

A small, wistful smile melted over her face. "But boy, what a kiss. It was a good thing I was sitting down or my knees would've given out."

Addie leaned against Phoenix's end of the couch. "That romantic, huh? Were there rose petals involved? Soft music in the background?"

"Nope. High, itchy grass that gave me a rash that took two weeks to go away. Sweat stains. And the only music around was the loud thrum of about a million crickets—one of which got tangled up in my hair and East had to go spelunking to get it out. It was the best."

Addie let out a genuine laugh, her eyes twinkling in the dim lighting. "What? High, itchy grass, bugs, and sweat stains?"

"Without a doubt. Summer days at Emilio's farm weren't just an escape from the city, but from everything. I swear even to this day that that place is magical. You could have the weight of the world resting on your shoulders, and the second I stepped into that barn and climbed into the loft, it all melted away."

Addie's gaze caught Phoenix's and they shared a knowing look.

"That does sound magical," Addie admitted slyly.

Naiomi snuggled deeper into East's hold and the two lovebirds quickly lost themselves in each other, whispering and sneaking kisses.

A little devil took a seat on Phoenix's shoulder. He patted

his lap and flashed Addie an inviting grin. "I saved the best seat in the house for you, love. VIPs only."

"So the pretty brunette was a VIP?" Addie kicked up a teasing eyebrow.

"No, she was a lap crasher." He amped up the Naughty Nix charm. "This seat has been reserved for you and only you since the day I opened my apartment door to a very incessant knocker."

"You know I've been sitting in my own seat for years now without problems."

"Suit yourself. Just know that it's an open invitation. Anytime you want it, the spot's yours." He grinned coyly. "And just so you know, in this lighting, your gorgeous eyes almost *sparkle*."

Fewer than six feet away, a small group of friends, hearing their exchange, giggled and whispered amongst themselves before the tallest of them broke away with a seductive smile. "I'd love to claim the best seat in the house if she isn't taking it."

"Sorry. You heard the man." Addie lowered herself sideways onto Phoenix's lap and wrapped her arm around his shoulder. "This seat is reserved for *me*."

"Fuck yeah it is, love." Phoenix guided her fully into his embrace and tucked his face into the curve of her neck.

"Now who's sniffing who?" Addie whispered with amusement.

"I fully admit it and don't care in the least because you smell fucking amazing." Phoenix drifted his mouth closer to her ear. "And did it just get hot in here, or is that your possessiveness warming up the joint?"

She turned her gaze on him and . . .

It was a good thing he was sitting down because *damn* . . .

The mixture of heat and mischief dancing in her green eyes

stirred something other than his dick—although that was definitely waking up, the longer she sat on his lap.

The corners of Addie's lips lifted as she used the damp napkin around her drink to wipe at what must have been remnants of the groupie's unwanted kiss.

"It wouldn't look like a fauxmance if I let some other woman sit on your lap—*again*. Would it?" Addie said coyly.

That fucking word.

Phoenix could kick himself in the ass for ever coming up with it.

Addie

Just saying *fauxmance* left an ashy taste in the back of Addie's throat, and she didn't need many guesses to figure out why. But what she did need was a bit of air and to be somewhere—even for a few minutes—that didn't assault her eardrums.

"I'm going to make a quick run to the bathroom." She regretfully climbed off Phoenix's lap and he moved to stand. "I think I can handle the bathroom alone, rock star."

Phoenix didn't look thrilled, but Addie leaned down, giving him a spectacular view of her cleavage. She was probably flashing someone behind him, too, but she couldn't bring herself to care as she tilted Phoenix's chin up and kissed him.

His hand slid to the back of her head and held her close, making what she'd planned to be a quick peck into something a hell of a lot more. It physically pained her to pull back.

"Try not to let anyone else sit in my seat while I'm gone, okay?" Addie teased.

"Oh, bathroom break!" Naiomi stood at her side. "I pregamed way too much water and now I'm paying for it. I'll go with you."

"Be careful. You both have your phones?"

Nai rolled her eyes. "Yes, Dad. We do. Let's go before he decides to follow us."

They asked one of the servers to point them toward the restrooms and got directions to a more private one a little farther away. When it came to women's bathroom lines and Naiomi's overfilled bladder, shorter was paramount.

There was no line at the door, and Naiomi immediately ran into the closest stall while Addie waited by the sinks, just needing a little quiet time.

Nai emerged a minute later looking much more comfortable until she glanced in the mirror. "Well hell. Why did no one tell me I looked like a hot mess?"

"Uh, because you don't. You're stunning. As always."

Nai scoffed and started pulling makeup from her little clutch. "You have to say that because you're faux fauxmancing my older brother."

Addie's mouth opened and closed as she struggled to form words.

Naiomi laughed. "Oh, don't let flies in your mouth, babe. I approve."

"It's—"

"Not real?" Nai challenged with a lipstick in her hand. "Temporary? An 'arrangement'? Yeah, Phoenix tried telling me that once, too, and I didn't believe him then, and I sure as hell don't believe it now."

"Naiomi . . ."

"Deny it all you want, Adalyn Whitlock, but to anyone watching from the outside, it is as obvious as the nose on your face. Or should I say *big gold sign linking the two of you together*?"

"The 'big gold' *what*?" Addie's stomach dropped.

"Golden link. Neon sign. Whatever you want to call it," Nai continued, not registering the slight panic her words elicited. "There's never been any two people better suited for each other than you and my brother—except for myself and East, obviously. Stop with the freaking *fauxmance* nonsense already. The only people you're fooling at this point are yourselves."

Crap. Was she right?

Did part of Addie know it and that's why the words, the denial, failed to come out of her mouth? She couldn't argue that Phoenix had become a big part of her every day. To keep up their fauxmance and perform as his Muse, it had been necessary.

But now?

He nearly had a complete song—one he seemed extremely proud of—and there hadn't been an article written by Evelyn Sinclair in days or a social media post from Karleigh. For the first time in ages, the HEF phones rang for something other than cancellations and refund requests.

Both Phoenix and Addie seemed to have gotten what they'd set out to get, and yet she hadn't once tried to bring an end to the FAMA.

At some point, everything had started blurring. Maybe it was triggered by the first kiss, or the first article of clothing being shed. And maybe it had started the second she banged on his apartment door and he answered wearing nothing more than a low-slung pair of pants and a wicked grin.

The large bathroom shrank inch by inch, walls slowly closing in around her as she looked for an exit. "I'll meet you right outside," Addie said, hustling from the bathroom and struggling not to hyperventilate.

Her head screamed for her to run, but her heart begged her to stay.

With Phoenix.

Addie leaned against the wall, her eyes closed, and slogged through all the unfamiliar emotions getting in her way of making a well-informed decision.

Someone joined her.

Her eyes opened and she immediately recognized Karleigh Kinkaid's father.

His typical high-end suit fit his large body like a glove. His expensive watch flashed in the club's lighting as he fixed his tie and tucked his hands casually into his pockets. But Addie knew better. There wasn't a casual bone in the man's body.

He didn't say a word, and Addie took that as a sign to do the same, hoping luck was on her side and he wouldn't recognize her as the woman who had "ruined" his daughter's magical day. She briefly considered firing off an SOS to Phoenix, but thought better of it.

He didn't deserve to be dragged into her messes.

"They look every bit the rock stars, don't they?" Mr. Kinkaid broke the blessed silence.

"Excuse me?" She instantly regretted acknowledging him as he shifted his attention toward the center of the room where Phoenix laughed and talked to East, Xavier, and Gavin.

"Yes, they do." She kept it short and agreeable, her eyes trained on Phoenix as he chuckled at something Easton said.

"Now they just need to get with the rest of the program and act like it."

Addie looked his way reflexively as unease curled in her stomach. "Sorry?"

"But now that you've uncorked whatever it was that was wrong with our Nix, things will head in the right direction." He turned with a fake smile plastered on his face. "That was brave of you to take on the role of his Muse, Miss Whitlock.

Most people with your views on love and attachments wouldn't even dare risk it."

There was a lot in the man's words for her to unpack and it took a little extra time for her to put two and two together.

Mr. Kinkaid was the music executive, the label owner who put constant pressure on Phoenix to come up with the next panty party song.

"My views on love and attachment?" Addie parroted him as she digested the second half of his statement. "What exactly do you mean by that?"

"Come now, Miss Whitlock. You don't have to pretend to be something you're not. At least not now that you've fixed our Nix and your little arrangement has come to an end." He paused, head tilted innocently, but on him, looked anything but. "I mean, your arrangement has ended, right? It's been quite some time since I've had contact with a Muse, but I vaguely remember that the shorter the involvement, the best for both parties. Something about codependency and blurred lines."

Addie's breath stalled.

It was obvious Kinkaid was trying to play her right now. She wasn't stupid and he wasn't exactly tactful.

But he wasn't wrong, either . . .

It was why Muses had contract limitations. If one Muse couldn't get the job done in a matter of weeks, another filled the position. The line kept moving until someone completed the assignment.

A cold sweat peppered Addie's brow and her stomach churned, sick with the realization that Naiomi was wrong. She and Phoenix didn't have a link.

What they had was Muse Sickness.

It explained *everything*.

What had started as an intense physical attraction had

slowly morphed as they spent more time together, thanks to their FAMA. Throwing intimacy into the mix upped the stakes, and then Muse Sickness did the rest.

It formed a bond.

Intensified feelings.

Hell, it could alter their brain chemistry and have them thinking—and doing—things that they wouldn't normally do . . . like actually contemplate the existence of *love*. Hell, maybe that's why she'd started seeing gold toga ropes all over the damn place.

Addie's stomach lurched. "Excuse me . . ."

She sprinted back toward the bathroom, pushing past Naiomi as she exited.

Alarm widened the brunette's eyes. "Addie, are you—"

Addie barely made it to the toilet before the first wave hit. Naiomi was by her side in a second, holding her hair away from her face as she heaved her throat raw.

"Are you okay?" Naiomi handed her a wet napkin what felt like hours later, watching her with heavy concern.

As Addie thought about what she had to do, the nausea returned, tilting her stomach over again and again because only one thing cured Muse Sickness.

The total separation between Muse and Musician.

Addie needed to walk away.

Because if she didn't, she'd lose Phoenix for good.

24

SILENCE

Phoenix

Something was wrong. He didn't know exactly what that something was, but he had felt it the instant Addie returned from the bathroom with Naiomi earlier that evening.

She was way too quiet, and although after the party she smiled and joked around with East and the guys, it was obvious—to him, at least—that something had changed drastically from the start of the night until now, when they were in an actual limo still fully clothed and with about six feet of awkward silence between them despite sitting right next to one another.

Phoenix drummed his fingers against his leg, forming a game plan on how to approach the topic, when the limo came to a stop outside their building. Addie was out of her seat before the driver even opened the door.

Fuck. Whatever this was, he already knew he wouldn't like it.

They made their way up to their floor in total silence, Addie artfully avoiding his gaze at every turn. As she opened her apartment door, she gifted him a small, flat smile that sent a chill straight to his gut.

The smile didn't reach her eyes.

Normally glittering with excitement and challenge, her gaze shifted from his and looked anywhere but in his direction. This wasn't the Addie he knew. Wasn't the woman he'd grown to care about so damn much.

He couldn't take it anymore.

He'd give her anything she wanted.

An explanation.

A declaration.

He opened his mouth to ask her what was wrong, and she beat him to the punch.

"I think our arrangement should probably come to an end now," Addie said in a rush, her words tumbling together, so fast he had to roll them back in his head and replay them.

"What?" He hoped to hell he'd heard wrong.

She fiddled nervously with her keys, hesitant to meet his gaze. "You're writing music—and if your late-night humming and your full journal are any indication—a lot of it. And things at Happily Ever Forever are going great. Bailey texted me that we got two new bookings just this morning from consultations we did last week, and the Anti-Aphrodite name is finally starting to disappear. It's everything we both wanted out of our FAMA arrangement."

Fuck.

Fuck.

Phoenix treaded carefully as he focused on her. "Things are definitely better than they were when we first started."

She nodded. "Right. So we don't really need the agreement anymore. Why monopolize each other's time unnecessarily?

We're about to both be so busy it'll be difficult to even catch a breath."

Hell, he could barely breathe now.

Every word out of Addie's mouth was another knife plunge to the chest, and yet he'd done it to himself.

How many times had she warned him that she didn't do love? That she didn't believe in it? It's what necessitated their arrangement in the first place. But somewhere along the way, so focused on how he felt and the feelings she conjured in him, he'd lost track of that.

He hadn't allowed himself to believe that everything she made him feel wasn't—at least partially—reciprocated.

Standing in the middle of the hall between their two apartments, Phoenix's heart broke. There was no other way to describe the pain in his chest, the all-consuming agony that had him fighting to suck in each breath.

He'd give her anything she wanted.

An explanation.

A declaration.

A retreat.

"Adalyn, are you sure—"

"Yes." The word came way too quickly, but even though her face paled, her shoulders lifted with a hint of the stubborn woman who'd once banged like hell on his door. "I was so focused on trying to be Muse-like, and doing what we needed to do to get the Anti-Aphrodite thing to disappear that I forgot a few integral things about Muse and Musician agreements and . . . I'm sorry."

Tears shone in her eyes and it nearly broke him.

"Addie." He stepped forward, hand reaching out to wipe away the first tear, but she stepped back . . . away from him. "What are you talking about?"

"Everything we're feeling?" Addie struggled through each word. "Everything we think we're feeling . . . it's not real. It's—"

"Like fucking hell it isn't," Phoenix growled. He closed the distance and cupped her cheek, gently urging her to look at him. "Addie, what I feel for you is the realest thing I've ever fucking felt in my life."

She was already shaking her head, a new wave of tears falling. "It's Muse Sickness, Phoenix. It's . . . it's the reason why Muse agreements are meant to be so short, and we went over the usual allotment by . . . a lot."

"Like fucking hell."

"There shouldn't be any . . . lasting effects," Addie continued as if not hearing him. "But it'll be hard the first few days and—"

"Addie, don't do this. Please. There is no fucking way that this is—"

Addie held a hand out in front of her, as if they'd just sold a car. "Thank you for helping me out of a jam, Phoenix Cross. And I was glad to help you get your musical mojo back."

The awkwardness grew until she dropped her hand to her side with a softly muttered apology.

Phoenix couldn't stand the physical distance one second longer.

He inched closer, one small step at a time. Green eyes widening, she countered his moves until her back pressed against the wall.

The second he cupped her cheek, her eyes fluttered closed before opening and locking on him. "What are you doing?"

Her chest heaved with each breath, matching his own erratic pace as he searched her face. Her eyes. He savored the soft skin of her cheek beneath his palm as he brushed his thumb over her lower lip.

"If this is the end, I want to permanently etch every facet of you onto my soul," Phoenix admitted unashamedly. "Adalyn Love Whitlock"—he slowly brushed his lips against hers in a whisper of a kiss—"you will always and forever be *my* goddess of love."

She brushed the tips of her fingers against her mouth and turned toward her door with a silent sob. And fuck, it took everything in him not to barge through the door and run after her.

Phoenix forced his feet back toward his own apartment, working his way through the anger and disappointment, and the white-hot pain ripping through the center of his chest. If he hadn't just had a checkup, he'd think he was having a heart attack.

Although this was worse.

It didn't feel like it was just his heart breaking.

It felt like something a fuck-ton more.

Not long ago, he opened this door and stepped into a bright, music-laden world filled with hope and possibility . . . and Adalyn Whitlock. Now, as he closed the door behind him, with Addie on the other side, the opposite happened.

His world was too damn silent.

25

APHRODITE! APHRODITE! *BEETLEJUICE!*

Addie

Addie pulled the puffy blanket over her head and sank deeper into her mattress, wishing the damn thing would swallow her whole and she wouldn't have to listen to the insistent knocking on her apartment door. It stopped for a short minute before starting up again with renewed vigor.

Do-Re-Mi huffed next to her, their three heads tunneling beneath her blanket fort to give her identical judgmental looks.

"Don't look at me like that," Addie demanded. "I deserve a day or two off with how much I work."

Do chuffed and Mi took a big sniff before wrinkling his nose.

Addie gasped in indignation. "I don't stink! I showered yes-ter . . . wait, no. The day before yesterday, but it's not like I've been doing any strenuous activities where I've sweat."

The person on the other side of the door knocked again, this time more aggressively.

Addie shoved her face into her pillow with a groan. "I give

you permission to eat whoever is making that horrific noise . . . or at the very least scare the shit out of them so they go away."

Do glanced at his brothers as if contemplating her offer before they all three released doggie sighs and trotted away, way too timidly to be heading to scare the crap out of any uninvited guests.

With a dramatic fling of her comforter and a string of curses, she stalked to the door, already preparing to give the person on the other side a piece of her damn mind.

"Unless the building is on fire, I suggest you go away," Addie yelled, opening the door with a flourish.

Bailey and Maxi stood on the other side, Bailey's fist poised to knock down her door with another series of bangs.

"Holy shit." Bailey's nose wrinkled as she snuck a quick glance to Max. "It's worse than we thought."

"Excuse me?" Addie propped her hands on her hips. She got a whiff of something . . . unpleasant . . . and took a quick sniff of herself, her face nearly matching Bailey's expression. "Whatever. I'm conserving water. Why are the two of you here? I took some personal days. I'll be ready to go tomorrow for Naiomi's big day."

Just the thought of Naiomi's big day . . . and running into Phoenix . . . nearly sent her running back to her blanket fort. Seeing the uncertainty on her face, Bailey and Max pushed their way into her apartment.

"Okay, first things first." Maxi looked all stern business as she closed the door. "And first is you getting into the shower and literally showering the stink off you. While you do that, Bailey and I will open windows to . . . air the place out."

"It is not that bad."

At their matching scoffs, Addie glanced around her apartment. A few empty takeout cartons from the Chinese restaurant down the block sat on the kitchen table, and a pizza box that may or may not have been empty rested on the counter. The dishes piled in the sink almost teetered onto the counter.

Okay, so maybe it wasn't the greatest, but she'd get to it all . . . eventually.

"Look, I appreciate the concern." Addie half-heartedly began picking up empty cartons. "But it's not necessary. I got a little tingle of pre-sickness ick, and wanted to head it off with some extra sleep and vitamin C. I can't afford to get the full-blown icks with Naiomi and Easton's big day on the horizon."

Both Bailey and Maxi stared at her with twin looks of disbelief.

"That's what you're going with?" Bailey challenged. "Staving off the icks?"

Addie shoved the takeout boxes into an already overflowing garbage bag and contemplated jumping in after them. "Yes. Because that's the truth."

Exchanging a frustrated look with Maxi, Bailey threw up their hands. "Tag! You're it!"

"Addie"—her sister used her soothing voice—"you know we both love you, right? And we want nothing but the best for you."

"Same."

"What would you do if the roles were reversed, and it was me or Bailey who'd been holed up in our stinky apartment after breaking up with our fake boyfriends, only to realize that at some point during the fauxmance, it started becoming real and we realized that perhaps we were wrong about *love* not being real?"

Addie glared at her sister. "That's a really long run-on sentence, Max."

"You're making me do it, aren't you?" Maxi's eyes narrowed.

"Do what?" Addie asked warily.

"Just know that I do this out of love. And because you leave me absolutely no choice."

Max commandeered Addie's full attention now, her heart galloping in her chest like a thundering herd. "What are you—"

"Aphrodite," Maxi blurted unapologetically.

Addie's eyes bugged. "No, no!"

She chased her sister around her coffee table. On the second round, she stubbed her toe and yelped. "Maxine Sonnet Whitlock! Don't you dare summon her!"

"Are you going to admit that love exists?" Maxi walked backward, easily staying out of her reach while Addie hopped after her.

"Look, there's more to it than you realize and—"

"Will you admit that you fell—hard enough to give yourself another concussion—in *love* with Phoenix Cross? And that's the real reason why you're hiding under your weighted blanket and avoiding all forms of personal hygiene?"

"No," Addie growled.

"Aphrodite," Maxi drew out their mother's name like a freaking song lyric.

"Please, Maxi," Addie pleaded. "Bringing Mom into this won't help anything. It'll actually make things ten times worse."

"Actually, Ads, I think this is probably the one time that Mom really can help. I do this for your own good." Maxi took a deep breath before finishing her summoning of Beetlejuice—er, their mother. "*Aphrodite*."

Addie's groan didn't fully escape her throat before their mother blinked into the apartment.

Wearing a white fluffy robe and slippers, Aphrodite sported gold under-eye gel pads and a hydrating face mask. She dangled a water bottle at her side, notably filled with water and cucumber.

"Sorry it took so long, my dear. I was in the middle of a much-needed massage and—" Aphrodite turned toward Addie and froze. "What on Hades Hellscape happened to you?"

"Nothing," Addie answered too quickly.

Max sighed. "She fell in love."

Aphrodite's eyes widened before she beamed wide, her skin practically radiating with her goddess glow.

"No, I did not," Addie denied, dimming that glow.

"Then explain why you've been hiding in your room and not showering, and by the smell of this place, haven't so much as cracked a window?" Maxi demanded.

"My allergies are acting up," she retaliated without much heat, arms folded over her chest.

"Adalyn," Aphrodite said in a soft, knowing whisper. "Sweetheart."

"It's not love," Addie denied, the denial sounding weak even to her own ears. "It's . . . something else."

Her mother shot her a sympathetic look.

That's what did it.

The tears she'd barely held at bay escaped in a tsunami. Floodgates opened. Snot running, Addie flung herself into her mother's open arms and immediately felt her mother's warmth seep into her skin. She held on tighter, fingers latching on to the back of her terry robe until she probably resembled a red-eyed zombie from *The Walking Dead*.

She hiccupped, accidently wiping her snot-laden face on her mother's lapel.

"Sorry." Addie grimaced, trying to swallow around the lump lodged in her throat.

"Not a worry." Aphrodite snapped her fingers and the robe,

the gel pads, and the face mask disappeared, leaving her in a pair of chic pink sweats. She ushered Addie to the couch and wrapped a supportive arm over her shoulders. "Now tell me what happened, and then we'll brainstorm ideas to fix it."

"There's no way to fix it, Mom."

"Sometimes the impossible seems that way. It's what entices you not to try. Now, talk to me."

"I thought I was falling in . . ."

"Love . . . ?"

She nodded and took a deep, cleansing breath. "I seriously thought maybe I had it wrong . . . that maybe it does exist, and . . . then it was brought to my attention."

"What was?"

"Muse Sickness."

Aphrodite paused as if waiting for more.

"You do know what Muse Sickness is, right?" Addie asked.

"Of course I do, but, sweetheart, I don't think it's possible for you to have it."

"Well, it's possible because I have it!" She yanked the *Muse for Dummies* text she'd gotten at the library and flung it open to the pages listing symptoms. "Phoenix and I have every single one of them. *Every* one. Inexplicable attraction—check. An intense, severe need to be in the other's presence—check. And that's just—"

"Honey."

"Don't *honey* me, Mom. I know what I'm feeling and that's all of this." Addie shook the book.

"Let's get to the bottom of this, yeah? It's always best to go right to the source." Aphrodite cleared her throat and called loudly, "Eunice. Eunice. Eunice."

Bailey muttered next to Maxi, "Do all goddesses get called like in *Beetlejuice*?"

Eunice popped into the room right next to Bailey, making Athena's loin-spawn jump. "My, my, are we having a party and I wasn't invited?"

Aphrodite kicked up a golden eyebrow. "You're here, aren't you?"

"Ah. That I am." Eunice looked toward Addie and did a double-take, her mouth opening to say something. "Oh, my . . ."

"Yeah, yeah," Addie beat her to it. "I look like shit, but it says here on page ninety-two that that can sometimes happen during Muse Sickness's first withdrawal wave."

Eunice glanced to Aphrodite with a silent question, the two goddesses seemingly having an entire conversation telepathically.

Finally, her mother nodded. "That's why I called you here."

Eunice took a seat on the other side of Addie, her face pensive as she reached for her free hand. "First, I want to remind you that I told you that a crash course in Musing in one single afternoon isn't exactly ideal."

"You did," Addie admitted.

"And I told you that being a Muse is a little more complex than the average person thinks."

"You told me that, too, yes."

Eunice cleared her throat and tightened her grip on Addie's hand. "What you're feeling—and I know you said that you're experiencing all the symptoms written in that book—but it's not Muse Sickness."

"But—"

"It's not Muse Sickness, Adalyn Love Whitlock. You're not a Muse. Yes, you are a gorgeous, softhearted, and talented young demigoddess with loads of inspiration to give, but you're not a Muse. Muses are *born*. Therefore, you—and anyone you're in contact with—cannot be afflicted with Muse Sickness."

Maxi and Bailey whispered on the other side of the living room as Addie struggled to comprehend everything. "Then what the hell is this all-consuming, simultaneously thrilling and scary-as-hell feeling that washes over me whenever I think about Phoenix Cross? It's not . . . natural. It's too powerful and overwhelming and it's—"

"Love."

Addie scoffed at her aunt's response, but her humorless laughter died in her throat when she glanced at her mom. "Is she serious?"

"Very," Eunice answered instead.

"And she's also very right," Aphrodite agreed.

Addie took a deep breath and her entire body—and her heart—trembled.

Did she love Phoenix Cross? The weight-crushing pain and her struggle to take full breaths—not to mention her sudden *Planet of the Apes* and *The Princess Bride* binge-watching—would indicate yes.

As improbable as it was, and as much as she tried denying it, she was, without a doubt, *in love* with Phoenix Cross.

In love with his wicked smirk and that panty-dampening dimple. In the way he protects—and teases—his family. His nipple piercings and every single tattoo. In the way he holds her, his strong hands gentle as if they possessed something precious in his arms.

Hell, even now, thinking about his ridiculous pickup lines, her heart did a little flip.

She couldn't even pinpoint the exact moment it had happened. It could've been when he'd taken care of her after the Jones Beach incident, or when he first opened that apartment door and half-jokingly asked her to be his Muse. Hell, it could've been when he remembered she liked her coffee piping hot with a single ice cube thrown in.

"Oh. My. Goddess. I'm in l-love with him," Addie murmured softly. The truth hit her in the face like a two-by-four and the impact teetered her sideways. "I need to sit down."

"You *are* sitting down," Aphrodite mused, and pushed her upright.

"Oh. Good for me then."

Somewhere nearby, Max and Bailey whispered their shock at her admittance.

Addie dropped her head into her hands and sighed, feeling as if her heart was breaking all over again. "He's never going to speak to me again."

"Why on earth not?"

Addie snorted humorlessly. "Well, because first he tried telling me how he felt and I played it off like we both just had a case of the cooties. Then, I basically told him that I got what I wanted from him so I don't need him anymore, tried to shake his hand, and after he kissed me, I holed up in my room and blocked his number because I didn't trust myself not to call him."

"Dang," Bailey muttered.

"Well, that isn't ideal." Aphrodite grimaced, but quickly patted her hand. "But it's not irreversible. You tell him you were wrong and—"

"That you were an idiot," Bailey added pointedly.

"But you've since realized your error and wish to make amends."

"Mom," Addie sighed. "People don't just walk up to people and say things like 'I wish to make amends.' I fucked up. Bigtime. Phoenix was trying to tell me how he felt, and he was so damn sure, but . . . so was I."

A new wave of tears threatened to fall.

"I was so quick to believe that what I felt for him couldn't be possible that I latched on to the only other feasible excuse—or so I thought." Addie glanced to her mother for her input. "What about that screams *love*?"

"Everything." Aphrodite smiled. "Love is scary. Love is blind. And more often than not, love makes absolutely no fucking sense."

Addie rubbed her eyes, trying to wipe away the gritty sensation. "It would've made things so much easier if I had just seen a damn link."

"A link?" Maxi asked from her spot leaning against the chair.

"Unlike the gold cords I've seen linking all the other couples, I've never once caught a glimmer of one between me and Phoenix. Not a gleam or flicker. Nothing."

The silence in the room was deafening.

Addie glanced to her mother, to Bailey, and then to Maxi.

It was her sister who broke the silence first. "*Golden* cords? Do you mean that all those times we were out in public . . . at the café, and during that brunch . . . you saw *actual* links tethering people together?"

Addie nodded, unable to admit it aloud.

"Are you freaking kidding me?" Maxi squealed. "I've been poring over client files and dealing with raiding police officers and fraudsters and you've been seeing freaking soul tethers?! How the hell could you deny love—true love—after seeing them?"

"In my defense, I thought—and so did my eye doctor—that something was wrong with my contacts," Addie mumbled.

"That's why you started wearing your glasses," Bailey whispered.

"Except it didn't work, and I've seen more since." Addie

turned to her mother. "But there's a very obvious one that I haven't seen, and maybe it's a little chickenish of me, but I don't think I can put myself out there without knowing for absolute sure that it's the real thing."

"Oh, sweetheart." Aphrodite reached for her hands and gave them a firm squeeze. "A Cupidess can't see her own soul tether—at least not until you make that fated leap of trust without a safety net. Trusting that your love will catch you. Don't ask me why. It's just one of those things that is what it is and I'm not sure there's an actual reason."

"Well, that fucking sucks," Addie mumbled grumpily.

And it in no way helped her with her situation in the least.

"I can't believe you can see soul tethers." Maxi shot her a stern glare. "When East and Naiomi's ceremony is over, we're having a sit-down and talking about changing things up at Happily Ever Forever. I mean, let's face it. I'm probably more suited for the event planning side anyway. I know the difference between antique white, pearl white, and airy white."

Addie groaned, but grinned wanly. "For the last time, there is no difference. They're all white."

Aphrodite wrinkled her nose. "Your sister may have a point. It may be time to shake things up . . . and I'm not just talking about things at Happily Ever Forever."

Phoenix.

No doubt she meant Phoenix, or her love life, or lack thereof, but she just didn't know how big of a leap she was willing to take without that damn safety net.

Phoenix

Phoenix brought his sticks down on the snare drum a little harder than necessary, his foot a little heavy on the bass. East snuck him a questioning look as they continued with the recording of their umpteenth party song.

By the time the chorus came around, the damn mallet went through the kick drum with a loud thud.

The producer's voice bellowed through the comms. "What the hell did those drums do to you, Nix?"

He grunted and shrugged, knowing the guys were watching him. Hell, they'd been sending looks his way ever since he walked into the recording studio grumpy, cranky, and more than a little eager to pound away on his drums. His idea to wail on the set had evidently worked a little too well.

The people in the lounge cleared out as the producer sent someone to find another drum. Phoenix and the guys took this moment to drop themselves onto the nearby couches where he avoided all eye contact.

East kicked the side of his boot—and it fucking hurt since the bastard was currently in gargoyle mode.

"What the hell, man?" Phoenix shot at him. "No harsh physical contact in stone form. It's one of the rules."

East flickered into his skin suit and kicked him again, this time in the shin. "There. Better?"

"No, asshole." Phoenix rubbed his sore foot and shin. Now he wouldn't be able to pound on the bass drum too hard. "Look, I'm sorry about fucking up another take. I'll get it on the next one, okay? I'm just . . . a little out of sorts."

The guys exchanged a series of looks, and that's when Phoenix realized.

He sent a glare to East. "You fucking told them?"

Easton shrugged his broad shoulders. "You didn't tell me I couldn't, so yeah. Figured they should probably be aware why you're acting like a cranky toddler who didn't get their afternoon nap for the last few days."

"It's not a big deal," Phoenix repeated for the tenth time since his and Addie's hallway conversation. Each time he said it didn't make him believe it any more, but a guy could try. "We had an agreement. We each delivered on our end of the deal. Now it's time to move on."

And there was the problem.

He wanted to move on *with Addie*.

He wanted more bedroom snuggles. More evening strolls in the park. Hell, he'd even subject himself to weekly fucking carousel rides at Coney Island if it meant keeping her in his life.

And yeah, in his heart.

It fucking ached whenever he thought about her, a real, visceral reaction that'd been plaguing him for the last three days, and no amount of banging his sticks seemed to take it away. The only thing it did do?

Kept him up late into the night—and early morning—leaning against the shared wall of their apartment while he wrote more lyrics and melodies, churning out song after song until he had damn near filled his current notebook.

All because of her. Fucking *Muse Sickness*.

He still didn't believe it, but he sure as hell could see how she did, someone who always had one foot poised to run in the other direction if shit got too real.

"For the first time since we were in my parents' garage, I've been writing real music," Phoenix admitted, stealing a glance at his friends since childhood. He took the time to look each of them in the eye because they deserved that much from him. "And I'm not sure I want to stop. I know I don't want to stop. And yeah, I could do it while also drumming with the Stone Talons but—"

"You don't want to," Gavin finished, surprising him with his astuteness.

"I love you all like brothers," Phoenix said quickly. "You *are* my brothers, my family, and I don't want to let you all down, but . . . yeah. My heart hasn't been in it for a long time now, and it wasn't until recently that I realized that I'm not doing any of you any favors by sticking around and holding you back."

The guys exchanged a few looks before Gavin nodded. "Let's see this latest song . . . and not the one you gave Marcus to appease Kinkaid. Let's see the one you've been writing with stars in your eyes."

He glanced at the guys, getting two additional nods, and dug into his bag for the notebook. The spine bulged with the additional pages he'd stuffed inside when he'd run out of room.

East whistled. "Damn, man. You've been busy."

Phoenix chuckled warily. "Yeah, well, it's been a wild few weeks . . . and days."

He opened the book to the song that had started it all, the one inspired by the demigoddess that stole his heart—and if he was honest with himself—that he'd freely given. He sat back and waited, watching East stand behind Xavier as they all read the lines and Gavin hummed the melody.

It felt like eons until they were done, and by the time they got to the end, Phoenix was fidgeting in his seat and felt seconds away from throwing up. "Is it fucking horrible? Tell it to me straight. I can take it. Maybe."

"You wrote this about Addie?" Gavin's gaze flicked up to him and back to the open book.

"Yeah."

"Well, fuck." He closed it with a sigh. "If I could write something like this, I'd want to branch out and do my own thing, too. This is fucking amazing."

He saw each of them nodding in agreement.

"Don't get me wrong," Gavin added, "it'll fucking suck having to get used to someone else's drum style, and I'm already dreading searching for one even half as good as you, but you should definitely chase this, man. The songwriting. The girl. All of it."

Phoenix chuckled humorlessly. "Yeah, well, I'm not so sure chasing the girl will work when the girl doesn't believe in love and thinks what we have is some freaky Olympus thing . . ."

"Then find a way to prove to her that it exists . . . and that it isn't."

Phoenix shot his friend a look. "Who the fuck are you? Because you're being awfully mature and way too insightful for you to be our Gavin."

The griffon shifter tossed him his notebook. "Whatever, asshole. But tell me I'm wrong."

East cleared his throat. "Since we're all being insightful and understanding, and talking about making grand gestures and following new paths, I decided that I really do want to open my own School of Rock for Kids. Naiomi's about to get her PhD, and I don't know what will happen in the immediate future, but I do know I want to be around for it. And her. I can't do that while on tour."

They all joked, not bothered in the least—at least for now—over their groundbreaking admissions.

Gavin chuckled. "Anyone else have any grand declarations?" He shot a look to Xavier. "What about you, man?"

"Actually . . . I've been offered a position as a spokesperson for the Animal Preservation Society, and if they'll have me, I'd like to be more involved and actually have my boots on the ground."

They all blinked before all eyes slowly turned toward Gavin.

"Well, don't look at me for any grand announcement." He laughed. "Although I admit, I kind of like the idea of going solo. It's very Harry Styles–esque. I kind of dig it."

Did that mean . . .

East glanced around the room, locking eyes with each of them. "So this is actually happening?"

They each slowly nodded, and Phoenix was the first to break into new—real—laughter. "Please let me be the one to tell Marcus. I want a front-row seat to watch his head explode."

They all laughed, and Phoenix couldn't help feeling at least a little bit lighter than he'd been a few minutes ago.

Except for one very large anvil hanging over his heart.

Addie.

He dropped his head onto the back of the couch with a groan. "How the fuck will I survive coming face-to-face with Addie tomorrow and not make a fucking lovesick fool of myself?"

"Maybe that's exactly what you should do," Gavin suggested. "Let me ask you a serious question."

"Is it actually serious?"

"Are you in love with her?"

"Without a fucking doubt," Phoenix answered without missing a beat. "Head over heels and all-in, tattooed on my fucking soul."

His friend nodded. "Then I have an idea."

"That should scare the fuck out of me," Phoenix admitted. "But?"

He shrugged. "But I'm all ears."

26

TRUST FALL

Addie

It was Go Day, and for every hiccup, something went shockingly right. Maxi handled every surprise with effortless foresight and ingenuity when Addie would've been huddled in the corner of the former tack room—now converted bridal chamber.

She was more certain now than ever that Maxi taking over Happily Ever Forever's event services was the right move. As for her, she'd dive into her new role as the *Anti*-Anti-Aphrodite and try her hand—with her mother's guidance—directing people to their perfect matches.

Goddess help them all.

Almost literally.

But as Maxi said, if the feds didn't show up during a pairing and haul someone away in handcuffs, she'd already be one step above her sister's track record.

Now showered and armed with an emergency sewing kit and mini fire extinguisher, Addie was ready to tackle the day and whatever came next.

Okay, so she was showered.

And her emergency kit was bulging and ready to go. If another cake went up in flames, she was prepared. A torn seam? Easy peasy lemon squeezy. She even had extra-large hand wipes and a vat of Purell in case someone stepped on a stray mound of horse poop they'd somehow missed during cleaning.

The only thing she wasn't prepared for was seeing Phoenix Cross.

Gavin and Xavier had shown up early that morning and helped with the last of the twinkle lights in the kissing tree, and East and Phoenix had arrived a few hours ago, but they'd headed right up to the main house where they'd be getting ready before the ceremony.

After the big L.O.V.E. revelation, Addie couldn't evict her mother's words from her head.

A fated leap of trust without a safety net.

That was scary as hell. Even thinking about it sent her heart into palpitations, but maybe that was the point. As special and magical as love was, it *should* be scary. If it wasn't, it wouldn't have the power to heal even the worst wounds.

But knowing it, and letting yourself fully accept it, was something entirely different. Just when she thought she was inches away from doing so, all those old doubts and worries reared their ugly heads and latched on to the only thing she'd erroneously thought was her safety net.

Muse Sickness.

Goddess, she wanted to kick her own ass, especially after reading more of the information that Aunt Eunice had left for her. If Phoenix never spoke to her again, he'd be well within his rights. She should've trusted what she felt, but damn it, after a lifetime of doing the exact opposite, reflexes kicked in and got in the way.

Bailey rounded the corner and nearly collided with Addie. "Uh, we have a problem."

"All problems should be directed to the new head of events," Addie stated with a smirk.

"Who the fuck do you think told me to get you? Maxi is in the bridal room with Nai and she's freaking the hell out—Nai, not Max. Although now that I'm saying it all aloud, Maxi looked a bit pale, too."

"Shit." Addie hustled into the barn and knocked once on the guestroom door before letting herself in. "What's going on?"

Nai was indeed freaking, breathing into a brown paper bag as her chest heaved.

"What the hell happened?" Addie dropped to a crouch in front of Phoenix's sister. "Nai?"

"I don't know." Maxi sounded frustrated and at a loss. "One moment we were putting the final touches on her makeup, fixing a loose button, and then *bam*. Meltdown."

Addie gentled her voice as she looked her new friend in the eye. "Nai, what's all this about? You're about to forever link yourself to your soulmate. That shouldn't require a paper bag."

"I don't know." Nai pulled the bag away from her mouth, her words breathless. "I just . . . suddenly started thinking about how we're finally here—after everything that happened—and then this intrusive thought slipped into my head that maybe there was a reason that things kept happening. Maybe this isn't the path we were meant to take."

"Are you freaking kidding me?" Addie scoffed gently. "I can honestly say that I have never met two people more suited to being together than you and Easton."

Did she repeat words Nai once told her not that long ago? Yes. But it was the truth.

"You have to say that because you're the event planner."

Addie laughed. "With my event history, what's one more botched wedding? No. I'm saying it because it's true."

She glanced up at her sister, getting a small supportive nod before she continued. "Nai, I'm looping you in on a secret, one that a select few people have the privilege of knowing. Hell, I figured it out not that long ago."

Nai's breathing evened as her gaze remained locked on Addie. "I love secrets. What is it?"

"True love *does* exist, and I know, without a shred of doubt, that yours and Easton's souls are a perfect match. You're tethered. I've seen it . . . as the daughter of Aphrodite," Addie said truthfully. "And your link is an immaculate dark gold, so thick and strong, and it's a never-ending loop. It's unbreakable."

Tears slipped down Naiomi's cheeks.

Maxi was already reaching for the makeup bag and pulling out the pressed powder and setting spray.

Nai gripped Addie's hands tightly. "You really mean it?"

"I've never meant anything more in my life."

She'd seen their link less than two hours ago, when botched arrival times had them nearly running into each other on their way to their individual ready-rooms.

They hadn't laid eyes on each other, but they'd been close enough that Addie had seen their link right there in front of her eyes, so bright and strong she wasn't sure how she'd missed it before.

"So what do you say?" Holding onto Nai's hand, Addie coaxed the bride to her feet. "Are you ready to exchange vows with your soulmate? Because unless my former event planner senses have already gone haywire, there's probably a very nervous gargoyle groom standing near a very special kissing tree."

Naiomi laughed, gently drying her tears. "Let's fucking do it. It's about damn time I claimed my man."

It was time to get this ceremony started.

Phoenix

It was finally happening. Two of the people that Phoenix loved most in the world were officially declaring their love in the place that started it all.

Addie had outdone herself, making the spot by the kissing tree even more magical than it had been to begin with. White lights and lanterns hung from the massive willow, and Nai and East stood beneath a brilliant white arch adorned with colorful wildflowers, the same kinds of flowers that filled Nai's bouquet. The two lovebirds recited their heartfelt vows just as the sun set in the background, gifting everyone a beautiful sunset filled with warm pinks and purples and dashed with a spectacular golden glow.

Or maybe the glow was coming off Addie.

As Phoenix listened raptly to his father—who became officially licensed to perform ceremonies for this specific purpose—his gaze drifted to the back left corner where Addie stood, Maxi at her side. A soft, sweet smile hovered on her lips as she occasionally dabbed her happy tears with a tissue.

Everything in him longed to cross the distance and wipe them away himself, but knowing they were happy tears, and that she rejoiced in East and Nai's love, gave him hope that maybe Gavin's harebrained idea wouldn't end in a disaster of epic proportions.

As if sensing being watched, Addie's water-filled eyes tilted toward him, and held. He couldn't look away even if he tried, willing her to see straight into his heart. A flurry of emotions flickered over her face until she darted her gaze away and leaned over to whisper something in Maxi's ear, and then disappeared somewhere behind the wagons.

Below the arch, East and Nai gave the crowd a kiss for the record books, and when they finally came up for air, his best friend whooped loudly and immediately scooped Nai up in a bridal carry. The audience laughed and cheered as East practically levitated back down the flower-strewn aisle.

The wedding party—kept small and intimate with just family—followed closely behind. Addie's disappearance was explained as she stood by one of the wagons and ushered them all into the back. Phoenix and his father helped everyone navigate the short steps, and once everyone was safely tucked away, Phoenix's father climbed in as well.

Turning toward Addie, Phoenix chiseled his tongue off the roof of his mouth. "You coming with us?"

She shot him a startled look, looking like a deer in headlights, her gorgeous green eyes rounded. This was the first time they'd been so close in days and his body practically vibrated with her nearness.

"Um. Yes. Bailey's already back at the barn and Maxi is staying here to make sure all the guests get on the wagons."

"Then let's get you loaded up, love." The nickname slipped out as he reflexively gripped her hips and effortlessly hoisted her into the wagon where Gavin took her hand until she steadied her balance.

Phoenix jumped up next and closed the gate, and then they were off on a magical hayride, a blanket of stars peeking out from the dark sky. Everyone watched the cloudless sky while Nai and East only had eyes for each other.

Phoenix's attention was stolen by the sassy redhead sitting almost directly across from him on the other side of the wagon.

Addie's eyes caught his more than once, and she looked away, her cheeks pinking instantly. Fuck, he missed the way she flushed, especially after a kiss, or even brighter after he made her come.

Next to him, Gavin elbowed him in the side. "You ready?"

Draping his arms on his propped knees and stretching his fingers, he took an unsteady breath. "Ready as I'll ever be to put my heart on the line in front of a crowd. As good of an idea as this is, I was half hoping Naiomi would nix it."

Gavin snorted. "Like she'd do that. Hell, I heard her talking to East about it and it sounded like she was taking nearly full credit for the idea. I mean, she did think of the other thing, I'll give her that, but let's not forget the real mastermind here."

"Like you'll let anyone forget it," Phoenix joked.

"True." Gavin shrugged.

In just a matter of hours, Adalyn Whitlock would know that his heart would forever belong to her . . . and he'd find out if hers could ever belong to him in return.

27

THE CHRONICLES OF AN *ANTI*-ANTI-APHRODITE

Addie

The night was almost over and nothing had burned down, no police had shown up to arrest a ceremony guest, and no one accidently stepped in a steaming horse patty. Now, Addie sipped her wine and celebrated a beautiful couple whose souls were destined to complete one another.

It was a perfect ending to a perfect day.

Almost.

Standing next to Maxi, Addie's gaze strayed past the dancing guests and toward the other side of the barn, immediately landing on Phoenix as if already knowing exactly where he stood. He leaned against one of the columns, white dress shirt open at the neck and sleeves rolled up casually to reveal his corded arms.

Each of the Stone Talons looked the same, even East, who'd been thrilled at the notion of a more casual look for their ceremonial festivities. But it was Phoenix who took her breath away, and if she was being honest with herself for once, had done so since their first run-in.

The man should come with a warning label, one that read DANGER: WILL MAKE YOU FANTASIZE ABOUT HAPPILY EVER FOREVER.

Because that's exactly what he'd done, and not just any happily ever forever, but *theirs*. With their friends and families standing by their sides. It didn't take much imagination to picture the two of them having their own ceremony here on Emilio's farm.

"You okay?" Bailey eyed her curiously.

"Yeah." Despite the barn's open doors, Addie's next breath lodged in her throat, making her a little bit dizzy. "I'm going to go grab some fresh air. I'll be right back. Set off an alarm if anything happens and I'll come running."

Bailey snorted. "We'll be just fine. The curse is broken, remember?"

Addie turned toward the rear, her gaze once again stumbling directly over Phoenix, except this time he was staring right back, his heated gaze without a doubt watching her every move. It warmed the back of her neck and followed her as she skirted the dance floor and made a beeline toward the exit.

It distracted her so much that she nearly collided with Phoenix's mom, Lani.

"Addie!" Lani pulled her into an immediate bone-crushing hug. "I cannot express my thanks enough to you and your team for making this the most magical of days for our girl and East. It was nothing short of perfect. Stunningly, breathtakingly perfect."

Addie smiled sincerely. "It was my absolute pleasure. I'm not so sure I've met any two people who deserve their perfect night more than them."

Lani grinned mischievously, the smirk looking so much like

her son's. "Oh, I don't know. I could probably think of at least one or two more people."

"You know, I need to go check on something outside. Make sure you and Judd find the photographer later and have him take your pictures. East and Nai will want them as mementos."

She nodded and hugged her one more time, and then Addie hustled, the walls of the large barn starting to close in around her.

By the time she stepped into the warm open air, she practically panted, closing her eyes to the sky as she focused on every inhale and exhale until the world finally stopped spinning.

She told herself that she'd come clean to Phoenix about everything . . .

About how she felt . . .

About how much she loved him . . .

But after weeks of telling him that love was a farce, what would make him believe her now? She had no fucking clue, which was why it was easier to steer clear of him altogether, at least until she found the right words to explain how she felt and what he meant to her.

Addie lost track of time, and turned, finally somewhat ready to face the music, when a blur of cotton and lace bolted from the barn as if her dress were on fire.

Naiomi, panting heavily, latched onto her arms in a frantic death grip. "Thank the gods you're still here. For a minute, I thought you'd left already, and I—"

"Why would I leave?" Addie chuckled. "There's still a lot of celebrating to do."

"Right. Yeah. That's what East said, but when I looked around and you weren't there and then Bailey said you stepped out, I thought, Ah! *Runaway Bride* moment."

"Except you're the bride tonight, Nai."

"Right." She laughed nervously, the sound a little high-pitched.

"Are you okay?" Addie studied her with full event-planner concern. "Did someone spike the punch fountain or something?"

"No! Well . . . maybe. I did see Gavin standing over there for an exorbitant amount of time looking all sneaky, but honestly, that's his typical look so maybe he was just thirsty."

"Nai."

"Sorry. Um, there is something that you should probably be present for. It's not a problem per se, but it is a little unexpected—for some people. Who weren't expecting it."

"You know I have no earthly idea what you're talking about, right?"

Nai grinned. "I know."

The brunette dragged her back into the barn where the crowd of guests parted and an anticipatory silence filled the room. No music. Hardly any conversation.

Dead silence.

"All right, Dread Pirate Roberts," Nai exclaimed. "I got her here, now the rest is up to you."

Addie shot the brunette a confused look. "What?"

Her gaze drifted to the small stage where the band had been playing for the majority of the night, and instead of the High Topps, there stood Phoenix—alone except for the acoustic guitar strapped over his shoulder and the microphone standing in front of him.

Gaze locked on her, his lips twitched into that coy smirk that never ceased to make her stomach flip. "I'll take it from here, sis. Thanks."

"Anytime," Nai answered, making the crowd around them chuckle. The brunette flashed Addie a conspiratorial quick wink. "Talk to you later."

The bride was gone in a blink, leaving Addie standing in the middle of the dance floor, a floor that no one was currently dancing on, their gazes bouncing between her and Phoenix as if waiting for something to happen.

Onstage, Phoenix gulped. The sound was picked up by the mic and he chuckled nervously. "If you all will bear with me for a bit, I'm used to hiding behind a massive drum set when I'm on a stage like this."

"Not so easy, is it, big guy?" Gavin taunted from the sidelines, earning more than a few chuckles.

Phoenix rolled his eyes and turned his attention back to the crowd, his gaze always returning—and staying locked—on her.

"Music has always been a big part of my identity, so much so that I revolved my entire life around it, commandeered my parents' garage, formed a band with my best friends." He shot a glance toward the guys. "And it's been a wild ride full of ups and downs. But despite the dips, I was always able to fall back on music. It was my security blanket. And then one day, that music just . . . stopped."

Addie's gaze was transfixed on Phoenix as he opened his heart for all to see.

"Suddenly, I was living in a quiet world, with no earthly idea how the hell to get that music back." Phoenix's gaze once again returned to Addie. "And then late one night, a gorgeous, redheaded spitfire came banging on my door, and the moment I opened it, my world lit up in surround sound. I found my music again. *In her*. In the way she smiled at me—when she was done glaring."

There was a chorus of chuckles, and Phoenix's mouth twitched.

"In the way she snorted at the end of a laugh. At the way her eyes twinkled when she was teased. Not only did this beautiful, loving woman bring music back into my heart, but she *became* my music. This is my newest Phoenix Cross original, and I'm calling it 'My Heart & Soul' . . . and I'm dedicating it to her."

He didn't say her name, but there was no denying to whom he was talking. All eyes shifted to her before turning back to Phoenix the second he strummed the first chord. He stopped once and took a deep breath before starting over again.

His voice, rough with emotion and yet smooth like aged whisky, sang the first words, and as the song progressed, so did the emotions. They swelled from Phoenix and were absorbed by her . . . until he hit the chorus.

Looping around his fingers and lifting from the strings of his guitar, shimmered an ethereal golden glow, and this time, Addie's eyes didn't burn, blur, or ache.

They welled, full of such all-consuming emotions she didn't know where to go with them. The gorgeous gold soul tether wrapped playfully around Phoenix and swirled through the air as if dancing with his words.

Before you, the world was dark and grim.
A silent battlefield.
The quiet, overwhelming.
And then you opened the door,
Walked into my heart.
My before and after.
My fresh start.

You are my music.
You are my stars.
You are my moon.
My heart and soul are no longer mine.
They belong to you.

Before you, my world was dark and grim.
A lonely battlefield.
The silence overwhelming.
Then you walked into my heart.
You brought music.
You brought love.
With you, our happily forever can now start.

Silence blanketed the room as Phoenix slid from bridge to chorus to refrain and played the last, soft note.

Bailey leaned closer to Maxi and used the hem of Maxi's sleeve to mop up their mascara, and they weren't alone. People sniffled from every direction.

One of them was Addie.

Tears slipped down her cheeks, but she couldn't move, frozen to the spot and barely breathing as Phoenix hopped down from the stage and tossed his guitar to a waiting East.

He closed the distance between them, that ethereal cord moving with him. Hazel eyes filled with so much longing, longing she felt just as intensely, he didn't look away from her even once.

He stopped an inch away from touching her. "I promised that you'd hear it."

Addie struggled to clear her throat from the ball of emotions clogging it. "It was worth the wait. That was quite the song, rock star."

His lips twitched. "That wasn't just a song, love."

"No?" Something like hope blossomed in her chest, and Addie glanced down, seeing the beautiful glowing link slowly wrapping around her waist. "Sure sounded like a song to me. It rhymed and everything. Mostly."

Phoenix cupped her cheek and her heart nearly sang, her

knees quaking as she fought to keep her eyes open and on him. "That was more than a song, Adalyn Love Whitlock. That was our beginning."

Addie's heart hitched.

"This isn't Muse Sickness," she blurted out. "Just . . . fuck. I was so, so wrong and I—"

"I know."

"You know?"

"There was no doubt in my mind about what I felt," Phoenix admitted. "No way in hell that the feelings I have for you could be considered a sickness."

Tears slipped down Addie's cheeks as she wondered what the hell she'd done to deserve this man.

"Adalyn Love Whitlock"—Phoenix's lips twitched, and his thumb reached out, gently sweeping away the moisture on her cheeks—"I am, without a doubt, one hundred percent in love with you. Hearts and sky and all the moon, in *love*. And from the moment you opened that door, and until the stars cease to shine in the sky, my heart and soul will forever belong to you. I want you in my life, however you'll take me . . . but admittedly, I hope it's in a way that involves a lot of naked time and a happily ever forever."

Phoenix wrapped his free arm snugly around her waist and drew her flush against his body. "So what do you say?"

Her lips twitched in a teasing smirk while happy tears fell down her cheeks, her entire being bursting with love. "I say . . . *sparkles*."

Phoenix whooped much like Easton had earlier and dragged her into a kiss that literally swept her off her feet. Time froze. The air stalled. Everyone else melted away until it was just the two of them, their bodies entwined in that gorgeous glowing soul tether.

They kissed until they were both breathless and panting.

"Leave it to a rock star to prove to me that true love exists," Addie teased wryly.

Phoenix grinned coyly. "I am a man of many talents . . . but you do know what this means, right?"

"What?"

"The media will have to find something else to focus on other than the chronicles of an anti-love Aphrodite. Either that, or you'll need a new nickname. How about . . . Cupid?"

Addie wrinkled her nose. "Hard pass."

"Come on. Think of all the possibilities."

"I am. It'll already take massive patience until I can get my matchmaking legs underneath me—maybe a minor miracle. Let's not add to it by throwing nicknames around. Could you imagine? A Cupid Dilemma."

Something flickered in the background, and standing at the rear exit against a starry-sky backdrop, stood Addie's mother.

Aphrodite, wearing her Goddess of Love white toga and a gold leaf crown, watched them with a warm, loving smile. She blew a kiss in Addie's direction and Addie sent one right back.

No one saw her except for Addie . . . until.

"Is that who I think it is?" Phoenix's face paled slightly as his head swiveled from the back of the barn to her.

"Oh. Um . . . maybe?"

"Shit." Phoenix looked panic-stricken.

"What? Why?"

"Your dad was pretty pissed off I hadn't introduced myself to him when he thought we were dating. How will your mother feel when she finds out that you're in love with a former rock star?"

Addie blinked. "Former?"

A slow smile spread over Phoenix's face. "Surprise. You're

not the only one in need of a new nickname because you can't call me *rock star* anymore. How does *melody master* sound?"

Addie groaned and shook her head.

"No? Okay . . . *lyric illuminator*. Or—"

Addie pulled him in for a quick, deep kiss. "How about I just call you mine?"

He smirked wickedly and brushed his lips over hers. "That works, too."

EPILOGUE

"You ready?" Addie glanced to Phoenix standing next to her and gave his hand a firm, supportive squeeze.

"Sure. Yeah. One hundred percent ready." Phoenix's voice cracked slightly.

From Addie's other side, Bailey snorted. "He looks greener than my morning matcha smoothie and we haven't even stepped through the portal yet."

Her cousin wasn't wrong. Addie watched Phoenix worriedly as the sweat peppering across his forehead intensified.

"Seriously, I'm good." Phoenix cleared his throat and, squeezing her hand, offered her a brave smile that brought out that dimple she loved. "It's not every day a guy gets to meet his girl's extended family."

"Just remember what I said and you'll be fine," Addie reassured him.

Phoenix nodded. "Eat anything Hades offers me and try not to look as though I'm eating rocks."

"Exactly. Other than your father, no one takes his grilling skills more seriously than Hades, and he only goes for one kind of doneness—briquette. And you're going to love Aunt Persy. She's the absolute sweetest."

Maxi added, "And just humor Grandpa Zeus and laugh at his dad jokes—we all know they're horrible but, well, he controls the lightning, so it's just best to laugh."

Phoenix's head bobbed as he went through the Gods 101 CliffsNotes he'd gotten on the way to the gardens. "Eat rocks. Love Persy. Laugh with Zeus."

"You're going to be fine." Addie pulled him close and lifted onto her toes, gifting him a slow kiss that she felt down to her toes. "They will all love you just like I do."

Addie glanced to Bails and her sister, and with a faint nod, they each laid a palm on the arch. The stone pulsed and glowed, the center shimmering as it came online.

"State your lineage," a disembodied male voice—that instantly sounded familiar—chimed.

Withholding a soft giggle, Addie cleared her throat. "The children of Athena and Aphrodite—and special guest—humbly seek entry to Olympus."

The portal shimmered brighter as the god on the other side of the portal made them wait.

"Special guest, huh? What makes him so special . . . and deserving of a daughter of Aphrodite?"

Next to Addie, Phoenix muttered a string of soft curses.

Addie rolled her eyes. "Because the daughter of Aphrodite loves him with all her heart and soul, and if the uncle of Aphrodite's daughter does anything to make him nervous or feel unwelcome, then I'll be forced to retaliate in the form of sending in said uncle's wife to deal with the matter."

From the other side of the portal, Hades chuckled. "Well, when you put it that way . . . you may all enter. And I'll be on my best behavior. I even have your human's plate all prepared."

Maxi entered the portal first, followed closely by Bailey, who jumped in with a wink in their direction.

"You ready to go portal jumping with me, Phoenix Cross?" Addie wrapped her arms around his waist and squeezed.

Phoenix's arms tightened as he dropped a sweet kiss to her lips. "Love, I am ready, willing, and able to go jumping anywhere with you. Lead the way."

"Don't worry. I'll hold your hair back when you puke," Addie said a split second before tugging Phoenix through the portal. "Again."

ACKNOWLEDGMENTS

Every book has its own publication story. Some pretty much write themselves, others not so much, whether from internal or external reasons. For *The Cupid Dilemma*, it was very much both, and if it weren't for the wildly supportive people around me during its drafting, I'm not sure you'd even be reading these acknowledgments.

This past year has been . . . a lot. It tested me in ways I haven't been tested before, and reminded me that I'm surrounded by amazing people who never cease to encourage me and lift me up when I need it.

Mom, you are my biggest champion. You are strength, and resilience, and the personification of everything I strive to be both now and in the future. I've been blessed to have you as my biggest cheerleader and am so glad that my children have you as their biggest inspiration.

Snort-bert & Squirrel (aka, The Children). You push me to keep going and not only keep me humble but up-to-date on all the young people lingo (and social media trends).

Sarah E. Younger, this is number twelve! Get your email

fingers ready because I'm already prepped for twelve more! I couldn't do it without you!

Tiffany, Ashley, Sara, Marissa, and the rest of the amazing St. Martin's Griffin team, you all are rockstars and I hit the author jackpot to have you help bring this book into the world.

Tif Marcelo, you are a woman of many talents and roles. Bestie. Critique partner. Therapist. Cheerleader. And my Honey, No person. Because of you keeping me on track, I was finally able to write The End on this baby.

And to all the readers, thank you so much! I'll never be able to find the right words to express how much your support means to me. Because of you, I'm able to chase my dreams and show others—especially my children—that dreams are meant to be followed.

ABOUT THE AUTHOR

Amie Otto

USA Today bestselling author **April Asher** was hooked on romantic stories from the time she first snuck a bodice ripper from her mom's bedside table. By day, April dons dark-blue nurse's scrubs and drinks way too much caffeine. By night, she still consumes too much caffeine, but she does it with a laptop in hand. She pens rom-coms with a paranormal twist but also writes high-octane romantic suspense as April Hunt. She lives out her own happily ever after in Virginia with her college-sweetheart husband and their two children.